EASY

EASY

A DOGS LIFE

RUSSELL SHAW

Library of Congress Control Number:		2011914732
ISBN:	Hardcover	978-1-4653-5135-7
	Softcover	978-1-4653-5134-0
	Ebook	978-1-4653-5136-4

This book was printed in the United States of America.

To order additional copies of this book, contact:
Xlibris Corporation
0-800-644-6988
www.xlibrispublishing.co.uk
Orders@xlibrispublishing.co.uk
302473

Chapter 1

Bill, the mastiff, was a big, strong, street fighter. Yet again our paths were to cross; only this time I had no back-up.

A year's incarceration in the concrete hellhole had left me underweight and weak. Even fully fit, I was no match for this vicious killer.

My time was up.

Nine Months Earlier

Phew, it was hot. It must have been six in the morning, and already the sun was up. I could feel the heat rising from the road as it soaked up the morning sunshine. It was going to be another scorcher. We were heading for town with about two kilometres to go.

We kept to the side streets and shadows, trying not to draw attention to ourselves, ever watchful for the catchers. We are rough and tough and came from Dalman, which is a seaside resort in southern Turkey. Our reputation is such that other gangs were wary of us and tended to keep out of our way.

There were five members in our gang, though we preferred to call ourselves a team, and we reigned supreme in this area. Our leader was Bernie. He liked to be called Bernie, as for some strange reason, he thought he was a St Bernard. Between you and me, he was a mongrel like most of us. Mind you, having survived on the streets all his life by knowing how to duck and dive, there was very little you could teach him. He was a master of his craft.

Then, there was Harry, a pure bred husky who liked to be called Harold. He had it really cushy till his owners decided to uproot and leave town. Finding himself on the streets, he soon learnt to adapt and fend for himself.

The problem with him was the way he strutted around and the snooty attitude he put out. Quite frankly, he was a bit posh and didn't quite understand that you had to fit in if you wanted to survive. I found him very irritating when listening to his constant rhetoric of 'We are a team, we're team players, and we must all pull together.' 'Yak, Yak.' What a pain! I wished he would just shut up! I think the hot weather had fried his brains.

I mean huskies should live in a cold country, but he didn't seem to realise that or chose not to. Quite honestly, between you and me, he was a bit thick. All that constant rhetoric—we must pull together as a team, work as a unit—everybody knew that's what huskies do, pull . . . I suppose you had to make allowances for him, given his history. I could have done without his never-ending lectures. Boring . . .

Then there was Jack. Jack was a collie . . . sort of . . . He was very quick-witted, had fast legs, and extremely sensitive ears. They say his dad was a Doberman and his mother a collie. What a combination to have around! Bernie said he's our early warning system. Nothing—and I do mean nothing—got past those ears. The ladies liked him too. It must have been his colouring. Slick, glossy black fur covered his body, and a white, evenly matched patch was on both sides of his ribcage. What I wouldn't have given for those looks!

The fourth member was Barney. That's the name everyone called him. He was my saviour, my mentor, and my friend—my personal hero. Don't get taken in by the name. I think because of his laid-back nature and friendly disposition, other dogs and people tended to take him for granted, which he liked. He said it gave him an edge when other dogs underestimated him. I must say he was very kind and protective towards me. He looked like a Labrador with long legs and floppy ears. Somewhere in his ancestry, he inherited genes from a greyhound. He said he found me by the rubbish dump half starved and felt sorry for me and took me under his wing. I think there's more to it than that, because when I ask him about my family, he is very vague and steers off the subject. If I persist, he tells me, 'We'll talk about it someday.'

Then, there's me. Speed—that's what they called me, because I was small and very quick, hard to catch, able to get in and out of small spaces, and a perfect foil for Bernie's strategy. They say I'm too flash and cocky for my own good. Well I could afford to be, couldn't I, with the team I had around me. There you go—team . . . That was dopey Harry's influence. He said I resembled a Jack Russell except for my colouring—a white nose and paws, same colour chest, plus the tip of my tail had a white streak. As I said, when Barney found me on a rubbish skip, I was about three days old and starving. I was fostered by his friend Lulu for the first three months of my life until her owners moved. That's when I joined the team. Barney must have felt I could contribute something to the gang. That's why he introduced me. Much later, he was proven right.

If I say so myself, I was flash and full in your face. You see, in this day and age, you had to look after yourself. Otherwise, you would get trodden down and wouldn't survive.

I don't remember much of my first meeting with Barney except for that gnawing pain in my stomach and an insatiable thirst. Apparently, I was in a pretty bad way—my ribs were sticking through my skin, I was riddled with fleas, and ants were crawling out of my sores. Barney said he wasn't sure I would make it.

He had a hell of a job convincing the gang that I could be very useful to them. They weren't at all happy. The overall opinion concluded that I was another mouth to feed and would slow them down—too much of a liability. But Barney persisted and finally convinced them. It was agreed, providing Barney took full responsibility for me, and they didn't want to see or hear from me until I could take an active part and pull my weight with the rest of the team members.

So, there I was on my first job. Leading our group was Jack. The reason he was selected for this position was obvious—his quick feet and keen ears . . .

Following him was Harry three metres behind, put there because Bernie said that was the safest position and he could keep an eye on him.

With Bernie following Harry, that left Barney and myself, walking together, bringing up the rear.

As we approached the main intersection into town, Harry piped up, 'I say, chaps, there's a garbage bin just across the junction. Let's have a look, might be something interesting inside.'

Harry proceeded to break formation, 'Cool it, you dumb mutt. How many times have I told you to stick to the plan? Never ever break formation. That's a no-no! The last thing we need is to have the council pest control on our backs, and we will if we draw attention to ourselves. Get back in line, stupid: If you're caught, it will be curtains for you and probably have serious repercussions for the rest of us.'

Barney had drummed it into me to keep clear of the council catchers because if you're caught, they have a way of making you disappear. Rumour had it that nobody had ever returned from the pound. The council considered dogs to be a pest and an annoyance to holiday makers, and once the season finished, they poisoned or electrocuted all dogs without a collar or an internationally recognized microchip. I wasn't sure but suspected that's what happened to my mum and dad.

Chapter 2

Bernie and his gang weren't the only ones up and about on that hot, sunny morning.

Abraham Burder arrived at his restaurant early. Today was Saturday, the busiest day of the week. Halfway through the season, and profits were up compared with last year. He had inherited the family business in which he had worked since the day he left school. He had started from the bottom, clearing tables in the evenings, then worked as a waiter at weekends till finally his father passed away, and he became the proud owner of the establishment. It was his first and only full-time job. He sighed as he looked up at the awning. Burder's Restaurant, it said.

Abraham married his childhood sweetheart, Sophia. They had two children, a boy and a girl. Abraham was very proud of them. Asra was the eldest, a boy of twelve years, whilst Lithia was ten. Of course, when they come into the business, they will be known as Allan and Lisa. The reason being most of his clientele were English, with a sprinkling of French and Dutch, so it made sense to have names that his customers were familiar with.

For the first time that he could recall, Sophia was in serious disagreement with him. Sure, they had fallen out on various occasions over the years, but this time, she was standing her ground and refusing to back down on the issue of the children's education.

Abraham had always assumed that Asra, on leaving school, would join him in the family business and his daughter, Lithia, would work as a waitress under her father's watchful eyes until she found herself a husband and moved on to raise a family of her own, but the previous evening, Sophia made it known she had other ideas. She wanted both children to go on to further education.

Women, he thought . . . They should come with an instruction manual.

As he stood admiring his new patio, he saw that Dennis was already hard at work hosing down the front of the premises.

'Morning, Dopey, you're nice and early.'

'Yes, Boss,' grinned Dennis. Why does he persist in calling me Dopey? After all, I can write my name and count up to ten. True, my concentration is not good. Apparently, he knew my family. He said they were all dopey, and when I was a baby, my mum was changing my diaper on the kitchen table. As she reached for the baby powder, I rolled off and landed on my head. It's not true, of course. My mother is the best in the world. Still, best to keep my mouth shut and get stuck in my chores. It's hard work cleaning, bagging the rubbish, then being stuck in the kitchen all day, washing up the cutlery and pots and pans, sometimes even cooking when Michael, one of the chefs, is too drunk to work. This has been happening more frequently lately. I'll have to ask for an increase in my salary. Mind you, to be fair, Abraham is a hard task master but pays well.

Abraham noticed Dopey's hair. It was black, lank, and greasy, hanging down to his shoulders. I must have told him a hundred times to get it cut. His Levi's are tattered and threadbare. It may be fashionable but not suitable for the job and the type of clientele I am trying to attract. Why is he wearing trainers for work? He could easily slip over when in the kitchen and hurt himself. Mind you, it's not him I am worried about. If he breaks his leg or something else, I would be hard pressed to find a replacement for him. After all, he's a hard grafter.

Dennis continued to clean the front of the café. That's what he called it, as he had worked at better places. Prior to returning to Turkey, he had worked at a proper restaurant off Bayswater Road in London—Queensway, to be precise—a sort of cosmopolitan area, upmarket, a hive of activity. There, they provided him with a proper uniform. Wiping his hands on his off-white apron, stained with various food products from yesterday, he thought, I must remember to change because Abraham will scold me for being untidy. Well, that's finished. The front patio is clean.' Putting his hands on his hips, he looked down the road. Not many people about, he thought. Mind you, it was still early.

Already his T-shirt was clinging to his skin. He was sweating like a pig, still only another fourteen hours to go, and he would be finished for the day. Disconnecting the hosepipe and curling it up neatly, he made his way to the kitchen to sort out the food swill, bag it up, and place it in the yard for the garbage men to collect. Must remember to keep an eye out for those stray dogs. If you're not on your toes, they can cause havoc, he said to himself.

The waiters usually arrived about ten o'clock to prepare for the lunchtime rush. James and Julian were their names. Dennis found them a bit smarmy with their slicked-back hair and grovelling attitude to the customers. There again, he had very little to do with them. Mind you, they were immaculately turned out, always on the lookout for single ladies or even unaccompanied married ones. They both seemed to do well in that department.

Michael was already in the kitchen with his assistant, Robert, both preparing food. Luckily, Mike was sober. He was very temperamental. When things were not going well, Robert took the full brunt of his temper. I'm told most chefs are highly strung, but it was inexcusable the foul language that Michael sometimes used—you know, the F and C words. Still, it was none of my business; I keep my head down and carry on with my work.

The lunch menu was fairly mundane—the usual fish and chips, steak and kidney pie, sausages and mash, hamburgers served with various salads, more chips topped up with tomato sauce. I mean, what is it with the English? Always tomato sauce. Robert said it ruins the food. Occasionally, someone asked for brown sauce. Then Michael would say, 'We have a posh one here.' Even on Sunday when the chefs cook various roasts, most diners still persisted in drowning their beef with the red stuff instead of the usual tartar sauce.

Michael made his Yorkshire pudding the traditional way, roasting the beef on a spit, allowing the juice from the meat to drip on to the puddings, thus giving them their renowned flavour They say in the old days, way back in time in England, the poor people who were unable to afford much meat invented the pudding so as to fill the workers up. After all, the main ingredients are flour and water.

When he got to the small cupboard at the rear of the kitchen, Dennis put the hose away and picked up the overflowing garbage bags. Cramming the contents down, he tied them off, then took them out to the rear yard. Today was collection day. The garbage men usually arrived around midday.

Chapter 3

Jack pricked his ears. He turned and said to us with some urgency:

'Hold still. I can hear a garbage lorry coming up fast behind us . . . and another vehicle following it . . . ' He stood still listening. 'And it's stopping every time the truck does.' It meant nothing to me, but it obviously did to the others.

'Scat and hide,' Bernie barked.

This situation we had rehearsed many times. The plan was to run in different directions and hide till the coast was clear and meet up at a pre-arranged destination where we felt safe—the old boathouse.

Barney nudged me saying, 'Leg it back to that derelict villa we passed.'

I didn't need to be told twice. With Barney leading, I was flat out heading for cover. Then he disappeared through a broken piece of fencing. I skidded to a halt, overshooting the gap, but in a heartbeat, I was through the fence and face to face with a panting Barney.

'Phew! We made it,' barked Barney. We hid, cowering in the overgrown front garden of a dilapidated old villa, panting for breath, gasping for air.

'Did you see where the others went?' I asked Barney.

'I'm getting too old for this,' he said between sharp intakes of breath.

'Jack took off like a rocket. I think he went left, heading for that disused garage. The others I'm not sure. We'll lie low for a couple of hours, then meet at the old boatyard as agreed.'

We were well hidden from any unseen eyes. I lay down next to Barney. When his breathing returned to normal, I asked him what we had been running from. He explained that if it was a garbage truck on its own, no problem, but when it had a vehicle following it, you could be sure it belonged to the dog pound. It was the van that took the dogs away never to be seen again.

'We have time to spare,' said Barney. 'We should take a nap until we are sure the coast is clear.' I made myself comfortable, curled in between Barney's legs. That's where I always slept. I felt safe and secure there. Within a few minutes, we were sound asleep.

Sometime later, I was roused by a faint rustling sound. I kept quiet and looked to Barney . . . He was gone. What had happened? Don't panic, I told myself, but my heart was slamming in my chest. The noise grew closer. I became fearful. I could feel the dampness running down my rear leg. Oh my god, I was wetting myself. Still the noise grew closer. In my head, I was screaming for help Barney, Barney, where are you? Frozen to the spot, I thought I would pass out. It's the council pest control. They're going to impound me and make me eat poison. With my whole body shaking and totally confused, I was scared to move. Then just in front of me, the long grass parted. This is it. I'm finished, murdered before having a chance to live or see life.

Feeling totally alone and desperate, I wanted my mum. I don't know why that came to mind as I didn't know her. Mum, mum, help me, please. I'm scared. Unable to bark, I became aware of a hissing sound, and as the long grass parted, my eyes stood out on stalks. Rooted to the spot, unable to breathe, there in front of me stood the most hideous sight—a thin, lean, mean, feral cat, his face cut and bruised, giving the impression he had been in many a battle. Drawing himself to his full height, he hissed, 'This is my manor, so piss off or I'll take your eyes out.'

'I can't. The pest controllers are outside.'

'That's your problem, I said piss off. This is my turf, and I have babies to look after.'

'Be reasonable,' I said. 'Let me stay just for fifteen minutes till the coast is clear.'

He moved a step forward and retracted his claws.

'I'm warning you. It's your last chance. Git!'

'Hold it,' said a voice. 'I've only left you for five minutes, and already you're in trouble.'

Seeing the size of Barney, the cat's attitude changed somewhat, especially after noticing the juicy lump of meat in Barney's jaw.

Addressing the cat, Barney said, 'I appreciate this is your turf, but if you let us stay awhile, I'll share our food with you. Should be enough left to feed your young-uns.'

It was then I noticed how thin and scrawny the cat was. He looked half starved.

'What's your name?' I said.

'My friends call me Molly.'

Oh, I thought . . . I didn't realise he in fact was a she.

Molly made up her mind immediately. The dogs didn't seem to pose a threat, and there was a free meal in it. Considering she hadn't eaten for days, it was an offer she couldn't refuse.

When they had finished eating, Molly said, 'I must be off.'

'Take those few scraps with you for the youngsters,' said Barney.

Molly made to leave. 'By the way, what are your names?'

'I'm Speed and this is Barney.'

'Nice to meet you.' Then she was gone.

'So glad you came along when you did Barney. I was so frightened.'

'All part of the learning process,' he replied. 'We better be on our way. I've had to scout around and the coast is clear. We better make our way to the meeting point.'

They set off back down the way they came towards the junction. Barney reminded Speed to keep to the left-hand side of the road as the motorists could see them more clearly. As in most European countries, they drove on the right.

Trotting behind Barney, Speed was totally absorbed with the new sounds, smells, and the constant activity of a large bustling town; after all, it was all new to him. Even at that relative early hour, the roads were busy, people were going about their business, and there was the noise of traffic as they made their way to work. Lorries were hooting and honking. They all seemed to be in a hurry to load or offload their goods. The pace of life was much quicker compared with the laid-back style where the gang squatted on the edge of the National Park just out of town. It was Speed's first experience of a thriving town and was he excited! Wow, he thought, I would love to live here.

There had been some talk from the gang about taking up residence in the town, basically to be nearer a food source. But this had its drawbacks—mainly the constant threat of the council's dog catchers—and finding somewhere suitable to bed down away from prying eyes.

As they approached the road junction, Speed noticed the garbage bin that Harry had been interested in. The lid was open, probably emptied by garbage men whose truck they had fled from. Barney said, 'Stay close to me when we cross the junction. These roads are dangerous, especially for animals. People driving are in such a hurry that they couldn't care two hoots about us, as there are no penalties for running animals over. The law says, if we don't have a collar, we're strays. They don't even have to report it to the police unless we are dead and blocking the road.'

The more I learnt about humans, the less I trusted them.

Having safely crossed the road junction, we proceeded at a steady pace forward, heads down, trying not to draw attention to ourselves. It was a lot more difficult than you would have thought. My sensitive nose picked up a delicious aroma. Barney noticed it too.

'Keep walking. We are passing a baker's.'

'What's a baker?' I interjected.

'Concentrate,' said Barney. 'I'll tell you later.'

That smell was playing havoc with my senses. If this is what towns smell like, I would definitely love to live here.

'About fifty metres on the left, we'll make a turn,' said Barney. 'You see that red and white pole hanging over that corner shop? That's where we turn.'

'Why is the pole over the shop?' I said.

'Because it's a barber's—a place where humans go to have their hair cut, and stop asking dumb fool questions. We are nearly there so stay close.

This will lead down to the marina. With luck, the gang should be waiting for us.'

As we turned the corner, I became aware that except for the barber's, we were entering a residential street about one hundred metres long. The sun was quite low given the early hour rising in the east and shining directly in our faces. We were about a quarter of the way along when simultaneously, Barney and I saw what appeared to be five or six shadows standing at the end of the road. With the sun in our eyes, we were unable to distinguish what they represented. A little further on, Barney slowed. As I caught up to him, he whispered, 'Trouble.'

It was then I realised that standing at the end of the street were six dogs, strays no doubt, and they were blocking our exit.

'Keep moving,' said Barney. 'Don't show any fear.'

'No problem,' I said, trying to appear confident and at ease, but really, my insides were churning over.

Barney seemed to be full of confidence as we made our way forward, his head up, tail wagging.

'Here's the plan,' he said. 'A few more steps, and I will stop, turn, and pick a fight with you. What you need to do is bark and yelp as loud as you can. Hopefully, this should confuse them as they will expect us to run for it. While they're wondering what's going on, this will distract them, giving us a split-second advantage. Then you leg it as fast as you can straight through the middle, follow your nose, and head for the marina and meet up with the others.'

'What will you do?' I said.

'Don't worry about me. I'll outrun them and catch up with you later.'

It was then I realised the large shadow in front of the rest was a bull mastiff who was no stranger to street fighting, judging by the scars on his body and half of his left ear missing.

'Now,' barked Barney, growling and clamping his jaws around my neck. Hissing, he said, 'Yelp as loud as you can.'

I didn't need any urging. He was hurting me at the same time, shaking me from side to side. After about fifteen seconds, he let go.

'Now scamper. Don't look back.'

I set off as fast as I could. I was almost out in the open when this little sausage dog brought me down. I think it was a whippet. All that shaking had disorientated me; I was just not quick enough. Then there were two of them biting, snapping, tearing at my flesh. God, it hurt. I knew I was in serious trouble, overpowered, and about to incur lethal damage. Out of the corner of my eye, I saw Barney doing battle with the huge mastiff, with two other dogs snapping at his legs to bring him down. It looked like he was holding his own, but it was only a matter of time. He was outnumbered three to one. I tried my best but could feel myself getting weaker. My whole body was racked with pain. This is it, this is the end . . .

'Stop!'

'Stop!' roared a loud booming bark. Everyone froze.

The two dogs attacking me ceased and stood back. The mastiff let go of Barney. His confederates cowered. I couldn't believe my luck. Inches away from permanent injury, I was free. Looking up and to my surprise, and I must say utter relief, stood Bernie, standing tall, with an air of total confidence as he strode toward the bull mastiff, whose tail and head had now dropped.

'You know who I am?'

'Yes,' said the mastiff.

'In that case, you should know better than to mess with my team.'

'But, but I-I wasn't to know they were with you.'

'You didn't think to ask before you attacked them?' said Bernie.

The Mastiff squatted down and lay on his side.

'Please don't hurt me, I-I, I'm sorry.'

Bernie placed a huge paw on the mastiff's neck and said, 'Piss off, if ever—if ever I see you again, I'll tear your guts out.'

With that, the mastiff and his cohorts were up and legging it as fast as they could. Barney and I barked our thanks.

'No problem,' said Bernie, 'but be careful in future.'

Still shaking, but feeling much more confident, Barney and I trailed behind Bernie as we made our way towards the southern corner of the marina to meet up with the rest of the gang.

As we trotted along the quayside, I was enthralled by the sheer beauty unfolding before me. The sea was flat and, as far as the eye could see, azure blue. It was difficult to see at what point on the horizon the sky started and the sea ended. They seemed to blend together. I asked Barney about the boats moored up against the sea wall. They were about twenty metres long with rows of seats and a canvas canopy above them. On some of the boats, the sides of the canopies were rolled down. Apparently, if the weather turned, the people sitting inside would be protected from the rain. The same applied if the sun should get too hot. Barney said, 'The boats were owned by the council and were used to ferry the tourists to the various beaches dotted along the coastline.'

Further out in the bay I noticed a sheltered inlet, where moored were the sailing yachts that spent most of the summer season sailing around the Mediterranean Sea and the Greek islands. Those people must be rich, but I bet they don't have pets travelling with them.

'Barney, do those people take their pets when they go sailing in their big boats?'

'Of course they do—cats, dogs, parrots, all sorts.'

'I wish I had an owner to care of me and take me sailing.'

'Hold up, I'm bursting for a pee.'

'Can't you wait?' said Bernie.

'I was okay a minute ago, but passing by that large palm tree sort of gave me the urge.'

'All right,' said Bernie, 'but hurry up. We haven't got all day.'

We made our way towards the southern corner of the marina. There stood a disused boathouse—the agreed meeting place. Already the market traders were setting up their stalls, hoping to attract the tourists who were heading or returning from the beach or just shopping for themselves, perhaps looking for presents and souvenirs to take home.

With the hustle and bustle and general activity of people going about their business, little attention was paid to three stray dogs that appeared to be wandering aimlessly. The odd trader would shoo us away, thinking we were scavenging. But they would be wrong; that day we had more important things to do.

We headed towards the rendezvous point behind the derelict boathouse, once a thriving business until the council took it over and built a new all-purpose workshop, catering for the repair work or trade from the sailing fraternity who, for whatever reason, visited this beautiful part of the country, which indeed it was. The town was surrounded on three sides by mountains that sloped gently down to the marina, a hive of activity.

Bernie said that in the old days, a long time ago, it had been a thriving fishing community before the onset of tourism. Indeed, a few families still worked the nets, keeping up the ancient traditions of the seafarers, but there was no stopping progress. A few diehards would argue against that. True, the living was hard, but life was so much simpler then as opposed to the complications of the modern-day. As their children grew and reached an age when they were able to work, most of them drifted into tourism or left for the big cities like Istanbul or Ankara to work in large air-conditioned offices behind computers, eventually having to wear glasses or having arthritic hands from typing all day.

As we passed by a road sweeper, he shouted, 'Scat,' and at the same time, brandished his broom at them. 'Be off. There's nothing around here for you.'

As we scooted past, we heard him muttering, 'Bloody dogs. The council should exterminate all of them—pissing and shitting all over the place. It's me who has to clean up after them.'

It never occurred to him that sweeping up the litter was what the council paid him to do. Without them, he would probably be out of a job.

As they neared the boathouse, Bernie picked up the scent of Harry. The three of us rounded the corner, and there he was.

'I say, chaps, where have you been? I've been quite frantic with worry. It seems hours since we split up.'

'We had a spot of bother with Big Bob the mastiff and his gang,' said Barney. 'Lucky for us, Bernie was on hand to sort them out.'

'Think nothing of it,' said Bernie somewhat modestly.

'What happened to you, Harry?' I asked.

'I hid in a ditch up a sewer pipe till it was safe to come out.'

'Phew, I thought you stank a bit,' I replied.

'Cheeky little blighter, you would smell the same stuck up a sewer pipe for an hour.'

I couldn't resist the temptation, 'I meant regardless of the sewer.'

They all laughed except Harry. He didn't seem to get the joke. I always knew he was a bit thick, I thought.

'Has anyone seen Jack?' Bernie said to no one in particular. There was a chorus of no's.

'Well, this is the agreed meeting point. We had better settle down and wait,' said Bernie.

Barney and I found a cool patch of shade beneath the hedgerow. Harry squatted beneath an olive tree and started preening himself. Bernie was pacing up and down quite agitated, obviously worried about Jack. They didn't have long to wait. About thirty minutes passed, and along he came, grinning all over his face, bouncing along, tail wagging.

'Where have you been?' they all barked at once.

'Well, you remember that French poodle I used to knock around with?'

'Which one?' said Bernie sarcastically.

'You know, Mimi, the one with the pink bow who lives in that big house on the corner of Ismir Street?'

'Oh, that poodle,' replied Bernie.

'Yes! When the garbage men appeared, I hid in her garden. She was a bit peeved as last time we were due to meet, I stood her up. Unfortunately, I had arranged to see another lady at the same time. She was a little annoyed at me, but I soon talked her round and one thing led to another. You know how it is. Time passes and here I am.'

So glad we are all safe, Barney thought. Typical of Jack. He's quite incorrigible.

Chapter 4

George sat up and looked at his bedside clock. Blimey, he thought, better get up and have a shower. Looking down at Mary who was fast asleep, gently snoring, he was amazed at her beauty. It never failed to impress him. She still had a natural elegance about her. There were a few wrinkles playing around her eyes and lips, but she didn't look a day older from when they first met. She stood about five foot eight, weighed in at around nine stone, although in fairness that tended to vary at times depending on what state of mind she was in. Being a depressive, she tended to binge eat when going through a bad patch.

We had met at a day hospital in Fulham, London. She was recovering from a nervous breakdown. My first impression of her was mixed as she sat huddled in the corner of the day room. This was where the patients go in between classes run by the OT's (occupational therapists).

The classes were compulsory to attend. They varied from current affairs, pottery, creative writing, arts and crafts, cooking, exercise, and a few more I can't remember.

Many patients were back in the institution after a few months. As once discharged they had great difficulty adjusting to the real world. It was my third visit in as many years .My mother spent most of her adult life in and out of mental hospitals with very little help from doctors, whose main course of treatment was rest and electric shocks delivered to the brain, (ECT). All that achieved was to make the patient forget. Sometime during the sixties antidepressants became available for psychiatrist to administer. These drugs have a proven record in the majority of cases.

There she sat in the corner. Around the table were a few other patients in various stages of recovery.

'Does anyone have a cigarette to spare?' she said.

Smoking is very prominent with people suffering depression. Nobody answered except me, offering her one. I was obliged to hand them around to the rest of the group. From that moment, our romance blossomed.

Me, I'm fifty-seven, six feet tall with a thick mop of white hair. My wife had passed on leaving me with four children to raise, two boys and two girls. Years before, she fell foul to that insidious disease—alcoholism. It killed her five years previously. The doctors diagnosed cirrhosis of the liver. We had married young, eighteen years of age to be precise—I loved her dearly. Even now, I wonder if the pressure of raising four children eventually had its effect on her. I like to think it was the worry that turned my hair white. In fact, it was hereditary as my mother, aunts, and uncles all went white prematurely, except for my two brothers. My dad, who I could hardly remember, passed away during World War II. He contracted TB (tuberculosis), a very prominent illness at that time due mainly to malnutrition.

Better wake Mary up or we will both be late for breakfast.

Over the years, we had cultivated a group of friends who for different reasons had attended the same hospital as us. One of the ladies called Patricia had married and divorced an inhabitant of Turkey, so she was fluent in the language. As we were all keeping well and feeling fairly confident, it was suggested we should holiday in Dalman, south Turkey.

Chapter 5

'Let's go over the plan one more time.'

'But Bernie, we know it by heart,' said Harry.

'Listen to me, you dimwit. We can't be too careful. You know the consequences if we are caught. They have no compassion, the council exterminators.'

Bernie chose that word to be more dramatic.

'They'll have you down the pound before you can shake your leg. Then it's the stun gun or poison and goodbye, Harry.'

'I say, old chap, are you directing your remarks at me?' said Harry.

'Yes, because you're such a dunce, so can it while I go over the plan once more.'

Harry thought, One day I'll have my own gang and won't have to take orders from that big lump.

'Now listen up,' said Bernie. 'At 9.55, I will be waiting at the southern corner of the street outside the supermarket. At 9.58, you, Harry, will wander down from the north and be in position. By 9.59, that's thirty metres from the hit, you'll sit down and pretend to sleep. Make sure you stay awake, keeping one eye open in case the dog catchers are out early. I have been watching the place for weeks, and they never show till the earliest at 10.30. By then, we will be gone. Jack, your job is to approach with Barney from the rear of the premises, under the fence by the olive tree, where you will find a small opening I dug last night. It'll be a tight squeeze but shouldn't cause you any problems. Once you are inside the compound, you draw the bolt on the gate, leaving enough room for Barney to step through. Don't open it too far so to draw attention to yourself. Once Barney is through, you will have two minutes in which to operate. At precisely 9.59, I will amble down the High Street so as to be outside Abraham's at ten sharp, meeting up with Speed, who will approach from the side alley next to the restaurant at the same time. Now, Speed, this is your first job, and I am aware how nervous you are.'

'I'm not nervous,' said Speed with more confidence than he felt.

'Well, be that as it may, I have every confidence in your ability. When the town hall clock chimes ten on the first bell, we go into action. At that point, I will turn and attack Speed, whose job will be to bark and yelp as loud as he can. The noise of the fracas coupled with the chimes from the town hall clock will bring Abraham and Dopey Dennis out of the café to see what's going on. Then and only then, Barney and Jack will check out the bins in the back yard with two minutes to sort through the garbage sacks. Take only what you can drag safely. Don't be tempted to take more as that will slow you down. Once you have made your selection, head for the disused pump house in the old bramble field behind Abraham's cafe. Whatever happens, stay put till we all arrive. Then we will share the spoils—okay, any questions? . . . No! So everybody is clear on what they have to do. Right, then let's make a move. Jack, you go first followed by Barney, Harry, then Speed, and myself. We'll leave at one-minute intervals so as not to draw attention to ourselves; off you go, Jack.'

Abraham stood in the doorway of his restaurant feeling quite pleased with himself. His wife was happy. She had been elected on to the PTA (parents and teachers association), the children were doing well at school, and his business returns were up on last year. That night, he knew he would be very busy as he had recently installed a large screen television and satellite dish, enabling him to show the big match. Two rival English teams were due to meet—Chelsea and Manchester United at Old Trafford. The screen was to be erected outdoors on the patio. That allowed Abraham to put in extra chairs for the paying customers. The football teams were so well known in Europe that other nationalities would come to watch, women as well as men. This didn't surprise him, as in recent years, he had noticed an increase in women supporters. After all, his daughter played for the school girls' team.

'Yes,' he sighed, 'life is good.'

Casting his eyes down the street, he noticed a dog lying in the sun, nothing unusual about that. But what he found strange was that the dog appeared to be a husky. You don't see many of those around in Turkey as they normally reside in cold countries like Canada, Iceland, or countries close to the pole caps. As long as the husky was alone, Abraham didn't foresee any problems. His mind drifted back to his restaurant, thinking if the staff would be able to cope with the extra clientele he was expecting that evening. He had hired two more waiters to cope with the influx of people he expected to watch the match. Mind you, he would have to think about expanding once Turkey was accepted into the common market. After all, the government was already set up for entry and just waiting for the European council to vote them in. His eye latched on to a large dog, looking like a St Bernard, approaching from the supermarket. Abraham watched as it ambled along. The animal stopped and did a large crap right outside his patio. What luck! Dopey Dennis had just washed that down, but before he could shoo it away, haring around the corner straight out of the alley came a little whippet-like mongrel that ran full pelt into the St Bernard and tried to mount him. All hell broke loose—they were snapping, biting, and the little one was yelping. The clock in the tower was chiming. It was bedlam.

'Take it easy,' said Bernie to Speed. 'You're hurting me. Don't get carried away.'

Just then, the chefs and Dennis rushed out to see what the commotion was about.

Meanwhile, Jack had taken his cue, ducking under the fence by the olive tree. He ran to the gate and clasped his teeth on the bolt, drawing it back, thus allowing Barney to step through, remembering to leave the gate open.

'Come on, Speed, let's get to it. You take the four trash bins on the right. I'll handle the rest.' The pair of them set about their task.

The first bin Barney pulled over had nothing but potato peelings and rotting vegetables. The second was more successful—plastic bags full of, if his nose was to be relied on, meat scraps, bones, and chicken carcasses. The third was the same. He was aware of Jack rummaging through the other bins. They would have to hurry because the noise they were making would surely bring someone to investigate.

By then, Dennis had connected the hose and turning on the tap, proceeded to spray Bernie and Speed with a powerful jet of water.

'Time to go,' said Bernie, running past Harry at full pelt as he and Speed tore up the road. Taking his cue, Harry got up and followed.

Barney became aware that the noise in the patio had stopped. He barked at Jack, 'Grab what you can carry and leg it. I'll meet you at the pump house.'

Bernie, Speed, and Harry reached the southern end of High Street puffing and panting. Barking to the others, Bernie said, 'This is where we split.'

As Abraham would be using his mobile to ring the council dog catchers, it would be more difficult for them to be caught if they went their separate ways. Also the townspeople were out and about, as well as a few early risers—those who hadn't been drinking the night before and who were genuinely here to see the local geological attractions as opposed to the boozers whose aim was to get drunk every night and enjoy themselves. If you could call it that, Bernie thought rather cynically. Still, everyone to their own preferences as to how they spend their annual two weeks' holiday.

'OK, let's split and mingle and meet in a few hours at the pump house.'

'Bernie,' Speed piped up, 'I think I've broken my leg.'

'Can you walk on it?'

'Yes.'

'Then it's not broken just sprained. Hobble down to the marina, find a secluded spot, and sit in the water for an hour or so. That will bring out the bruising.'

'But I can't swim.'

'Well, find a shallow spot and just sit,' said Bernie somewhat tersely. These youngsters, he thought, they're so inexperienced they need wet nursing 24/7. Mind you, for his first job, he's performed very well.

'You okay, Harry?'

'Fine,' he replied. 'I'll just mingle and wander around,' he said, thinking, People seemed to like huskies and often gave him titbits. Perhaps it was his good manners.

'Right, scat,' said Bernie. 'See you at the pump house in two hours. Make yourselves scarce and watch out for the dog catchers.' So they split. Harry made his way to the ruined mosque, headed for the marina, and Bernie made his way out out of town—the best place to be if the catchers were about—out of sight, out of mind. Jack finally made it to the pump house huffing and puffing, dragging the two plastic goodie bags.

'You took your time,' said Barney. 'I've been here five minutes.'

'So!' replied Jack. 'I had to lug two bags.'

'Big deal,' said Barney. 'I carried three.'

'Yeah! You're bigger and stronger than me. Anyway, let's have a look to see what we have.'

'Better not,' Barney said. 'Wait till Bernie arrives. You know the rules.'

'But I'm hungry.'

'You'll just have to wait. Bring the bags over here, and put them with mine in the corner.'

Jack dragged them over. His stomach churned with the odour emanating from the bags.

'Can't we open one?' Jack asked. 'Who's to know?'

'That's not the point, Jack. This gang is based on trust, and without trust, you are unable to function as a team.'

'S-s-pose you're right, but I'm starving.'

'Lie down and have a nap till the others arrive. Think about your friend Mimi, the poodle. That'll take your mind off your stomach.'

Jack curled up in the opposite corner to the food and tried to sleep. He was just starting to doze when Barney said, 'Are you sure you weren't followed?'

'Of course, I'm sure. What do you take me for—a bloody novice?'

'Just asking,' replied Barney.

Except for the birds and the occasional fox passing by, it was quiet and cool inside the pump house as the two dogs relaxed with their own thoughts. Jack thought about Mimi and the possibility of an entertaining evening when they met later, Yeah, Mimi was special. Sure he had plenty of other girlfriends, but Mimi knew the right buttons to push where Jack was concerned. Yeah, she certainly did. He sighed.

Barney was finding it difficult to sleep. For some reason, he was worried about Speed. Had he made his getaway? Did he panic? Was he safe and had the council men captured him? Already he had started to 'what if' himself—what if this happened, what if that happened. Calm down, my son. There's nothing you can do at this moment in time but wait for a couple of hours and see if he shows up.

Speed was like a son to him, a son he never had, as he was neutered when he was a youngster. Having taken Speed under his wing, Barney was determined to teach him all he needed to know to survive—and survive he would.

Harry was minding his own business as he wandered around the ruined mosque when he bumped into a young couple.

'Hey! Look, Rose, there's a stray dog over there. If I'm not mistaken, it's a husky. What's a husky doing in a hot country like Turkey?'

'Dunno!' said Rose. 'Call him over. See if he comes.'

'Here, boy, come,' said Peter.

Harry knew how to play the game, so he trotted over. After all, his previous owners had taught him all the commands—sit, come, stay, heel, fetch, so on and so forth. You never know. There might be a treat in it for him. What was the saying? Never look a gift horse or something like that, so there he was.

'Sit,' said Peter.

That's precisely what Harry did, wagging his tail at the same time.

'Oh! Look, Pete, he's obeying you.'

'They always do if there's food about,' he said.

'Give him a piece of that ham you have in the picnic basket. Go on, he's so friendly.'

Pete suitably obliged.

After eating the ham, Harry rolled over on his back with his legs in the air and tongue hanging out of his jaws.

'Oh, he wants us to stroke and play with him,' said Rose.

The pair played and walked with Harry. After a while, Peter said, 'We had better be going if you want to sunbathe on the beach.'

'Can we take him with us?' said Rose.

'Be practical, Rose! He doesn't have a collar. For all we know, he could have rabies or distemper.'

'I suppose you're right. It's such a shame. He's a lovely dog.'

'If you really want a dog, I will get you one when we get home.'

'But I want this one.'

'Well, you can't have it.'

'But I want it.'

'Stop being a spoilt brat. You can't have it and that's final.'

Rose and Peter walked away still arguing.

Well, it was nice while it lasted. Mind you, time's getting on. I better make my way to the pump house.

Bernie drifted out of town. He wasn't in a hurry. After all, he had a couple of hours to kill. Keeping to the side roads and in the shade, he felt safe. I wonder how the others made out. The job seemed to go smoothly enough. No problems from my end. If Jack and Barney stuck to what we rehearsed, all in all, it will have been a productive morning. As he rounded the bend in the road by the old deserted villa, he thought he heard a sound. His ears pricked up, so he stopped to listen. Must be my imagination, he thought as he continued on. There it was again. It seemed to be coming from the overgrown garden in front of that villa.

Sounds like a mewing, he thought. I'll just keep on walking and mind my own business. The last thing I need is trouble. The words had barely crossed his mind when, to his utter dismay, a lean, mean feral cat appeared out of nowhere, its back arched, hissing through its teeth.

'Stay back or I'll tear your eyes out.'

'Pardon?' What Bernie didn't need right now was a confrontation with a half starved, lunatic, feral moggie.

'Whoa! Hold up. Where did you come from?'

'Never mind that. This is my manor and you're trespassing,' hissed the cat through clenched teeth.

'Look, I was passing by minding my own business when you leapt out of nowhere and threatened me. I think you're pushing it, to say the least, so out of my way and let me pass.'

'I'm warning you,' said the cat.

'You're warning me,' Bernie replied. 'That's a laugh. I could eat you for breakfast, no problem.'

'Yeah,' said the cat.

'Yeah,' Bernie replied.

'Well, come on, then,' said the cat, 'you fat lump.'

'Come on what?'

'Try to eat me.'

'Look, this is getting us nowhere. Move aside and I will be on my way.'

'How do I know you won't come back and cause trouble?'

'You don't, and if you don't move your arse, you'll have more trouble than you can handle.'

'Yeah?'

Here we go again, thought Bernie. Then he heard it again, the same mewing noise.

'What's that?' asked Bernie.

'What's what?' said the cat.

'That mewing sound.'

'What mewing sound?'

'Bloody hell! Are you deaf as well as obnoxious?'

'Who are you calling obnoxious?' said the cat.

'Quiet!' boomed Bernie. 'I'll have a look.'

'Oh no you don't! It's my kittens and they're hungry.'

'Why didn't you say so?'

'Because you never asked.'

'Look,' Bernie said. 'I'll be passing this way with my gang later, and I'll bring some food back for you and your family.'

The cat's attitude changed. 'Is your name Bernie?'

'Why?' Bernie said.

'Well, I met two members of your gang earlier on, said their names were Barney and Speed. Barney, the bigger dog, shared some food with me. He spoke very well of you.'

'Be that as it may,' said Bernie feeling somewhat embarrassed, 'take my word for it. I will be passing by in a few hours, and will bring some food back with me. You can rely on it.'

'Thank you,' said the cat. 'I can't leave the young-uns to hunt. It's too dangerous and I'm not able to produce any milk to feed them as I am too undernourished.'

'We'll soon take care of that. Just be patient. I will be back.'

Bernie realised time was getting on, and he should make his way to the pump house, so turning around, he said goodbye to the cat, reminding it to stay out of sight as the catchers were about. Looking over his shoulder and addressing the cat, he said, 'I never caught your name?'

'It's Molly.' Then she was gone.

Bernie and Harry went their separate ways, so Speed thought he would do what had been suggested—make for the marina and sit in the water. Bernie said it would help his sprained leg. He should know. After all, he was the boss.

But how will I know if it's shallow, he thought. I suppose there must be a way of finding out. Come to think of it, what does shallow mean? Anyway, I should get there as soon as possible. As he hobbled towards the marina, a feeling of loneliness enveloped him. He felt lost and alone without the others around him. Limping down the hill towards the quayside, once again his senses were alert. With the stall holders and tourists milling around, nobody seemed to notice a poor crippled pup. Oh dear, he thought, now I'm feeling sorry for myself. Not far now. The sooner I get in the water, the better. With about fifty metres to go, Speed noticed a group of dogs blocking his path. Pay no mind, he said to himself.

'Oi! What do you think you're up to?'

At a glance, Speed realised it was Big Bob the mastiff and his motley crew.

I'll have to front it out, thought Speed. After this morning's fracas, I have no chance if they start a fight

'Mr Oi, to you,' he retorted. As the words left his mouth, he thought, Shit, why do I have to be so flash? It's okay when the gang is around to back my play, but now I've no chance. They'll kill me.

'Well—you're that little runt we had a "run-in" with this morning.'

'Yes,' Speed replied, thinking on his feet. 'Look how you left me, with a broken leg.'

'You're lucky we didn't break your neck.'

'We've hurt him enough,' said the little whippet, 'and he is under Bernie's protection.'

'S'pose you're right,' said Big Bob. 'Let him pass, but in future, stay off my patch.'

'I'm only going for a dip in the water.'

'Well hop off—get it? Hop off,' laughed Bob, looking at the rest of his surly crew. They all sniggered and pretended to laugh. Anything to keep Bob happy, thought the whippet.

Speed was so relieved to get away that before he knew it, he was up to his belly in water. Big Bob called his band together and meandered off.

This is a nice little spot I've found, thought Speed. Not too many people about. I think I'll stay here and see if my leg improves. The water felt cool, just as well as the sun was directly overhead. As he squatted down, he thought, Nobody to bother me except for some children in the marina about a hundred metres further down the quayside playing. So engrossed in their game they were totally unaware of Speed.

About fifteen minutes had passed and he was dozing off when suddenly he heard someone shout, 'Help! Help!—There's a dog drowning!'

Speed looked up. Where? he thought. Then he heard and felt an almighty splash right beside him, and before you could shout Jack Robinson, a few pairs of hands had hold of him and he was hoisted out of the water. Hold up, thought Speed. I'm not drowning. Put me down. By then, he was surrounde by a group of children all yelling, 'We've saved a dog! Hurrah!'

'But I didn't need saving,' barked Speed.

'Leave it to us,' a burly voice said. 'We'll look after him.'

Oh no, Speed thought. There stood two men by a white van with the rear doors open and what appeared to be a large steel cage in the back. They were the dog catchers.

'Don't let them take me. I'm dead once in that cage,' barked Speed.

'Leave him to us. We'll take care of him.'

'No! No! No!' Speed barked as loud as he could. 'Don't let them take me.'

'Hand him over,' said the second man. ' That's good boys, he will be safe with us.'

The boys handed Speed to the man with the burly voice. At that precise moment, the man gave a yelp and dropped him on the floor. As he landed, he noticed the whippet who spoke up for him before had sunk his teeth into the catcher's ankle. Speed didn't need any urging. He ran it as fast as he could, which was pretty quick considering his bad leg.

Chapter 6

Abraham was pissed off. He had rung the council about the dogs. Mind you, he laid it on a bit thick—the animals were vicious and a danger to the public and for all he knew, they could be rabid. It never occurred to him that there had never been one case of rabies recorded in the immediate area as far as anybody knew in living memory.

The chief pest control officer had dealt with Abraham before and was quite familiar with his attitude, implying that he and his staff were underworked and overpaid.

'I pay my rates and taxes. I backed the council in the last election, so I am entitled to a decent service from you.'

Mohamed Izmik thought to himself, Being chief of the pest control unit was proving to be more demanding than he was led to believe. Mind you, it had its perks—a nice three-bedroom villa on the edge of town, away from the general hubbub of the market and the constant melee of holidaymakers, a four-door saloon car supplied by the mayor's office, petrol paid from the council coffers, and in addition, a liberal expense account. Even with all of that, he still had to appease Abraham Burdur. Speaking into the phone, he said, 'Yes, Mr Burdur, I'll send my best men around immediately. You can rely on the full cooperation of my department. Yes! Yes! They will be there in fifteen minutes.'

Putting the phone down, Mohamed thought, There's very little I can do after the advent except to advise Abraham on tighter security.

Mohamed radioed his two more accomplished controllers, who he had sent to the marina to investigate a reported incident concerning a drowning dog. Privately, he named them Bill and Ben. They were brothers, dedicated to eradicating all the feral cats and dogs that lived in and around Dalman They both considered all animals vermin. Needless to say, they were not very popular with the locals, who had a fondness for pets.

'Car AC 1, are you there? Pick up and call in.'

Bill, who was nursing a sore ankle, said to Ben, 'Answer that call. It's old slobber-chops.'

It was the name they had bestowed on Mohamed, as he tended to spit and dribble when speaking, especially if angry.

Ben flicked the switch on the radio and answered, 'Yes, Mr Izmik. Benjamin here. Can I help you?'

'Drop whatever you're doing and get over to Abraham Burdur asap. There's been an incident there, some sort of problem with wild dogs. He's been on the phone bending my ear again.'

'Sorry, Mr Izmik, no can do.'

'What do you mean no can do?'

'Just as I said. That job you sent us to at the marina, the reported drowning dog.'

'Yes,' said Mohamed.

'Well, while we were in the process of putting the beast into our van, a small sausage-like animal bit William on the ankle, so we are heading for the hospital, over.'

'Never mind the hospital. Get round to Burder's straight away.'

'As I said, Mr Izmik, no can do. Union rules state if any members in the course of their duties incur any injury, they are to report to the police and make their way immediately to hospital to receive treatment for tetanus or rabies.'

'What do you mean rabies? There hasn't been a reported case in living memory.'

'Be that as it may, I can't take any risk. I could easily be infected and just as easily pass it on to the others. Then the whole department could be put out of commission.'

'Don't be stupid,' said Mohamed.

'Who are you calling stupid? I'm just obeying the rules.'

'All right. Take Bill to the hospital, then make your way over to Abraham Burders.'

'Can't do that,' replied Ben. 'William may already be affected and could have passed the infection on to me.'

The radio went dead. Mohamed was furious. Talk about job's worth! He would have to ring Abraham Burder and make excuses as to why his men would be late.

Thinking about what he would say, a brilliant idea came to him. Picking up the phone, he rang Abraham's number.

'Ah! Mr Burder' I am quite worried about your problem' so I will be coming around immediately to sort it out. See you in fifteen minutes.' That should appease him, thought Mohamed, personal service no less.

Chapter 7

Shaking Mary gently by the shoulder, George said, 'Wakey, wakey, time to get up.'

Mary yawned, 'Five more minutes.'

'Come on,' said George. 'It's past eight and we need to shower before breakfast.'

'I thought the agreement was, even though we came as a group, we could still do our own thing.'

'That's right,' said George, 'but I think it would be appropriate for all of us to have breakfast together on the first day of our holiday. I've made you a cup of tea.'

Like most holiday complexes, the apartments had tea and coffee facilities. 'A nice cup of tea and your first cigarette of the day, and you'll be raring to go'. George was a non-smoker. He gave it up ten seconds past 12 a.m., New Year's Day, three years ago, due to health reasons. Well, not really. He was just neurotic and a hypochondriac, to boot. In all fairness, he had no problem with those who chose to smoke, not like some people. As far as George was concerned, it was their choice.

Having worked hard all his adult life, bringing up four children and nursing an alcoholic wife plus coming from a deprived background, he was aware how much money you could save over a period of a year. If you smoked thirty cigarettes a day, about £2,200, it would pay for a decent holiday every summer. Indeed, during the first year of his departure from the joy of inhaling nicotine, he religiously, every morning, dropped £7.50 into an old giant, plastic, imitation coke bottle, his reasoning being depending on what brand of cigarette you smoked, they cost about five pounds a packet of twenty.

Mary came from a middle-class background. I know what you are thinking. It's not true; you still have a class system in England even though the middle classes are the ones feeling the pressure in the current financial situation—no growth in the economy, two and a half million unemployed! But I digress. She is vegetarian, loves all animals, and once owned her own horse called Heathcliffe. I can hear the cogs in your brain turning, putting two and two together and making five, thinking, How could they sustain their relationship, coming from different backgrounds?

At breakfast, George and Mary decided they would seek out the local stables and do a spot of riding, which they both loved. Mary was an accomplished horse person, and George was, well . . . a novice really. They had heard that in Turkey, they rode Western-style saddles. That would be a first for George. He was quite looking forward to the ride. As he had only ever ridden European style. They spent most of their spare time riding in north Wales, finance permitting. They had found a stable in the middle of a national park situated at the foot of Mount Snowden. At that time, George had never ridden before, and the funny thing was he felt totally at home with the idea of horsemanship, even though he didn't have a clue what to do with regard to trotting, cantering, and tacking up.

'What would you do if the lead horse in a party took off into a gallop? Your horse would surely follow?' said Mary.

'No problem,' said George. 'I would jump off.'

'Don't be silly. You would hurt yourself, even possibly be killed.'

'Don't talk daft,' replied George. 'I've seen plenty of cowboy films. It's easy.'

Mary gave up! George would have to learn the hard way, and learn he did.

Over the next few years, they spent as much time riding as they could. Even though George enjoyed himself, he never really mastered horsemanship. Mind you, riding Western-style really appealed to him.

'Come on, Mary, hurry up! I can't wait to get to the stable.'

Chapter 8

Bernie started back to the rendezvous point, the old pump house, as ever careful to keep to the back streets and a wary eye out for the council catchers. As he had time to spare, he thought he would check out the dirt road between the two hotel complexes. He had been there before and was pretty sure it was a dead end. In a way, the road would suit their needs. Being a dead end, nobody would have reason to use it, so if the gang did move to town, they would pretty much be undisturbed. The main drawback being the councils pest control department. If they found out that a pack of feral dogs were hanging out there, it would be fairly easy to ambush them with only one way in and out. Well, thought Bernie, can't do any harm to check it out.

As he neared the town centre, he knew at some point you had to cross the main road. Unfortunately, there wasn't any way of avoiding it. It was where you were most vulnerable. The utmost care had to be taken—one eye on the road the other on the dreaded council catchers. Slowing his pace and with his ears on red alert, he waited for a lull in traffic and proceeded to amble across, thinking that way he would appear to any nosy parkers that as he wasn't rushing, he probably knew his way around and belonged to someone local.

On reaching the other side, Bernie quickened his pace up to the next right turn that led down to the hotel complex. Having made the turn successfully, he was able to relax a little and take in the sights and scenery. To the uninitiated, this would probably seem a little frivolous, but to Bernie, a necessity, as you never knew when information concerning your locality would be useful, especially in a tight spot. Immediately as he turned, on the left-hand side of the road was a parade of shops. He counted seven, all catering for tourists. There was a Minimart with cooler cabinets outside stocked with mineral water as the local water was undrinkable unless you boiled it. As in late August/early September, it has been known for the temperature to reach forty-four degrees, the tourists needed a constant supply of fresh water to sate their thirst.

Next to the Minimart was a shop trading in leather goods, handbags, wallets, purses, even handmade leather cases containing backgammon sets. The men of Dalman were very much into board games.

The third shop was selling ladies dresses, T-shirts, underwear, even parasols. The yellows and pinks and other pastel shades made the frontage very attractive to the naked eye.

On the corner of a narrow alleyway was a green grocer's with a great variety of different fruit, apples, oranges, bananas, and the largest peaches Bernie had ever seen, apricots, melons, cherries, and virtually every fruit that you could think of.

Taking on board all he had seen, Bernie filed it away in his memory to be investigated when he had more time. On the other corner of the alley was a tobacconist-cum-paper shop and next to that, a gentleman's hairdresser, followed by a post office.

Turning his attention to the side he was walking on, Bernie noted he was passing a large car showroom with all the latest models lined up behind the glass frontage. Next to that, a large building lot stretched down to the end of the street, no doubt once again catering for tourists who could afford to buy a holiday apartment. Property was relatively cheap compared with other European countries. The same went for the cost of living, but prices would increase once the European community accepted Turkey into the common market.

On the other side of the road after the shops and leading down to the junction were all residential properties.

Reaching the end of the street and crossing the road, he continued on. Bernie could see it led to a blank end. On either side was the rear of the hotel complexes with the entrances in the adjacent streets. Running along both sides was an three metre wall. Attached to it was a hedgerow of bushes and long grass, which Bernie noticed with increased interest.

As he approached the end, he could see a wooded area matted with brambles and shrubs seeming to lead nowhere. Because the thicket was so overgrown, he was unable to ascertain the depth of the matted undergrowth.

On further investigation, Bernie found two very narrow paths which led out to the west side of the marina. Ideal, thought Bernie, an escape route. This appeared to be exactly what the gang needed should they decide to move to town. It certainly had his vote. The move depended on how the others reacted to his suggestion.

Engrossed in his observations, Bernie realised he was already running late to meet up with the team. Finally, he arrived at his destination, out of breath and thirsty. Passing through the door, he was greeted by a cacophony of barking.

'Quiet, you dumbos, else you'll have the catchers on our backs."

'We thought the catchers had caught you,' they barked in unison.

'I said quiet!'

'What happened to you?' said Jack.

'I'm only fifteen minutes late,' replied Bernie. 'I went to recce a possible new home for us should we decide to move to town, which certainly has my vote.'

'Tell us about it,' said Harry.

They all gathered around Bernie as he proceeded to recount what he had seen. When he had finished, Barney, ever cautious, reserved any comment on the proposed move until he had given the area the once over. Jack, Harry, and Speed were very enthusiastic, all reasoning if it was good enough for Bernie, it was good enough for them. After all, Bernie knew his way around the area.

One after another, they related their experiences as to what happened to them after the successful heist.

When Speed told his story, he was careful to leave out his lack of understanding of shallow water. It was generally agreed that he was very lucky to escape from the dog catchers, and if it wasn't for the whippet's intervention, he might not be there to tell the tale.

'The whippet used to run with us until he changed allegiance to Big Bob's undisciplined mob,' said Bernie.

'I suspect if the truth is known he regrets the move,' said Bernie. 'Anyway, on to more important things. Time to share the spoils. How did we do?'

'Five bags altogether,' said Jack. 'We might have done better, but we were pressed for time, plus I could only manage two.'

'Bring the bags to the centre of the room and we'll have a divvy up,' said Bernie.

They all sat in a circle while Bernie emptied each bag in turn. Well, it was a nice little haul—spare ribs, steak bones, some chicken bits, and fish pieces.

'That'll keep our bellies filled for a couple of days. Save some of the chicken as I promised a friend of mine who's hit on hard times I'd bring her some food.'

'Well said,' said Barney. 'There's life in the old boy yet.'

'It's not what you think,' came the reply, but Bernie declined to explain his reason, not wanting to appear soft.

'We'll stay here until dark, and when you've all finished eating, settle down and take a nap. I'll wake you when it's time to leave and show you the new hideout.'

Chapter 9

Abraham put the phone down on Mohamed, thinking to himself, Perhaps I was over the top mentioning rabies. If Mr Izmik is coming himself, he must be worried about the situation. Moving from his office to the kitchen where Dopey was industriously cleaning the cooking pots. he said, 'Dennis, check around and make sure that everything is spick and span. I am expecting a visitor from the council, a very important man.'

'Yes, Boss, right away,' he said, thinking to himself, I bet it's Mohamed Burder, the pest controller. They've known each other since they were kids.

Indeed, Abraham and Mohamed had grown up together, went to the same school. Even as adults, they still maintained a keen competitiveness as to who had fared better in their chosen careers.

Mohamed left his office, telling his secretary he would be out for an hour or so to attend personally to an urgent case. Should there be any problems that she was unable to deal with, he could be contacted on his mobile.

Driving directly to the café, as Dennis, Abraham's long-suffering employee, called it, he thought, Old Abe! his nickname for Abraham, suffered from delusions of grandeur. A restaurant indeed! Everybody knows it's a café. Still, if it keeps Abe happy, then let it be so.

Pulling into the public parking lot on the opposite side of the street, adjacent to the ice-cream parlour, he got out, locked the car, and carefully straightened his tie. He crossed the road and entered the café, nodding to Dennis as he passed.

Abraham was seated in his office looking around, feeling quite pleased with himself; he had come a long way since he inherited the family business. The restaurant was doing so well he was thinking of expanding. Who knows? In a few years, he could be the proud owner of a chain of restaurants. Yes! He had certainly done well. Looking around his office seated on his reclining chair at the recently installed oak desk, he noticed an intercom plus a large well-stocked drinks cabinet, his own private bathroom, and his latest purchase, a computer. At that time, more for show to boost his importance, his children were teaching him how to use it.

He knocked on the office door and at the same time reminded himself when conversing with Abe to refer to the premises as a restaurant. In spite of their differences, Abe had really worked hard since taking over the restaurant from his father. Certainly he had increased his clientele and had a reputation for serving good traditional English food.

Most of the tourists liked the street dogs as they all seemed well fed and very friendly.

Last year during the winter, when food was not so plentiful, the council had passed a resolution to round up the strays and have a vet give them a clean bill of health. Those who passed were recognised by a green tag stapled in their ear. The others were put down either by poison or electrocuted. That way, they were able to control the animal population. Obviously, some dogs and cats escaped through the net. Those were the ones causing the problems. It was quite an investment for the town council, but they reasoned the ends justified the means.

During the last year's holiday season, they conducted a poll amongst the holidaymakers and found to their amazement that the majority of tourists were in favour of the idea. That is the tagging, not the cull. When asked what happened to the others, they instructed their pollsters to say wherever possible that each dog was found a decent home, which was completely untrue. The strays were rounded up and taken to a pound two miles east of Dalman and exterminated.

As the poll suggested, the tourists found tagging acceptable providing the remaining animals were housed. According to council records, the tourist that were approached some 80 per cent were British, who apparently loved their animals, mad dogs and Englishmen and all that . . . By adopting this policy with the strays, the council had found that tourism had increased over the last two years by 30 per cent due to the rise in prices of the other major holiday countries or because the cost of living in Turkey was 40 per cent below the rest of them, and the weather was just as good, plus the beaches and night life was excellent.

Of course, there were other places on the south-western shores where people could holiday at a much more leisurely pace. That part of Turkey was very Westernised as opposed to the inner areas that were still very old world.

As an added bonus, you were able to catch the ferry to the Greek Islands or even Greece itself at Canakake, north-west Turkey, there you could board a ferry to Venice, taking about twenty-four hours.

Chapter 10

Mohamed rapped smartly on the office door. 'Enter!' said the voice. It was all part of Abe's business persona, even though he knew it was Mo, his nickname for Mohamed.

Closing the door behind him, Mo held out his hand. 'Nice to see you, Abe. Too long. Much too long for old school friends to be apart. I came as soon as I could. We are very busy at the moment. All my people are out on calls. Being as we go way back, I thought it was best to attend to your problem myself.' That should appease him, thought Mo. 'What exactly is the problem, Abe?'

'We will get to that in a minute. Please sit down and make yourself comfortable,' came the reply. He pointed to the brown leather, stiff-backed armchair, somewhat smaller than his.

'Drink?' said Abe, opening his well-stocked cabinet.

'No thanks,' said Mo, 'not on duty.'

'A coffee then?'

'Yes, thank you. That will do nicely.'

Clicking the intercom that connected to the kitchen, Abe barked, 'Robert, bring in two coffees . . . No, you idiot! Not café leche, Turkish coffee!'

Mo noticed he didn't use the word 'please'.

In general, both Mohamed and Abraham kept to Turkish traditions, but when speaking to each other, they conversed in English, their second language, that they were both taught in school; each one tried to outdo the other with his mastery of the Queen's English.

There was a tap on the door.

'Enter!' said Abe.

It was Robert. 'Your coffee, sir!'

'Yes, well, put it down, man. No! Not on my desk, you fool! On the coffee table over there.' He pointed to a mahogany inlaid nest of tables.

Getting up and handing a cup to Mo and taking one himself, he settled down in his plush chair.

'Right, to business,' he said, addressing Mo.

Abraham related the incident that occurred that morning down to the last detail, even compiling a few untruths to emphasise his annoyance.

'To add insult to injury, just prior to the fight, the big dog shat right outside my patio.'

'When you say big dog, could you be more specific and describe the animal?'

'Well, it looked like one of those dogs you see in pictures. You know, they have a small cask around their neck full of brandy and help to rescue people lost in the snow.'

'You mean a St Bernard?' said Mohamed.

'If not a St Bernard, a large dog that looks very much like one.'

'Um,' muttered Mohamed. 'It could well be a dog I've been trying to catch for a few years, but he's always managed to slip through the net. Yes, it's on my most wanted list. This is what I propose to do. As a start, I'll put on an extra patrol in this area and tell my informers to locate where it hides out. In fact, I'll offer a substantial reward to anyone who has information leading to the capture of the beast. I will have to okay this with the council, but I can't see it being a problem. They're well under budget this year.'

Getting up, offering his hand, and thanking Abe for the coffee, he said, 'Leave it to me. I'll be in touch soon.'

Leaving the office and making his way to the car, Mohamed pondered on the problem, thinking over the years he had had several run-ins with this dog, but it always eluded capture.

Chapter 11

At the pump house, the afternoon had drifted by and the dogs were beginning to stir. They were getting ready to do the evening rounds, begging food off the diners who ate at the various restaurants around the town.

'Right, now gather round,' said Bernie. 'You all have your separate eating establishments where you go to beg scraps, so at eight o'clock, start your rounds. As always, stagger your departure times. I recommend fifteen-minute intervals between each of you. Barney, I think Speed should stay with you.'

'That's not fair,' piped up Speed. 'I'm big enough to have my own patch. I want to go alone.'

'Quit it!' retorted Bernie. 'You certainly have grown these last few months, but you lack experience, so stick close to Barney, listen, and learn. I'll tell you when you're ready to go unsupervised.'

'But! But! I-I,' stuttered Speed.

'I said quit it, and that's my last words on the matter.'

Speed sat down staring sullenly at the floor thinking, My day will come, and I'll show them all. Didn't I do my bit when we raided Abraham's café? There again, it was my first raid. Bernie has a point.

'There will be one change to the routine this evening,' said Bernie. 'When you have finished your rounds, I want you all to meet at the bottom of Bodrum road.'

'Where's that?' barked Harry.

'You know,' replied Jack. 'There's a Minimart on the corner and next to that a shop that sells leather goods and on the opposite corner a post office adjacent to the car showroom, you dimwit.'

'Oh, there.'

'Oh, there,' aped Jack.

'Stop your bickering and pay attention,' Bernie said.

'I want all of you to wait till nightfall and arrive at different times. Sort that out amongst yourselves. Wait quietly in separate hide holes till I arrive about eleven o'clock. As I said before, there's plenty of cover and it's a dead end.'

'Isn't it dangerous?' said Barney.

'No. There are two concealed paths that lead down to the marina, and the thicket is too dense to see into. Any questions? No! . . . Right, Jack, you go first, fifteen minutes after me.'

'Where are you going?' Barney said.

'I promised to meet someone,' said Bernie as he picked up the leftover chicken pieces and left.

Chapter 12

Mary and George caught the bus going to the riding stable, situated five kilometres along the road leading to Ortarco a mining town The stables were sited behind an exotic restaurant that was constructed on two levels around a pair of small lakes. Each level had six areas that projected over and around each lake with a table that could cater for twelve people. Apparently, in the evenings when the restaurant opened, you could dine under the stars surrounded by flamingos, storks, and all manner of bird life whilst being entertained by a traditional Turkish band. One of the more interesting features of this remarkable restaurant was that as you entered through a narrow arch, there were flowers on both sides and running across the top of what could be described as a tunnel. As you passed through the tunnel, on your right side, there were two women kneading dough, which they baked in an open kiln and served with your starters. The menu consisted of traditional Turkish fare and a good selection of main courses from most leading European countries.

George noted the name: Lake Hous. It was their seventeenth anniversary on Saturday. Maybe I'll book a table and surprise Mary, thought George.

They entered the stable courtyard to see other people standing around dressed in summer clothes—T-shirts, sandals, flip-flops. Not ideal—footwear without heels, thought Mary. On the right-hand side were nine horses already tacked up.

'Mary!'

'Yes!'

'They're not very big, are they, compared with those in Wales?' said George.

'No, silly. They're a different breed. They're mainly used for herding.'

'Oh! I didn't know.'

'So now you do,' chided Mary, forgetting that George was relatively new to riding.

From a small wooden cabin exited a tall, lean, tanned man who looked as though he worked the land for a living. Holding out his hand, he introduced himself as Ilias.

'Are you experienced riders?' he said in rather stilted English.

'My wife is a very accomplished rider,' said George proudly. 'As for myself, I manage.'

It soon became apparent that Ilias's English was very sparse, limited to short sentences, such as 'Mount up', 'We are off', 'Stop', 'Go', and so on.

Mary had the foresight to bring their riding helmets; just as well, as Ilias didn't offer any. She doubted if he had insurance to cover the customers. As they mounted, George exclaimed, 'Look, Mary. That chap is sitting arse about face. He's having a laugh. He can't be serious.'

'Don't be so critical, George. More than likely it's his first time on a horse.' Mary nudged her mount forward and spoke to the young man who was obviously very embarrassed about his predicament.

'I feel such a fool,' he said. 'This is my first time on a horse.'

'Not to worry,' said Mary, and to ease his discomfort said. 'That happened to me on my first ride. Let me hold the reins, then slide off.'

The young man who looked about twenty years of age, and was clad in a white T-shirt on which was printed a picture of Che Guevara on the front and Fidel Castro on the back. His jeans were faded and torn. Mary had noticed that quite a few young people were wearing their jeans rather tattered. They couldn't all be poor. It was probably a fashion statement, mused Mary. After all, when she was young, didn't she wear mini skirts and ridiculous four-inch heels and had her hair cut in a Mohican style and dyed red, white, and blue. In those days, she thought she was the cat's whiskers. She sighed to herself. Oh! To be young again. Still, she thought, there was very little to gain dwelling in the past.

'Now come round to the left-hand side of the horse,' she said to the young man. 'Put your foot in the stirrup pointing to the horse's flank. That's right. Now clasp the saddle with your left hand and swing your right leg over the horse's rear. That should land you in the seat.'

She noticed he was trembling as he swung himself up, and unfortunately landed on the horses' rump.

'Not bad for your second attempt. Now shuffle forward till you're in the saddle. Then put your right foot in the other stirrup and take the reins in your hands. Whoa! Don't hold so tightly. There you go. Now you're ready to gallop and jump.'

'What!' exclaimed the boy. 'I can't do that!'

'Only kidding,' chided Mary. 'Remember, next time you ride, make sure your footwear has heels attached as it can be quite dangerous if your feet slip through the stirrup, especially when you're moving fast.'

'Moving fast? No way,' said the boy. 'There won't be a next time.'

She didn't bother to tell the lad that the herdsman rode one-handed, leaving the other free to manoeuvre the livestock.

'By the way, I'm Tom,' he said, holding out his hand.

'Mary!' she replied as she shook it warmly, thinking, If Tom is so scared, why is he riding? It doesn't make sense. Well, mine's not to reason why.

'I suppose it would be too much to ask, when we get going, to keep an eye on me as I'm a little frightened.' In fact, he was more than a little frightened—he was petrified.

'No problem,' said Mary, pondering on Tom's words.

George trotted up. 'Is everything all right?'

'Fine, I was just giving Tom here a helping hand.' With that, she stooped down to tighten Tom's horse's girth a few notches. As she pulled on the strap, the horse trumpeted a loud resonating fart.

'Charming,' said George. 'How come ours never did that when we made the adjustment?'

Mary shrugged.

At last, they set off. The only ones who looked happy were the three children whose parents presumably the other two riders were trying to remain anonymous.

The children, whose ages ranged from eight years to twelve, so George thought, pretended to have guns. Ilias had magically turned into an Indian brave, who they were determined to shoot. Inappropriately, the sounds they made were more like modern machine guns than pistols of the old west, except for the youngest, a girl who was trying her best to imitate the boys. She was having considerable difficulty, owing to the braces on her teeth. She was constantly spitting over the horse's mane.

The noise coming from the non-existent pistols was irritating to say the least. They can't keep this up much longer, thought George rather optimistically. If they do, surely the parents will tell them to quieten down.

The make-believe guns continued as the children fired at each other or at Ilias, the Indian chief. About thirty minutes into the ride, they stopped as the trail led into a narrow path that wound through the foothills. The riders were reduced to proceeding in single file, with Ilias in front and Mary bringing up the rear. This gave the adults a chance to view the wonderful scenery unfolding as they meandered along. The children remained silent. The horses were determined to take advantage of the long grass bordering both sides of the track. With their heads down munching, the children, their mothers, Tom, and the horses remained stagnant.

Mary hoped Ilias was a strict Muslim and wouldn't understand the foul language the non-riders were shouting.

The only ones unimpressed were the horses, who were grazing quite happily.

Ilias turned around and noticed no one was following. So he trotted back. He didn't have to say a word. The horses pricked up their ears and continued walking. Even the children were impressed so much so, they ceased swearing.

They had been ambling along with no major incidents, if you don't count the loss of flip-flops and low overhanging branches, when the trail widened to reveal a wide tract of land.

The horses knew they were on their way home and became friskier. Also, to Mary's dismay, the other riders seemed to have gained undeserved confidence and bravado. One person, who shall remain nameless (George), imagined he was on the home straight in the Grand National with cheering crowds as he galloped past the winning post. All these ideas vanished as Mary shouted, 'The horses could and would go faster as they near home.'

Ilias looked worried, Mary thought, though she noticed a slight smile appear on his serious face.

'Trot, canter, gallop,' he murmured vaguely.

At least he has them in the right order, thought George, gripping his horse's mane and closing his eyes. He wasn't the bravest of people.

There was silence, even from the children. Everyone glanced at each other to see if they understood correctly.

'Grab your manes,' Mary yelled.

Half of them held their own hair, not knowing what a horse's mane was. This was disastrous as it left their reins loose, and horses took full advantage of the situation, breaking into a trot and heading for the stable.

The eldest boy was riding the laziest, smallest, and fattest of the horses, who had been at the stable the longest and knew every trick in the book. It was aware that it wasn't necessary to exert yourself to unseat a rider. Thus, allowing an easier, lighter journey back to the stable, it had decided to use an old favourite. Tobias (the boy mounted on his back) had a fit of giggles watching his sister heading into the distance. His horse put into practice his tried and tested dismount, the whether-you-want-to-or-not technique. With no time wasted, he dropped to his knees and rolled in the grass.

Poor boy! (if you are feeling generous and kindly since there are many other words you could describe Tobias) He found himself quite disorientated sitting in the grass.

The horse (mission accomplished) contentedly trailed after his friends.

Mary, who had stayed back to help anyone in need, asked, 'Are you hurt?'

'No!' replied Tobias putting on a brave face.

'Good! Well, up you get and catch your mount.'

From afar, a familiar voice range out, and, for some reason, reminded Mary of a wildlife programme she had seen on the television about orangutans. She dispensed with the uncharitable thought, realising George was in trouble. He was heading straight for a large tree, making unusual yelling noises. Mary galloped towards him, but time was not on her side.

Horses! At least riding school ones have more sense of self preservation than you might think, and just before impact on hard wood, the horse swerved around the tree, unseating George, who found himself pirouetting like an ungainly ballerina towards the ground. Mary, although concerned, had to stifle a giggle.

Ilias, never far from the disaster, was openly laughing and shouted, 'Bravo!' at George's balletic performance and clapped his hands.

George, now standing on two feet although landing on one, took a bow. He never missed an opportunity to show off. His horse, whose name was Dancer, headed for the stable. Ilias kindly, or hoping for more laughs, caught up with him and returned the animal to George, who was then limping.

'I would love to remount but I've injured myself,' he said, trailing his left leg.

Ilias refrained from comment; he had seen this ploy used many times when riders had lost their confidence.

All the riders had reached the stable except for the other lad, whose horse had decided to fulfill its lifelong ambition of pretending to be in the rodeo. He bucked playfully two or three times till he heard a bump, and then he trotted off after his friends where he would find peace, rest, and a good feed.

Those who arrived first were still in their saddles, not sure what to do. So they waited for Ilias and Mary. Ilias dismounted, and to complicate the situation, his knowledge of the English language had mysteriously disappeared. He seemed to be enjoying himself, nodding and smiling, expecting Mary to join in.

At last, they had all dismounted, and the horses were safely tethered to the hitching rail. George's limp had miraculously cured itself. Once the horses were settled, it was time to leave, but not before paying Ilias for the ride. Gathering around, they handed him their money, refusing any change. The couple standing apart from the rest said in unison, 'We'll pay for the children.'

George thought, That sounds like a declaration of parenthood. There again, he could be wrong.

George was the last to pay. Resurrecting his limp and reaching for his wallet, he gave Ilias the thirty euros, the cost of his and Mary's ride. Ilias, who had thoroughly enjoyed himself watching two dancers together, took the money thinking, I'll be dining out on this story for weeks.

As the group made their way to the bus stop outside the Lake House, Mary heard Tobias say to his sister, Jessica, 'I say, Chesky, I think my horse farted.'

'I know it did as I was right behind you,' she replied. 'I didn't know horses farted.'

Mary couldn't resist it, she said in a low voice, 'They do fart and very loudly.'

The children looked suitably shocked at that word coming from an adult.

Chapter 13

Bernie had a lot on his mind. First, he had to ferry the chicken scraps to Molly and her kittens. With the plastic bag containing the food clasped in his jaws, he headed for the old villa, the greasy scraps smelt delicious as the aroma wafted up to his sensitive nostrils, making his jaws water. A promise is a promise, he said to himself.

He had other problems to contemplate—the fact was time passes. Now at the ripe old age of twelve, which he kept to himself, his legs ached. He no longer had the energy he used to have.

All he wanted to do was to sit in the shade and dream of large juicy steaks and huge meaty bones. By far, his biggest worry was the constant fear of the dog catchers. It nagged him like a fierce toothache. Also, he had to find a new base for his gang, although he hoped he had solved that problem for now. He couldn't be certain until they had stayed there for a few nights and thoroughly checked it out.hopefully, he should arrive around 11 p.m., sometime after delivering the food to Molly and her kittens.

As he made his way to the old ruined villa, his nose picked up the scent of the cat. Molly wasn't the cleanest of cats and the smell hung in the air. As he neared her hiding place, his ears latched on to the same mewing sound he had heard before, and from out of nowhere appeared Molly, whose eyes were so sharp she had spotted Bernie fifty metres away.

'Is that you, Molly?' he barked.

'Who do you think it is?' said the cantankerous cat. 'The pest controllers?'

'Don't joke aboutt! That's not funny.'

Molly immediately honed in on the chicken Bernie was carrying. 'Is that for us?'

'Yes! For you and your family. How many kittens do you have?'

'Four. I did have six, but one passed away last week, and last night, I lost another.'

'I'm so sorry,' said Bernie. 'I hope this food helps you out, and I will endeavour to bring some more every other evening.'

'That's very kind of you.' Molly's whole demure softened. 'I really am very grateful. Once I can build myself up, I will be able to suckle the kittens and hunt for myself.'

'Think nothing of it! May I see the young-uns?'

'I would rather you didn't as the sight of you would scare them to death, and they're halfway there already.'

'Perhaps another time then.' Putting down the plastic bag, Bernie made his excuses, 'I had better be off as I'm due back at our new hideout.' Bernie turned and said, 'See you in a couple of nights. Bye,' and was gone.

It was close on eleven o'clock when he reached the top of Bodrum Road; the Minimart was still open—a must if you want make a living, when you consider the new supermarkets stock everything these days at very competitive prices. Plus, the tourist season only lasted four months, sometimes running into the second week of October. Most of the smaller businesses closed during the rest of the year, leaving the owners and staff to seek other work in the big cities.

Bernie felt tired as he trotted down the street, careful to look both ways as he crossed the junction. I'm definitely slowing up, he thought. Perhaps I should consider stepping down and letting someone else take over, but whom? The obvious choice is Barney. There again, would he want the additional responsibility—leading the pack plus keeping an eye on Speed? I think I'll hang on at least till the gang settle into the new hideaway. That's assuming they agree to stay. Well, I must say, they have certainly hidden themselves very well. His thoughts were interrupted by a soft bark coming for a clump of bushes on the left.

'Over here.'

That sounded suspiciously like Jack, he thought. Bernie made his way to the sound. A head appeared between two low branches.

'It's me—Jack. There's enough room for two of us in here, and you can't be seen from the street.'

'Where are all the others?' said Bernie.

'I don't know. We agreed to find our own spot and lie low till you arrived.'

'Okay, Jack, follow me. It's dark now, so we shan't be seen.'

Leaving the cover of the bushes, Bernie and Jack proceeded down the left-hand side of the secluded street. A little further on, they came upon Harry, fast asleep under an overgrown olive tree.

'Would you take a look at that!' exclaimed Jack. 'If I hadn't seen it with my own eyes, I would never have believed it.'

'Wake up!' growled Bernie. 'I said, wake up.'

Harry lifted his head and yawned, saying, 'I say, chaps, it's a bit late to be waking one up.'

'Waking one up, you, you stupid mutt! Anyone passing by can see you.'

'Nobody comes down this end of the street,' said Harry.

'That's not the point. There's always the odd chance that someone could pass by and report you to the council catchers, thereby endangering all of us,' growled Bernie.

'Oh, I never thought of that,' said Harry.

'Oh, I never thought of that,' chided Jack, 'you bloody dumb arse.'

'Quiet, you two! The last thing we need is to draw attention to ourselves. Let's find the others.'

The three of them continued down to what appeared to be a dead end, then they turned right along the edge of a hedgerow. About five metres futher, they stopped at a small gap in the grass as they heard a low panting sound.

'Is that you Bernie?' It was Barney.

'Yes! Are the others with you?'

'Yes!'

'Is Speed with you, Barney?'

'Of course I am. Where else would I be? You said I wasn't experienced enough to go it alone and to stay with Barney, so that's what I'm doing.' Bernie detected a touch of irony in Speed's manner.

'Good man,' said Bernie. He almost said, 'Good boy,' but stopped himself in time. The last thing he wanted was to put his foot in it, with Speed being so touchy about his independence.

'As I said before, I've checked this end of the road out. There are two little paths leading down to the marina. The rest of the area is covered with thick bamboo and prickly, overgrown shrubbery. Once through this gap and a few metres in is a clearing where the five of us can bed down for the night,' Bernie said.

Bernie found it a tight squeeze because of his size, but once inside, there was ample room for the five of them.

'Okay, lads, settle down and make yourselves comfortable. It's been a long day. Let's get a good night's sleep. In the morning, we'll talk about making this our new home—night all,' he said.

By the sound of the snoring, the others were already in the land of nod.

Chapter 14

Monday morning at eight o'clock sharp, Mohamed entered the briefing room, making his way to the small desk that stood beside a large map of Dalman mounted on the wall. Standing next to that was a board that had a variety of pictures pinned to it. Opening his briefcase, he took out some papers, which he shuffled. Why he did that he wasn't sure, but deep down, there was always a feeling of insecurity having to address his staff who were gathered there expectantly waiting to hear what he had to say. Glancing around the room and noting all those present, he thought, No absentees today. Word must have got around about the importance of this meeting.

His staff consisted of four pairs of animal welfare teams, the name given to his catchers. He had changed their title as it made them sound more caring. Except for Bill and Ben, who hated animals, the other three teams couldn't care less; it was just a job to them. Then there was the vet, a rather grumpy man just seeing out his time, and his keen assistant, ready to step into his shoes when he retired, two female admin staff, plus two pest controllers, who handled anything from rats, mice, infestations, bee colonies, mosquitoes, and such.

'Ladies and gentlemen, before I begin, are there any unusual reports from last week I should know about?' Mo didn't think there would be. There were a few gripes and grumbles that were to be expected from his overworked staff. Then Ben raised his hand.

'Yes,' said Mo.

'You will be pleased to know that William and I have both had our rabies and tetanus shots plus blood tests. We will have the results in four weeks.'

'Excellent,' replied Mo. 'I am pleased to see you both well, and I hope there are no unpleasant side effects.'

Mo always praised the deadly duo. After all, they were his most efficient catchers; they really loved their jobs. Even knowing there had never been a case of rabies or tetanus in recent recorded history, Mo felt obliged to keep them happy. Mo addressed the assembly, 'It has come to my notice that there has been a recent increase in the raids on restaurants in Dalman. The main culprits would appear to be led by a large dog.' Picking up a pointer from his desk, he honed in on a picture of Bernie pinned to the board. 'I've had several reports about this particular mongrel, which seems to be getting bolder by the day. I've known about him for years, but he has always eluded capture,' said Mo, striking the desk with some vehemence, thus having the effect of grabbing his staff's attention. 'It has to stop!'

The fact is he only had one complaint, and that was from Abraham. Well, it could do no harm to keep his staff on their toes. Addressing the catchers, he said, 'As you know, every week, I alternate the areas you patrol. So you can familiarise yourselves with each other's territory. This week, I want you to concentrate on your own areas, and you will need to be ever vigilant if we are to nail this perpetrator.' Mo thought that word sounded dramatic. Yes, I'll file that away for future use. 'So from this moment on, I want you all to double your efforts. Any sightings or unusual behaviour report to me immediately. No action to be taken without first informing me. Is that understood'.

The catchers nodded their heads in unison.

'That's all for now. So let's get to it'.

That afternoon, after checking the animal pound and briefing the staff on the expected increase in captures, Mohamed was due to meet with the town council and hoped to prise out of them a substantial reward for the capture of the St Bernie look a like and his gang. Should he be successful with his request and knowing his informers where money was concerned, they would double their efforts. and the fact that he had three people who were animal-haters, of dogs in particular—Faruk, the road sweeper, Mrs Fethyde, who ran the post office, and Oli Atalya, who owned the local auto repair shop.

That afternoon, with success ringing in his ears, having persuaded the council to put up a reward of three hundred euros for information leading to the capture of this brute. The word he used was chosen to impress the council of the urgencies of the capture. He arrived back at his office to find a message on his desk from Mrs Fethyde at the post office: 'Could he pop in to see her?'

My, he thought, already the word was out concerning the reward. There again, it could be another matter entirely. Mo had promised his wife to be home early to attend the PTA meeting. Still, he had to pass Bodrum Road on his way home; so he decided to look in on the old nosy parker. He made calls to his catchers for an update as to what progress had been made, telling his secretary he was leaving. If necessary, she could contact him on his mobile.

Driving through town, Mo was constantly looking for stray animals. Not surprisingly, he saw none. The reason was probably down to the heat of the day. Making a left turn into Bodrum Road, he stopped the car outside the small post office. The main office was situated in the high street, not far from the town square.

Mrs Fethyde had been the postmistress at this little sub-station ever since her husband died. Apparently, as far as Mo could remember, he never had a day's illness, yet he went to bed one evening and never woke up. That's the way to go, he thought. The coroner's verdict: natural causes. Some people said she nagged him to death. She had a reputation as an old gasbag, with her nose permanently in other people's business on matters that did not concern her. Practically anything that happened in Dalman she knew about.

As he entered the post office, a voice called, 'Mr Izmik. I'll be with you in one minute.'

Mo looked up and smiled. To his right were three chairs up against the wall. Two were occupied by elderly citizens. Most of the locals conducted their business at this little post office. They preferred the personal touch compared with the town office, where they treated you like a number. The very fact that the chairs were nice and comfortable for the older people to sit on whilst waiting their turn was proof that their custom was appreciated. Mrs Fethyde appeared at the end of the counter, and lifting the hinged flap, beckoned him through.

'Come in,' she said as she ushered him into a small but airy room.

'Please sit down. Coffee?' she asked.

Mo sat—'Well I am in rather a hurry.'

'Turkish, of course, none of that leche nonsense,' she replied.

Mo sighed to himself, I better appease the old bat.

'That'll be lovely.'

Pouring two cups of thick black coffee and handing one to Mo, she sat in the seat opposite.

'How good of you to come so quickly. I hope the information I have will be of some use to you.' Then, rather hesitantly she continued, 'I-I er believe there's a reward for information leading to the apprehension of the dogs that raided Abraham Burder's café?'

'Yes,' replied Mo.

'Well, I'm not sure if this will help, but last night whilst taking my evening stroll, it must have been around 10.30, as I passed down the end of this street, I came upon a husky dog curled up asleep under an overgrown olive tree.'

'You did? And where exactly was that?' said Mo.

'About thirty metres on the left—past the road junction.'

'You mean this road?'

'Yes!'

'But it's a dead end.'

'I know, but there it was.'

Mohamed's mind was churning over. Hadn't Abraham Burder mentioned a husky asleep when his café was raided? This is too much of a coincidence, he thought. How many huskies can there be in Dalman? That breed of dog usually lives in much colder countries. Gulping down the remains of his coffee, Mo stood up.

'Well, thank you, Mrs Fethyde—a very useful piece of information. I must be off as I have another appointment,' he lied. As he made to leave, Mrs Fethyde said, 'If what I saw helps in any way, you won't forget the reward?'

'Rest assured,' replied Mo, 'you'll get what's coming to you'.

Chapter 15

As the sun rose behind the high-ridged, purple-coloured hills, Bernie roused his team.

'Wakey! Show a leg. Time to move before anyone is out and about.'

One by one, they stretched and yawned.

'Another ten minutes,' murmured Harry.

'I said up!' barked Bernie. 'We can't stay here all day as we'll draw attention to ourselves. Now listen up. I did a lot of thinking last night and came to the conclusion that this new hideout suits our needs. The only drawback I can see is we can only access it when the sun goes down for obvious reasons. Are we all agreed? . . . Jack?'

'Yes.'

'Harry?'

'Spiffing new home.'

'Speed?'

'Er! Me . . . yes!' Speed was quite taken aback that Bernie had asked his opinion. All of a sudden, he felt important. Puffing out his chest, he said, 'I'm with you, boss.'

'I'll take that as a yes,' said Bernie thinking, I played that well by allowing Speed to voice a vote. He was acknowledging that he was maturing and by implication becoming more responsible.

'Barney, do you have any objections?'

'It's fine with me and like you said, access only when it's dark and leave at sunrise.'

'Well, that's agreed then. Let's disperse at five-minute intervals and meet back here tonight. One more thing, go about your normal business, keep a low profile, and stay out of trouble, and Jack, a word in your ear. Watch yourself with that French poodle. You could be biting off more than you can chew.'

When Bernie left, he made his way down to the old boathouse, where he could find some shade and catch up on his sleep, as he had precious little sleep the preceding evening. He arrived fifteen minutes later, finding himself quite a shady spot, where he wouldn't be disturbed. He lay down and tried to sleep. But still, he was unable to nod off.

There was something at the back of his mind that didn't sit right with him. It concerned Molly and her kittens, and he just couldn't put his paw on it. Eventually, he fell into a troubled sleep.

He awoke with a start; the burden of leadership didn't sit well with him. Once again, he thought about handing the responsibility over to Barney if he could be persuaded to accept. But as before, his instincts told him Barney was fully occupied nurturing Speed along. That's why he involved Speed this morning in decision-making. The quicker he matured and became streetwise, the sooner he could approach Barney about taking over.

The sun was directly overhead, and the few hours' sleep he had managed left him dehydrated. So the first port of call was the disused pump house, where the old machinery still leaked fresh water. As he stood up and stretched, a voice yelled, 'Oi! You! . . . You! Piece of vermin, hop it. What are you doing skulking around here? I'll have the dog catchers on you.' A broom head landed on Bernie's back, wielded by Faruk the road sweeper.

Bernie yelped and dashed off. That hurt! he thought. If proof was needed, that incident sealed it for him. Not only was he getting old, his once acute hearing was now a distant memory.

Harry was last to leave. As he exited the hideout, he noticed the sun was high. Damn, he thought, I must have fallen back to sleep. I better make haste in case I'm seen. He scampered down Bodrum Road heading towards his usual stomping ground, the old mosque. His mind wandered back to the previous evening, thinking that Bernie overreacted just because he nodded off under the olive tree. After all, nobody went down that end of the street. It was quite safe with the two hotel complexes backing on to each side of the road, shielded from view by the high walls and hedgerow, plus the tangled web of bamboo trees, brambles, and matted undergrowth that sealed the bottom end. Yes, he was sure it was safe.

Arriving at the mosque that was located close to the market, he was surprised to see it so crowded. He joined the throng of tourists as they jostled around looking for bargains, bartering with the stall holders, leaving him feeling quite claustrophobic and longing for his old home, now a distant memory since his owners had upped and left. Where he originated from was a mystery to him. Bernie had suggested Iceland, somewhere north, where for most of the year, the temperature was sub-zero, whatever that meant. All he could remember of his puppy-hood was his owners' house in Dalman, with the air conditioning installed for the hot summers. He felt very hurt that they upped and left, tossing him out in the street to fend for himself. He was quite ignorant where street life was concerned, and when his owners had left him near the market, he hadn't realised they were abandoning him. He thought they would be back later and were allowing him sometime to mooch about and enjoy himself. When it was dusk and the stall holders had ceased trading, closed down, and drove away in their vans, he realised something was amiss. So he made his way back to where he lived only to find the house deserted. Even then, he thought there must be an explanation to this event. Perhaps they had gone to visit friends and forgotten him. But after three days of waiting, starving, and being alone, he realised something was definitely wrong.

What to do? he wondered. He hunted around to see if he had buried any bones, but to no avail. He remembered the gold fish pond in the rear garden, so he was able to sate his thirst even though he wasn't too sure about the purity of the water. Even the fish were listless, and the pond was beginning to stagnate as a dirty green film of algae was forming on the surface.

Sitting at the front gate feeling sorry for himself and wondering what to do, he noticed this collie walking down the street towards him. As it drew nearer, he realised he was mistaken. At a distance, it seemed to have the marking of a pure-breed; up close, Harry realised the animal was a mongrel with collie markings.

Being somewhat reticent to strike up a conversation with a mere mongrel, Harry held back and waited to see how the mutt reacted. As the dog neared, it spoke directly to Harry, 'What's up, mate? You seem rather down and forlorn?'

'Yes. I have been waiting three days for my owners. They've disappeared.'

'Oh,' said Jack, 'have you thought of looking in the windows? That might give you a clue.'

'Good idea,' said Harry. 'Two brains are better than one. Let's pull together.'

Harry headed towards the nearest window and stood below it as Jack trotted up to him. He realised Harry was waiting for instructions.

'Put your paws on the window sill and look in.'

Harry's nose was pressing against the glass, his eyes widened, and he dropped to the ground.

'Well, what did you see?' asked Jack.

'Nothing,' said Harry.

'Nothing?' said Jack.

'Nothing, nothing.'

'Nothing, nothing,' said Jack.

'Nothing, nothing, nothing.'

Jack thought, This is stupid. I'm not playing this game. And being much smaller, he was unable to see for himself. Instead he barked curtly, 'Describe the room to me.'

'There's one, two, three, four, five, oh no, four blue walls, five windows, and um . . . um a white ceiling, and a cement floor.'

Jack pondered on this mystery for at least five seconds and came to the only possible conclusion; this mutt's family had left, taking everything with them apart from the dog, who didn't seem to realise the implication of no furniture in the room. How could he break the bad news gently? He looked at the husky's stupefied face and heard him say, 'Nothing, nothing, noth . . . '

At this point, Jack could stand it no longer and snapped, 'They've left, and by the looks of it, they ain't coming back.'

'Left? Left! . . . left forever? Oh no, no, they must have forgotten me.'

'Yes,' replied Jack, hoping to make up for his short temper a minute ago. 'They must have been in a rush and thought you were in the car or something.'

'But they dropped me at the market.'

'Oh!' Jack said, trying to change the subject. 'By the way, we haven't been introduced. My name is Jack and yours?'

'Harold, and I'm a husky.'

As if I didn't know that, thought Jack. To lighten the mood, he said, 'You don't see many pure breeds these days, especially a husky. You're in the wrong country, mate.'

Harry, not knowing why or where he belonged, kept quiet.

'Look, there's nothing here for you, so why not tag along with me?'

'That's very kind of you. I'll do just that.'

As the pair of them sauntered down the road, Harry looked over his shoulder. Somehow, he thought that was the last he would see of his safe, comfy home. On reflection, Harry thought he was lucky to run into Jack, who seemed to know his way around.

'I say, Jack, where do you come from?'

'Dunno,' Jack replied. 'I've always lived on the streets.'

'Where'r your parents?'

'Dunno,' said Jack, 'I don't remember.'

'Oh,' said Harry, 'how sad.'

'I'm all right,' said Jack. 'I run with a gang and we get by,' adding, 'I'm footloose and fancy-free and do what I want, when I want. I'm on my way to the rubbish tip. Why don't you join me?'

What had he to lose? thought Harry. Rubbish tip, what's that?

'After the tip, I'm meeting up with Bernie, our leader and organiser. You never know. He might ask you to join us, though I must say he is very picky when recruiting a new member.'

Harry was quite bemused—rubbish tip, organizer, recruiting. Having nothing else to do, he thought he'd tag along. Jack seemed a nice fellow—a bit rough around the edges, but he could live with that.

They had little success at the tip. Jack remarked, 'Big Bob has probably been here first.'

'Who's Big Bob?' asked Harry.

'He's the leader of a rival gang that Bernie doesn't see eye to eye with.'

'Really,' said Harry, not quite knowing what Jack meant by eye to eye, but again, he thought he would keep quiet and take in all he could.

At that moment, Harry was destitute, alone, and very scared, not knowing where his next meal was coming from, so his best bet was to stay with Jack and see what developed, realising there were no other options.

Jack led them through a maze of side streets, keeping to the shadows all the time, moving out of the town till they finally arrived at a nature park. Down a little footpath under a bridge, they followed a slow meandering stream for about four hundred metres, and quite suddenly, Jack turned left through a thicket out into a little copse and stopped. He barked twice and waited.

Through the undergrowth appeared two dogs, one much larger than the other. Harry guessed it must be Bernie as he had a similar stature to a St Bernard. The other to a certain degree resembled a labrador.

'Hi!' said Jack, addressing them both, 'this is Harry.'

'Hello,' said Harry meekly. 'I'm pleased to meet you both.'

Before another word was said, Bernie barked, 'How many times have I told you, Jack, not to bring strangers into our hideout? We know nothing about him. He could be a spy for Big Bob.'

'I don't think so,' replied Jack, who then went on to describe the circumstances under which they met, adding quite honestly, 'I felt rather sorry for him.'

On hearing the story of Harry's plight, Bernie's attitude softened. 'Well, he can stay here for tonight, and I'll reassess the situation in the morning. By the way, this is Barney,' said Bernie, nodding towards the labrador with the legs of a greyhound. 'He's my number two.'

Once again, Harry said, 'Hello.'

Barney replied, 'Pleased to meet you.'

'Have you eaten?' Bernie asked.

'Not for a few days,' replied Harry.

'Well, there's a few scraps over there under that tree,' nodding to his left. 'That should suffice till morning.'

Harry didn't need to be told twice. Within a couple of minutes, he devoured the lot.

'My, you were hungry,' said Barney. 'I've never seen food swallowed that quick. It never touched the sides of your jaws.'

Sometime later, when Jack and Harry were asleep, Bernie nudged Barney, 'What do you think?'

'About what?' said Barney.

'Harry, for God's sake.'

'Well, he's very naïve, which could be turned into an advantage for us as nobody would suspect a pure-bred husky of any skullduggery, the perfect foil for us when going on a raid.'

'I take your point,' Bernie said. 'I'll put it to him in the morning.' And that's how Harold became inducted into the team.

'Yeah, you do that,' said Barney casting his mind back to how he first teamed up with the gang.

For as long as he could remember, Barney had worked the streets on his own before Dalman had become a tourist attraction, but as the town became more popular and street dogs more plentiful, he began to notice more and more of his acquaintances disappearing, and it was getting increasingly difficult to survive operating alone as there was no one to watch your back. So he resolved at the first opportunity, he would find someone to team up with. Then one day whilst eyeing up a van delivering meat to the supermarket, thinking that as the driver loaded his barrow and then entered the rear doors, he would strike. He heard a deep voice bark, 'Clear off. This is my pitch.'

'What do you mean—your pitch?' he said, turning his head to see what appeared to be a St Bernard lying in the undergrowth. 'I was here first,' said Barney.

'That may be so, but it's my pitch.'

'I don't care. I was here first, so you clear off.'

'I won't tell you again. It's my pitch. I always work here.'

'And I won't tell you again! I was here first,' Barney replied, 'so hop it.'

'What do you mean, hop it, you sorry excuse for a labrador? Look, the driver has one load left. Because of your bickering, I've nearly lost my chance. The van is almost empty.'

'My bickering?' retorted Barney. 'You're the one who's bickering.'

'Oh, shut it,' said Bernie. 'Look, this is our last chance to score. If we don't hurry up, we will both leave empty-handed. Tell you what, I'm willing to take a chance—I'll block the door to the supermarket by lying down and pretending to be asleep while you snatch what you can from the van.'

Barney thought, He's right. If they didn't hurry, they would both end up potless.

So began an unlikely friendship.

Over the next few months, Bernie and Barney worked together. As they were both street dogs, they experienced very little difficulty in adapting to each other's methods.

It was late September and the tourist season was drawing to an end. They had just finished rummaging around the Taj Mahal, the only Indian restaurant in Dalman. Using their usual ploy, Bernie begging around the tables, that sat under a large canopy outside the main dining area, their system worked well. Bernie eased up to a well-stocked table and sat panting. If the diners fed him titbits, in his hurry to snap them up and being so large, he would accidentally bump into the table, thus spilling some of the food on to the floor, enabling him to indulge his appetite still further.

He would always pick a table furthest from the main entrance, thus ensuring the waiters, who were constantly in and out serving food, had a longer distance to travel when shooing them off. This ploy worked very well as Barney kept watch for any potential danger, like the restaurant manager, who may have witnessed this action before and could ring the dreaded council catchers.

At the next venue, it was Barney's turn while Bernie played lookout. They never worked the same venue more than once a week as there were plenty of eating establishments in Dalman catering for all tastes—French, Italian, Chinese, and the usual fast-food outlets.

They had had their fill and were heading back to the nature reserve as usual, using the back streets, keeping in the shadows. They became aware of a commotion emanating from the fried chicken shop on the edge of town. It was situated on the corner of a small dead-end road. On the adjacent side was a tobacconist. As they neared a small crowd gathered there, they noticed the white dog catcher's van next to the pavement a few yards down from the fast-food outlet and a consistent barking coming from the dead-end street, which sounded in dog terms like, 'You rotten bastards! You'll never take me alive. I've heard about how you kill off all the strays when the tourist season ends.'

If it wasn't so serious, it was almost funny, reminding Bernie of the old 1940s gangster films.

Barney and Bernie stood across the street opposite the dead end. By standing on his back legs and leaning on the wall, Bernie was able to see over the small crowd. He wasn't happy with what he saw. There were two catchers, one wielding a large net on the end of a wooden pole, the other with a metal adjustable noose attached to an extended telescopic rod, trying to corner what appeared at first glance to be a collie, who was frantically dashing up and down trying to evade capture and at the same time barking out rude expletives at the council men.

'We can't let him be captured,' said Barney.

'I agree,' Bernie said, 'but what can we do?'

'I have an idea. Bernie, if you and I start a fight at the back of the crowd and cause a diversion drawing the catchers and peoples attention to us, it might just give the collie a chance to slip away.'

'Good idea,' said Bernie, 'but we will have to make it loud and appear vicious.'

'No problem, Bernie, for two old campaigners like us. Right, Bernie, let's go for it. If the collie escapes, we'll split up and meet at the reserve.'

'Right on,' said Bernie.

The pair of them went at it hammer and tongs when a gruff voice shouted, 'What's going on?'

A chorus of voices replied, 'There's a fight. Two large dogs are tearing pieces out of each other.' A slight exaggeration.

'Let us through,' shouted one of the catchers. 'Leave it to us. We'll sort it out! Out of our way.'

As the catchers pushed through the crowd, Barney noticed the odd-looking collie limping out of the dead-end street and down the road.

Having the full attention of the catchers and crowd, Bernie said, 'Split and I'll see you later.'

Barney and Bernie went in different directions, making it harder for the council men to catch them.

Sometime later at the hideout, whilst discussing the day's events, they were interrupted by a bark that said, 'Can I come in?'

'Who's that?' said Barney.

'It's me,' replied the voice.

'Who's me?' said Bernie.

'Jack, the collie you helped earlier on today.'

'Well, show yourself.'

From out of the undergrowth appeared a dog limping and somewhat resembling a collie.

'You look in a sorry state. How did you find us?' asked Bernie.

'I followed the labrador. I can't thank you both enough for what you did back there.'

'Pleased we were able to help. How did you acquire that limp?' said Bernie.

'I crashed into a fire hydrant when fleeing the council men. If I hadn't done that, I would have outpaced them easily.'

'You were lucky. Had they caught you, it would have been straight to the pound, then extermination as that's the policy of the council once the tourist season is over.'

'Really.'

'Yes, you're not from around here, are you? We pretty much know every dog in Dalman.'

'That's where I am?' said Jack.

'You mean you don't know where you are?'

'No, I originate from Ismabul. Unfortunately, I left town in a hurry.'

'Why was that?' said Barney.

 77

'Erm! . . . Well . . . er! I . . . em! It's a bit embarrassing. To be quite frank, I'm in a bit of bother with the ladies.'

'Oh, I see,' said Bernie. 'You won't survive long in this town if you don't know your way around.'

'I'll survive,' said Jack. 'I have good ears and when my leg's better, no one is as quick as me.'

'That may well be, but the council is stepping up their policy of total extermination of all stray animals, especially dogs and cats without collars. Have you considered joining a gang? That would give you some security,' Bernie asked.

'Not really. I've always worked alone. Anyway, what have you in mind?' asked Jack.

'Well, us,' said Bernie, looking over at Barney and getting the nod.

'If it is as difficult as you say it is, it might well increase my survival chances. Tell you what, let's give it a try for a couple of weeks and see how it goes.' Two weeks later, it was the rebirth of the Three Musketeers.

Chapter 16

Jenny was a black Heinz 57 (a mixture of many breeds), who Jack hadn't seen for a few months, having bumped into her whilst making his weekly trip to the dump he noticed she was heavily pregnant but rather underweight. Keeping the conversation light, he remarked amiably, 'When's the happy day, Jen?'

'Anytime, Jack,' she replied. 'I'm keeping as close to the tip as possible so should there be any scraps of food left at the dump, at least I'll have a chance of first pickings.'

'Well, good luck. I'll see you around.'

'Yes,' Jenny said rather sadly.

As he walked away, Jack felt rather guilty. Maybe, just maybe, he could be the father. Dismissing that thought from his mind, he reminded himself that after all she was the local ride, but the guilt persisted. Some three days later, Jack decided to revisit the dump and asked Barney to go with him.

'But you were only there a few days ago.'

'I know,' said Jack and went on to explain how he felt. Plus he needed moral support.

As the pair of them neared the skip, they became aware of frantic barking.

'That's Jenny,' said Jack hurrying.

'Whoa! Hold it. Let's sneak up slowly. We don't know what's going on.'

Jack hesitated. 'You're right,' he said, 'but I'm really worried Jen's in trouble. I know it.'

About fifty metres from the tip, they stopped and squatted down.

'Look,' said Barney, nodding towards a white van. 'It's the council catchers.'

The van stood to the left of the tip, from the way they were facing, the rear doors were open, revealing a metal cage. They were some seventy-five metres from where the van stood and unable to see what was insid, if anything.

'Let's creep a little nearer and make for that broken, dilapidated, kitchen table lying on its side. Once safely behind it, we'll be in a better position to access the situation.'

Jack nodded.

As they crept slowly forward, Jenny's plaintive barking became unnerving. She seemed to be saying, 'My babies! My babies, please don't take them, oh please! Oh please, won't somebody help me? Help! Help!'

Making it to the safety of the table, Jack, who by then was very agitated, wanted to charge straight in.

Barney said; 'Calm down, Jack. Let's try to see exactly what's happening. Then we'll form some kind of rescue plan. There's no point in dashing in unprepared. We could put ourselves in danger.'

'I don't care. Jen's in trouble,' and to reinforce his point, Jenny's barking became more desperate, crying, 'My puppies, my puppies, leave them alone, please, oh! Please . . . '

Jack could stand no more. He stood up bristling.

'That's it. I'm going in.'

Barney acted quickly, clamping his large jaws around Jack's neck and shaking it violently.

'All right!' All right! Stop, you're hurting me.

Letting go of Jack's neck, Barney barked, 'I'll stop when you're calm.'

'Okay! Okay! I'm calm,' said Jack.

'Right!' Barney said. 'Look over there,' nodding to his left. Coming over the tip were two catchers carrying what looked like bundles of black fur.

Jack had an idea, saying to Barney, 'You take the one on the left. I'll take the one on the right. If we sink our teeth in their legs, they'll drop what they're carrying, giving us a chance to rescue Jenny.'

'Not a good idea,' said Barney.

As the two men approached the van, another man appeared with Jenny, her head enclosed in a wire noose attached to a metal pole, still barking tearfully, 'Oh please! Oh please! Please don't hurt them. They're only three days old.'

'Stop that yapping,' said the third man, aiming a vicious kick at Jenny, who yelped painfully.

The man tightened the noose and dragged Jenny towards the van. By then, she could barely breathe, let alone bark.

Another van pulled up and parked near the first. Jack heard the driver say, 'I don't think you'll have enough room for all of them in your van. Put the big one in mine.'

With that, the two men threw the two black bundles into the cage and slammed the door shut. Then closed the van's rear door. You could hear the hurtful yelping of what must have been Jenny's pups.

Jack was beside himself. He thought, What can I do? What a useless piece of shit I am. The last he saw of Jenny was her pleading eyes as she was bundled into the second van.

Barney tried to think of something to say that would ease Jack's pain but to no avail. They waited there quietly. Both vans turned and passed within ten feet of the dogs with their windows opened. They heard the passenger in the front vehicle say into the radio, 'Yes, Mr Ismik. It's William. Mission accomplished. We're heading for the pound.'

The vehicles picked up speed along a flat straight road heading west. Very soon, they were approaching a steep hill. The vehicles slowed, and the gearbox clunked as Ben changed down. On reaching the crest of the hill, Bill said to Ben, the driver, 'How many of those mangy mutts did you count?'

'Eight, I think.'

'I thought nine,' replied Bill.

'Eight or nine, what's it matter if there is another one? It won't survive more than a few hours. All in all, a good day's work. We should be proud of ourselves, ridding the town of those filthy animals. Cull them all and incinerate the bodies, I say! Lousy vermin.'

Barney and Jack lay still until the vans were out of sight. Not knowing what to say, Barney stayed quiet, hoping Jack would make a move. After a few minutes, Jack said, 'Suppose we had better get going.'

'Suppose so. There's no point hanging around. There's nothing we can do,' said Barney.

'No, but I feel so useless. If only . . . '

'Stop it!' said Barney. 'Once you go down that road, you'll end up driving yourself mad. If only this, if only that . . . next you'll be running round in circles chasing your tail. There's no end to it.'

Jack fell quiet, lost in his own thoughts, trying to come to terms with his sorrow. No matter how he tried, he was unable to erase the feelings of utter guilt. He had totally convinced himself that he was the father of those poor little pups, and no amount of reasoning from Barney could quell his sadness.

The two dogs looked at each other, both waiting for the other to move. It seemed as if the whole world had stopped. Instinctively, both dogs lowered their gaze. Once again, Jack was in a world of his own, and Barney's thoughts drifted to a time long ago, remembering when he was young.

So much time had passed since his youth. Like most mongrels, he had no recollection of his father, but one incident he recalled when living on a small farm. That particular day, he was feeling rather adventurous. Whilst his brothers and sisters were playing in the barn and his mother was keeping a watchful eye over them, he decided to find out what was on the other side of the sty, the place his mother had always forbade him to go, which of course aroused his curiosity. After sneaking past his mother and crossing the rice field, there it was—the forbidden sty. Well, she did say when he was six months old that she would show him what was on the other side. Sure, he wasn't six months old, but five and a half is near enough. Putting one foot tentatively on the step, he hopped over, finding himself in a lane.

Apparently, according to his friend, the old ass that pulled the farmer's cart, a lane is a long stretch of open smooth ground that has twists and turns in it which terminated in a town. That's where people lived in houses very much like the building the farmer lived in with his wife and children, except they were all clustered together.

'Very unhealthy,' said the old ass. What he neglected to tell Barney was that a lane, as well as being a means of travelling from one town to another, one of its primary uses was for traffic. What he didn't explain and Barney was about to find out—motor cars. Wandering to the middle of the lane and looking to the east, he found the glare of the sun interfering with his vision. A noise he was unfamiliar with seemed to be getting louder and louder, and before he knew it, what appeared to be a large monster was thundering down on him. Scared, no—petrified, yes! He was unable to move, transfixed by this massive contraption not unlike the farmer's tractor, frozen to the spot as it propelled itself nearer and nearer.

'Mum, Mum!' he barked. 'Help . . . '

Then he heard a deep growl followed by a loud bark. He recognized his mother's voice, 'Barney, stay where you are and squat down.'

The words had barely penetrated his brain as the monster was about to devour him. Closing his eyes and waiting for the inevitable, the noise was deafening as the monster passed overhead. The next thing he knew was that his mother was standing beside him.

'You stupid pup, how many times have I told you not to cross the sty.' She said. 'One! You're not six months. Two, tell you I said, not show you. Now follow me back to the barn.'

Barney trotted after his mother, tail between his legs as he murmured, 'I'm nearly six months.'

His mother turned and barked, 'I heard that. Don't give me any of your lip, else you'll be for it.'

They continued in silence as they made their way back home. Barney's early life was fairly uneventful. His brothers and sisters were given to friends and family. On reaching the age of four, there occurred a double tragedy in his life. His mother passed away. She died peacefully in her sleep. She had prepared him for this possibility so he was able to pass through the grieving process fairly smoothly. About that time, the government subsidy dried up and farming was no longer a viable living, so the owner decided to sell up and move to Dalman. His children had grown and moved on. One year later, his wife died, leaving him with a defunct farm and a dog. So that day, they were on their way when tragedy struck. As the old lorry made its way down the mountain five miles from Dalman, the off-side front tyre blew, sending the lorry plundering down the mountainside. Over and over it rolled. Barney was flung clear as the lorry came to a stop.

Picking himself up shaken and bruised, he made his way limping to the blazing inferno. It was obvious nobody could survive that heat and fire. Feeling quite disorientated, Barney hung around till the fire burnt itself out and the the ambulance and police arrived. He kept out of sight till he regained his senses, rested up, and the next day, made his way to the town, where he had been on the streets ever since.

Jack's soft bark snapped Barney out of his daydreaming;

'Did you hear that?'

'Hear what?'

'That sound,' said Jack.

'What sound?'

'That sound!'

'Don't hear a thing,' said Barney.

'Listen, there it is again.'

They both kept quiet.

'I can't hear anything,' said Barney.

'There, hear it,' replied Jack.

'I told you I can't . . . '

'Shhh, it's coming from over there, just past that mound. Let's have a look.'

Thinking that Jack was losing his marbles and most of all to keep him happy, Barney followed him. Stopping for a second, he thought he heard something. There it was again. Catching Jack up, Barney said, 'I did hear something. It sounded like a whimper.'

The dogs stood together on the mound, the sound quite audible now.

'It seems to be coming from over there.'

Both dogs sensed something as they neared an old suitcase. The lid was closed but not locked. Jack pawed it open. To their amazement, lying curled up in a ball, was a tiny, black, whimpering puppy. On closer inspection, it had white paws and a white chest. It lifted its head and cried, 'I want my mum. Where's my mum?'

Through all his years on the street, Barney had experienced many things, but this little ball of black fluff tore at his heart strings.

Jack was standing with his jaws wide open staring dumbstruck, finding his voice and to cover his embarrassment, Jack said, 'What shall we do with it? I think it's hungry. We better get some meat for it to eat.'

'Don't be silly,' Barney said. 'Whelps can't eat meat. They need their mother's milk.'

'Where are we going to get that?' Jack asked.

'I don't know. Hold on, let me think a minute. Didn't you say that a friend of yours, what's her name, you know, that poodle, who gave birth last week?' said Barney.

'You mean Lulu.'

'That's it.'

'And what an assortment they are,' said Jack.

'I wonder,' pondered Barney.

'Wonder what?'

'It's worth a try.'

'What's worth a try?' Jack asked.

'Well—do you think you could persuade her to take care of Speed for a while?'

'You're confusing me. Who's Speed?'

'This little black ball of fluff.'

'How do you know its name is Speed?'

'Well it must have been fast to evade the catchers, so I've named it Speed.'

'But that's a boy's name. What happens if it turns out to be a girl?'

'My gut feeling tells me it's a boy,' replied Barney. 'Look, Jack, you nip round to Lulu's and see if she will help, then on to Bernie and tell him what's happening. I'll wait here with the pup till you get back.'

'I'm not sure how she will react as I've let her down a few times.'

'To make it simple, tell her it's one of mine. That way, you won't implicate yourself. Use your natural charm. Make her believe you have remained faithful to her.'

Barney thought, If I massage his ego, it may give Jack a lift, subsequently boosting his somewhat flagging confidence.

'Yes,' said Jack, 'no problem. I can do that.'

'Great, so shift it and get back as soon as . . . '

Jack legged it round to Lulu's and found she was housed at the bottom of her owners' garden. Squeezing through a hole in the fence he always used and padding quietly to the door of the garden shed, he barked softly, 'Lulu, it's me.'

A voice replied, 'Who's me?'

'Jack.'

'Jack who?'

'You know, Jack.'

'I did know a Jack once. He was a loving, caring dog who would never leave a lady on her own especially when she was giving birth. But he disappeared some time ago.'

'I didn't disappear. I've been away on business.'

'Been away sowing your wild oats, no doubt,' said Lulu.

'Sowing wild oats—that's rubbish. I've been trying to secure our future.'

'Really, Jack?'

'Yes, really.'

'I would love to believe you, but you are always telling porkies!'

'I'm not telling porkies. It's true. You know you've always been the only one for me, and I need your help. I'm in trouble.'

'What do you mean trouble?' she replied with a little edge to her voice.

'Well, it's not me. It's a friend. You know Barney?'

She had known Jack and his reputation a long time, but she still loved him.

'You mean Barney who runs with Bernie?'

'Yes!'

'Well, you better come in.'

The doors opened. Jack entered to see Lulu sitting in a basket surrounded by her litter. At a quick glance, he counted seven, all of different shades and markings. Making straight to Lulu, he licked and nuzzled her ear. Lulu's defence melted.

'I see you haven't lost your touch. Now tell me about the trouble Barney's in.'

She had known Barney as a friend a long time, and over the years, he had helped her on various occasions.

Jack related the whole sorry business to Lulu, implying that Barney and Jenny were partners.

'How strange,' said Lulu. 'I would never have thought Jenny was his type.'

'You know, Lu, it takes all sorts.'

'It certainly does,' she replied with a touch of irony.

'OK, Jack, I'll do it. Bring the pup around about ten o'clock when it's dark.'

'Thanks a million, Lu!' he licked her nose and was off, heading straight to Bernie to put him in the picture.

Barney was a little worried. Sitting in the middle of the tip looking at a suitcase was inviting trouble. The catchers might come, though he doubted it. Two of the teams had gone to the pound, which left the other two to make their rounds around the town. Possibly Big Bob might show up with his gang, and then again, Faruk, the road sweeper, might appear as he always emptied his container at the tip. No, he thought. It's not safe. I had better find a more secluded spot.

Barney surveyed the surrounding area to be sure he was alone. He clasped his jaws gently around the pup's neck, lifting it clear of the suitcase.

A small voice whimpered, 'Are you my mum?'

Not knowing what to say, he made his way to a clump of trees, out of sight of prying eyes. Settling down to wait for Jack, again the pump whimpered, 'I want my mum.'

'Hush now. She won't be long,' he lied.

As Barney settled again, for some reason, his inner eye conjured up a picture of a particular sunset he had witnessed some years previously as the red orb disappeared behind the purple hills. For a brief second, the sky was awash in a green hue. Rather weird, he thought. He had heard about this phenomenon. Apparently, it occurred in the Caribbean countries that lay along the line of the tropics. He felt privileged to have witnessed such a scene, his brain trying to remember the name of the spectacular event. Ah! That's it. I'm sure. 'The Greenflash', well, that was something to tell the puppy when it grew up, if it ever did.

'I'm hungry,' said the little one.

'Try to sleep, then when you wake up, you'll be with your mummy, and she will feed you.'

Jack appeared a few minutes later, he looked around the tip. Unable to find Barney, he started to panic. What if. .. ? Don't start that, he told himself. Think! If Barney's not here, there must be a logical reason.

Then he heard a low, soft bark coming from a clump of trees beyond the tip. There it was again. I better investigate. As he made his way towards the trees, there was another bark. It was Barney.

'Over here.'

Jack hurried forward to where the sound came from.

'There you are!' exclaimed Jack. 'You had me worried for a minute.'

'It was to dangerous to stay in the open, and I wasn't sure how long you would be.'

'How's the pup?' said Jack, a little concerned.

'As far as I can tell okay. He's fast asleep now but very hungry,' replied Barney. 'How did it go with Lulu?'

'Well it wasn't easy, but I stuck to the story we agreed.'

'How did you explain away the fact that you've been on the missing list?'

'Simple,' Jack replied. 'I told her I was away on business.'

'And she swallowed that?' said Barney.

'Yes! How could she possibly resist my undisputable charm?' replied Jack jokingly.

'So! What's the plan?'

'I suggest we wait until dark, then I will take the pup to Lulu.'

'Not a good idea. If she see's you with Speed, she'll just put two and two together and make four as anyone can see the pup has the same colour and markings as you,' said Barney.

'Yes, you have a point. I'll head back to the gang, and you drop Speed off,' said Jack.

Much later, they made to move with the fading light. Barney took Speed by the scruff of his neck and started out towards Lulu's.

A sleepy voice said, 'I'm hungry.'

'Won't be long now,' said Barney.

Padding away quietly, eyes and ears ever vigilant, Barney made his way to where Lulu lived, as usual keeping to the back streets. On arrival, he found the hole in the fence that Jack had mentioned. To his dismay, his bulk was much too large to squeeze through. The garden shed was situated some eight metres to his left, the rear of the house a further thirty metres to his right. The shed backed on to a high wall. The hole was as near as he was going to get.

Barney considered enlarging the aperture but that meant tangling with the wire fence, which in turn meant putting Speed down and probably making a noise. The lights were on in the house. It was a fair assumption the family had not retired for the evening.

The rear door opened to reveal a man carrying a rubbish bag, his outline silhouetted by the glow of the kitchen light. Barney instinctively drew back and waited. Walking down the two steps, the man deposited the bag in the nearest bin of three. Then looking up to the sky, he murmured something Barney was unable to make sense of even with his acute sense of hearing. The man climbed the steps and re-entered the house, switching off the kitchen light.

As Barney moved closer to the hole, still not knowing how to resolve the entry problem, he became aware of a rustling sound emanating from the rear of the garden. At that precise moment, Speed chose to whimper, 'I'm hungry.'

'Ssssh !' said Barney.

A soft bark caught his ear.

'Jack, is that you?'

'No! It's me, Barney.'

'Where's Jack? Shirking his responsibilities, I suppose.'

Barney's mind raced. 'Not exactly, Lulu. We had decided to split as the dog catchers were about.'

'What! This time at night!' she replied.

Knowing full well Jack had no intention of appearing, Barney changed the subject and said, 'Thank God you came. I'm unable to squeeze through the fence.'

'Wait there. Do you have the pup with you?'

'Yes.'

'How is it?'

'Very hungry,' replied Barney.

'Poor little mite,' she said, appearing at the fence. 'Pass him through. You'll have to be quick as there's not much cover here.'

'Here you go. He's all yours.'

Lulu clasped Speed in her jaws as Barney withdrew his head.

'I'll be on my way and try to pop back in about a week's time.'

As he went to leave a little voice said, 'Are you my mummy?'

'Yes, dear,' said Lulu.

'I'm hungry,' whimpered the pup.

'We will soon sort that out, and when you've been fed, there's a nice warm basket where you can sleep.'

'Thank you,' yapped the little voice.

Chapter 17

Barney returned to the nature reserve and updated Bernie and the team. They were pleased that at least one pup had survived. Taking Bernie to one side, Barney whispered, 'A word in your ear. I'll be missing for a day or so. Thought I'd let you know. A spot of personal business needs my attention.'

Bernie knew better than to question Barney. Part of their sustained relationship was built on a mutual trust.

'When do you intend do to leave?' he enquired.

'Sunrise tomorrow,' Barney replied.

'Well, you take care, and I'll see you anon.'

Turning to the others, Bernie said, 'Time to bed down. Sleep well. See you in the morning.'

Barney woke early. As the sun rose, he left the comparative safety at the nature park and headed out on his quest. After a sleepless night pondering on what to do, still he was unable to come up with a concrete plan.

Bernie, ever alert with one eye open, silently watched him leave. Whatever his mission, he dearly hoped Barney was successful. They had been friends for a long time and had grown very close.

Barney's first objective was to pass through Dalman before the residents were out and about. Once safely through, a further three kilometres had to be covered to reach his goal. He had considered bypassing the town, but that would add a further eight kilometres to his destination, plus the time involved, which he could ill afford as it was a matter of some urgency that he arrived at his destination early. The journey to Dalman was uneventful. Again keeping to the side streets, he navigated his way successfully. Now out of Dalman and heading east, he estimated the journey would take an hour, providing it was incident free. He didn't anticipate problems, as the road was relatively free of traffic and led nowhere other than his destination. Thus he was able to push on.

He knew the layout of the building that figured in his plans, but as of yet, he was unable to formulate a strategy, hoping something would be in place by the time he arrived. Having been incarcerated some years previously, the experience left him deeply traumatised. He managed to escape. Since then, the council had rebuilt the pound. It was now said to be escape-proof.

The building was rectangular in shape and measured some eighty by forty metres. The quarters that accommodated the staff was located on the right of the entrance. Against the north-eastern wall stood the holding pens. A walkway separated two rows of six cages. Inside the compound doors, a driveway led to the parking facilities. Beyond that was the office building. In the north-west corner stood the slaughterhouse, where rumour had it the guards murdered the adult animals with a steel rod capable of delivering an electric shock of some fifty thousand volts and used a large water tank for drowning puppies and kittens. A door in the southern wall led through to the incinerator where they disposed of the bodies. A wire fence connected the holding pens to the abattoir. The rest of the perimeter was constructed out of brick. Why a wire fence was a mystery. It was said the council had exceeded the budget and were unable to complete the brick structure, so the fence was a cheap option.

Barney noticed that between the holding pen and the slaughterhouse stood a hitching rail running parallel to the fence. Having circled the pound carefully, he hid behind a clump of bushes about three metres from the fence and waited.

It was not quite eight o'clock. He knew the guards began the slaughter of strays early Monday morning after a hectic weekend of rounding up the dogs. As there were only twelve cages, room had to be made for the next intake of unfortunate animals captured.

Barney hadn't long to wait. A few minutes had passed when the holding pen door opened. A guard appeared pulling a bedraggled looking mongrel on a tight metal chain, which he hooked on to the hitching rail. Next out was Jenny, being yanked along by a second man. She looked so sad Barneys heart went out to her. Head down, her tail drooping, her very posture suggested she was resigned to her fate.

Having hooked her to the rail, the men returned to the pen, closing the door behind them. Seizing his opportunity, Barney edged closer to the fence. A loud bark attracted the two dogs' attention.

'Jenny, it's me, Barney.'

She looked so subdued, no doubt absorbed in the fate that awaited her. She knew her puppies were dead, drowned. Life was meaningless.

He realised that time was not on his side and he could easily be heard. There again, the guards might think the noise came from one of the dogs hooked to the rail. He chanced a louder bark.

'Jen, it's me, Barney.'

She lifted her head.

'Is that you, Barney?'

'Yes!' he replied.

'What are you doing here? You shouldn't have come. It's far too dangerous.'

'Never mind that. How are you holding up?'

'Not very well. They drowned my puppies earlier this morning. Now it's my turn. I'm frightened, but there's nothing to live for now. My pups are dead.'

Barney felt her anguish as for many years, he had nurtured strong feelings for Jenny. As a confirmed bachelor, he had never mentioned what was in his heart. Time was running out. The men could appear at any moment.

'Jenny! I have some news. One of your pups survived.'

'Survived?' she replied.

'Yes!'

'Really?' she said excitedly.

'I found him in a suitcase at the tip.'

'How he managed to crawl in there, heaven knows. Anyway, he's safe.'

Still not knowing the sex of the pup, Barney took a chance, remembering not to mention Jack's part in the discovery for obvious reasons.

'Who's feeding him?' she said.

'Lulu.'

'That old tramp,' she exclaimed. 'She's the biggest tart in Dalman —'

Barney interrupted Jenny's outburst, 'She agreed to feed him as one of her own. Her litter was born last week.'

'What's he like?'

'The same colouring as you. He has the same markings.' It was a blatant lie. He knew there was no way he could mention Jack.

'Promise me you will look after him, Barney! Promise me!'

'Once he is weaned, you have my solemn oath, I will never leave his side until he reaches maturity, and I'll teach him all I know.'

Before any more could be said, the door opened to reveal the men leading two dogs that they hitched to the rail. Then untying Jenny and the mongrel, they led them into the slaughterhouse. Barney turned and left. He had hardly covered any ground when a high-pitched whining reached his ears. As much as he tried, he was unable to detach himself from the lamenting sounds of the dogs as they were slaughtered. His mood sombre, he slowly headed back to Dalman and the team, muttering to himself, It's so sad, so sad.

Chapter 18

On his way to work, Mohamed was deep in thought wondering how to solve the problem everyone seemed to know about, namely the particular group of stray dogs that appeared to be led by a St Bernard look alike. His mind distracted from his driving, he nearly ran over Faruk, the road sweeper, who managed to jump out of the way, landing on his knees. He clambered to his feet and brushed himself down. Mo wound down the driver's window to apologise, 'I'm so sorry. I could have killed you. My mind was on other things, and quite honestly, my attention was totally distracted.'

'No harm done, Mr Ismik. I was hoping to bump into you, not literally of course,' said Faruk with a nervous laugh.

Mohammed thought, Another piece of tittle-tattle Faruk had probably picked up.

The sweeper continued, 'As you know, I'm in charge of keeping the marina clean.' He puffed out his chest, full of his own importance.

'And a very important job it is too,' replied Mohamed, playing the game.

'Well, yesterday, or perhaps it was the day before, actually, I'm not really sure. Well, I'm fairly certain it was yesterday, there again I could be mistaken. Erm ! . . . let me think.'

For Christ's sake, get on with it, thought Mohamed.

'Well, whatever, I was going about my business, you know, sweeping, and I reached that section, you know, between the old boathouse and the public toilets, you know.'

Why does he keep saying 'you know'? Of course I know, thought Mo.

'Get on with it, man,' he said irritably.

'You know that section that backs on to the end of Bodrum Road, you know, the area that is covered in rotting bamboo, brambles, and long grass?'

'Yes!' said Mo impatiently.

'Well, there's a covered pathway that's well . . . hidden, where a dog can get through to the street, and yesterday, or was it the day before? I really can't remember.'

Mohamed's patience finally snapped.

'Stop dithering, you idiot! Get on with it.'

'Yes, right, er . . . where was I?'

'Sweeping the section between the old boathouse and the toilets,' replied Mohamed.

'Er, yes! Well just before that, when sweeping behind the old boathouse, I came across what looked like a St Bernard fast asleep.'

Mo's ears picked up;

'And?'

'And what?' said Faruk.

Mo was having a hard time controlling his temper.

'Finish what you were saying, man,' he said tersely.

'Where was I? Ah yes, this big dog was asleep behind the boathouse. Well, I wasn't having that, the filthy beast, so I hit him with my broom.'

'And?'

'And what?' said Faruk.

'Get it out, man. Tell me what happened next, you! You dithering moron!'

'No need to take that attitude. I'm only trying to help. Anyway, not much really. It darted off along that hidden pathway I was telling you about.'

Mo's mind was working overtime, Too much of a coincidence. The postmistress coming upon a husky asleep under the olive tree. The day Abraham's café was raided, he reported a husky asleep in the road, plus the St Bernard fighting with a dog outside his establishment. Now Faruk's story about a St Bernard lookalike disappearing into the undergrowth that backed on to the end of Bodrum Road. Yes, far too much of a coincidence. At last, a breakthrough, luck was on his side, the opportunity he had been waiting for. If I could catch this gang, my prestige would be sky high, he thought.

The sound of Faruk clearing his throat interrupted Mohamed's thinking.

'I hope I have been some help to you,' he said.

'Yes! Yes! Very helpful, very helpful indeed. Thank you very much. Should you notice anything else unusual let me know at once. Must be off now as I have a very busy day ahead of me, bye!'

'Ahem! . . . Just before you leave, a quick word, Mr Ismik.'

'Yes!' Mo's impatience returned.

'Well, er! . . . I mean, um . . . well, it's . . . '

'Get on with it, man.'

'The, the . . . erm, reward?' stuttered Faruk. 'You know, like er, information leading to the capture and all that?'

I wondered when he would get round to mentioning money, thought Mohamed.

'I can assure you that anything that is coming your way, you will get.' He would up his window so that the air conditioning was effective. Mo pulled away in a buoyant mood. After all, the day has started well, he thought.

'What I now need is a plan,' he murmured to himself.

On reaching his office, Mohamed asked his secretary to inform all his operational staff that they were to attend an extraordinary meeting the next day at 8 a.m.

This afternoon I think I'll take a drive down to the marina and have a look around. He didn't expect to find any dogs there, but it could do no harm to check out the path that Faruk had mentioned.

The marina car park was exclusive to the owners who had their boats moored there or those who had business concerning shipping. Finding a shady spot, he parked, locked the car, and sauntered down to the public loos to relieve himself. On his way out, he asked the attendant if he had seen Faruk.

'Yes!' replied the man. 'Eating his lunch behind the boathouse.'

Walking past the section of land that Faruk had mentioned, Mohamed noticed how dense the area was, matted with brambles, bamboo cane, and thick reeds overrun with climbing plants. Looking very carefully, he was unable to see a path of any sort.

On rounding the corner of the boathouse, he came across Faruk, who was packing what was left of his lunch away, muttering, 'I'll save that for later.' Looking up, he saw Mohamed approaching.

Very quickly, he tossed a half-empty bottle into his bin.

'Good afternoon, Mr Ismik. I was just finishing my lunch.' The bottle made a resounding thump coming to rest at the bottom of the bin.

'There's no accounting for some people. Very irresponsible leaving glass bottles lying around. It's quite dangerous, especially if children are about. They could easily fall on the glass and hurt themselves,' said Faruk, implying the beer bottle wasn't his, as you were not allowed to drink alcohol whilst on duty even if you were on a break.

This action didn't go unnoticed. As Faruk wasn't a member of his staff, it was none of Mohamed's business.

'I'm glad I ran into you, Faruk, as I wanted to see that hidden path you told me about this morning.'

'No problem. Follow me,' he said. Leaving his sweeping equipment behind and leading Mohamed by his coat sleeve, he ushered him around the corner of the boathouse.

'It's just along by the toilets.'

'Where?' said Mo as they walked along.

'About three metres past the toilets.'

That's where Mo looked before. All he could see was a mass of broken bamboo and undergrowth.

'That's it,' said Faruk. 'If you lift the bamboo up, you will see the beginning of a winding path that leads to the back end of Bodrum Road.'

'Well, I'll be damned!' exclaimed Mohamed. 'And this is where you saw the St Bernard enter?'

'Right!' came the reply.

'And you say the exit is in the rear end of Bodrum Road?'

'It must be, because once the dog went in, it never came out this side.'

Mohamed thanked Faruk, then walked to his car, and drove back to the pest control office. On his way, calling William and Benjamin from his mobile, he told them to drop whatever they were doing and meet him at the office asap.

They arrived some five minutes after Mohamed, who ushered them through the door and bade them sit. William and Benjamin were looking somewhat perplexed, both wondering what could be so important that they were ordered to report back immediately.

'Well,' Mohamed began, 'as two of my most efficient and effective employees, I am entrusting you with a very important mission. What I am about to ask you to do is not in your job description.' Mo chose his words very carefully, as he knew from previous experiences that the two where union men, who went by the book, so buttering them up was the right policy.

'Before I share with you privileged information, can I rely on your discretion?'

'Absolutely,' they both said in unison.

Mo went on to describe what he wanted of them.

'You will start as from now. I don't care how long it takes, but you must have the answer on my desk by 8 a.m. tomorrow morning, as I have convened an extraordinary meeting.'

'Er, one thing, Mr Ismik. If we have to work late, I trust union rates will be adhered to?'

'Of course,' replied Mo, 'also any out-of-pocket expenses will be paid,'

Chapter 19

After feeding the latest addition to her family, Lulu introduced Speed to the rest of her litter, who quite happily accepted him as one of their own. She was worried about what she would do if he was rejected. Sure, he was a little younger than the rest and possibly a little greedier, but that shouldn't cause too much of a problem. When Jack asked her to adopt the pup, no mention was made as to its sex. Well, she knew now she had three males to look after.

As they settled down for the night, all curled up like fluffy balls, Lulu's's mind churned over the day's events, True Barney is a long-standing friend of hers, and she knew he was a confirmed bachelor, but something didn't add up. But she just couldn't put her paw on it. Her intuition was making her think there was more to this caper than meets the eye. Soon all the litter was sound asleep, and she was about to join them when a little bark startled her. 'You're not my mummy. You don't smell like her, but you do seem very nice.'

'Shush, Now, and go to sleep.'

Those few little words reinforced Lulu's suspicion that something was amiss.

Two days passed and Lulu hadn't seen hide nor hair of Jack, her only true love. Sure he was a rogue, always in trouble with the ladies, disappearing for days on end, and when he did show his face, invariably it was a short visit—short or not, she couldn't wait until the next time. Many a bitch had tried to make him settle down, but he always ended back with her.

Perhaps, she thought, one day he would see the error of his ways and stay permanently. Who was she kidding? If pigs could fly, she thought.

Barney had been keeping an eye on Speed as he had promised Jenny, popping around once or twice a week to check on him. As the weeks passed, it became quite obvious to Lulu that Speed bore no resemblance to Barney whatsoever. In fact, Speed's markings were very similar to Jack's—white paws and a white chest, even the same temperament, cocksure and overconfident. The weeks flew by, and most of Lulu's litter had been found homes.

Speed had been promised to the ginger-headed boy next door and had confided in Lulu that he was not happy, as Carrot Head, the name he called the lad, had a habit of teasing him whenever his parents' backs were turned. One particular day when Carrot Head's parents were out shopping, he came to the shed to play with Speed—his favourite game 'chooky egg'. The game itself was designed so there was only one winner. It entailed tapping the top of Speed's head with a wooden spoon as though he was opening a boiled egg, hence the name. Speed was getting hurt. He decided it had to stop, so he bit Carrot Head on the hand. As a precaution, Lulu's owners took him to the hospital for a tetanus jab.

Carrot Head's parents were very upset and refused to allow him to adopt Speed, and to aggravate the situation, insisted that the pup should be put down, their reasoning being if he could bite Sam, the boy's proper name, he could bite anybody. So keeping Speed alive wasn't an option.

Lulu was beside herself with worry. That evening when Barney came to visit, she related the whole sorry mess down to and including her owners' decision to terminate Speed's life.

'What am I going to do?' she wailed.

'Calm down now. Calm down,' said Barney. 'Let me think. Having decided on that course of action, when did they propose to do it?'

'They're taking him to the vet's tomorrow morning.'

'Hm! I see,' muttered Barney whilst scratching his ear with his paw. 'There is only one course of action we can take.'

'And what's that?' asked Lulu.

'Well! He will have to leave with me.'

'Leave with you?'

'Yes, it's either that or be put down. I'm pretty sure I can persuade Bernie to let him join our team, providing I take full responsibility for his actions, as Bernie and I go way back.'

'I suppose you're right,' said Lulu, 'but what will happen to me?'

'Come with us,' replied Barney. 'There's really not much left here for you now your pups have gone.'

Lulu thought for a moment. 'No, I couldn't do that. After all, my owners have been very good to me.'

'Well, if that's your decision, you had better bring Speed to me, and I will explain what's happening.'

'Okay, you wait there and I'll fetch him.'

Lulu was gone for about two minutes and came back with Speed in tow, telling the pup about the predicament he was in and the need to act with some urgency. It was left to him to say goodbye.

Barney tried to be discreet, standing a few metres away, but he couldn't help overhearing Speed as he said to Lulu, 'I know you're not my mum, but you have been very good to me. I'll never forget your kindness, and I will always remember you.'

'You will come back to see me sometimes?'

'Of course I will, as often as I can.'

Barney interrupted them, 'If we stand around here much longer. We will be seen.'

Lulu took one last look into the eyes of Speed, and all she could see was Jack. With a tremor in her voice, she said, 'Barney's right. Be off with you and make haste.'

She turned around. Her head and tail dropped as she slowly made her way back to the shed.

Chapter 20

At precisely 7.55, Mohamed entered the briefing room only to see his entire staff sitting and waiting for him. Prior to arriving at the office, he had taken a call on his home number from the town council chairman wanting to know if there were any new developments concerning the capture of the infamous St Bernard. The councillor had no hesitation reminding Mo that they had a vested interest in this mutt and expected results soon. This added to the pressure Mohamed was already feeling. Making his way to the rostrum, Mo thought, It never ceases to amaze me that in a small town like Dalman, how rumour spreads so quickly. The whole situation was in danger of being blown out of proportion. After all, he was dealing with a group of wild dogs, and there were plenty of those around Dalman.

'Good morning, everyone. Nice to see that you are all present and there are no latecomers. The reason why I called this extraordinary meeting today rather than wait till our usual time on Monday is because the council is now applying pressure on this department. They want results now regarding the feral dogs led by the St Bernard lookalike and his gang. By now, you are probably aware that the council has put up a bounty to be paid to anyone who has information leading to the apprehension of the leader and his motley crew. This is the main reason for this morning's briefing. I am fully aware that you are all engaged and working on your own particular projects, but unfortunately, they must be put on hold while you channel all your energies into finding this particular group of dogs. It will mean pooling and sharing any information you have or receive in the course of your investigation. We need to nail this one promptly. I know you are aware there's talk of cuts in our budget next year. Should that happen, all our jobs, one way or another, will be affected. We are not working completely blind on this particular issue for the reasons I am about to tell you.

'It has come to my notice that on at least two occasions, a pure-bred husky has been seen in the same location as the St Bernard. Coincidence? I don't think so. Also, various reports suggest we are dealing with a pack of four or five dogs. Two of our most trusted operatives were put on a special assignment by me yesterday. William, Benjamin, let's hear the outcome of your investigation. Which one of you is the spokesman?'

William stood to his feet, coughed nervously, and shuffled his notes.

'At precisely two o'clock yesterday, Mr Ismik briefed myself and Benjamin on an important mission we were to undertake.' He looked down at his notes, and once again, he emitted a nervous cough.

'At ten past two, we arrived at our destination, the stretch of marina that runs between the old boathouse and the public urinals. At 2.20, we started to check along that section. For those of you who are not familiar with the layout of the marina, this particular sector is made up of dense undergrowth, bamboo, and a network of brambles and reeds.'

At that point, William looked at Benjamin for confirmation and support. Benjamin, sitting bolt upright in his chair, nodded furiously, puffing out his chest and murmured, 'Yes, that's right.'

'By 2.40 . . . ' Mohamed was by then getting irritated with William's slow and meticulous oration. He felt like saying 'Stop dithering and get on with it,' but he refrained from doing so.

'You were saying, William?' Mo asked.

'Erm! Yes, now where was I?'

One of the other catchers, Steve, piped up, 'Get on with it. You were describing an area in the marina.'

'Yes, right, by 2.40, having checked about a third of the frontage, we came across a gap hidden under some broken bamboo.' On further investigation, we discovered a path that seemed to zigzag through the gorse and undergrowth where allegedly a St Bernard was seen entering and apparently never came out. Benjamin volunteered to go down on his hands and knees with total disregard for his own person, let alone the health and safety factor.

Steve interrupted. 'Yes, let alone the health and safety factor. Get on with it,' he said.

Mohamed thought he should try and hurry William along.

'Yes, William, and the outcome of this valiant deed perpetuated by Benjamin?'

Hearing this, Benjamin noticeably grew in stature.

'Well, the outcome, Mr Ismik, he—Benjamin—came out at the bottom end of Bodrum Road, covered in scratches and bruises from his ordeal.'

Everybody turned and looked at Benjamin, who on closer inspection was certainly scratched and generally bedraggled, with his chest so swollen with pride his shirt had lost a button.

'And in conclusion, I would like to add this person,' pointing at Ben, 'acted beyond the call of duty and should be rewarded from the public purse.'

There was a small round of applause as Ben stood up and took a bow.

'And finally—' Bill was about to prattle on when Mo interrupted.

'Good work, the pair of you, but time is against us.'

Addressing the assembly, he said, 'Is there any further information that can help our crusade?' At the same time, he was thinking, I bet Bill pulled rank on Ben and made him do the dirty work.

Steve stood up.

'Mr Izmik, earlier on you mentioned a pure-bred husky. There's one that hangs around the market. I've seen it there a few times. As he's well fed and has a collar, I assumed he belonged to a stall owner. After all, there can't be two pure-bred huskies in Dalman.'

'Exactly my thought,' interrupted Mohamed, thinking about the husky seen asleep under the olive tree at the bottom end of Bodrum Road. 'If there is no further input, I want you all to drop your present assignments and concentrate on locating the gang. Be especially vigilant, but on no occasion are you to try and capture the husky or the St Bernard, as I want to nip this in the bud and capture the whole gang. It's quite possible their hideout is concealed in that area between the rear of Bodrum Road and the marina. So, people, get to it and report to me anything that looks suspicious. William and Benjamin, a quick word before you leave.'

Mo waited until the rest of the staff left. Addressing Bill and Ben, he said, 'Excellent work. As the pair of you are my most trusted workers, I need you both to stake out the marina and Bodrum Road. William, you take the road, and Benjamin, the marina. We need to be sure that there is a den in that overrun section before taking any action. After all, we don't want to be seen as fools incapable of doing our duty. My suspicions are that the band of curs is quite cunning, and you won't see them at that site during the day. So I am authorizing you both to observe the area between 6 p.m. and 12 p.m. every evening.'

'How long for?' said Bill.

'As long as it takes,' replied Mohamed.

'Ahem!' interrupted Ben. 'You do realise that this is out of normal working hours?'

'Yes! Once we have completed our mission, you can take days off in lieu.'

'No can do, Mr Ismik,' replied Ben. 'Union rules state—'

Mo interrupted, he could see this coming.

'Okay! Monday to Friday time and a quarter, Saturday up to twelve in the evening, time and a half, Sunday double time, agreed?'

'Fine by us,' said Bill.

'Right, that's settled. As I said, be discreet and try to stay unnoticed. If this is where their hideout is and my intuition tells me yes, we will devise a plan to capture them all in one swoop.'

Chapter 21

Bernie was visiting Molly every two days as promised, more often than not with food. Already he could see an improvement in her. She had put on weight and generally looked in better shape from when they had first met. He had yet to meet the kittens, but she assured him they were doing well and were very grateful for his kindness. What troubled Bernie, and he wasn't sure why, was that something about Molly didn't add up. True, she was pleasant and certainly very grateful, but niggling at the back of his mind was an uncertainty.

That particular afternoon, as he headed back to town, his mind was turning over his last venture. He had put it on hold for a while, while he investigated the pros and cons of the latest escapade. On the edge of town lay a commercial centre where various companies rented factory space. Jacobs Meat Importers, a large industry that distributed their produce throughout the region, was one such company.

Bernie's team had successfully raided them four months ago. Since that venture, Jacobs had tightened their security. When offloading, the articulated vehicles, the lorrys, reversed into the large, empty freezers before opening their doors. Then they hooked up to a conveyor belt and proceeded to unload. As far as Bernie could see, at no point were Jacobs vulnerable. On the last raid, the lorries opened their doors and proceeded to discharge their cargo by using barrows to wheel the meat into the freezers, which in turn at some point left the vehicles unguarded.

With the new system, Bernie had to devise a completely new strategy, which would entail greater risks. He may have to abandon this project. Try as he may, he was unable to devise a workable plan.

Nearing the edge of town, Bernie thought he would pop in to see an old mate of his, Joshua, who hung out behind the gas station. They had known each other for years, and on one or two occasions had worked together. Joshua was a loner who liked to work on his own, his philosophy being—if you worked alone and something went wrong, you could only blame yourself, plus, you had only one mouth to feed and one person to take care of. Apart from that, he was quite a sociable dog.

He greeted Bernie with his usual bark, chiding him for not coming around more often.

'How are you?' asked Bernie.

'Still getting away with it,' replied Joshua, 'and you?'

'Fine,' said Bernie. 'Mind you, I'm starting to slow down. Old age is catching up with me. I'm seriously thinking of stepping down as leader and handing control to Barney, but it's proving difficult as Barney has that young whippersnapper Speed to look after and educate.'

'How old is he now?' asked Joshua.

'He must be close on six months, very headstrong and thinks he knows it all—a bit like us when we were young, eh?' replied Bernie.

'Yeah! Those were the days, Bernie, those were the days,' Joshua said with a sigh. 'But there you go. Time passes. Yes, time passes.'

'It's very difficult for me to approach Barney on the matter as he made a solemn promise to Jenny before she was murdered that he would care for Speed until he was old enough to care for himself, and at the moment, he's not ready.'

'What about that husky who runs with you, what's his name?! No, don't tell me. It will come to me in a minute. Let me see, Herbert! Henry! No, erm! Harry! That's it, Harry! I believe he's a pedigree.'

'Pedigree he might be. Unfortunately, he's as thick as two planks. Sure, he's willing enough but absolutely no sense, no sense at all,' replied Bernie. 'S'pose I'll have to soldier on for a while. Well, I'll say my goodbyes—things to do, places to go, you know the drill.'

'Before you leave, a word in your ear. There's been an unusual amount of activity coming from the council catchers around town today. Word has it that they have increased their stray runs and checks. Probably nothing to worry about. With the tourist season almost finished, the council likes to rid the streets of as many strays as they can before they close down for the year. Anyway, you take care and keep your wits about you, and don't be a stranger,' said Joshua.

'You know me, Josh . . . always the careful one. See you.'

I hope so, thought Joshua as Bernie departed.

Steve played a hunch. If Mr Ismik was right and the husky somehow was involved with the St Bernard lookalike, the chances were if he tracked the husky, there was a fair possibility that he would lead him to the big dog and maybe, just maybe, the reward. Steve pondered on those thoughts as he sat in his catcher's van at the far corner of the market.

He must have dozed off and woke with a start. A trader's lorry had backed into a refuse bin, spilling the contents over the surrounding area.

An argument had broken out between the driver, who was profusely apologising, and Faruk, who was heard to say, 'You stupid maniac, it's me who has to clean it up.'

Looking at his watch, Steve realised it was five o'clock and most of the stall holders had packed up and gone home. His shift had finished at 5.30, time he was back to the depot, with van parked, signed out and then home. Driving along, he noticed coming out of a disused builder's yard what appeared to be a dog, and if his eyes weren't playing tricks, a husky, no less. Quickly slowing to a stop, Steve waited to see which direction the dog would take. It stood for a moment sniffing the air, giving the impression it was making a decision on which way to go. Finally, the dog headed towards the van. It would be quite simple to catch it alive, thought Steve. There again, I have a few minutes to spare. I'll follow it to see where he goes. Waiting till the husky was well ahead, Steve made a three-point turn and followed. It looks like it's heading for the market, Steve mused. The likelihood that there were two huskies in Dalman just wasn't logical.

On reaching the market, Steve stopped his vehicle and watched. Twenty minutes passed, and all the dog did was sniff around and piss. It obviously wasn't going anywhere, Steve thought. Looking at his watch, he realised he was on his own time and should have been back thirty minutes ago. Starting his engine, he left the dog to his own devices and headed off.

Earlier that afternoon, Bill had parked up outside the car showroom facing down Bodrum Road toward the dead end and prepared himself for what might well be a long wait. Over the next few hours, nothing entered or exited the box end. The only time he left his post was to use the toilet in the car showroom. The manager, who on hearing his quest, was only too pleased to allow Bill usage of his company's facilities. As time passed, Bill waited patiently. One by one, the shops and businesses closed for the day with the exception of the Minimart at the other end of the street. It was dark, but the lights from the showroom reflected down as far as the crossroads. Glancing at the dial on his illuminous watch, Bill realised it was nigh on ten o'clock, and for a fleeting moment, he was tempted to call it a day. But, there again, he was being paid union rates, time and a half till twelve, plus the possibility if events were in his favour, a nice little bonus, the bounty money. Time seemed to stand still. Looking at his watch for the umpteenth time, he noted 10.40.

At precisely that moment, Bill became aware of a moving shadow on the corner of the crossroad. There it was again, only that time, the lights from the showroom picked out the silhouette of a dog as it turned down the dead end. I'll wait, thought Bill, to see if the mutt comes back. Ten minutes had passed when another moving shadow appeared on the opposite corner, which in turn was highlighted by the glare from the showroom. Yes, thought Bill.

'Yes,' he said to himself, 'that's another dog'.

Over the next twenty minutes or so, he counted five dogs. He had to make a decision. Should he go in to investigate or sit and wait to see if any dogs came out? Bill waited till twelve and was satisfied that no more dogs went down the dead end and pretty certain none came out. He started the van and drove slowly down to the junction, turned left, and waited till he could see the crossroads in his rear mirror before turning the car lights on and moving off.

Chapter 22

The next day, Mohamed arrived at his office bright and early, eager to see the day's events unfold. Even though operation 'Beastly Bernard' had only just got under way, he was hoping some progress had been made. His son had dreamt up the name 'Beastly Bernard'.

Wishing his secretary, Susan, good morning, he thought it had just turned eight o'clock. She normally worked nine to five. Maybe the meeting yesterday had motivated at least one of his staff.

'Morning, sir! Coffee?'

'Yes, please, Susan. Nice to see you bright and fresh this time in the morning. Is there anything that requires my immediate attention?'

'No, sir, other than Bill and Ben . . . sorry, sir. William and Benjamin are waiting in the briefing room to see you.'

That sounds promising. You can never be sure with those two, he thought. Even Susan had picked up on the pair's nickname, he mused.

'Okay, I'll take my coffee in the briefing room. Thank you.'

On entering, Mo was surprised to see the two of them deep in conversation.

'Good morning, sir,' grunted Ben. Then they both started talking together . . .

'Whoa! Slow down, one at a time, please.' They both fell silent.

'Well,' said Mo, 'Who's going first?'

Bill looked at Ben, who returned his gaze.

'You go,' said Bill.

'No, you,' replied Ben.

'I don't have a lot to say. I would prefer to go last,' Bill said.

'So would I,' said Ben.

'Stop it, you two! You're like a pair of fishwives backwards and forward. I have a very busy day ahead, so get on with it. Bill, let's hear from you first.'

'Yes, sir.'

Bill went on to relate his entire day. Mohamed was unable to see the relevance to operation Beastly Bernard, till he recounted the events on the Bodrum Road from six o'clock onwards.

'And you say five dogs entered the dead end and none came out?'

'That is till twelve, when I called it a day and went home,' said Bill.

'Hm! Interesting, and you Benjamin?'

'Well as you know, sir, my brief was to survey and report on any unusual occurrences relating to dog activity within the precinct of the marina,' said Ben with his chest so puffed up with self importance Mo thought his shirt button would fly off again.

'And?' said Mo.

'And what?' said Ben.

Here we go again, thought Mo.

'Your report, man.'

'Well that's just it, sir. There's nothing to report.'

'So am I to understand there was nothing unusual happening at the marina yesterday evening?'

'No! Sir, I sat by the toilets all day, and nothing came out of that path or any other part of the shrubbery.'

'Hm. Nothing, eh?'

'No, sir.'

'Well done, the both of you, excellent work. As of now, continue with your usual routine, and keep your eyes and wits about you, and once again, report to me if you notice any unusual activity where dogs are involved. That's all and thank you.'

There was a knock at the door.

'Come in.'

The door opened and Susan entered with Mo's cup of coffee.

'Sorry it took so long, sir. There was another power cut. That's the third this week.'

'Never mind, my girl, better late than never. Thank you.'

Susan left. Mo drank his coffee, then made his way to his office, deep in thought. Having learnt from Bill and Ben what he already suspected, it was time to put his plan in action.

He was feeling somewhat rejuvenated, as the previous evening he had precious little sleep thinking about the best course of action to take. If his suspicions were confirmed, it would mean involving all of his catchers plus help from the council's traffic department.

Mo rang the highways manager and requested a meeting that very afternoon, briefly outlining his request. The manager wasn't at all pleased with Mo's proposal, saying, 'I just can't drop everything I'm doing just to meet the local rat catcher.'

So that's how they saw him, a rat catcher indeed. Mo kept his temper. After all, he thought, without the cooperation of the traffic department, his plan was unworkable. Pulling out his big guns, he said, 'I have the full backing of the town council on this matter. If you have a problem and are too busy to meet me, I'll ask the council chairman to call you. I'm sure he can find someone to deputise for you whilst we discuss my news.'

'That! Er . . . that's not necessary,' spluttered the manager. 'Would three o'clock suit you?'

'Excellent,' replied Mo, 'see you at three.'

Putting down the phone, Mo was feeling pleased with himself, very pleased indeed. Mind you, he had better be right, or he would have egg all over his face. Rat catcher indeed . . .

The very next day, Mo's plan was put into action. It involved erecting six interlocking metal crowd control barriers across the junction point in Bodrum Road. As well as locking horizontally, they also connected vertically. As the barriers measured three metres by one, doubled up, you now had a metal wall measuring eighteen times two metres.

Mo was careful to leave the last barrier at an angle with a gap, as Bodrum Road backed on to the hotel complexes and the walls, separating the road from the buildings. This sealed the bottom end of the road, except for the gap left to allow the tree surgeons in with their equipment. That's what you would see written on a large board situated next to a sign warning: Danger! Men at work, dated two days hence. In actual fact, on the big day, the barrier would be pulled shut, thus sealing that end of the road.

Housed in the confined area would be four of Mo's catchers armed with nets and noose poles. By putting in place the barriers two days before the proposed work on the trees, the dogs would be used to seeing the entrance to their den being sealed except for the gap and wouldn't connect it to the fact that they were being ambushed.

Sealing off the marina side was a different kettle of fish. Somehow, it had to be done without alerting the dogs. Having given this a lot of thought, Mo had decided to erect the barriers the same as the ones in Bodrum Road, leaving a small gap where the path met the quayside, putting in place a cage to catch the animals. The cage had to be in place at the same time on the same morning as Bodrum Road was shut off, one hour before sunrise.

Two days later, just before dawn, the dogs were awoken by the clattering of bin lids coming from the road. Before panic set in, Bernie said, 'Jack, creep down the path and see if the marina is clear.'

Jack was back in a flash.

'It's blocked off,' he gasped.

'Okay!' Bernie said. 'Follow me and we will get out into the roadway. Take it steady, and above all, don't panic.'

Bernie led, followed by Harry, Jack, and Barney, with Speed bringing up the rear.

The moment Bernie exited the undergrowth, he saw the barriers and realised they were trapped. Barney assessed the situation immediately. Turning, he said to Speed, 'Quick! Back to the hideout.'

Speed didn't need to be told twice. He turned and ran with Barney, hot on his tail, both arriving back simultaneously.

'What are we to do?' barked Speed, with more than a hint of desperation.

'Quiet! Let me think,' said Barney. He already knew what to do. He had promised Jenny and a promise is a promise! If he had to sacrifice himself, then so be it. Turning to Speed, he said, 'Now listen up. You know the other path, the one that only you use as we are all too large for it?'

'Yes—yes,' said Speed tentatively.

'Well, you take that one and stop about two metres from the road and wait for my signal. I'll go down the usual path, and when you hear me barking, make a dash straight out and head for the barriers. With any luck, you're small enough to squeeze underneath. Once you are free, head for Molly. You remember that flea-bitten cat we met at the old villa? She'll know what to do, okay?'

'But what about you?' said Speed.

'Don't worry about me. I can take care of myself. Now off you go. Time is not on our side. See you later,' he added, knowing full well that would never happen.

Speed positioned himself almost at the end of the narrow path. He hadn't long to wait as his thoughts were interrupted by a ferocious barking coming from Barney, the signal! Speed leapt out into the road, tail between his legs, racing flat out towards the barrier.

The council catchers were caught napping, totally unaware of the other exit. This gave Speed an edge, precious second's advantage as he bounded on, swerving around one catcher holding a net, only to be confronted by another with pole and noose attached. His heart pounding and at full tilt, he saw the barrier and the gap underneath rushing towards him. At the rate he was moving, he was unable to check himself. His only option was between the third catcher's legs. Closing his eyes, he went for it. Before the man realised what was happening, Speed sped through. With the barrier looming up, he managed to check and squeeze under. He was free. Seeing that happen, Barney gave up, snarling and barking and waited for the inevitable. Barney heard Bill say to Ben, 'I've got the bastard! Open the cage.'

Speed never looked back or slackened his pace. He was moving like a bat out of hell, caution thrown to the wind, and heading straight for the abandoned villa, and hopefully Molly. Once clear of the town, he slowed and tried to make sense of the past twenty minutes. One moment he was woken by an ear-piercing clattering noise, the next he was trotting towards

Molly's hideaway. As his breathing slowed and his heart resumed its normal pumping rate, realisation took over.

'I'm on my own,' he murmured to himself. 'What will I do?'

The last thing he remembered was Barney saying, 'Go to Molly. She'll know what to do.' He tried to make sense of the whole business. Where were the others? Had they been caught by the catchers? Would he ever see Barney again? His mind was in turmoil.

A feeling of utter loneliness swept over him. Maybe, just maybe, things weren't as bad as he thought. Once he had met up with Molly and rested for a couple of days allowing events to quieten down, he'd go to town and check out some of their old haunts and try to make contact with his buddies, at least find out what went down today. Yeah that's what I'll do, he thought.

Feeling a little perkier, he trotted on. Within a few minutes, he was in sight of the old villa. As he neared Molly's hideaway, he became aware of a low-pitched hissing sound. His ears picked up. Then, out of nowhere, she appeared.

'Who are you?' she said.

'I'm Speed. You remember, we met some time ago?'

'Ah yes, you were with that big fella, what's his name? Barney, that's it, Barney. Where is he?'

'I don't know.' Speed went on to relate what he could remember of the morning's events.

'It doesn't look good,' said Molly.

'What do you mean?' replied Speed.

'Well, from what little you have told me about the barriers in Bodrum Road and the fact you have lost touch with the others, it's more than likely they have been caught.'

'That doesn't make sense. Barney had said not to worry about the barriers as they were there to stop people wandering down the road when the tree surgeons were working.'

'Don't you believe it. I've been around the block a few times and heard of this ploy before, especially if the council believes that the feral animal problem is getting out of hand. They have to be seen to be doing something to keep the rate payers happy.'

Speed replied with a touch of annoyance, 'Bernie is too shrewd to fall into a catcher's trap.'

'Be that as it may, the only way to find the truth is for one of us to go into town and check it out.' It can't be you, for obvious reasons. You stay here and I'll go, okay? Sit behind that wall and wait for me. I'll be as quick as I can.

At a blink of an eye, Molly was gone. Speed settled down by the wall to wait.

If it was a trap, Bernie, Barney, and the others would be too shrewd to fall into it. I'm sure they would have got away, and at this very moment, they are in the process of regrouping, and no doubt, Barney was on his way here. Yeah—that's what has happened. I'm pretty sure of it. Molly will be back with the good news, and in a few hours, we will all be reunited, he thought. But Speed couldn't rid himself of those lingering doubts rooted in the recess of his mind.

Another thought occurred to him, Molly had made no mention of her kittens, as to where they are, and how they were doing. I suppose, after losing two, she had them well hidden and out of harm's way. The time seemed to drag, and Speed drifted into an uneasy sleep.

Mohamed was back in his office and was humming to himself. This little coup of his would increase his standing with the town council, he thought as he reached for the telephone to inform the chairman of this morning's success. Pity about the little dog that escaped. Still, he wouldn't last long on the street, too small to fend for itself. I'll give him two weeks at the most before either a truck will run him over or it will starve to death. Having asked his secretary to type up a letter of thanks and to distribute a copy to all personnel who took part in the operation, with a special thanks to the traffic department, all that was left to do was to thank Bill and Ben personally for their part in the mission.

Mo found them at the marina, sitting on a bench eating sandwiches, having their lunch break.

'All safe and delivered to the pound,' said Benjamin. 'Pity about that small one escaping. Still, it won't last long, a few weeks at the most.'

'Exactly my feelings,' said Mo.

'Tell you what,' said Bill, 'that labrador-cum-greyhound took a hell of a beating. If I didn't know better, I would swear he was trying to hold our attention so the little one could escape. When we offloaded them at the pound, Ben had to drag the bastard out of the cage. It looked half dead. Mind you, if it dies before morning, think what the council will save on electricity,' he laughed.

'Everyone okay?' said Bernie as he turned around in his holding pen.

'Yes,' said Jack.

'Harry, are you all right?'

'A few lumps and bumps, not so bad.'

'Barney, how are you?' barked Bernie.

Jack interrupted, 'He was in the same van as me. He looked terrible.'

Bernie tried again, 'Barney, answer me. You all right?'

No reply.

'Speed? Speed, how are you?'

No answer. Jack barked again.

'I think Speed got away. Barney was causing so much trouble barking, biting, and running around, it took four catchers to subdue him. That allowed Speed time to leg it and squeeze under the barriers.'

Well, Bernie thought, Barney must have created a diversion to give Speed a chance. Addressing his remarks to Jack, Bernie asked, 'Did Barney say anything in the van?'

'Very little. He was pretty much out of it, drifting in and out of consciousness. He did say they had broken his leg and several ribs before he passed out. I noticed he was bleeding from his jaws quite heavily,' said Jack.

Bernie had thought it possible Barney had sustained mouth injuries, but more than likely, the probability of a punctured lung could not be ruled out. Best he kept his thoughts to himself.

'What will happen to us?' said Harry.

'You know the answer to that,' replied Jack. 'Tomorrow, they'll fry us.'

'What do you mean fry us? In a pan?' said Harry.

'What Jack means is they'll electrocute us. That's their usual method of eliminating unwanted animals.'

The three of them withdrew into themselves to contemplate the full consequence of their capture.

Suddenly the atmosphere was interrupted by a low pitched whine. Three pairs of ears picked up and listened. Before anybody could speak, Bernie said, 'Hush . . . is that you, Barney?'

Nothing . . .

'Barney, is that you? It's m, Bernie . . . '

Through the intense silence, the three dogs became aware of a rasping, gutterous sound as if someone was struggling to breathe. Harry and Jack picked up on the urgency in Bernie's bark!

'Barney, talk to me. It's Bernie.'

'Bernie, I'm hurt real bad,' came the stuttering reply. 'I ache all over, don't think I'm gonna make it,' said the pained voice.

'Sure you'll make it. A bit battered and bruised maybe, but you've had worse than that,' said Bernie, trying to lighten the mood.

'Did Speed get away?'

'Of course,' replied Bernie, 'straight under the barriers like a bat out of hell.'

'I—I promised Jenny . . . ' the words tailed off.

The silence was like a vacuum in the holding pens. A minute had passed. It seemed like an hour to the three entrapped dogs before Bernie said, 'Barney . . . Barney, speak to me.' Unable to control his grief, Bernie emitted a mournful howl.

Molly returned to the villa to find Speed waiting patiently for news of the others.

'Tell me all,' said the dog.

'There's not a lot to tell, really. The bottom line is they have all been captured.'

'All of them?' said Speed.

'Yes, I'm afraid so.'

'I'm not having that. We will have to work out an escape plan.'

'That's impossible,' said Molly. 'Nobody has ever escaped from the new pound. It's impregnable. It's manned 24/7, surrounded by a high wall, except for the section between the dog pens and the abattoir. You have to face it, Speed, there's nothing we can do.'

'There must be something.'

'Be sensible,' Molly replied, 'with just the two of us and you being barely six months old and me a cat that's seen better days . . . no, I'm afraid we're stymied.'

She had yet to tell Speed about the condition of Barney, thinking of the dogs' tender age. He would have difficulty coming to terms with it. So she made up a lie, 'Anyway, Barney managed to pass on a word to a friend of mine before they put him in the van to say on no circumstances were you to try anything. His orders are for you to stay with me and my kittens, because the catchers know there were five of you, and they have been told to bring you in.'

'Well, I suppose if Barney said that, he and Bernie probably have a plan,' Speed said dejectedly. 'By the way, where are your kittens?'

'Funny you should mention that.'

'What do you mean funny?'

'I mean, it's like this. There aren't any kittens.'

'Oh, I'm sorry, they're all dead then,' said Speed.

'Noooo . . . '

'What then? Have they all been cat-napped?'

'No, not exactly,' Molly replied.

'Well, you're their mum. You must know what has happened to them.'

'That's just it. There never were any kittens.'

'No kittens, I don't understand. Barney and I heard them when we first met, and Bernie's been bringing them food. Are you saying you deceived us? If that's the case, I'm out of here. How can you stoop so low? If it wasn't for the fact you are a female, I'd tear your tail off. So you've been scoffing the food yourself, eh!'

'Well, it's no and yes.'

'No and yes!'

'That's right!'

'Explain yourself,' said Speed. 'I want an answer and I want it right now.'

'Keep calm. Don't get your tail in a twist.'

'Get my tail in a twist, you-you-you fraudster! Either you tell me what's going on, or I'll tear your tail off.'

'Okay, okay. No! I'm not a female. Yes, there were never ever any kittens, and before you turn violent, let me explain. I had accidentally eaten some poisoned meat because I was so hungry. Fortunately, I realised something was amiss before I finished it but was left half dead and unable to fend for myself. Out of sheer desperation, I came up with the idea of pretending I was a female with starving kittens. Luckily for me, Bernie came along and swallowed my story, and with his help, I regained my health. I was going to tell him the truth today. But the catchers got him first. If it wasn't for Bernie, I'd be dead. I owe him a huge debt of gratitude, which now I will never be able to repay.'

Speed stayed silent and pondered to himself, thinking, I would probably have done the same thing had it been me ill and starving.

'But the mewing,' he asked, 'how did you manage that?'

'It's quite easy really. Listen . . . ' Molly went on to reproduce the noise of the kittens.

'Well, I'll be!' exclaimed Speed. Who would have thought!

'Now that you have heard my the story, what do you intend to do?'

'I don't know,' said Speed. At the same time, he was thinking to himself, Can Molly be trusted? There again, Barney had said to him make for her. She'll know what to do. Speaking out loud, he said to Molly, 'What's your real name? I feel stupid calling you Molly.'

'It's Tiger,' came the reply.

'Right, if you don't mind, I'll hang with you for a while, at least till I find my feet.'

'No problem,' said Tiger. 'We're pretty safe here at the old villa. It's out of town and nobody comes this way. What you need to do is to chill out for a few weeks till things calm down. I should be able to scrounge enough food for the two of us. Give it some time, and when you're feeling safe, reassess the situation.'

'Yes, I suppose you're right,' said Speed, feeling a little apprehensive.

'Okay, that's settled then. Tomorrow morning, I'm leaving early as I have some unfinished business in town. I'll be gone before you are up. Should be back about midday.'

'Okay,' said Speed.

The sun was rising over the eastern wall of the animal pound. Harry, Jack, and Bernie had been left to their own devices and were fully aware of what the morning would bring. Held in the cages without food or water, they had plenty of time to ponder their fate.

The morning sun came streaming through, casting eerie, foreboding, dark areas everywhere, the pen itself taking on an air of surrealism. Harry gave a nervous bark.

'When do you think it will happen, Bernie?'

Trying to play down the seriousness of their predicament, Bernie remarked, 'I really don't know. Still, we have a nice day for it.'

'Bernie!'

'Yes, Harry.'

'I'm real scared.'

'What's there to be scared about?' said Jack with more bravado than he felt. 'They lead you into the abattoir, jab you with an electric pole, and it's all over. Kaput, finished, gone—gone forever, as though you never existed,' his voice tapered off.

'Shut it,' said Bernie.

'Does it hurt?' said Harry.

Before Bernie could reply, the bolts of the main doors were drawn, the door opened revealing two men whose outlines were silhouetted by the sun's rays as they stood in the doorway.

'This is it,' barked Jack, 'the short walk.'

'Hush,' said Bernie, 'don't let them see you are scared.'

Jack still nursed this idea that sometime within the next twenty minutes, there would be a window of opportunity to escape.

The two men entered the pen, one man holding a pole with a noose at one end that once over the dog's head could be tightened around its throat, if necessary, cutting off the supply of air. The other man held a short chain with a leather loop at one end through which his hand was protruding. The other end of the chain had a metal locking device.

The men advanced, one saying to the other, 'We'll take the big one first.' They unlocked Bernie's cell and came in.

Around Bernie's neck, there was fastened a metal collar attached to a short sturdy chain, which in turn was locked on to a metal hoop embedded in the corner of the concrete cell.

The noose was passed over Bernie's head and tightened. No point in struggling, thought Bernie, I'll only choke myself. The other man disconnected Bernie's chain from the metal hoop, at the same time connecting his own chain to Bernie's collar. He was taken outside and attached to the hitching rail.

The two men went back inside to fetch another dog. At the same time, Bernie became aware of a mewing sound coming from the other side of the fence behind a clump of bushes.

'Bernie, it's me, Molly.'

'Molly, what are you doing here?'

'I've come to tell you that Speed's with me.'

'You mean here with you now?'

'No, back at the old villa.'

'Thank goodness,' said Bernie. 'Barney wouldn't want him to witness our last remaining moments on this planet.'

'Of course not,' replied Tiger. 'By the way, how is Barney? Heard he took a helluva beating when helping Speed to escape.'

'He's dead,' said Bernie glumly. 'They beat him to death. I don't want Speed to know about it, so keep that information to yourself. By the way, how are the kittens?'

'Great,' lied Tiger, 'they send their love and thanks for saving them. Without you, they never would have survived and the same applies to me.'

'Think nothing of it, old pal. Now be off. I can hear the jailors coming.'

'Okay,' said Tiger, 'you take care.' What a dumb thing to say, he thought as he left.

The two men appeared with Harry, who had the sense not to struggle as he was hitched next to Bernie.

One of the men remarked, 'This one didn't fight either. How strange. They always kick up a fuss.'

Finally, Jack was brought out and hitched up with the other two. Bernie quickly related to Jack and Harry the conversation he had with Molly as the men made their way back to the pen, wheeling a barrow only to find it was too wide to fit through the cell's main door. Leaving it outside, they entered to reappear a few minutes later, dragging Barney by the chain round his neck. The men lifted the body, then dumped it unceremoniously into the waiting barrow.

'That should set them off,' grunted one man, sweating with the exertion. Immediately, Bernie barked to the others telling them, 'Cool it, don't give them any satisfaction.'

They stood silently as Barney was wheeled towards the furnace. Harry noticed Bernie's reaction and said quietly, 'Steady on, old chap. Chin up, don't let the side down.'

The sight of his oldest friend being thrown into the barrow, his head hanging over one side with his tongue hanging down from between his jaws, the broken leg at an acute angle to the rest of his body, it was too much for Bernie as he let out a mournful howl.

'There,' said the man to his co-worker, 'that's more like it. I told you so. We'll leave the big one till last.'

Tiger heard Bernie as he set off for town to try and scavenge some food before heading back to the old villa. Try as he may, he was unable to erase the image of the large dog chained to the rail, contemplating the last moments of his life. It kind of put things into perspective and set him wondering how he would meet his end. Tiger's main problem at present was explaining to Speed the demise of his companions. Sure, Speed knew about the animal pound and the probability that his friends had been incarcerated there, but he doubted that the pup would fully comprehend the fate of his four pals. How could he? The young one was just starting out on life's great adventure. The concept of death is the last thing a youngster thought about. On reaching the town, Tiger headed for a restaurant he knew whose hygiene was very questionable. Squeezing under the yard gate and up the kitchen steps, his luck was in. The cook had left the large fridge door open. As quick as a flash, Tiger was in and out with a piece of steak that had yet to defrost and on his way back to Speed. On arrival, Tiger thought he would be met by a barrage of questions, but no. Speed eyed the meat that had more or less defrosted saying, 'Is that for me?'

'Not all of it,' replied Tiger, thinking, Typical youngster—belly first, questions later.

After relieving himself and having a full tummy, Speed lay down and curled himself up with one eye open. Then the inevitable question, 'Did you find out about my friends?'

'Yes!' said Tiger. 'Unfortunately, they were caught.'

'Where are they now?' asked Speed.

'Being detained at the pound.'

'What will happen to them?'

This was the question Tiger wanted to avoid or somehow lessen the blow, even though he suspected Speed already knew the answer. On the spur of the moment, Tiger said, 'I don't really know what the council's policy is this year. It's quite possible they will be found new homes. So get some sleep now, and we will talk about it tomorrow.'

Speed tried to stifle a yawn, but already his head was nodding.

'Okay,' he said as his eyes closed.

The next morning, Tiger was hoping to leave early, but Speed was awake with more questions that needed answers.

'Are you going to find out what's happening at the pound today?'

'Yes! So stay in the vicinity and keep your head down till I come back.'

'Okay, but it's boring hanging around doing nothing.'

'I know it is, but it's just for a few more days until the heat dies down,' said Tiger. At the same time thinking to himself, That's another lie.

Moving towards town, going his usual way, a route he had travelled many times, Tiger was thinking about the events of yesterday and wondering the best approach to answering Speed's inquisitive questions. As he neared the crossroads where the rubbish bins were located, he realised they had disappeared. For a fleeting moment, he thought he was lost. As he endeavoured to cross the junction, his mind preoccupied thinking about Speed, the driver in a lorry failed to notice him as he was adjusting his rear-view mirror. The lorry hit Tiger with a resounding thump, sending him flying. He landed some fifteen metres up the road. Death was instant. The lorry roared on, totally oblivious to the cat twitching in the gutter.

Speed waited all afternoon and the next day for Tiger to appear. By then, he was starving, so he decided the very next morning that he would make for the town.

Chapter 23

Mary and George had four days left of their holiday and decided that today they would shop for presents and souvenirs to take home to their family and friends. This in itself was problematic for George, as shopping didn't figure highly on his list of things to do. As long as the intended purchases were practical, the right price, and he didn't have to queue, he would be in and out of the shop like a flash, satisfied and with the rest of the day to himself.

George had already decided to use his usual ploy when Mary invited him to shop.

'Look, dear. There's no point in dragging me along. I'll only get in your way and slow you down. You carry on. You're much better than me at souvenir hunting and have the knack of knowing what people will appreciate.'

Not for one moment was Mary taken in by George's backhanded compliment. She had heard it dozens of times. It suited her purpose knowing if she exceeded her budget, George wouldn't complain, as her answer to any objections would be, 'You should have come and kept an eye on me.'

With the unspoken agreement, Mary was free to indulge herself. George retired to the hotel pool with the latest best seller.

After a hectic day, Mary returned to the hotel laden down with bags. George had just finished showering when there was a rap on the door.

'Just a moment,' said George.

'Hurry up,' replied Mary, 'these bags are heavy.'

George groaned inwardly, How much has she spent this time? He knew only too well he couldn't grumble. Opening the door, he said, 'How on earth did you manage to carry that lot up? You should have left some bags in the lobby and asked the receptionist to ring me. I could have come down and helped you.'

'Never mind. I'm here now so give me a hand.'

'You must be absolutely knackered,' said George. 'Why don't you get out of those sweaty clothes and freshen up in the shower?'

'That's exactly what I intend to do.'

'Good. Me, I'm going to have a nap before we eat this evening.'

'Once I've cleaned up, I'll join you,' said Mary.

Two hours later, the pair of them, suitably attired, made their way down the stairs and out of the hotel.

Either side of the entrance lay a flowerbed running the full length of the hotel frontage. The owner's wife was a keen gardener and took immense pride in her botanical efforts. Eyeing the array of different blossoms, Mary's eye caught sight of what appeared to be a black-and-white piece of material lying against the wall amongst the flowers. That won't stay there long, she thought as the owner's better half watered all her blooms first thing in the morning and just before sunset.

They ate well at Abraham's. Their taste buds didn't extend to Turkish food. They preferred traditional English fare. Having paid the bill, they decided to take a stroll around the marina before retiring for the evening.

The sun had almost set when they arrived back at the hotel. Much to Mary's surprise, the owner's wife, instead of watering her plants, was thrashing them with a broom.

It wasn't that Mary was nosy (mind you, George would disagree with that), it seemed strange when a person spends so much tender loving care on her hobby that she would be damaging them. She just had to ask.

'Excuse me, is something wrong?' she said, addressing the woman.

'No,' she replied in perfect English. 'It's that bloody black-and-white pup that keeps sleeping among my flowers.'

So that's what she saw earlier, thought Mary, who was quite impressed with the woman's command of the mother tongue.

Most of the local business people were able to converse in an assortment of European languages due to their dealings with the different nationalities that for many years spent there holidays in Dalman. They wished her a pleasant evening and went to their room.

As the night progressed, Mary was having problems sleeping. Something was playing on her mind. Tossing and turning, she just couldn't get comfortable. She decided to go for a stroll. Having dressed, she took the key off the dressing table and left a note for George to say 'Unable to sleep, gone for a walk, back soon.'

Making her way down the stairs, she passed the night porter dozing in a chair. She didn't want to wake him, so she slipped quietly outside. The sky was clear with a full moon and the visibility was good. On reaching the main gates, she passed through and paused, wondering which way to go. It was then she heard a noise, a whimpering sound. It appeared to be coming from the flower beds, in fact, the very spot the owner's wife had been beating with a broom earlier. She approached cautiously. There it was—a small, black-and-white pup, not unlike a Jack Russell. It looked so thin and weak she immediately picked it up and, placing it under her coat, made her way back to her room. She crept in without waking George, placing the pup in the shower room. She opened the fridge and took out a carton of milk. Taking down the spare blanket off the top of the wardrobe, she arranged it at the foot of the bed and placed the saucer beside it.

Fetching the puppy from the shower, she settled him down. The pup was on his third saucer of milk when George awoke. Seeing Mary sitting on the floor, he said, 'What on earth are you doing sitting down there?'

'Feeding my pup,' said Mary.

'Did I hear you right?' said George, jumping out of bed, 'Feeding a cup?'

'No, silly, feeding my pup.'

'Feeding your what?' said George.

'My pup, feeding my pup! Look, George, isn't he lovely? Four white paws, a white nose and chest, it's adorable and very hungry.'

'I don't care if it's a Crufts winner, it can't stay here. If the owners find out, we will be thrown out of the hotel.'

'Please, George, don't be so grumpy. I promise I'll keep it quiet and smuggle it out in the morning after breakfast.'

George knew that Mary was very single-minded where animals were concerned, a vegetarian, and quite recently, her pet Doberman had died, leaving her very upset. George relented.

'Okay! But if there's any noise, it goes. I want no part in it. Tomorrow, when there's no one around, sneak it out and take it to the animal welfare centre, and if it messes in the room, you clean it up.'

With that, George returned to bed, and just before he nodded off, his intuition told him that Mary had other plans. Remembering two years previously, whilst holidaying in Cypress, they had found a stray mongrel chained outside the riding stable. It was in a pitiable state, but Mary had fed it and found someone to adopt it. The situation caused so much friction between them that they had nearly parted company.

It would have meant flying the dog to England, six months' quarantine, not to mention vet bills. That information was supplied by DEFRA, the governing body that applied the rules for importing animals into Great Britain. The government was paranoid about rabies crossing the Channel, seeing that a good part of the British economy relied on the cattle farming industry. The pup would have to go. I'll make sure of that in the morning, thought George as he drifted into an uneasy sleep.

The next morning, George woke to see Mary still sitting at the foot of the bed nursing the pup.

'Come on, Mary, get ready. It's breakfast time. Have a quick shower, and we'll go down.'

'Tell you what,' she said, 'you go to breakfast and bring me back a plate of hard boiled eggs and any meats that are available.'

'I can't do that,' said George.

'Yes, you can. If anyone asks, say I'm having breakfast in bed.'

George wasn't a happy man. He met the rest of the party in the dining room.

Trisha said, 'We're all going to catch the boat to Turtle Beach for the day. Would you and Mary like to come?'

'Nice of you to ask, but Mary's feeling a bit peaky, so I'm taking her up some breakfast. If she improves, we might see you later,' he lied!

Finishing breakfast, George loaded a plate of food for Mary. Returning to the room, George found her showering, and the pup was asleep on the blanket.

'Shan't be long,' she said. 'I'll dry off and get dressed. Then we will take the pup to the marina and feed it.'

'I hope it hasn't made a mess up here,' said George.

'Nothing, nothing at all,' she replied. 'It's as though he's house-trained already.'

'It's a he, then?' George said.

'Of course, dear. Now pass me my clothes, then we can get cracking.'

Some fifteen minutes later, they had passed through the hotel foyer successfully and were on their way to the marina. Having concealed the food in a plastic bag and placed it on the top of her shopping basket in which the dog was concealed, they made their way to the marina. Selecting a bench that was furthest from the market, they fed the pup.

'Look, George, look! Can you see how happy he is?'

'I must admit he's an attractive little fellow.'

Having eaten, the pup lay down. Mary produced a bottle of water and a saucer she borrowed from the hotel room,

'Just in case he's thirsty,' Mary said to no one in particular.

They sat there for the best part of an hour, watching the boats sailing in and out. The sun was hot, but the offshore wind made it bearable.

'The council must have a problem with the stray dogs wandering around,' said Mary.

'Look over there,' replied George, pointing toward five or six dogs trotting along the quayside, heading in their direction.

'If I'm not mistaken, the one in front is a bull mastiff.' With that, the pup's ears were on red alert. The pack of dogs picked up their pace. They must have been thirty metres away when the pup sat bolt upright, whimpered, and dashed off.

Chapter 24

Nearly two days had passed since Tiger had left for town. By then, Speed's tummy was rattling due to the lack of food. Something was amiss. He thought, If he doesn't show this evening, I'll have to chance it and go into town and try to scavenge some food.

The sun had started to set. Speed's mind was made up, and he had to move, otherwise, he would starve to death. So leaving the relative safety of the old villa, Speed headed towards the town, using the same route that Barney would have taken and at the same time wishing he had paid more attention to what Barney had tried to teach him. The obvious lessons he remembered, such as keeping to the shadows, avoiding people, watching out for the council catchers, and keeping an eye on the traffic when crossing the roads. The main crossroads were relatively simple to cross at that time of evening. The traffic had thinned considerably. Having safely mounted the pavement on the other side, out of the corner of his eye, a little way up from the junction, Speed saw what appeared to be a bundle of fur lying in the gutter. As there were very few people about, Speeds natural curiosity took over he thought, I'll have a look. Nearing the bundle, he was aware of the endless noise of buzzing flies, and on closer inspection, realised it was a dead animal.. Within two metres of the body, he stopped. The awful realisation hit him. It was Tiger lying in the gutter—Tiger, who was going to look after him was dead. He couldn't look after himself. Panic started to set in. Get a grip. There's nothing you can do. Best get out of here, pronto, undercover somewhere and think this through. Move yourself, Speed, he said to himself and ran to the nearest clump of bushes, where he hid and he tried to make sense of what he had seen.

What would Barney do? He always said, 'Weigh up the pros and cons before you make a move.' Don't rush into a hasty action that later you might regret.

Realisation suddenly dawned upon him. Tiger was gone, and if he was honest, there was a high probability that Bernie, Barney, and the rest were incarcerated at the pound, if not already executed. He had no one. A feeling of utter despair settled over him.

The day faded into night. The darkness seemed to engulf him in its foreboding shroud. Let's face it, I'm on my own—no home unless I use the old nature reserve, which really isn't an option too far out of town. I need to be where the action is. It's too dangerous to go back to Bodrum Road, no doubt the council will be keeping an eye on the old haunt. Right! My immediate need is food. At this hour, the only place I'll find it is at the tip, a large area where all the garbage and waste collected by the council was dumped. Once I've eaten something, I'll feel better and be able to think more clearly. That's the first course of action. Standing up, he headed for the dump, sticking to the same route Barney would have taken. On arrival, he started foraging around. After a considerable time searching, he found nothing, zilch, a fruitless waste of time and effort.

With his stomach making rumbling sounds, he knew something had to be done. Then it hit him. I'll leg it to my foster mother's, Lulu. She'll help me. Leaving the tip, he broke into a fast trot, heading for Lulu's house. In a few minutes, he was outside the hole in the fence. Surprisingly, he was still able to squeeze through. Softly, he padded down to the shed at the bottom of the garden and gave a soft bark.

'Lulu, it's me,' no answer. He barked again, a little louder.

'Lulu, it's me, Speed!' Still no answer. He noticed that the shed door stood ajar. Gently pushing it open, he went in.

'Anybody here?' he barked. Still no reply. As his eyes became accustomed to the gloom, he realised the shed was empty. How odd, he thought, I'll have to nose around outside.

Passing through the shed door into the garden, he looked up, noticing the house was in darkness. On further investigation, he realised the whole place was deserted. The owners must have upped and left, he thought. Still, his stomach rumbled. Moving back down to the shed, he decided to spend the night there. At least he was comparatively safe for the time being. Settling down, he pondered on his next move. An idea suddenly struck him. Barney always said there was safety in numbers. First thing tomorrow, he would seek out Big Bob, the mastiff, and offer to join his gang. Yes, that seemed to be a sensible idea. In spite of his hunger pains, Speed still managed to fall asleep.

He was up at first light and on his way to the marina. If anywhere, that's the place to find Big Bob. On arrival, the marina was empty except for one stall holder setting up. Better keep out of sight until the marina is busy, he thought. Making his way to Bernie's old haunt at the back of the old boathouse, he settled down to wait.

Sometime later, he ventured out to find the place teeming with activity. Making his way to the launching ramp, Speed spotted Big Bob and his motley crew. As he approached, Bob saw him and growled, 'What do you want?'

Speed halted and barked back somewhat tentatively.

'I come to offer you my services.'

Cocking one ear, Bob replied with a snigger, 'Say that again.'

Speed repeated himself, 'I've come—'

Bob cut him off with a growl, 'Your services! How can a little runt like you be of service to me? Piss off!'

'But . . . but . . . !' stuttered Speed.

'I said piss off,' he said, at the same time ordering his gang to attack.

Speed was off like a flash, hotly pursued by Big Bob and his crew. He managed to lose them. He wasn't called Speed for nothing. In truth, Bob had called his crew off. There was no point wasting his time on a little runt. He had more important things to do.

Finding himself in the vicinity of the disused pump house, Speed thought he would hang there till he could come up with another idea. At least it was cool inside. Still, his stomach rumbled.

Settling in his favourite corner, trying to remember the advice that Barney had endeavoured to pass on to him, how he wished he'd paid closer attention to what was said. Once again looking at his options, Speed thought, Options! There are no options. The truth is I'm homeless, hungry, and destitute. Depression threatened to engulf him. I've got to snap out of it, try to join another gang. The trouble was he didn't know any, and to compound the situation, Big Bob was after him. If I could work the old haunts—impossible on his own, he thought. One thing Barney always said about people—they were a source of food, especially the English. They are a nation of dog-lovers.

That's it! Suddenly, the beginnings of a strategy popped into his head. If he remembered correctly, there's an English tea garden opposite the Isparto Hotel. Barney had mentioned, that when he was younger, he would sit outside and beg off the Brits as they indulged in their quaint habit of afternoon tea and scones. Apparently, they were suckers for a friendly dog with doleful eyes and a wagging tail.

Okay, I'll wait till later and give it a try . . . Well, would you believe it? thought Speed as he sat outside the tea garden furiously wagging his tail whilst crouching down. Only two or three minutes had passed, and already a little girl sitting at a table said, 'Look, Mummy, look . . . there's a poor little puppy over there,' pointing at Speed. 'Isn't he lovely? I bet he's hungry. Can I feed him?'

'Yes, dear, if you must. Throw it a piece of your scone.'

'A big piece?' came the reply.

With that, a large dollop landed at Speed's paws, which he hastily gobbled up. Two hours went like a flash. By then, his tummy was full, true full of cream cakes. There again, beggars can't be choosers. Then he needed to sleep it off. The ideal place was opposite a flower arrangement that ran along the outside wall of the Isparto Hotel. That will do nicely, he thought. Trotting over and selecting a suitable spot in the shade, he lay down. Within minutes, Speed was fast asleep only to be woken by some mad woman bashing him on the head with a broom and at the same time mouthing obscenities.

'Get off my flowers, you! You! Filthy mongrel.' Bash . . . bash.

That hurts, thought Speed. Bash. Bash.

'Off with you, you mangy cur. I said off, you stinking street dog.'

Speed wasn't putting up with that. He was tempted to give her a nip, but thought he had found a source of food, so a hasty retreat was in order. He could always come back later and guard his pitch . . . and that's where Mary found him and took him into the hotel.

Chapter 25

Speed was quick off the mark, but he was not fast enough. Perhaps having a belly-full of food slowed him down. He had covered very little ground before Bob's gang had him surrounded. He crouched down, eyes darting every which way. The snarling and barking was coming at him from all angles, so much so that a crowd had gathered to see what the fuss was about.

A group of children playing at the end of the street came dashing over shouting, 'Dog fight, dog fight!'

It was then that Bob growled the order, 'Move in.'

The dogs inched forward, yapping, snapping, and baring their fangs. This is it, Speed thought, his eyes darting left, then right, then left again, his whole body shaking with fear. As he looked for an avenue of escape, there was none. It could well be the end, no way out. Oh, how he wished Bernie would come to his rescue and save the day! There was no chance of that happening. He was locked up at the pound.

As he cowered and waited for certain death, then out of seemingly nowhere appeared Mary, striding through the circle of dogs and standing over Speed, shouting and waving her straw bag.

'You naughty dogs, be off with you. Pick on someone your own size. I won't tell you again. I said off!' she roared.

The crowds were amazed at the sheer nerve of this Englishwoman walking into a circle of feral dogs. She could be seriously hurt, even killed. For Mary, there was no danger. All she saw was a group of dogs misbehaving.

The pack quietened and looked to Bob for direction. Bob, who was totally unimpressed by this unhinged woman's shouting, he barked, 'Kill!' Then with a louder bark, 'I said kill!.'

At that precise moment, the mad woman stepped forward, and to Bob's amazement, grabbed him by the scruff of his neck and said, 'You're the biggest, and by the looks of it, the ring leader.' The rest went silent, watching to see what Big Bob would do.

Baring his fangs and snarling, at the same time thinking, The effrontery of this person! Who does she think she is dealing with? I'm Big Bob, leader of the hardest gang in Dalman. Before he could made a decision as to a course of action, she grasped his neck even tighter, bent down and looked him square in the face, at the same time, wagged her finger at him and said, 'I won't tell you again. Stop that posturing, you silly dog, and be off, and take your scruffy friends with you.'

Bob was stunned. He dare not bite her with the crowd watching. Then again, he couldn't afford to lose face in front of his gang. An idea came to him. Barking to his team, he said, 'We had better get out of here. Someone will have called the catchers. They could be here any second. Let's move.' As they parted, Bob barked at Speed, 'You were lucky this time. We know where you hang out. We'll have you yet.'

George stood on the edge of the crowd, full of admiration for Mary. She showed no fear in entering a circle of wild hungry dogs and telling them off. Mind you, she did love all creatures, and they seemed to love her.

The crowd cheered, exclaiming, 'Bravo!' With all the commotion going on, Speed had ample time to slip away unnoticed and made his way to the safety of the pump house.

'You took an awful risk walking into that pack. You could have been seriously injured or maimed just to save a wild puppy.'

'Don't be silly, George. They were just excited dogs playing around.'

If you say so, thought George.

'By the way, where is the pup?'

'I don't know. It must have been frightened and run off. I didn't see it go,' he said.

'You should have held on to it.'

'How could I?' George answered. 'I was too worried about you.'

'That's no excuse, George. It's lost and we'll never find it. You stupid man.'

'Don't start, Mary. What if it was me in that situation? You would have probably saved the dog, I suppose.'

'Don't be stupid, George. Now let's look for it.'

Anything for peace and quiet, he thought.

'I'll take the main street and all the side turnings. You look around the marina, market, and all the open spaces. If you find the pup, meet me back at the hotel.'

'Okay,' said George. 'See you later.' He knew from the previous evening that this pup meant trouble for him.

Mary was gone. Having searched the marina and market with no luck, George proceeded to look further a field. Dalman, once a thriving fishing village, was the centre of activity of this small community. Accessed by two roads, one led to the main highway. Once reached, to the east lay the city of Ankara, to the west, the airport. George reasoned that the pup would not wander far as it needed to be near a source of food, so he chose the other road. In reality, it was little more than a lane that meandered through the surrounding fields As he trundled along, George had time to appreciate the natural beauty of the surrounding countryside. The mountains formed a half-circle terminating at each end as they tapered down to the sea, which formed a natural harbour. The wildlife was abundant—everywhere different-coloured butterflies and through the hazy sunshine, he could hear the various calls of mating birds. For some reason, he always imagined the country to be quiet and subdued, but this was totally different. With very little traffic, the unaffected nature had not changed in centuries, the whole area giving an impression of half a sunken volcano. As the mountains interlocked, it seemed as if someone had sculptured a series of camel humps locked together to form a crescent shape that backed into a deep blue sky. Around the peaks floated little white fluffy clouds. On the lower slopes, the deep green vegetation appeared to the naked eye like a sea of grass. Certain parts of the lush green surface were broken with very little plant life, probably formed by earth movements ages past, leaving steep, sharp crevices, and if one looked carefully, they could see the occasional mountain goat grazing on the sparse surface.

George was so engrossed in the magnificent panoramas unfolding before him that he never saw the rotting tree root protruding from the ground and tripped, falling on his knees.

'Ouch!' he said.

As he stood up and dusted himself down, his eyes fastened on to a beautiful array of violet plant life. George's knowledge of nature's natural abundance was very limited, so he was unable to ascertain if they were flowers or weeds That really was of no consequence. As his eyes surveyed the terra firma, he realised that the variety of colours were wonderful—reds, yellows, mauves, all manner of different shades seemed to unfurl like rolled-up carpet. The sheer grandeur of nature's constant beauty reminded him of the Wordsworth poem 'To the Daffodils'. Yes, George thought, a poet could not but be gay in such jocund company.'

He searched till nearly sundown as the light around the mountain tops turned into a purple haze. George realised he had better make his way back to the hotel. His efforts fruitless, perhaps Mary had had better luck. Feeling deflated, he had to admit there was something about that little whelp that stirred him.

On reaching the hotel, he asked around to see if anybody had seen Mary. It was of no surprise to him that she hadn't returned, knowing how tenacious she was. Whatever it took, she would find the pup. Going to his room, he quickly showered and changed, then went down to the bar-come-coffee shop to wait. It was nigh on ten o'clock, and George realised he was hungry, so he ordered a pizza with a green salad. Nursing a cup of coffee, he had a feeling this would be a long night.

Halfway through his coffee, the pizza arrived. Quite impressive, he thought, very prompt service. He soon devoured the food and managed to empty the salad bowl—some achievement for him as he wasn't too fond of vegetables. Mary, being a vegetarian, was forever telling him he needed a balanced diet.

'You need to eat more veg and fruit,' she kept reminding him.

Ordering more coffee, he settled down to read his book. Time passed. Looking at his watch, George realised it was almost 1 a.m. Glancing up, he noticed the barman was smiling at him, trying to convey that he was closing for the night as the bar was deserted. George called over and said, 'Sorry to have kept you, but I'm waiting for my wife,' at the same time, indicating by yawning it was bed time.

The hotel policy was such that if the bar was in use, it would stay open. As George was the only customer, he thought it inconsiderate to keep the barman away from his bed. Wishing him goodnight, he left for his room.

Half an hour later, feeling quite agitated and unable to settle, George decided to look for Mary. Leaving the room key at reception, he left the hotel, not sure in which direction to proceed. He decided that informing the police was the best course of action. The police station was situated in the town centre. On arrival, he found the building closed and a notice written in various languages saying: 'In case of emergencies, call this number'.

As of yet, though very worried, Mary's absence wasn't exactly an emergency. After all, she often went on long walks as she was one of those people that seemed to manage on very few hours' sleep. She would often go for days just catnapping. Having a quick look around the small town, he made his way back to the hotel. He passed the night porter, who was snoring, asleep behind the reception desk. So as not to wake him, George helped himself to the key hanging on the board. He made his way to their room, careful not to lock the door. Once inside, he fell on to the bed exhausted.

A noise interrupted his fitful dozing. Looking at his watch, it was past three o'clock. The door clicked shut, and there stood Mary.

'Where have you been!' exclaimed George angrily. 'It's gone three. I've been worried out of my mind.'

'You know where I've been,' she answered, 'looking for the pup, stupid.'

'I'm not stupid. How would you feel if I went missing and arrived back at this hour?'

No reply.

'Well?'

'Well what?'

'Did you find it?'

'Of course not, you idiot. Would I be standing here empty-handed if I had, you bloody moron?'

By 8 a.m., Mary was shaking him vigorously.

'Wake up, wake up, George. Let's get going.'

'Going where?' he said, not fully awake.

'To find the pup, silly!'

'Oh yes,' he yawned. 'I've barely had four hours' sleep and it's time for breakfast.'

'We don't have time for that. Come on, get dressed and let's get going.'

George thought he would make a stand, 'I'm not going anyhere till I've eaten my breakfast.'

'Typical,' said Mary. 'At an important time like this, all you can think about is your stomach.'

'You've heard the saying Mary, "An army marches on its stomach."'

Exasperated, Mary replied, 'You're not exactly an army, are you?'

'True, but I'm hungry.'

'Well, if you must stuff your face,' she said rather wickedly, 'I'll see you at the post office in an hour, so chop chop and get moving.'

'All right! All right! Give me a chance. See you later.'

Being a stickler for time, George arrived at the post office exactly an hour later to find Mary drinking coffee at the café next door.

'Well, you took your time,' she said.

To which George replied, 'I said one hour and one hour it is.'

'Stop arguing about the time and let's get moving.'

George wasn't letting it go at that, 'Who's arguing? I'm only making a statement of truth. It's bang on one hour and I'm here.'

'Why do you always have to start an argument, George? Just move your arse.'

'I'm not starting . . . ' George stopped himself. The conversation was going nowhere. He had learnt many years ago it was pointless to argue with Mary. Like most women, she had to have the last word.

'Yes, dear, you're right. You're always right,' he said with a touch of irony.

This was not lost on Mary as she smiled inwardly. 'Right, let's get moving.'

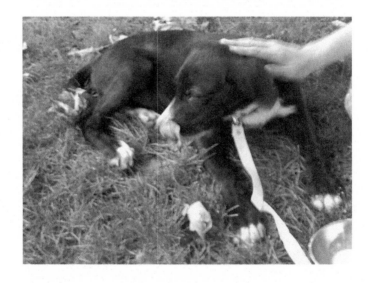

Easy as a puppy when I found him in Turkey.

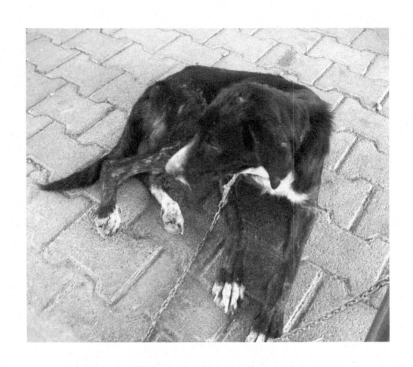

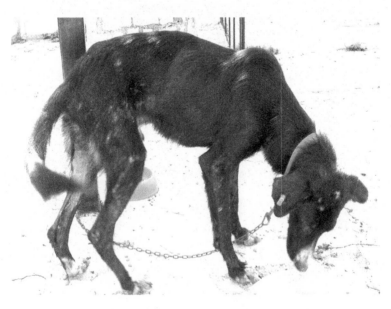

Easy one year later weighing 7.5 Kilos taken on the day I rescued him from the bogus animal charity, run by an English woman. Having parted with a considerable amount of money for his keep and vet bills.

Easy enjoying life living with me.

Easy today.

Chapter 26

They spent the morning and most of the afternoon searching, still no luck. Feeling hungry, they decided to take a late lunch and to review the situation. They shared a green salad and a plate of chips. Mary ordered a gin and tonic, George a coffee; being a recovering alcoholic, he was quite happy to stay with tea, coffee, or the occasional soft drink.

'The point is we're getting nowhere. We've looked everywhere with no luck. I have an idea. Let's have some posters made and distribute them around town with the hotel phone number printed on them,' said Mary.

'That's a good idea,' said George, trying to sound enthusiastic. 'It might work.' Inwardly thinking, The town is full of stray dogs. Nobody will remember one black-and-white pup, if indeed they are interested.

It was then it occurred to George it might be worth a try if they went back to the marina and waited by the bench where they had last fed him. This he suggested to Mary.

'S'pose it's worth a try,' she said with a despondent note in her voice.

They settled the bill and started toward the marina, both of them feeling somewhat deflated. On arrival, they made their way towards the bench. About halfway there, Mary complained of tiredness, saying, 'It's pointless. I'm going to sit on the grass and rest. You can see from here there's nothing there.'

'Yes, you're right,' he said, sitting down.

Mary joined him and proceeded to light a cigarette, not offering one to George because three years earlier as Big Ben sounded in the New Year, George had stubbed out his last cigarette and hadn't smoked since.

The thing Mary admired about George was his good looks and his natural tendency to care for other people. Tenacious by nature, he would not give up till he had exhausted every possibility.

'You sit there and rest. I'll wander over and check the bench and surrounding area.'

George ventured on, thinking to himself, This is a pointless exercise, even if we find the pup, we are leaving Turkey on the late evening flight in two days' time. Had she thought about the implications of once having made friends with the dog, it would be heartless to desert it, leaving the animal once again to fend for itself? George neared the bench, his mind preoccupied with this problem; he noticed a slight movement in the long grass under the bench. He was sure something was moving. Proceeding stealthily, George realised his mistake. Just the wind blowing through the grass, he thought. Never mind, I'm nearly there, might as well check it out. There it was again. Just wishful thinking, he said to himself. Still, he hurried forward just to dispel any illusions that the pup was there. Then he saw it curled up in a tight little black-and-white ball.

George couldn't believe it. There it lay asleep. 'Well, I never . . . ' he said aloud. 'Who would have believed it?' Picking it up, he shouted, 'Mary! Mary! Come over here.'

'What for?' she yelled back.

'I've found it,' he answered.

'Speak up. I can't hear you.'

I'm the one who's deaf in one ear, not you, he thought.

'Get over here,' he yelled even louder.

'All right, I'm coming. Don't panic.'

She moved towards him, shouting, 'What is it?'

'I've found the pup, you dumbo.'

Increasing her pace and with the broadest smile George had ever seen, she said, 'Oh, George, you've found him,' at the same time almost tripping over in her eagerness to get to the pup.

'I can't believe it. You actually found him!' she said, almost snatching the pup from George's hands. She began smothering it in kisses and crooning;

'My poor little orphan waif, you're safe now. Mummy will look after you.'

Oh my god, thought George, that's more attention than I get.

Giving the pup back to George, Mary reached into her straw bag and, to his amazement, pulled out a collar and lead, fitting it around the pup's neck.

'Now,' she said, 'everyone will know it has an owner.'

'When did you get that?'

'This morning while you were at breakfast,' said Mary. 'The first thing is into town to buy Easy some meat. There's a supermarket at the end of the high street.'

Setting the pup down and striding out with renewed energy in the direction of the shop, some ten minutes later they arrived. Once inside, Mary brought a packet of frankfurters, off cuts of meat, and a juicy steak. As George waited outside with Easy.

'What's all that for?' inquired George.

'Well, the frankfurters for now and the rest for later.'

George wished he had never asked.

Mary said, 'Let's walk him back to the hotel,' which in turn meant, down the high street being the quickest way.

With that, they set off; the pup now with a full belly took on a different persona. Strutting along, head held high, as much as to say to the shop owners and the other strays, Look at me with my brand new collar and adopted owners. I'm no long a street dog.

About halfway down the street, the pup stopped and to George's astonishment, squatted down and did the biggest shit he had ever seen, giving the impression he was cocking a snoot at the street traders.

'Now, look what he's done,' said George.

'Good boy,' Mary said.

'Good boy!' George exclaimed. 'We'll be the laughing stock of the town.'

With that, Mary produced two plastic bags from her basket. With her hand inside one, she scooped up the pile and placed it in the other, wrapping the pooh up and dropped it in the nearest bin.

My God, thought George, that pup could shit for England.

Mary, quite unperturbed, continued on her way. As they neared the hotel entrance, she suggested they stop for a cup of tea at the English garden café opposite.

'Mind if I bring the dog in Reg?' she said to the proprietor.

'Not at all. Would it like a bowl of water?'

'Thank you, that will do nicely,' said Mary, as they both sat down.

'The usual for yourselves?'

'Yes, thanks,' replied George.

Having eaten her scones and into a second cup of tea, Mary lit a cigarette. George thought, Now is the appropriate time to tackle her as to what she intends to do with the pup.

'Well,' she said, 'Easy will stay with us tonight.'

'Be that as it may,' interrupted George. 'I'm talking about in the long term. We're leaving in two days, and we can't take the dog with us.'

'Stop fretting, George. Let me worry about it. Now you run along and find the hotel owner and ask if Easy can stay with us tonight.'

'I'll do my best to persuade him,' said George, 'but you know how his wife hates dogs.'

'If necessary, tell him I'm prepared to stay out all night rather than lose him again,' she said.

Knowing Mary, that's exactly what she would do, he replied, 'Okay, I'll go over to the reception and ask them to page him.' George stood up to leave. 'By the way, how on earth did you come up with the name Easy?'

'It's from the book I'm reading about the gangs in New York, Harlem in particular. One of the member's name is Easy.'

'Oh, I see,' said George.

As he departed, Reg appeared with the bill.

'Everything to your satisfaction?' he asked.

'As always,' said Mary, rifling her purse for the money. Having paid Reg, she asked if she could sit there till George returned relating the problem of housing the dog for the night.

'Stay as long as you like and good luck with Mr Yuris. As a matter of interest, that looks like the same pup that was outside, begging yesterday.'

'Oh, really . . . ' said Mary, tongue in cheek.

Some thirty minutes had passed and no sign of George. Mary wasn't worried; she had Easy to occupy her attention.

Mary looked up to see the hotel rep approaching.

'Hello, Mary, had a good day?'

'Lovely, Brett, thank you,' she replied, and without pausing for breath, she went on to relate the saga of Easy.

Brett, like all good hotel reps, listened patiently to all his customers, and when Mary had finished, he offered her the use of his office if the owner of the hotel refused to allow the pup in her room, adding much to Mary's delight that his mother ran an animal charity and that he would call her right away to see if she could take care of the pup. He dialled her number on his mobile; a brief conversation followed, which as far as Mary could make out, it was conducted in Turkish even though Brett was English through and through.

'No problem,' he declared. 'Be at the marina by ten o'clock tomorrow morning. I'm taking a group of tourist on the seven-island trip. The first port of call is Balgarese, where my mother lives. Don't forget to bring the pup,' he said with a smile, 'and my office is at your disposal should you need it.'

'Thank you, Brett. That's so kind of you. Thank you very much.'

As Brett departed, George came hurrying down the road with a broad grin on his face.

'Good news, Mary!' he exclaimed. 'Mr Yuris, the owner, has agreed to let the pup stay with us, providing he doesn't disturb the other guests.'

'Well done, George. I have a surprise for you too,' Mary recounted the conversation she had with Brett, 'so there we are all done and dusted.

Right next on the agenda, a shower, change of clothes, then out for a meal to celebrate.

'What about the pup?' asked George.

'He can come with us. The restaurant owners won't mind, providing he's on a lead. If they do, we'll take our custom elsewhere.'

As they passed through the hotels foyer, they noticed Easy was having difficulty staying on his feet, the reason being his nails were to long; he was unable to apply any grip to the floor.

On reaching the marble stairs, Easy thought, What are they, and he hesitated, not knowing what to do, so he sat down and waited. As George and Mary started to ascend, he endeavoured to follow, but try as he may he was unable to negotiate the obstacles; the stair risers were too tall for him.

Mary, noticing Easy's predicament, said to George, 'The pup's confused. Pick him up and carry the poor thing.'

Sometime later showered and changed and Easy fed, they made their way down from the first floor. This time, Easy found it less difficult; he simply slid down on his full belly.

They dined at their usual restaurant, no problems with the dog. Leaving a sizeable tip, they decided to take a stroll around the marina before turning in for the night, thus allowing Easy to do his business.

Next morning with their ablutions finished, they were ready for breakfast when George drew Mary's attention to the fact that Easy would not be allowed in the dining room.

'No problem,' she said. 'You eat first while I take the dog for a walk so he can relieve himself, and I'll feed him. When you're finished, let's say half an hour, we'll swap over. You stay with the dog while I eat.'

'Okay,' said George 'that's funny.'

'What's funny?'

'Well, the dog. It doesn't seem to have messed anywhere. Have you cleaned up after it?'

'No, I haven't,' said Mary. 'See, George, it's already housed trained.'

Thirty minutes later, they had changed places. As Mary entered the dining room, she noticed that the rest of their group was arriving, so they breakfasted together. They listened intently as Mary updated them on the Easy situation. Finally, she informed them of her intent to take Easy back to England.

The group listened politely; nobody wanted to point out to Mary that logistically it was nigh on impossible. First, you had to get the dog out of Turkey. If you were able to overcome that obstacle, you were faced with the British laws governing the importation of livestock on to Enlish soil. It was common knowledge that the British government was paranoid about the possibility of Rabies crossing the English Channel. She had little chance of success; nobody said anything not wanting to pour water on Mary's dream.

All three arrived at the marina ten o'clock sharp. They found Brett who greeted them then ushered all three

onto a half-empty boat that was ready to disembark.

'Make yourselves comfortable. Our first port of call is Balgarese, should take about forty minutes. My mother will be waiting for you on the quayside.'

As the boat moved off its mooring and gathered pace, Brett began his commentary.

Chapter 27

As he lay at Mary's feet, Easy thought, So much has happened to me in the last few days. The hunger pains have gone, my belly is full, and these nice people are taking care of me. Mind you, I must remember to eat everything that's offered as I can't be sure how long my good fortune will last, so this is what it's like to ride in a boat. Just as well I'm lying down as I feel quite queasy. I wonder where we are going. Hope, it's not too far. My bladder feels full, I need a pee. .. Trying not to think of his bladder, he drifted into a relaxed state. He wondered what had happened to his pals, if what he had been led to believe they had probably been found homes or exterminated. Mind you, Tiger had said they might find homes for them, but in truth, that could take months, even years.

I can't see the council spending public money on stray dogs whilst waiting for them to be adopted. Let's face it; there's a very high probability that they are already dead; Bernie, Jack, Harry, and his mentor and benefactor Barney—dead. I'm on my own now inside a boat, heading who knows where; I'm still alive. Thanks to these nice people.

I must try to think positively, that's what Barney would say. Make the best of what you have. He felt a little fearful not knowing where his future lay. Snap out of it, who knows what will unfold in the next few hours.

Finally, he drifted into an uneasy sleep, only to be woken by a nasty little jolt; the boat had stopped. Mary gave his lead a gentle tug. 'Come on, Easy. We've arrived, up you get.'

Standing and stretching, he looked around; it appeared that the craft was tied up next to a little pier. Already, people were disembarking and milling around on the quayside. He heard Brett say, 'We sail in one hour, so don't be late. The market is straight on this road about four hundred metres on the right.'

Brett walked over to George and Mary saying, 'If you and your dog would like to wait over there', pointing to his right at a pretty dock side open-air cafe, 'order whatever you want and put it on my tab.'

'That's not necessary,' said George.

'I'll fetch my mother shortly. At the moment she's with another client,' said Brett pointing to another cafe, one of several dotted around the quay. 'That's her, the lady wearing the yellow top, white jeans, and trainers. She shouldn't be long. Once she has finished, with those people, I'll introduce you to her.'

'Thanks,' said Mary.

Brett made his way to where his mother was sitting.

George caught the waiter's attention and ordered a coke plus a gin and tonic for Mary.

'Would your dog like a bowl of water,' asked the waiter.

'Yes, please,' replied Mary.

The waiter made off to fetch the order.

Mary said to George, 'Easy needs a pee.'

'How do you know,' said George.

'I just do,' answered Mary. 'Take him over to those bushes behind the water fountain.'

'Ok Easy come" said George standing up and leading the dog.

Phew! At last, thought Easy. Once in the bushes, he had a sniff around, then peed.

What a relief, he thought. He stopped at the fountain for a refill on his way back.

They returned to the table to find Mary sipping her gin and tonic with a bowl of water at her feet.

Some fifteen minutes later, Brett returned with his mother and made the introductions.

'George, Mary, this is Katie, my mother. They all exchanged handshakes.'

'Sorry, I have to leave,' said Brett, but it's time to round up my day trippers. 'See you back at the hotel later.'

'We're leaving tonight,' said George, 'so if we miss you, "thanks for everything".'

'Goodbye,' Brett called back to his mum.

Mary asked Katie if she would like a drink.

'A cup of tea will be fine'.

Signalling to the waiter, George ordered a pot of tea and the same again for Mary and himself.

As the two women chatted, George had time to observe Katie—a heavily built, busty, woman, about fifty years of age, hair gray, the colour of steel; tied back in a bun her face tanned and lined by the sun, her expression somewhat severe. She was saying to Mary, 'I married a Turkish man some twenty-five years ago. We set up business together, then Brett came along. Unfortunately, things didn't work out, so we divided our assets; he left for Istanbul; well, me, I set up a charity for abandoned animals and street dogs. Like most charities the major problem I have is money. I am completely self-sufficient; the government doesn't contribute at all, so I rely totally on animal lovers to support me. What usually happens, people like yourselves, whilst on holiday find a stray and take it in hand for the duration of their vacation, then either they let it free to run wild again or ask me to look after them, which is completely unfair to the animal and a tremendous strain on my finances.'

'I see,' said Mary, 'we have no intention of doing that. George and I have discussed this at length. We will leave you some money, our phone number, and email address, and if at any time you incur additional expenses, say vet bills etc., then call us and we will wire the money to you. "You have access to a computer and a phone?"'

'Of course,' Katie replied.

'Good,' said Mary, 'and we will be back next year to see how Easy is fairing.'

Discuss what? Thought George, which was news to him.

Writing on a piece of paper, Mary gave their details, while Katie did the same.

'The important thing is, how much do you need from us right now?'

Katie didn't hesitate;

'Five hundred euros should cover his cost for a year.'

'George! Give Katie the money.'

'But!'

'No buts.'

'What I was about to say Mary is it will leave us short of cash.'

'Never mind that, we're leaving this evening,' she replied.

George dutifully counted out the money.

'That should keep him for a while,' said George as he gave Katie the cash.

'That's very kind of you,' said Katie, thanking them both. 'Well, that's it then,' She said, bending down to pick up Easy and place him in a deep basket attached to the rear of her tricycle, which stood up by the wall.

'By the way, I forgot to mention that I have a piece of land down by the river, and once I've built a fence around it, I intend to move all my dogs there. Bye!' With that, she mounted her bike and was gone.

George was somewhat perplexed and said, 'What was that all about ? We didn't discuss anything.'

'Well, I had to say something. I knew you would agree anyway. Come on let's find the bus station and get back to the hotel. We have to do our packing.'

Once they were on the bus and heading back to Dalman, a thought occurred to George, looking at Mary he saw a tear running down her cheek.

'Never mind, love, we'll keep in regular contact with Katie and come back next year as you said.'

George didn't like to admit it, but he was quite choked himself having to work hard to stop a tear forming in his eye. He decided not to voice his doubts as Mary was already upset. But he found it strange that not once in the hour or so they were with Katie did she pat or pet the poor dog.

Probably an overreaction; obviously, she was preoccupied with the welfare and logistics of running a charity. Mind you, she admitted to say if she had any volunteer helpers. As soon as he was back in England, he would check out her web site.

And check it out he did; everything seemed to be above board and legal.

Chapter 28

This is odd, thought Easy. There I was dozing on a boat between those nice people who brought me my new collar and lead. The next thing, I'm sitting in a basket on the back of a tricycle being peddled along by a lady. She must be a friend of theirs. Maybe they've gone away for a few days and she's taking care of me. Well, as far as I know, I don't have to worry about the dog catchers any more.

Things must be okay as she seems to know lots of people, waving, passing comments as she peddles along. I wonder where we are going. By the looks of it, the town is somewhat smaller than that of Dalman, and this street we are on appears to be the main road, leading out of town as the dock is behind us, and we're heading up a hill.

Shame about those nice people though; I was getting very attached to them. The lady was so kind to me, so was the man although he appeared to be a little gruff, but no doubt when they collect me, I'll be able to get to know him better.

Phew! It's hot again, mind you; sitting in this basket doesn't help. It must be around midday. I hope we haven't far to travel because it's a bit cramped back here in this basket. Ah! There's a line of trees coming up, which reminds me I could do with a pee.

That's a bus shelter ahead, and if I'm not mistaken there's a dog asleep in the shade. That's the best place to be at this time of day. As we pass, I'll give him a few barks just to draw his attention to my lovely new collar and lead.

'Woof! . . . woof! . . . woof!'

That's strange; there's no reaction. Perhaps, he didn't hear me. There again, maybe he can't be bothered. He looks very emaciated as though he hasn't eaten for days. I'll try again.

'Woof! . . . woof! . . . woof!'

'Shut up, you mangy creature,' the lady said sternly.

Did I hear her right? Is she talking to me? No . . . no, I must have misheard. I'll try one more time. 'Woof . . . woo'

'I said shut up, or I'll get off this bike and give you a belting.'

She is talking to me. That's strange maybe she's having a bad day or something. Best to keep my mouth shut, I don't want to upset her.

Some twenty minutes later, after riding down a network of small lanes, Katie stopped outside an old dilapidated stone house. Placing the tricycle against the wall, she dismounted and produced a set of keys. After fumbling with them for a while, she finally found the one she was looking for and let herself into the house.

Easy noticed that the building was in a state of disrepair, one of the windows was broken, but boarded up from the inside to keep creatures, animals, or people from getting in. Still, he thought that didn't reflect on the general condition; at least he had a home and two meals a day to look forward to, he hoped. He heard a commotion from inside the house and the woman say, 'I said sit and you behave.'

There must be other dogs in there, he thought, and then again, it's possible she has children.

She appeared at the front door, walked over to where Easy sat in the cramped tricycle basket, lifted him out, and walked into the house through what appeared to be a living room. What a pong, thought Easy. He had enough time to notice two dogs, one sitting in an armchair and the other one stretched out on a dirty rug full of holes. Before he could take in any more, he was whisked through to an untidy, smelly kitchen, plonked on a table, and told to stay. She unfastened his collar and his lead and put them both in a cupboard, and then she slammed it shut.

'Oi!' barked Easy. 'That's my new chain and collar!'

'Shut it!' she retorted. 'You won't be needing them here.'

What does she mean? I won't them! He barked back, 'But there mine give them back.'

'Right, that's it,' she said, picking up a metal road, and with one swoop, she whacked Easy straight across his back.

'Ouch,' he yelped and cowered down.

I'd better play it cool. That really hurt and is still stinging. Maybe she really is having a bad day. There again, why would she take it out on me. I've done nothing to upset her. What I'll do is keep a low profile till I can sus—out the situation.

'You don't want to mess with me, you mangy piece of shit. I'll cut your balls off and put them in the mincer and then feed them back to yer.'

Oh my gawd, thought Easy, I think she means it. What a nasty piece of work she is. What on earth have I got myself into now?

Easy lay still as he glanced around the kitchen, which was also in need of repair, the ceiling brown with cigarette smoke; the paint flaking; the wallpaper peeling in places; and so dirty you were unable to see the pattern through the grime. A pile of dirty crockery in the sink and the cupboard above hanging open; the left hand door was minus a hinge, the right one without a handle. Under the window stood a rusty old twin-tub washing machine, and as for the refrigerator, it must have come out of the Ark; it was so dilapidated. The whole scene unravelling before his very eyes was depressing to say the very least.

Easy watched as Katie unbolted the door that presumably led to the garden; the foulest stench wafted into the kitchen. Then moving back to the table, Katie gathered Easy up and threw him out of the door down past two steps until he landed on a concrete patio.

Fortunately, for him, he was very agile and was able to twist in the air and land on his paws. Stripped of all dignity, his temper got the better of him. Climbing on the first step, Easy started to bark. Five minutes went by with no reaction. Just as he was about to stop, the door flew open, and whoosh, a dirty bowl of water hit him straight on, knocking him down, and the door was slammed shut. Everything had happened so quickly.

Shaking himself down, he looked around except for the patio the garden consisted of matted smelly undergrowth surrounded by a crumbling brick wall, probably about three metres high. To the right of the kitchen door, protruding from the wall, was a rusty tap dripping into a drain and next to that a wooden tub filled to the brim and floating on top a green stinking slime. Curled up next to the tub was a rotting hosepipe, next to that also curled up was what appeared to be a grotesquely emaciated whimpering dog. From behind him, their came a soft bark. On turning, Easy was appalled to see what had once been a big, muscular Bull Terrier, but now looked like a pile of walking bones.

Easy barked, 'Who are you?'

'My name is Boris,' replied the barking skeleton.

'What's happening?' asked Easy. The words had hardly left his mouth, when he became aware of a cacophony of sound as more dogs appeared from the tangled undergrowth. There were too many to count, but one thing was apparent—they were all starving and had lost at least half of their body weight.

'Keep the noise down out there. If I have to come out to you . . . you know what to expect.'

At the sound of Katie's voice, the dogs immediately quietened down.

'Will somebody tell me what's going on?' The dog's started to bark in unison.

'I shan't tell you again,' said the voice from behind the kitchen door. 'Shut it! I said shut it.'

'One at a time,' said Easy. 'Boris, you be the spokesman and tell me what's going on?' Though he was only six months old, Easy emitted an air of confidence which the other dogs seemed to recognise.

'Well,' said Boris, 'you can see from our condition that we are all absolutely starving.'

'You mean she doesn't feed you?'

'That's right, now and then, she throws us some bones that she scrounges from butchers in Balgarese, but there's very little meat on them. At least one of our number dies every single week, either through disease brought on by malnutrition or the infected water from that tub over there.'

'How long have you been here, Boris?'

'Two years. I'm one of the longest survivors.'

'If one of the group dies every week, what does she do with the body?'
Easy asked.

'Well,' said Boris, 'Old Bill over there says she cuts them up and boils
them, then feeds the meat to her two pets, which are inside the house, and
throws us the scraps. I'm not sure if that's true, but Bill is convinced.'

'Well, she ain't going to cut me up,' said Easy. 'I'll escape.'

'No chance,' replied Boris, 'If there's a way out of here, we are yet to
find it. The height of the walls makes it impossible to jump over.'

'Have you tried digging?'

'Yes, but the foundations go down at least a metre. One of our numbers
tried that last year when he first came, he dug down about thirty centimetres
while he was fit and healthy, but she saw him through an upstairs window,
came down, hit him with a spade, almost took his head clean off.'

'That's terrible,' said Easy. 'There must be something we can do. Have
you tried rushing her when she opens the kitchen door?'

'She rarely does that. She throws the bones from the first-floor window,
and all the ground floor windows are bared.'

'What happens when she removes your dead comrades?' asked Easy.

'Oh, she's very sly. Usually, at night, she opens the door, but it's on a
heavy chain, leaving just enough room to drag a body through, and her
two well-fed pets keep watch. You can't blame them, of course. They know
which side their bread is buttered. I would do the same in their position. If
they don't do it, she'll chuck them out here with the rest of us.'

'How did you all get here in the first place?'

'Well, most of us are strays who have been adopted by holidaymakers,
who when their vacation is over can't take care of us. Turkey being a non
EU country, their dog passports are not recognised in Europe. The others
here are house pets whose owners have moved on and don't want to take
them along with them. She advertises and pet owners bring their animals as
she is the only so-called charity in the area,they put them in her care, often
leaving a substantial amount of money for their welfare. She tells everyone
that the money they give her, helps with the feeding and the vet's bills. She
also tells them she owns a piece of land that contains a natural pond which
is fenced all around, where the dogs live, each one is provided with a kennel

of its own, and of course, this needs more money for the general upkeep. But she keeps all donations for herself. As time goes by, if people ask for a photo of the dog they have left, she tells them their animal fell ill and died. On the odd occasion when a benefactor asks to see the animal, she makes a lot of excuses. Things like, 'I'm away on business or there's an outbreak of some contagious disease,' or makes sure she simply is not available. I know there is no financial support from the local council as they consider us pests, and their policy is to exterminate us all, once the holiday season is over.'

'Yes, I know all about that. My friends were rounded up in Dalman and killed.'

'I'm sorry,' said Boris. 'I'm not sure what's worse, slow starvation or electrocution.'

'Well, that's not going to happen to me. I'll find a way out of here if it kills me.'

'It probably will,' murmured Boris, as he turned and slouched off.

Slowly, the other dogs disappeared into the undergrowth; Easy remained alone. The sun was beating down on his back. There wasn't any shade except for the tangled mass of rotting vegetation. He needed to drink, so walking over to the tub he tentatively put one paw in, to push away the green slime, and held his breath, from the filthy water emanated a stench that was overpowering; if I drink, that I'll catch dysentery. Looking around, he espied the old rusty tap next to the rotting hose pipe; sure enough, there was a steady but slow leak. Trotting over, he put his tongue out to catch the drop, it was certainly clean water. He must have stood there twenty minutes or so, his thirst still not sated. By this time, the heat was unbearable. Panting, he made his way to the undergrowth to dig a hole to lie in and cool down. He heard a bark saying, 'Don't dig there, dig it elsewhere.'

After several attempts, he found an unoccupied spot, dug a hole, and settled down to review the day's events.

He knew he was in trouble; one minute, life was looking rosy, a full stomach, new-found owners, not to mention and collar and leash. Now, he was imprisoned in a brick and cement jungle with a woman warder. Who knows what's in store for him next? According to Boris, death, by starvation or even dehydration. The future certainly looked grim. Who was he kidding, what future?

How would Bernie react in this situation? He'd come up with something, some kind of plan. Life hasn't been the same since his friends disappeared; he was still not convinced his old mentor Barney had died. There was a faint ray of hope that somehow he had survived, and at this very moment was looking for him. What a great gang of friend we once were; Bernie, Barney, Jack, and of course, dopey Harry; our friendship short lived but great while it lasted.

All this remembering was unproductive because he still had to find a way out of this hellhole. The heat of the day made him feel listless and sleepy. I'll take a nap, and, when it's cooler, I will try to make contact with the other animals.

His thirst not quenched and the beginnings of hunger pains, Easy found it difficult to sleep. His ears were picking up low whimpering sounds that emanated from all around him. He dozed fitfully as the afternoon dragged on; eventually, the sun moved across the heavens and looked for a resting place somewhere in the west. The day's heat abated making way for the welcomed cooler air of twilight time.

Now, thought Easy, I'll have a mooch around and see what's going down. Moving carefully through the matted undergrowth, he made his way to the cemented area, hoping to connect with Boris again. That in itself was difficult, trying to avoid dog faeces, at the same time pushing his way through a network of tangled reeds and low bushes.

As he emerged from the brick jungle, his eyes were drawn to an appalling sight, where the rusty tap protruded from the wall stood a ragged line of skeleton, thin, starving dogs, apparently queuing for the miniscule drops of water that fell slowly from the corroded faucet. The scene before him was surreal. Easy tried to look away, but his eyes were transfixed to the ghastly scenario unfolding before him. It reminded him of a photo he once saw taken at a concentration camp during the latter end of the last World War.

'How could a human inflict such suffering on these defenceless animals,' he asked himself. Is this how I will end up, not if I can help it? As he drew nearer to the tortured animals, he noticed that their ribs were protruding through their skin, they had clumps of fur missing, and what looked like bite marks that oozed puss. Some of the dogs had maggots and ants crawling around in their wounds, and at least two dogs were dragging broken limbs.

By the tub lay a small Terrier in the same condition as the others, with his tongue hanging from his jaws.

'I know what you're thinking,' barked a quiet voice behind him. Turning around, Easy came face to face with Boris. Nodding in the direction of the Terrier, Boris said, 'Yes, he's dead, passed away this afternoon.'

The dogs moved closer to the unfortunate hound, already a black cloud of flies swarming over the prone body.

'How can this happen?' said Easy. 'And why are the others covered in open wounds?'

'That's because we're lucky if she feeds us twice a week. You can guarantee Saturday afternoon as one of those times, as the butchers close for the weekend, she cycles around and begs for any leftovers they may have, which is very little, as they are quite frugal with their meat. If it can be pared off the bone, they package and sell it. Usually, she throws us the bare bones. The dogs then fight over what little there is. We are all undernourished, our teeth are falling out, so we are unable to chew the marrow out of the bones. We can never be sure what other day she will feed us, but as I said this morning, it's nearly always the day after one of the inmates has passed on. Bill, who you met earlier, is certain she chops up the dead and feeds it to us the next day after her pets had had their fill.'

The light was fading fast, still the thirsty dogs jostled for a few drops of precious liquid dripping from the rusty tap, and all Boris and Easy could do was look on.

'Judging by those black clouds gathering over the mountains, it will probably rain tomorrow. If we get a heavy downpour the pot holes and crevices fill and keeps us supplied with water for a week or so,' said Boris.

A fight had started next to the tap as the dogs squabbled to gain an advantage. Suddenly, the woman's voice shouted, 'Shut it! I said shut it.' The thirsty dogs quietened . . . an audible click was heard, a hush descended in the yard as the door slowly opened inwardly to reveal a thick chain tethered across a twenty-five-centimetre gap. Every dog froze and waited; the silence was deafening. The door stood ajar for what seemed to be an eternity. Easy and Boris watched, as slowly a steel rod with a large hook at its end inched through the gap toward the dead Terrier. A gasp exuded from the once silent dogs, watching the metal hook probing the unfortunate dead animal. Finally, it came to rest around the neck of the corpse.

The head jerked as the body was pulled toward the open door. As it reached the two steps, it seemed to slither upwards, giving the impression the dog was alive. A grunt was heard as the Terrier was squeezed through the gap, then the door slammed shut. The silence was broken by the frantic barking that followed.

Easy was visibly shaken; he could take no more. Turning away, his head dropped, thinking, that's my future, he made his way sadly back to his dug-out.

That night, the heavens opened and the rain lashed down with such force that in a matter of minutes, the potholes and crevices were full to overflowing, seeping into the tangled undergrowth and the dry ground sucked up the remainder. Easy watched his dug-hole steadily filling up.

After two hours of continuous rain, the prison hellhole was awash. Earlier that evening, the incarcerated animals were fighting over a few drops of water; now the situation had completely changed, most of them belly deep in the life-giving liquid. The smaller dogs were trying to find higher ground, as they were in danger of being totally submerged by the deluge.

The rain penetrated through his fur to his skin, leaving Easy saturated, cold, and miserable. He was at a loss, not knowing what to do to ease his discomfort, one thing he was sure of, something had to be done or he would die in this hellhole.

As the sun slowly emerged from behind the mountains in the east, the water began to subside in the flooded undergrowth.

Easy shook himself to dislodge the loose water that had settled in the outer layers of his matted fur. Making his way to the concrete patio, he spotted Boris drying out by a pothole full of water.

'Morning, Boris, you were right, wow! What a downpour last night.'

'With the small amount of fur left on my body, I was drenched in a matter of minutes,' replied Boris.

Trying to sound cheerful, Easy said, 'Any plans for today?'

'The only plan I have is to lie here and guard my waterhole, and if you have half a brain, find one for yourself, as in a few days, water in this shit hole will dictate whether you live or die, as those thirsty canines, who are unlucky not to have a supply of their own, will resort to any means, even ganging up to attack and dispossess any dog of their water. So get along and find yourself somewhere. It's still early and the weaker dogs are not out and about yet.'

Easy sensed the urgency in Boris. Thanking him, he moved quickly around the patio to find a supply of his own. He found a pool that had formed in the uneven surface of the cracking concrete near to where he had dug his shallow hole.

Settling down and making himself comfortable, he waited, his eyes constantly sweeping the area for any would-be usurpers.

As the long hot day cooled, and as evening approached, a few undernourished dogs passed by; none of them seemed remotely interested in his supply of water. Easy thought after the torrential rain last night water was in abundance; he didn't anticipate any problems just yet, but he was aware that as the days passed and the water dried up, the danger to his being would increase. Lying there, Easy pondered on the fate of the animals imprisoned in this concrete compound. What they need to do is organise themselves, ration the water so everyone has a fair share of what was available, and the same with the food. The thought of food made his stomach emit a noisy rumbling sound. Gawd, was he hungry! He could kill for a piece of meat! Hopefully, it won't come to that, at the moment still strong, fit, and able to take care of himself.

In a few weeks time, who knows what condition I'll be in? His thoughts were interrupted by the sound of a window opening. Looking across the patio, he saw the first-floor window, situated above the back door, had been raised. At the same time out of nowhere, the whole concrete patch was a seething mass of hungry dogs howling like a pack of wolves. Above the din, the woman's voice shouted, 'Quiet! You mangy curs.' Even louder came the voice, 'I said, "Quiet!"' Slowly, the sound diminished. 'That's better. Can't hear myself shout around here.'

Easy stood up. What's going on? he thought.

Though the hungry pack had quietened considerably, they were milling around constantly, snapping at each other as they pushed and shoved to gain a better position under the window. Then Easy noticed Boris, who somehow had managed to work his way to the front of the ravished mob; at that precise moment, Katie appeared at the window holding a bucket and threw the contents over the starving mob. All hell broke loose as the dogs fought whilst trying to consume the substance that had landed on their backs.

Easy looked on amazed, not knowing what to do if anything, standing there transfixed by the bizarre event taking place. Never in his short life had he experienced this situation being played out before him. Still, the unruly mob fought, snarling, snapping, and tearing at each other, trying to devour whatever was available.

Sometime had passed and the noise abated as the dogs dispersed making their way from whence they came, a few remained, milling around, searching.

Easy sat down; the event he had witnessed stamped indelibly in his brain, leaving him feeling nervous and frightened. Still trying to make sense of the situation, it occurred to him, perhaps, Bill was right about the dead Terrier from yesterday. Whatever was contained in that bucket he was unable to tell. One thing was for sure, it definitely was food of some kind. Once again, the thought of food played hell with his stomach, as now he was suffering with severe hunger pains.

Think I'll wait a while till things are back to normal. Stupid dog, he thought, Normal! None of what had witnessed by any stretch of the imagination is normal.

Time passed and Easy thought, See if I can find Boris, perhaps he could explain this morning's events. He found him sitting by his waterhole.

'Hello, Boris, how are you?'

'How do you think I am?' Look at me, I'm slowly deteriorating through the lack of food and dehydration. Sure I have water now, but in a few days, this pool will be empty, then what will I do? Fight for a few drops coming from that tap?

Easy thought he would change the subject. 'What was all that commotion earlier?' he asked.

'I told you yesterday,' said Boris. 'Saturday, she feeds us with what little she acquires from the butchers, and one other day, she throws us scraps, from the first-floor window.'

'And I told you,' said a third voice, it was Bill who had quietly padded up to join in the conversation. 'Those scraps the mob was feeding on are the stewed remains of the Terrier that died yesterday.'

Easy froze. 'I can't believe that nobody can be that wicked.'

'Believe what you want. I'm certain of it,' replied Bill.

What we need to do is get organised,' said Easy. 'Boris you must know every dog in the compound. Put the word about that at midnight a meeting is being held. Those dogs interested should assemble at the far wall away from the house.'

'I can only but try,' said Boris, 'but it's all been done before.'

'Tell them that I have new ideas, and it would be in their interest to listen. What about you, Bill?'

'I'm prepared to speak to anyone interested, but honestly, I can't see many dogs attending, as Boris says they've seen and heard it all before.'

'Well, do your best,' replied Easy. 'See you both at midnight. Bye for now.'

Easy left, thinking he would have to think of something new to convince those who showed up tonight. Preoccupied with his thoughts and his stomach still rumbling, he ventured back to his precious little pool of water only to find a skinny, long-limbed lurcher drinking out of it.

'Oi! That's mine. I don't mind you drinking some, but don't take it all.'

'What do you mean it's yours? I've just found it, so it's mine.'

'No, it's not. I discovered it this morning and left it for a few minutes to talk to my friend.'

'I don't believe you,' said the lurcher. 'Piss off, you little runt. Shan't tell you again.'

'You piss off. I've told you it's mine,' said Easy, edging nearer.

'Be that as it may, now it belongs to me.'

A few interested dogs had appeared and were watching to see the outcome of this confrontation. Trying to compromise, Easy ventured, 'Let's not squabble over a half-filled pool of water. We can share it.'

'Share it!' barked the lurcher. 'Share it, you! You, miserable little squirt. I said piss off. That's the last time I'm going to tell you.'

The lurcher was aware if he left the water to chase this pup off, the other dogs milling around would claim it, so he stood his ground.

Easy could see the lurcher had no intention of moving and a distraction was called for, but what?

The lurcher snarled and bared its teeth. 'You still here?'

'No,' said Easy as he bounded forward straight through the lurcher's legs, knowing the dog was very weak and in spite of his size, Easy played his ace; he came out from underneath the dog and nipped his tail.

'Ouch!' barked the lurcher and at the same time turning to snap at Easy.

Letting go of the tail, Easy went for the underside of the lurcher's throat, clenching his jaws, drawing blood, and he hung on for grim death. Already weakened by malnutrition and lack of water, whatever the lurcher tried, he was unable to extricate his neck from Easy's tightly clenched jaws. The lurcher sped off with Easy clinging to his neck, and the lurcher's blood oozed from his jaws. The lurcher barked, 'Enough! Enough! It's yours.'

Easy let go and raced back to his water pool, expecting the other dogs to claim it, but no, they saw what a fearsome predator this pup could be and left him alone. As he settled down once more, by his pool, he thought that was one lesson his mentor had taught him, which he had remembered, street fighting.

Easy remained beside his pool for three days; the only time he moved away was to relieve himself; even then, he kept it in sight. Eventually, with the heat and his thirst, the pool was dry.

During that period, he expected to be set upon by a pack of thirsty dogs and savaged, if not killed.

The strange thing was, that any dogs that came within his compass gave him a wide berth. The gnawing pain he felt because of the lack of food had finally disappeared, leaving him feeling empty, as his stomach began to shrink. Time to seek out Boris and thank him for his good advice, also to apologise for not attending the meeting he had asked him to set up.

Easy found Boris lying in his waterhole that was also empty. Trying to sound upbeat, he barked, 'How you doing, Boris? What's happening? Sorry about the other evening. I couldn't leave my pool unattended. Did many dogs show?'

'According to Bill, no one. They were either not interested or so weak they didn't have the energy. That's the way I feel. My days are numbered. Lack of substance has taken its toll,' said Boris.

'The other day I saw you upfront when those scraps came through the window.'

'Sure I was, but that was the other day. To tell you the truth, I contracted dysentery about three weeks ago, and as each day passes, I get weaker,' said Boris. 'My time has come. I'll be lucky to see this day through.'

'Don't be so pessimistic,' said Easy. 'You'll get better, just wait and see.'

'No, I won't,' said Boris. 'I've seen the way this disease takes its toll, too many times.' And lowering his voice, Boris said, 'I need a favour from you!'

'Anything you want,' said Easy moving closer.

'When my time is up and I leave to meet my maker, don't let that wicked old cow drag me through her door and chop me up to be fed back to the rest of you.'

'Of course not, I promise' said Easy, thinking Boris was delirious and out of his head. 'Tell you what, would like me to stay with you for a while?'

'Would you do that for me? That's very kind of you.'

Easy thought light-heartedly, there's nothing else for me to do, might as well stay with Boris, not really believing he was on his way out. They chatted some more until Boris fell asleep.

Later that evening, Easy detected a foul stench emanating from Boris, as his eyes opened, then closed; his whole body shuddered and then was still. Looking closely, Easy realised Boris's ribcage had stopped moving as though he was no longer breathing. His eyes detected a thin stream of brown liquid oozing from the unfortunate dogs hindquarters. So this is what it's like to be dead! he said to himself.

Easy stayed with the body until daybreak; as the sun rose, he was able to see what he was about to do . . . keep his promise. Clasping his jaws around the neck of Boris and heaving with all his strength, inch by inch, he pulled the body towards the undergrowth. It was tough going for a pup, even though Boris was half of his natural body weight. Easy was constantly having to stop and gather his strength at the same time keeping an eye on the house in case that evil woman should look out and see what was going on. After his third stop, Easy sensed a movement in the undergrowth; turning, he found Bill walking towards him.

'What are you doing to Boris?' barked an indignant Bill.

'Nothing,' said Easy.

'Well, explain yourself,' replied Bill.

Easy told Bill about his promise to Boris, relating the whole story. Bill listened patiently and, when Easy had finished, offered to help him. With Bill's jaws clenched on the tail, Easy resumed his grasp on the neck, Bill grunted, 'I might be old and fragile, but between us, we should be able to drag Boris into the undergrowth.' Some twenty minutes later, the body of Boris was concealed.

Then began the task of digging a hole to bury him in, and fortunately, the ground was still soft from the deluge of rain three days earlier. Two hours later, Boris was safely interred.

The two dogs lay still, exhausted from all their efforts. For a while, Easy thought he may well have another corpse to deal with, listening to Bills wheezing, as they slowly began to recuperate their remaining strength.

Once again, Easy felt the dragging ache of his empty stomach, trying to remember the last time that he ate anything. Bill was old and his health was failing fast, but his survival instincts were still intact.

'Today is bone day scraps,' said Bill, to no one in particular.

'You mean its Saturday already?' said Easy.

'That's right. Sometime this afternoon, after she's been to the butchers, her usual routine, out of the window it comes, then it's a free for all. For those dogs that are lucky and able to secure something, they have to wolf it down or defend it with their lives, but in your case, that won't happen.'

'I don't understand?'

'Well,' said Bill, 'I heard you had a run in with Len the Lurcher and saw him off.'

'True, he tried to steal my water supply. I offered to share it with him, but he wanted it all. I had no alternative. Anyway, he was twice my size.'

'That's what I mean. Until that confrontation, Len was top dog around here, now you are. You've become a bit of an icon, especially with the ladies, so there's no need for you to get involved in the free for all this afternoon,' said Bill.

'I don't understand what have the ladies got to do with the food supply?'

'How naive can you get. The ladies need your help, the last thing they want is a litter of puppies, who if born would never survive because the females are unable to feed themselves properly. So by sharing any food they are fortunate enough to salvage, with you in return, they expect your protection,' said Bill.

'But I don't want to be top dog. I'm still only a puppy, but I'm happy enough to take my chances with the rest of you,' said Easy.

'Too late, the die is cast. If I were you, I'd take the position as it will increase your chances of survival. Sooner or later, a dog will appear that's faster and stronger than you, thus resigning you to the ranks, same as Boris. That's how he managed to survive for two years until Len took over.'

Easy felt very uneasy and insecure with his new-found position, but quite flattered. He had noticed the few dogs he had seen in the last few days all gave a wide berth with no eye contact.

Regardless to his new-found status, he was preoccupied with escaping. Saying his byes to Bill, he decided to give the hellhole the once over. By mid-afternoon, he had a good idea of the layout; the area was about fifty metres square, bounded on three sides that butted onto the rear wall of the house. The walls were three metres high, and according to poor old Boris, the foundations were one metre deep, and at the rear of the house lay the broken, concrete patio, visible from all the windows on the back wall.

As of yet, he was unable to see a chink in this fortresses' armour. One possibility occurred to him; while the ground was still wet, he might be able to dig under the foundations. He was aware it had been tried before without success, but he was young and still fairly fit. Worth a try, he thought. He would start late tonight in the south-eastern corner.

By mid-afternoon there was an air of expectation, as the dogs gathered on the patio, once again jostling for position. At about three o'clock, the window opened and out came a bucket full of bones, immediately a second load, and then the window slammed shut as all hell broke loose. The dogs were snarling, barking, tearing at each other to gain access to the limited supply.

Easy kept away from the fracas and waited, as hungry as he felt, Bill's age was against him, he knew his best policy was to stick with the game pup. By befriending him a few of the scraps that were definitely coming, the pups' way may well land at his paws.

Eventually, the noise dissipated, and those dogs lucky enough to claim some bones with a morsel of meat attached to it ran off, not before leaving a tiny piece for Easy's consumption, not enough to fill his empty stomach but at least the hunger pain temporarily abated. He knew, without a doubt, that these offerings would not sustain him; he had to come up with an escape plan.

Thanking Bill for his help in burying Boris and saying he was tired, he upped and left, arriving back at his dug out. He settled down to wait until dark. A few moments later, his ears picked up on a sound approaching from within the undergrowth. Immediately, he stiffened his body on red alert, not knowing what to expect. Then he heard it, the familiar soft bark of old Bill as his head appeared through the foliage.

'Do you mind if I hang around, as I get quite lonely on my own. Nobody can be bothered with an old duffer like me,' said Bill.

Easy really wanted to play a lone hand, but on consideration Bill had been very helpful and could well be of some use in the future, he replied, 'Sure, make yourself comfortable, but once the moon is up, I'll be off. I have an idea that needs investigating.' Easy wasn't about to reveal his plan in case it didn't work.

'I'll help you,' said Bill.

'Thanks, but no thanks, if it works, I'll come back for you, I promise.'

For some reason, Bill believed him, whatever the pup was up to, possibly he had an escape plan, he thought. It had all been tried before, and Bill was not about to dampen Easy's enthusiasm.

'Okay, do you mind if I wait until you return?'

'Sure,' said Easy, 'as soon as its dark, I'll make my move.' This all sounded very dramatic, considering his intention was to dig under them foundations.

He had already selected his spot, the wall furthest away from the house, less chance of being heard. He hadn't long to wait; as the heat of the day dissipated and the full moon giving out plenty of light. Getting up, Easy said to Bill, 'See you later.' Then he left, heading for the furthest wall, carefully avoiding any other dogs that came across his path.

He reached a spot that seemed suitable a place between two bramble bushes; after all he didn't want to make extra work for himself by having to dig around bush roots. He set to work at once, the first twenty centimetres were no problem, the second a little harder.

So far it had taken him about an hour. Not bad, he thought. I'll rest a while to conserve my energy. He felt a little tired, but was happy with his progress. Some fifteen minutes later, he resumed. It was then he hit his first obstacle, a large stone, too heavy to move, so he set about digging around and under it. That took time and effort. To his dismay, he hit an even larger blockage, stopping for a rest to regain his strength again. He resumed fifteen minutes later, only yo find another rock, blocking his progress. This is impossible, thought Easy, best I try elsewhere. He moved to another spot and tried again, but to no avail, he had the same problem; as soon as he dug down so far, his progress was halted by a layer of rocks. After his third attempt, he gave up; exhausted, frustrated, and disillusioned, he made his way back to his dug out to find old Bill waiting there.

'How did you get on?' he asked.

'No joy,' replied Easy, relating the whole sorry episode.

Bill understood the frustration of the pup. It had been tried before without success, and in Bill's experience, the youngster had to learn the hard way.

When the builders of these old houses laid the foundations, they back filled them with rocks so as to reinforce the walls; otherwise, over a period of time, the rain would find its way underneath, and it doing so would weaken the foundations. Even if Bill had mentioned what he knew, the pup would take no notice and still try. Oh, the impetuosity of youth, thought Bill.

By now, the sun was up; the exhausted pup fell into a deep sleep, only to wake up some time later dying of thirst. Making his way to the tap on the wall, with Bill in tow, he found to his expectation some fifteen or so dogs milling around. Joining them with the attention of waiting his turn, he was surprised when a very thin bitch approached him saying, 'Your turn.'

Once again in all naivety he replied, 'Mine? What about the others?'

'They'll wait till you finish.' Later he found out her name was Cissy.

The other dogs parted as he made his way to the tap to drink. His compassion for the other wasted animals left him with a sense of guilt. Easy felt greedy keeping the other dogs waiting. Though he was not fully sated, but feeling better than before he arrived, he moved away, leaving Bill waiting in the mix. He still had difficulty comprehending his would be seniority.

Heading back to his dug-hole, he began to think about plan B. To Easy, it appeared to be quite simple; the next time the rear door opened, that would be his cue. The pup was small, true, but he was thinner than the opening. Of course, there were two guard dogs to overcome, but the element of surprise was on his side. He would run for the door at full speed through the gap over the chain before the dogs, who would be caught unaware knew what had hit them, let alone the women. Once in the house, he would take his chance, who knows maybe a window or the front door may be open. He had to admit the whole idea was iffy; there again he could stay put and die of dehydration or starvation.

He had to wait three days before the opportunity came about. Bill reported that another dog had died by the tap. He reckoned on the same procedure, it will be dragged in the house by the lethal hook.

Easy thought, This is my chance. Making his way to the patio, he positioned himself as near to the door as possible, without drawing undue attention to himself. He lay down and waited; other animals were still jostling to get to the tap, oblivious of the dead dog spreadeagled on the concrete. Speed was of the utmost importance; the moment the door opened, he had to shift, as once the gap reached the point where the chain was taut, the two dogs would be in position and a matter of seconds would pass before the deadly hook came prodding through. It was chancy, but Easy's mind was made up; what had he to lose. He was tense, his body felt like a coiled spring as he waited patiently; time stood still, his heart pumping twice its normal rate, the heat of the day adding to his discomfort.

With his ears and eyes alert, he heard the scraping sound of a bolt being drawn, followed imperceptibly by a faint click. The door inched open, Now, he thought, go-go-go, he sprang to his feet in a few strides he was flat out his timing perfect as the door reached its maximum aperture, he was through the gap, over the guards dogs' heads. As he landed and skidded under the kitchen table, he caught a glimpse of the old cow standing with the pole in her hand, her mouth agape, stunned at what she had just witnessed. Gathering herself, she dropped the hook and slammed the door shut.

Easy slid on through the kitchen into the living room and landed in a tangled heap on the rotting carpet. Quickly regaining his feet, he looked for an avenue of escape, realising immediately all the windows were barred. Through the hallway arch, he could see the front door shut and the security chain in place; frantically, his heart thumping, he realised he was trapped. At the same time, through the kitchen door, came the woman clasping a steel rod, followed by the two dogs barking ferociously, not knowing what to do, and waiting for orders from the woman.

Outside in the yard the imprisoned dogs realised one of their numbers was making a bid for freedom; there was hope for them yet. A chorus of sustained howling filled the air as they endeavoured to encourage the would-be escapee. The noise was deafening, leaving the hag and dogs bemused. As Easy's eyes flitted around the room, he saw a staircase. Taking advantage of the woman's indecision, he bolted up the stairs. In the split second available to him, he saw four doors—three closed, one open. From the landing, he dashed full pelt into the room. Gasping for breath, he leant backwards as his weight closed the door behind him. A quick glance revealed a double bed, a dressing table, plus an old armchair, but before he was able to take on-board any more, the door burst open, knocking him head over paws, revealing the old hag brandishing the steel rod and her dogs baying behind her. He dashed under the bed, petrified, and quaking with fear. She yelled, 'You ungrateful piece of shit. After all I have done for you, given you a home, fed you, and this is how you repay me. Come out you . . . you mangy mutt. You're a filthy waste of space.'

Easy, though terrified, realised this woman was unhinged; still the deranged crone roared obscenities, 'I shan't tell you again, you rotting lump of canine puss, what are you?' With that, she thrust the steel rod under the bed, thrashing it around the tip caught Easy just above his right eye, stunning him; at the same time, the smaller of the two dogs crawled under the bed, snapping at his tail.

Panicking, Easy ran and jumped on the dressing table. Withdrawing the rod, Katie swung it in his direction; it came down with a swish . . . narrowly missing Easy as he jumped to the floor at the same time, the rod smashed into the dressing table's mirrors and imbedding itself in the dilapidated armchair.

'Now, look at what you've done,' she screamed. 'When I get hold of you, I'll chop your ears off.' Frantic with rage, she once again lashed out, but Easy wasn't hanging around.

The bedroom door stood ajar. Easy saw his chance and bolted through with the larger of the dogs hot on his heels. Down the stairs through the living room, into the kitchen trying to remember if she had closed the garden door . . . she had: With the larger dog guarding the kitchen door, he realised the game was up; he cowered, waiting for the inevitable. It came in the form of the raging woman brandishing a steel rod as she beat him unmercifully; the pain was excruciating, and finally, the relief came as he slipped into unconsciousness.

Somehow, the dogs in the enclosure knew that something was wrong because everything went quiet, till you could hear a pin drop. The silence was broken by agonising squeals of pain emanating from behind the garden door; eventually, they lessened into a whimper, then silence. Slowly, the animals dispersed back to their dug-holes; all was lost, dreams of freedom shattered.

Chapter 29

Once again, Christmas had arrived with twenty-one shopping days remaining, as the television kept reminding them. His children, some years ago, had upped and left and now had families of their own. For many years, prior to and after his wife's demise, life had been tough for George, bringing up four children; every day clean clothes for school, cooking, ironing, homework, the list was endless, at the same time holding down a full-time job. He was fortunate in some respects; he was able to work from home. This allowed him a certain amount of freedom to cope with the endless amount of chores that went hand in hand with family life.

In moments of solitude, he marvelled at, and now appreciated the old saying 'a woman's work is never done'—it's no wonder his wife had turned to drink, and ultimately, it took it s toll. George realised that children are a 24-7 responsibility.

With Mary, life was different; with one son, now an adult and self-sufficient, she was a free agent. They had been a couple for seventeen years, and now, they were living together.

Mary was a long-life vegetarian, and in George's eyes, she had an unhealthy love of all creatures, horses and dogs, in particular. Her Doberman had passed away a few years earlier. He had offered to by her another dog, but she declined saying the memories were still too vivid. On her last birthday, Mary had asked for a pet rat; this had caused a certain amount of friction between them, as George had always thought that rats were vermin.

'Don't be silly,' she argued. 'They're lovely and very intelligent.'

Surprisingly, George grew quite fond of Shifty, the name Mary had given the rat. Shifty had an infuriating habit of sneaking up on them and stealing their chocolates. He was clever enough to be able to lift the lid off the box, steal one then dashing off to hide it. You would have thought he had a special place where he kept his stash, but no! He was shrewd enough to stow them in the most unusual places. The life expectancy of a rat is short; when Shifty's time was up, once again Mary was very distraught.

Prior to visiting Turkey in September, Mary had hinted that she was ready to take on another Doberman. Through the internet, George had located a breeder whose bitch was expecting any time and the pups would be ready for adoption in fourteen weeks.

Christmas was out of the question, but the waiting period coincided with her birthday. Unaware of what George was planning; Mary was convinced they would be able to import Easy to England.

The whole process was a minefield. You needed a pet passport to take the dog out of Turkey, then another issued by an EU country, to import the dog into Enland. Plus the dog had been microchipped and vaccinated against rabies.

It transpired according DEFRA, the government department that controlled all imports and exports of livestock in England.

Even though the microchip and other relevant vaccinations were recognised in England, if implemented in Turkey, the animal had to be re-vaccinated against rabies, and another, a blood test taken. If the blood test was clear and the chip reread, then a period of six months had to pass before the animal could set foot on English soil. It didn't end there. Oh no, twenty four to forty eight hours before entering England, the dog had to be vaccinated for tick and tapeworm.

If these criteria were not adhered to, the whole process was implemented again in England and the animal would be quarantined for six months.

Secretly, George was hoping Mary would be happy to send money to Katie for Easy's up-keep and he could surprise her with the Doberman puppy. No such luck, as Mary had just put the phone down on Katie, who was now asking for three hundred pounds.

Apparently, where Easy was housed, the compound had a leaky roof that had to be repaired before winter set in. George was furious.

'Did she or did she not say she was building a fence around her land where each dog would have its own kennel. I bet she never mentioned vet's bills or vaccinations? Why didn't you let me talk to her?' said George.

'Because I was afraid of the way you would react.'

'React!' exploded George. 'What about all her other so-called benefactors? Have they all been sucked in and sent her three hundred pounds each, I doubt it. She knows that you're a soft touch, Mary.'

Mary changed tactics. 'Don't be so mean, George.'

'It's not a question of being mean. It's more about being conned, Mary.'

'I'm not asking you for the money. I'll send it myself.'

'That's up to you,' replied George, 'but I think that's an act of gross stupidity.'

'Don't call me stupid. Let's just drop it, okay?'

'That's all right with me,' he said, turning away, thinking how can she be so thick?

Christmas came and went, so did the New Year. In the previous September, George had enrolled at a local day college to study GCSE Maths and English, an opportunity he never had as a child. His mother a Second World War widow was left with five children to bring up; unfortunately, one contracted German measles and died, and the other a boy succumbed to tuberculosis, which was prevalent during and after the Second World War mainly due to malnutrition.

Subsequently, having spent five years with his younger brother at a school, whose primary concern was health not education, left George without any qualifications, and plus he had to leave school at the age of fourteen to support the family.

Now, well into the New Year, exams were due at the end of May. George thoroughly enjoyed the day classes as at his age; he was by far the oldest student and secretly got a buzz from competing with the youngsters. His teachers were younger than his youngest daughter. His results from the mock exams were excellent, achieving 74 per cent for English and 82 per cent for maths.

It was about this time Mary received another call from Katie, this she kept to herself. Apparently, Easy had been fighting with another dog and she needed two hundred pounds to build a separate kennel to house him, adding that way she could keep him safe, from any would-be attacker. No doubt in Mary's mind Katie's main concern was Easy's health. Once again, with no hesitation, she sent the money.

Mary's relationship with George had lasted seventeen years, through various ups and downs, and bouts of ill health, she had nursed him when his addiction to alcohol threatened his existence. Equally, he was always there for her when deep bouts of depression had engulfed her. They both maintained that their partnership had survived because Mary maintained her own apartment and wasn't reliant on George for money. She had a small but steady income dealing in her second love, after animals, antiques.

To George's consternation, he now had two rented garages almost full with bric-a-brac as he called it, waiting to be sold. On days when their partnership was severely tested, he would say, 'If you don't move that junk, I'll call the council and have them remove it.'

Like most couples, something's were best left unsaid, certainly the fact that she had sent Katie more money.

May and June came and went, George's passed his exams. He was delighted with the results 'A plus' in both subjects; 82 per cent in English and 90 per cent in maths. Having received notification through the post and on the last day of term when asked by his math tutor how he had fared, she was genuinely so pleased for him. The class exchanged handshakes and wished each other well. George was last to leave; thanking his tutor once again, he made his way to the classroom door, and Keeley (his tutor) called out to him, 'George, can you spare a minute?'

'Certainly,' he replied, he turned and walked back to her desk.

Then She stood and said, 'Something I think you would like to hear.'

An intrigued George said, 'Fire away.'

To his complete astonishment came the words, 'Had I sat the same exam, it would have been beyond my capabilities to achieve your pass mark.'

'Well, I never . . . ' said George shaking his head in bewilderment.

'Also the dean asked me to tell you that yours is the highest mark ever recorded in the college's history.'

George was absolutely flabbergasted, the words still ringing in his ears as he drove home.

On reflection, George thought, No big deal the learning centre had only been open for three years. But his mind's eye kept saying wow!

The new term started in September and George had thought to enrol for three A level subject, English, maths and History, bearing in mind, this would take two years of study and meant attending the college for three days a week, not to mention all of the swatting at home. He wondered if he could stay the course or in fact live long enough to enjoy the fruits of his labour. He mused, there again; it wasn't exactly labour, and having the chance to catch up on his lost education was something he never thought would happen. He was on the home straight in terms of life expectancy, a race he couldn't win. He knew a university degree was within his capabilities, a dream he had nursed for years. He also knew time was against him. Little did he know as he indulged in his reverie that events would change the direction of his remaining years.

About mid-August, Mary received another call from Katie to say the fence was nearly finished but needed another three hundred pounds to complete the job, quickly adding what did Mary think of the photos she had sent picturing Easy, 'Didn't he look well, and how he had grown?'

Mary replied, 'They had yet to arrive. When were they sent?'

'About two weeks ago, I sent them by registered post. They should arrive any day. Mind you,' said Katie, 'the Turkish post was notorious for its late deliveries, and if they weren't in her possession by the end of the month, she would ask her friend to email them. I would myself, but my computer is broken and I can't afford a new one.'

'No problem,' said Mary, 'George is going to Turkey early in September before college starts. He will bring the money with him. Also he has an old computer in perfect working order that's been sitting on his desk since he updated. I'm sure I can persuade him to let you have it.'

'Are you coming over with him?' asked Katie.

'As much as I would like to, but I have three important auctions that I really must attend. I do have a problem that you may be able to advise me on. The last time we spoke you mentioned your friends in Holland who had found a way around the six-month quarantine restriction imposed by the British government for non-EU countries.'

'That's right, I'll explain everything to George when I see him,' replied Katie.

'Wonderful,' said Mary, 'thank you so much. Speak to you soon, bye-bye.' Mary was bursting to tell George the good news.

George had spent the afternoon at his daughter's house, who was experiencing a few marital problems. He was trying to advise her on the best course of action she should take.

Mary could hardly contain herself waiting for George to return. She heard the key in the lock and the mechanism turn. George barely had his feet in the hallway as Mary, bubbling over, related the conversation with Katie.

'Whoa!' said George. 'Slow down, I can't take it all in. Make a cup of tea, then we can sit down comfortably and you can give me a blow-by-blow account of what happened.'

'Yes, you're right,' said Mary. 'Give me a minute.'

The kettle had already boiled, just needed reheating; in a matter of a minute, they were sitting in the lounge and Mary related the telephone conversation with Katie.

'Isn't that wonderful, George? Hopefully, we'll have Easy with us for Christmas.'

George had listened carefully and could feel the enthusiasm emanating from Mary's voice.

'Well, that's terrific. I'm so pleased for you.'

Thinking there's no way Katie is having my old computer let alone another three hundred pounds without seeing Easy and his new kennel, as for this so-called connection in Holland, being able to speed up the British quarantine laws—No Way.

That evening, Tricia rang to say that the flight tickets had arrived for their group holiday and as usual to meet at the check-in two hours before take-off, reminding George that departure time was twenty-two fifteen.

As it was a Sunday, Mary had already offered to drive George to the airport. The fact that Mary was unable to make the trip worked in George's favour; he was determined to look at this so-called charity more closely, as he wasn't happy about the whole situation and was sure something was amiss.

Once that was sorted, he would enjoy his vacation and make his mind up as to whether he was prepared to commit himself to a further two years of study. He was due back on the seventeenth of September, leaving himself plenty of time to enrol.

Chapter 30

As Easy slipped into unconsciousness, he became oblivious to the pain Katie had inflicted on his body. The inner eye reminded him of those nice people who took care of him, his new collar and leash nda full tummy.

Bernie, his old gang boss, had always said they pet you for a few days, and once their holiday is finished, they depart, leaving you once again to fend for yourself.

Easy knew, he sensed something about the kind lady, she would come for him. He remembered as she handed him to Katie she whispered something into his ear, not knowing what was said he felt the urgency in her voice.

Katie realised her guard dogs had ceased barking; she lashed Easy's prone body once more, the noise of the blow made her own pet dogs whimper.

'And that's for trying to make a fool out of me, you ungrateful, mangy excuse for a dog. Nobody and I mean nobody takes the piss out of me.' The force of the blow made Easy's whole body quiver.

Katie paused to catch her breath; she felt quite exhausted.

'That'll teach the dumb mutt to show me some respect,' she said to herself. 'What I need is a strong cup of coffee with a drop of brandy to revive myself.' She switched on the electric kettle, and then turning to her dogs, she said, 'Stop whimpering, unless you want the same treatment.' By instinct, they both knew she meant what she said; they cowered down silently.

Having made the coffee, adding a liberal amount of Brandy, she sat down. Taking a sip, she thought, Ah that's better. Her eyes strayed to the dog lying comatose on the floor—stupid, filthy street dog she thought, fancy thinking it could put one over on me. Looking a little closer, she realised the animal was not moving, probably dead, never mind, things to do, places to go. I must get on. Downing the remains of the hot coffee in one gulp, she moved quickly through to the lounge, and reaching the front door, she turned and, in a harsh voice, ordered her dogs, saying, 'Stay, guard!' making sure the door was secure. Katie mounted her tricycle and headed for the quay-side to continue her business, conning unsuspecting tourists out of their money to support her unregistered animal charity.

Bill sat in the foliage close to the concrete patio, but not close enough to be in the sun. The whole compound was silent, as the animals pondered on the fate of the gallant pup. A pup in stature, thought Bill, but in his eyes a full grown, mature dog, a hero, too brave for his own good.

Bill felt each blow that Easy had endured; now he and the whole community waited in silence as to the outcome of Easy's attempted escape. He heard the front door slam; the old cow had gone out, perhaps to fetch the vet. Fetch the vet, who am I kidding, thought Bill.

Some hours later, Katie returned, having met the boat full of day trippers, on an island excursion trip, organised by her son Brett. He is another ungrateful bastard, a product of an unsuccessful relationship with her Turkish husband.

As soon as Brett left college, he upped and left home and was now living in Istanbul with his wife and son, returning to Dalman for the tourist season. He had long since stopped supplying his mother with money, as he argued that with a large mortgage his wife and son to provide for, he could barely keep his head above water financially.

As usual, their meeting was brief; he had inquired as to how her charity was faring, unaware what she was up to. He introduced her to a Dutch couple, who had adopted what they thought was a cute little Pekinese, with its flat nose and a tail that curled over its back.

Katie thought, That's another mouth to feed. Relieving them of five hundred Turkish Lira, with the promise of more to come, she made her way home. Not a bad day's work. Could have been better, she thought, nevertheless a profitable one. Parking her tricycle against the wall, she lifted out the Pekinese and entered the house. Closing the door behind her, she made straight for the kitchen, opened the garden door, and threw the small dog out, who landed on the concrete with a resounding thump, three metres from where Bill was hiding.

The dog clambered to her feet nursing a damaged leg, looked around, totally bemused. She heard a soft bark and listened carefully. There it was again; it sounded friendly. She limped toward the source to be confronted by Bill, who introduced himself, informing her of the predicament she was in and advising her to acquire a hole to settle into. Having thanked Bill, she disappeared into the undergrowth.

Now rid of the loathsome Pekinese, Katie noted her dogs had not moved since she had left some hours before. Filling their bowls with water and placing them on the floor, she said, 'I'll feed you later,' as they lapped up the liquid greedily.

Her memory was such that she had completely forgotten the beating she gave Easy earlier that morning. Her eyes latched on to the prostrate dog, taking a few seconds to realise what had occurred, looking more closely she noted the lesions left by the steel rod. She thought, The little bastard isn't moving. How selfish can you get, dying in a person's kitchen. I'll have to move it; otherwise, by morning the rotting corpse will stink the house out. Best to throw it outside for the night.

Grasping Easy's body by its front and back legs, Katie dragged him to the yard door, and taking off the chain, she opened it enough to throw the body through, then quickly closing and re-chaining it.

As she sat in the living room counting her ill-gotten gains, her ears honed onto an increasing crescendo of dogs baying and yapping. The noise was deafening to a point where it became intolerable, and try as she may she was unable to quieten the brutes. She decided to leave the house and go to the local cafe for some peace and quiet.

Bill had waited all day, lying in the same position; his patience was rewarded as he heard the bolt draw and the chain rattle as the door opened a little wider than usual. Then to his amazement, Easy's body came flying through, landing with a thump at the foot of the stairs. The door closed shut and was re-bolted, and then the baying and barking started.

Bill waited until the noise abated, all the time watching the black, bloodied dog for a sign of movement; nothing, still he waited patiently. As the sun began to set, he thought he detected a movement; perhaps his old eyes were playing tricks in the half-light. There it was again, a rear leg twitched. Could it be the pup was still alive? No way, thought Bill. The way he landed on the concrete like a sack of horses' dung. There it was again, only this time a definite kick, probably a nervous reaction as he went through his death throes. Bill thought he'd wait until dark and investigate further. He didn't have to wait long; the half-starved dogs milling around the dripping tap began to disperse.

Creeping out from behind the foliage, Bill made his way to where Easy lay, thinking he'd need a hand to drag the dead pup into the undergrowth to bury him.

The dark sky lit up to show millions of bright twinkling stars caught in the reflection of the dying sun's rays.

Nearing the body, his old ears latched onto a low pitched grown. Impossible, he thought, could the pup still be alive. There it was again, only louder; stooping over the body, Bill quietly barked, 'It's me, Bill, talk to me, please.'

Easy was totally disorientated as he lay still, staring at the evening sky. Slowly, he regained his senses. The events of the morning, gradually returning to his consciousness, the attempted escape, the beating he underwent, the latter still fuzzy in his mind. It occurred to him as he stared up at the white twinkling shroud that seemed to envelope him; maybe this is that place they call heaven, he had heard so much about. If that's the case why was he hurting so much and why was he lying in a pool of goo. He tried to move his back legs; the pain was excruciating and shooting up the spine to the back of his skull.

Now fully awake, his body aching all over, Easy realised how lucky he was to survive; if survive, he did. Now trying to weigh his options, he thought, Who am I kidding, options! What options? It was then he heard the low bark, 'Easy it's me, Bill, talk to me please.'

'Bill, is that really you?'

'Yes . . . ' Bill nearly said how are you feeling, but quickly realised that was a fool question to ask.

'Bill, I ache all over.'

'I know,' said Bill sadly.

'What's this sticky mess I'm lying in?'

Bill was about to say blood, your blood, but changed his mind, saying, 'I can't make it out. It's too dark to see. Can you move at all?' Bill asked.

'I haven't really tried as everything hurts so much, even my jaw when I bark.'

'Give it a go,' said Bill.

'I can't. I'm so tired. I need to sleep,' came the reply. 'Will you stay with me, please?'

'Of course,' said Bill. 'You sleep, and I'll watch over you till morning.'

In a matter of minutes, Easy fell into a deep slumber. Bill had every intention of staying with Easy until morning, but had his doubts as to whether the pup would make it through the night. The hours dragged by as Bill kept his long, lonely vigil. He was acutely aware if Easy should die sometime during the day, the lethal hook would appear to drag him into the house. As the night sky disappeared and the new day began, Bill noted that Easy was still breathing; in fact his rib cage was rising and falling at a regular pace.

Bill hastened to wake the pup, once again in a low bark . . .

'Easy, wake up,' and again, 'It's me Bill, wake up.' Fully aware that time was not on their side, with more urgency he barked, 'Easy, wake up!'

The pup stirred and yawned, as he tried to stretch, he emitted a prolonged groan.

'Try to keep the noise down,' said Bill. 'The last thing we want to do is to draw attention to ourselves. Easy, you have to make an effort to get off this concrete and into the shrubbery before it's fully light.'

'I don't think I can,' came the reply.

'You're gonna have to try,' said Bill. 'If you don't, that evil crone will hook you in.'

That sentence set Easy on red alert. Struggling and in a lot of pain, he managed to stand; maintaining that position was difficult, as his whole body was shaking with the amount of effort it took him.

Bill breathed a sigh of relief. 'Is anything broken?' he asked.

'I don't think so. I hurt all over, but I can't feel any grating.'

'When you're ready, you'll have to move and hide yourself in the undergrowth.'

'There's no time like the present,' came the half-hearted reply.

Tentatively, he put his right paw forward, and step by agonising step, he inched his way toward the shrubbery. It seemed like an eternity, but finally, he made it. Hidden in the brush, Easy collapsed exhausted. Still in great pain, he managed to thank his loyal companion Bill.

Easy slept through the day and awoke early evening, just in time to be greeted by a deluge of rain as the heavens opened. Bill was still at his side, keeping watch, and as far as he was concerned, it had a twofold effect—not only filling up the various dug-holes with the life-saving liquid, also cleansing the open wounds, one in particular on the pup's head which was still seeping blood.

'How do I look?' asked Easy.

'Considering what you've been through, you're in pretty good shape.' Bill knew he was lying, but then his main concern was keeping the pup's spirits up. 'You'll be as good as new in a few days.'

'You think so?' said Easy.

'Positive,' replied Bill, and as an afterthought, he said, 'If you're up for it, we should make our way to your dug-hole before somebody claims it.'

'Sounds good to me,' said Easy making an effort to stand. As he straightened, a searing pain shot up the length of his spine. 'Oh my gawd, that hurts, Bill.'

'I know, but you have to make an effort. Come on, try.'

An enormous amount of energy was needed as he began to edge his way to the dug-hole. With Bill in tow, he eventually arrived.

He was pleased to note that nobody had commandeered the precious hole; also it was full of water. The relief was enormous; at least he had a water supply for a few days, his tummy rumbled reminding him how hungry he was.

'I don't know about you, Bill, but I'm starving,' he said, collapsing in an untidy heap.

'Nothing new in that,' said Bill. 'It's the story of my miserable life. Still we shouldn't have long to wait for food.'

'I don't understand,' said Easy.

'Yesterday, while you were trying to escape, she hooked that dead terrier, and by now, it'll be chopped up and stewed, ready to be thrown from her first-floor window later.'

'You can't be serious,' said Easy.

'I've told you before, having been here some time, mind you it seems forever, it's a regular occurrence. You wait and see.'

'Well, how will it affect us?' said Easy.

'Simple,' replied Bill. 'If you can make it to the concrete patio a little later, the other dogs will note your appearance, and for all intensive purpose, you are still top dog around here, so as before, the bitches will leave you food, as they consider it your due. You rest up and conserve your energy. I'm going to potter around the compound and put the word about that you're alive and never felt better.'

'But Bill, the other dogs would have seen me lying comatose.'

'Yes, but you can use that to your advantage.'

'In which way?'

'Well, I shall make it known the reason that you lay there so long was to fool the old crone, by playing dead, that way she would dismiss you as no longer a threat.'

'Do you think it will work?' said Easy.

'Sure, it will, as long as you are standing in the vicinity of the window when it opens, the other dogs will see you there, probably give you a cursory glance knowing full well, that you will get what's coming to you. As far as the crone seeing you, with all the baying and barking as the dogs jostle for position and the mayhem it creates, you'll be the last dog she'll be looking for, one dog will look like another to her. If we wait in the undergrowth as near to the window as practical, at the appropriate moment, you stand and let yourself be seen, I know it will take a huge effort on your part, but if you can stay on your feet for a minute or so that should do the trick. If she keeps to her routine and there's no reason why she shouldn't. In the two years I've been in this shit hole, she's been as regular as clockwork. Just before dusk, the window opens. By my reckoning, we have about an hour or so. Now you rest up and wait until I return. Shan't be long, I'm off to spread the word that you're alive and well.'

'Thanks, Bill, I'm very grateful for your help.'

'No problem, see you in a while.'

The rain had long since stopped; coupled with the heat of the day, the humidity was stifling. Easy lay still panting a little to help keep his body temperature down.

As the day began to fade into night, he pondered on the hand that fate had dealt him. Was he doomed to see out his young life in this hellhole, he might be lucky and survive for two years or so; perhaps it may well have been better if Katie had succeeded in beating the life out of him? There again he should try to be more positive, which was extremely difficult given his present situation.

There has to be a way out of here! There just has to be . . . Come on, Easy, quit it. Rest up untill Bill gets back.

A soft bark woke him from his troubled slumber.

'Easy, it's me, Bill, up you get. It's time to make a move.'

Slowly, Easy dragged himself to his feet. 'Oh! My gawd,' he moaned, 'it hurts, Bill.'

'I know, but you can do it. I've found a spot where we can wait. It's not far. If you follow me, there's a trail we can use that bypasses the other dogs, so they won't be able to see you struggling. Should only take a couple of minutes, come on.'

Easy steadied himself, with a huge intake of breath, staggered after Bill; every step was agony, but finally, he made it, collapsing on the spot that Bill had selected.

Peering through the undergrowth, Bill said, 'Already, the other animals are gathering beneath the window.'

Most of the old hands like Bill knew the procedure and were waiting expectantly.

'As soon as the window opens, you stand up, take a couple of steps forward—most of the dogs will be watching the window. As I put the word about that you are fit and well, they will expect you to appear, and after a cursory glance, they will be so absorbed in fighting amongst themselves for what they can scavenge, you're the last thing that they'll be worrying about. After a minute or so, we can make our way back to your dug-hole and . . . '

The sentence was interrupted by an audible click, slowly the shutters were folded back, and there stood Katie at the half-opened window; at that moment, a deafening cacophony of sound erupted as the dogs yapped, barked, and howled.

'Now!' said Bill urgently. 'Now get up and walk forward a few steps.'

Inwardly groaning, Easy was on his feet and moving forward into the open ground; by now, the noise had reached fever pitch. Easy could hardly believe his ears and eyes; the dogs were going berserk, as the bucket's contents came flying through the window, snarling, snapping, biting, anything to get a piece of what had been thrown down unceremoniously upon them.

Easy stood his ground; Bill was right—nobody gave him a second glance. Bill said, 'Hold tight and wait for the second bucket.' The words were barely out of his jaws, when the contents of the second bucket hit the compound floor.

As the dogs continued their on-going battle, Bill said, 'Time to slip away.'

Thank gawd for that. I doubt if I could have stood up much longer.

Back in the undergrowth, both dogs rested.

'Can't lie here too long. We have to be back to the dug-hole before the offering arrives.'

Back and settled, barely a few moments had passed when Len the Lurcher appeared, dropping a small piece of food, about three metres from where the two dogs lay. Before Easy could offer his thanks, Bill barked in his ear, 'Don't make eye contact or offer any words of gratitude.'

'Why?' barked Easy quietly.

'It will be mistaken for a sign of weakness.'

'Oh! I see.'

'Tell you what,' barked Bill, 'for a feral dog you're not very streetwise.'

'What do you mean not streetwise?' said Easy indignantly. 'I'll have you know I ran with two of the wisest dogs in Dalman.'

'That may well be, but I bet you've already forgotten half of what they taught you, so you had better remember fast if you want to survive in this dump.'

Easy had to admit to himself old Bill was right. A rustle in the bushes caught their attention; as the undergrowth parted, Easy noted it was the same bitch who befriended him before. She dropped her piece of bone next to Len's offerings, then said, 'How are you?'

For the life of him, Easy couldn't remember her name. Keeping Bills advice in mind, he still thought he owed the bitch. The least he could do was to nod his thanks.

Over the next hour or so, there was a consistent flow of dogs depositing little pieces of meat and offal, till finally it stopped. Bill had already informed Easy to be patient and wait until the food donations ceased, and then he could indulge himself.

There was hardly enough food for one dog let alone two, Bill was assuming Easy would leave a few morsels.

All through the long wait, Easy was dying to literally jump on the food and wolf it down, but he saw the wisdom of Bills advice.

'Okay Easy, go for it, but amble over, as though you are only half interested in case someone is watching.' As an afterthought, he added, 'You never know.'

Easy stood up and began to walk casually towards the food; each painful step took him closer. Finally, he was there and set about demolishing the small heap, totally oblivious of anyone or anything, the food never touched the sides of his jaws. Pausing for breath as he came up for air, he became aware of old Bill sitting patiently sitting opposite.

'Sorry, Bill, I am so hungry I forgot about you. Come on, eat your half.'

Bill was dumfounded; he hoped for some sort of hand out, but half was beyond his wildest dreams.

'That's very kind of you. I'm old and my stomach has shrunk. Consequently, it doesn't take much to fill it, but I appreciate your offer.'

'Without you, I would be starving, so take whatever you need.'

'Thank you!' Bill sat down and started nibbling the food very slowly, pausing to look up at Easy, then said, 'I can't eat as fast as most of my teeth are missing.'

'Take your time, eat what you can manage. I'll finish off.'

Having his fill, Bill asked, 'Did you keep a mental note of those dogs leaving food?'

'No, should I have?'

'Yes, you never know when you may need help in this dump, so it's good to know who your friends are. Anyway, I did, it's a habit left over from when I was top dog.'

'Well, I'll be . . . ' said Easy, looking at Bill with even more respect.

Chapter 31

The flight from Gatwick to Turkey was of four-hour duration. This never bothered George as whenever he flew he always carried his trusty companions—a 'giant-sized volume of crosswords, puzzles, and the most difficult Sudoku book he could find'. From George's point of view, the Sudokus had to be testing; otherwise, there was no point in doing them. He had yet to find a puzzle that could defeat him. True, sometimes, he would take as long as three days to solve one. When finally he completed it, he felt a great sense of satisfaction.

He thought back to the 1960s, when he first flew with Pan Am, to New York; he was so scared of flying that before boarding the long-haul flight, he would down half a bottle of vodka. Even then, the purser would allocate a hostess to board and sit with him for half hour before takeoff. She would stay with him till the aircraft reached thirty-five thousand feet, and then the same procedure before touchdown.

What, always amazed George was . . . having drunk that much vodka, the moment he sat in his allocated seat, he sobered up. No doubt a psychiatrist could come up with a logical explanation as to this odd phenomenon.

Even being aware of the amount of fatalities there were when flying, it was much lower than other means of transport; still this didn't alleviate his fear. Mind you, these days pilots are almost defunct; every manoeuvre can be carried out by computers. Ah that's progress, thought George. I suppose the feeling that you are not in control and relying on someone else, aggravated the fear, rather like sitting in a dentist chair, having a filling, the noise of the drill, making you think the dentist had fallen asleep, and the drill was penetrating your jaw, sends shivers down your spine, thought George.

Even more puzzling than that, one of his companions travelling with the groups had a morbid fear of needles, the injection kind, yet had showed no fear when being tattooed.

They landed in the early hours of the following morning, at the airport; the hotel had arranged transport which was waiting for them.

As breakfast was served between eight and ten, George, though tired, couldn't see the point of going to bed, as once asleep, you would lose best part of the day.

The temperature was well into the seventies, so George and his fellow travellers whiled away the time, swimming in the well-lit hotel pool, before showering and changing into light clothing.

Having eaten, the usual procedure was agreed—each member of the group did their own thing during the day. If so desired, should they want to dine together for the evening meal, to meet in the hotel foyer, seven o'clock sharp. Those of the group who made the deadline would then select which restaurant to use; for the others, it would be assumed they had other plans.

After breakfast, George decided that he would once again familiarise himself with the pretty, peaceful, family orientated holiday resort. As he wandered around, he felt quite at home, seeing people he had met on previous visits.

From midday until about five o'clock, the temperature climbed steadily; this time of the year, it had been known to reach in excess of thirty-five degrees plus, too hot to sunbathe; he had long since ceased to indulge in that dangerous ageing process.

George had been visiting this resort for many years and felt quite at home here. During the day, he had been thinking about which way to approach Katie, as on consideration there wasn't any hard evidence to prove she was a fraudster, although he had serious doubts. His instinct told him something wasn't right. He decided to phone her early evening. Once he made contact, he would endeavour to lull her into a false sense of security, by saying how much he admired the work she was doing, adding she could rely on his and Mary's full support.

The telephone seemed to ring for ages, perhaps he was a little anxious, why that should be, heaven knows. Mary had always said he had a suspicious nature. Pick up, for Christ sake, can't wait here all evening.

'Ah . . . hello . . . hello, Katie, it's me George. We met last year, and you spoke to Mary, my other-half, a few weeks ago . . . Yes, that's right. She's unable to make it this year, but sends her regards and to tell you that you can rely on the two of us to support your charity in any way possible. I was wondering when we could meet? . . . Anytime is convenient for me . . . Wednesday, great. I have a wonderful photo of you, Mary, and Easy, taken at the bus station last year . . . Yes, I'll catch the boat and see you at the dock . . . Yes, I know Balgerese is the first stop off on the seven-island tour. Look forward to seeing you and the pup, bye-bye.'

Putting down the phone, George thought to himself, I handled that well. How stupid can I get, what was there to handle, there's no big drama, just an ordinary phone call.

Once showered and changed, George was in the foyer just before seven. Tricia, Mark, and Tracey were there waiting; the four of them left shortly after to dine at Ali's restaurant. They all enjoyed a pleasant evening, but were glad to get back to the hotel to catch up on their sleep.

Finally, in his bed, he rang Mary to update her on his conversation with Katie, then wishing Mary goodnight, George settled down, thinking he could sleep for England. As his head sunk into the pillow, his eyes closed within minutes; he was in the land of nod.

George woke from a deep untroubled sleep, glancing at the clock, noting it was nigh on midday. Well, he thought, I've missed breakfast, never mind a cup of tea, then a shower will do nicely. Jumping out of bed, he put the kettle on. Might as well unpack, it will take a few minutes to boil; lifting the case onto the bed, he released the lock. There wasn't much to unpack; these days, he travelled light. Over the years, he had learned the hard way. During his early days of travelling George would cram a large suitcase full of clothes, half of which he never used; maybe it was some form of security, he mused. Anyway those days are long gone.

Unpacking finished, as the kettle boiled and clicked off. Making the tea, George grabbed his bag of toiletries, and then into the shower, he cleaned his teeth, no need to shave as he wore a short beard which was trimmed every three days or so. Selecting clean clothes suitable for the hot climate, he sat down to drink his warm tea, unusual of course, then that's the way he liked it.

His eyes chanced on a piece of folded paper by the door, stooping down George unfolded it and read: 'A few of us are spending the day by the pool. If you've nothing on, join us.'

I haven't planned anything, might as well. Grabbing a book, towel, and trunks, George was out of the room and on his way to the pool; he wasn't surprised to see the ladies there sunbathing in between games of Backgammon.

'Afternoon George,' they said in unison, 'overslept?' They laughed. 'Missing Mary?' they chided.

George smiled, replying, 'I can see you three are nicely toasted.' Selecting a spot under a large umbrella, he settled down to read.

On looking around the large pool, George was not surprised to see, maybe a dozen people, that in itself was not unusual, as most of the residents opted to use one of the two beaches available to them.

'Do you play?'

'Pardon!'

'Backgammon,' said Trish.

'Er! No,' replied George.

'Would you like to learn?'

'Sure.'

'When we've finished this game, I'll teach you.'

'Great,' he replied.

The afternoon passed into early evening as they whiled away the time reading, playing backgammon, and sunbathing. As usual, George stayed in the shade. About six o'clock, he decided to return to his room and ring Mary, and then get ready for the seven-o'clock deadline. That evening, George dined alone; this suited him, because it gave him time to think about the meeting with Katie tomorrow. As he passed through the hotel foyer, he left a note for Brett, saying he would be joining him on seven-island trip tomorrow and would be on the dock at 10 a.m.

At precisely nine fifty-five, George arrived at the quayside to seek out Brett. The excursion boats lay anchored and tied to each other—George counted twenty, all owned by the council—so effectively, the captains and crew were employed by local municipality, as opposed to the tour guides who worked for themselves.

George found Brett without too much trouble, ushering the last of his day trippers to their seats.

'Nice to see you again, George,' said Brett as they shook hands. 'This must be your fourth or fifth visit to Dalman?'

'Yes! There's something irresistible about this place. Over the years, I've visited most countries, but for some reason this little resort keeps luring me back. I've arranged to see your mother and would appreciate it if I could hitch a lift to balgerese . . . I rang her last night to let her know I was coming. She'll be there to meet me with the dog.'

'Of course, you met her last year. How is the pup doing?' said Brett.

'Well, I hope,' George replied, knowing full well Brett and his mother had long ceased their once close relationship. George decided not to inquire about Katie's health.

'Come aboard. We are about to weigh the anchor. There's plenty of room.'

As George sat down, he noted the craft, which housed thirty people, was half empty. The engine ticked over gently as the captain gave the order to cast off. Having completed this task, the two crewmen moved forward to midship, taking their places behind a small kiosk, selling a range of soft drinks, various alcoholic beverages, mini snacks, plus an assortment of confectionery.

The boat chugged out to midstream, heading for the sea. George made himself comfortable, gazing around once again, noticing what a beautiful part of Turkey this tiny resort was and why he kept returning year after year.

Brett had started to lecture on the points of interest and local history of this lovely bay. Married and living with his wife and son in Istanbul, the boat excursions being a seasonal job to help pay his way through college. He was unable to support his mother financially, and this had caused a huge divide between the pair of them.

Katie had mentioned to George the possibility of spending the day in Balgarese, as there was plenty to see other than the local market, and had booked him in a small pension run by a friend of hers.

When George had mentioned the puppy, Katie had said, 'No problem, my friend loves dogs.'

The cost was a minimal twelve euros; why not, he thought, knowing this part of the country was absolutely steeped in history.

With the warmth of the sun, the gentle throb of the engine, and Brett's voice droning on in the background, George was dozing until the jolt of the craft docking roused him, plus Brett's voice saying, 'Here we are, folks. The local market is a hundred metres to your left,' pointing up the main thoroughfare. 'Be back in one hour prompt as we have a busy day ahead of us.'

Clasping his overnight bag, and once again thanking Brett for the ride, George made his way to the open-air quayside cafe, where he had first met Katie. Finding a table in the shade and ordering a coffee, he sat down to wait for her and his dog.

One hour and three coffees later, she arrived on her tricycle; leaving it standing on the grass verge, she walked over, George stood and held out his hand, which she shook warmly.

'I recognised you by that wonderful head of gray hair you have.'

'Please, sit down. Can I get you a drink?' said George.

'Orange juice will be fine.' Catching the waiter's eye, he ordered the juice and yet another coffee for himself.

'It's nice to see you again. How's the charity fairing?'

'It's hard work raising money. With no government funding, we have to rely on donations from the public. The main problem is I'm overpaid and underworked.'

It took a second or two for her wry humour to sink in. George laughed. 'Really.'

'Talking about money', Mary said, 'you have some for me.'

 209

Straight to the point, thought George, who already had made up his mind not to part with any cash until he saw his pup.

'Yes!' he replied, quickly changing the subject and inquiring, 'How is Easy?'

'Who . . . ?'

'Easy, my pup.'

Of course, she answered justifying her hesitation by adding, 'I look after so many dogs. It's hard to remember their names, the little darlings.'

'I can see that must cause you problems,' said George. 'Did you bring the dog with you?' he asked, having already noticed the basket on her cycle was empty.

'Unfortunately, just as I was leaving, Easy and another dog started fighting. By the time I was able to separate them, Easy had sustained an injury to his rear leg and is limping badly. Hopefully by tomorrow, he should be well enough to travel. As you're staying a night in the pension, you can see him tomorrow.'

The excuse sounded quite plausible to George, but being of a suspicious nature, he was not totally convinced by her casual, confident explanation.

Suddenly, George realised he was hungry and thought, If I invited her to dine with me, there may well occur an opportunity to pump her for more information, especially if she drinks alcohol.

'Have you eaten,' said George.

'No,' came the reply.

'Will you join me for lunch?'

'I'd love to. I know a lovely little cafe that the locals use. It's very inexpensive, but they serve only Turkish food. Is that okay with you?'

George hesitated, feeling guilt that in all the years he had been visiting Turkey, he had never eaten the native food.

'Fine, but to be honest, you will have to order for me as I have no idea what to ask for.'

'Really!' said Katie somewhat surprised. Standing up she said, 'Follow me. I'll leave my cycle here. It'll be quite safe.'

George got up to follow, leaving enough money on the table to cover their beverages.

Five minutes later, they were seated inside an air-conditioned cafe, the food ordered and the pair of them supping the local fruit juice concoction.

'Are you sure you wouldn't prefer something stronger?'

'No, thank you, George. I've been teetotal all my life and have no desire to change.' She lied.

Feeling somewhat disappointed, bang goes any chance to pump her, he thought. The food arrived promptly; even though George was unable to make neither head nor tail of what he was eating and too embarrassed to ask, he thoroughly enjoyed it. Through the entire meal, Katie never mentioned the charity, dog, or the money Mary had promised. Instead the conversation veered around, expats living in Turkey, the British economy under a labour government, and to George's surprise, Katie's knowledge of English football, what was quite astonishing, she was convinced that the now the ex-Fulham manager had joined Liverpool they would win the premiership next season. She also advised George if he was a betting man to get on a sure thing. The next thing she was doing was apologising; she added that she was unable to show George around the local points of interest, as there were some matters that had come up that needed her immediate attention. George viewed her excuse with some suspicion, why though he wasn't sure.

The meal finished and as they drank their coffee, George made one last attempt to steer the conversation round to her charity. Reaching into his overnight bag, produced an eight by ten photograph of Mary, Katie, and Easy taken at a bus stop last year, handing it to Katie who stared at it for some time. George didn't attach any importance to that, thinking she was probably comparing her own figure from last year, as it appeared to George she must have gained at least two stones.

He realised he wasn't getting anywhere fast and called for the bill; he was pleased to note that it came to fifteen euros as opposed to thirty if you ate at the tourist restaurants.

Having given George directions to the pension, she thanked him for the lunch adding that she would meet him tomorrow, same time, same place, and should she be late, not to worry, and she had to attend the welfare of her animals and sometimes problems occurred.

The town was small; the main high street contained the market, where you could buy almost anything at inflated prices but still cheap by European standards. The high street extended into the main pedestrian square; in the centre stood a fountain in the shape of a lion, the water spurting from the creature's mouth. That's rather odd, thought George.

Other than the market, the town had very little to offer a sightseeing tourist. Though George had been reliably informed, there were plenty of sites that contained historic interest dotted around the outskirts of the little port.

Wandering around held a twofold interest for George; one, it gave him some insight as to how the locals lived before tourism, they were the main fishermen or goat farmers; he did notice in two places antiquated looms, with women busily weaving various fabrics. The other reason was to inquire about Katie's charity, and find out where she lived. This seemed quite simple as an officer at the local police station directed him, not until he asked what business George had with her. The surprising thing was, the officers spoke reasonably good English, but when he mentioned her charity, the policeman clammed up, his command of the mother tongue suddenly disappeared. To George's astonishment, Katie's house was on the opposite side of the road and two streets up, heading out of town, from the police station. The officer had said it was the second house down with the wrought iron rusting double gate.

Two minutes later, he was standing outside the building; indeed the gate was rusty, the whole house was in a state of disrepair. No surprises there, thought George. What he did find disconcerting was the noise, well at least the lack of it. Surely, he thought, if she was looking after forty or so dogs, as she claimed, you would have thought there would have been some sort of noise!

Back at the police station, George, forgoing mentioning the charity, instead asked the officer where she kept her dogs. He shrugged and pointing across the road to an estate agents, saying, 'Helen, she speak good English.'

Crossing the road, George entered the shop; the door had one of those old-fashioned bells that tinkled. Through an opening covered with hanging beads stepped a rather thin angular woman, smiling;

'Can I help you?'

'Yes,' said George, 'would you by chance be Helen?'

'That's right, and you?'

'And me what?'

'You're name . . . ' George blushed at his own stupidity.

'So sorry, George.'

'Good afternoon, George. What can I do for you?'

George was quite taken back by this tall, thin, English lady and stammered, 'Are you English?'

'Yes,' came the reply, 'what can I do for you?'

George was totally thrown by the middle class accent and the directness of Helen's question.

'Oh, I er . . . ! er . . . !,' he stuttered, ' . . . was wondering if you could help me with my inquiries, concerning a lady called Katie who runs an animal charity. The officer from over the road sent me here saying you had a good command of the English language, but omitted to say that you are British.through and through.'

'Yes, though I have lived here nearly a quarter of a century, my husband and I set up in business many years ago, he has since passed on. But I still manage to eke out a living, selling property, and once Turkey enters the EU, who knows the property business could well take off. You want to know about Katie. There's not much to tell really. Can you be more specific?'

Somehow, George was drawn to Helen; maybe because she was British, he felt they both batted for the same side. Briefly, he told her the whole story and bringing her up to date with the day's events and waited for her response. Much to his surprise, she said, 'Would you like a nice cup of English tea? I am about to close for the day.' Shutting the front door, she continued, 'Come through to the back and sit down, far too hot to be standing and chatting.'

George followed Helen through to the rear of the premises, sitting down on a wicker backed chair. As Helen switched on the kettle and busied herself making the tea, George noted the small, neat, and tidy room, all the usual things that could be found in an English kitchen, cooker, fridge, disposal bin, a food larder, a few pots hanging above the fitted sink and cabinets, and a ceiling fan rotating over a two-seated sofa.

'Milk? Sugar?' she asked.

'Oh! Milk, please. No sugar, thank you. I have to watch the old waistline.' He laughed.

Helen handed him a cup of tea, saying, 'Help yourself to a biscuit.' She sat down on the sofa, between them stood a small coffee table with a plate of biscuits. George selected a Garibaldi. Helen spoke, 'As I was saying, there's not much to tell really. Katie's well known around town, if nothing else for the complaints that have been made about her, always bothering the local traders for food she needs to feed her animals, and at the least twenty or so British tourists have reported her to the police for begging. This I know to be true, as the officer in charge usually asks me to translate when he write up a charge sheet. But the police's hands are tied because the people who claim money has exchanged hands are here on holiday for two or three weeks before returning home. As the wheels of justice turn very slowly in Turkey, there is no way those people are going to return and try to recover one or two hundred pounds they have parted with; what with the cost of the airfare and accommodation, it's not worth their while, not to mention the time involved.'

'But she is a registered charity. I've checked her out,' said George.

'That's true, but when people who have parted with money find out that the law says the charity must be registered for three years before they can solicit money to support it, then the problems start. I have heard of other people, like yourself being taken in and parting with considerable amounts on a promise of new kennels, leaking roofs, money to erect a fence around her property to protect the dogs, etc. As I mentioned, I've been in real estate going on twenty-five years and yet to locate this piece of land she claims to own.'

'What does she do with the animals she takes on?' asked George.

'Your guess is as good as mine.'

'Why don't the police step in?'

'As I've said, for the courts to sanction a writ against her to real her so-called property, the police have to bring her to court, which they can't do, as the tourists never come back to give evidence against her. Quite honestly, I think the reason her son left for Istanbul is the embarrassment she caused him.'

Thanking Helen for her hospitality, George took his leave, not before she handed him her business card saying, 'If I can be of further help, don't hesitate to call me.'

As he made his way to the pension, George's head was in a whirl. What should he tell Mary who had complete faith in the woman? The more he thought about Katie, the more he realised he was dealing with a charlatan and the pup was already dead.

George checked in, went straight to his room, and showered then into bed. He thought about ringing Mary, but decided to put that on hold, knowing that she would be devastated if he passed on the information that Helen had supplied. One thing he was sure of, he was not handing any more cash over.

George lay in bed thinking over his options and possibilities—the chances were that Easy is dead. Equally, there was no chance of recovering any money.

Something didn't add up; assuming she managed to con at least one tourist a week by taking on a stray animal and she did in fact dispose of them, she would have to get rid of the body, so, logically, it was only a matter of time before she was discovered. Helen had said she knew of at least twenty complaints that the police had to deal with; there was a high probability many more had gone unreported. George was fairly sure that Brett wasn't involved. If she turned up with Easy tomorrow, he would be in a stronger position to ask more direct questions and hopefully get some answers. If he told Mary what he suspected all hell would break loose, and knowing her, she wouldn't let the matter drop and would be on the first available flight. Yes, thought George, let's see what develops before I ring her. George was tired and realised there was no point in playing the whole scenario over and over and getting nowhere. I'll try and sleep and see what tomorrow brings.

He was sitting in the quayside cafe, punctual as usual, at eleven o'clock; much to his surprise, Katie arrived shortly after, parked her cycle on the grass verge and strode over to his table offering her hand, saying brightly, 'Morning, George, sleep well?'

With one eye on Katie's empty cycle, he shook her hand. 'Yes, very well,' he lied, then blurted out, 'Where's the dog?'

'Still not well enough to travel I'm afraid.' George was seething, struggling to control his temper. Before he could say anything, she said, 'I have business in Dalman. If you don't mind I'll travel with you on the bus, the route passes close to the land where I keep the animals. Are you ready to leave?'

'Yes,' said George standing up, having already paid for his coffee.

They boarded the Dalman bus at the main terminal. About five minutes into the journey, Katie nudged George, saying, 'You see that pylon over there. Just beyond it is my piece of land. There's a pond, and the house is situated behind those trees. I have yet to raise the money to finish the fence, but slowly, and surely, I'm getting there.'

Was that a hint for George to part with more money? She sounds so plausible, thought George. Then avoiding the money issue, he asked, 'How much land do you have?' Thinking, if any.

'About an acre,' she replied, 'plenty of room for forty or so dogs. My aim is one day every dog will have its own kennel, and with regular donations coming in, I will hire some help to assist me in running the charity.' George saw an opening;

'You mean all the animals are cared for by you? Are there any local volunteers to help?'

'No!' said Katie. 'It's a pity, but Turkish people are not really into dogs.'

'Oh, that's a shame. You must find it extremely difficult to manage on your own.'

'One does one's best,' came the reply.

George was thinking, She's good, really good; she almost has me believing her. The rest of the journey passed in silence, both absorbed in their own thoughts.

'I get off the next stop. If you ring me, at say, eleven tomorrow morning, I'll have news about Easy and how he's mending. If all's well, the three of us can meet up the next day.' Sounds too good to be true, thought George, as he blurted out, 'Great, I will bring the money Mary sent.'

The bus stopped.

'Bye,' said Katie, 'don't forget to ring.' Then she was gone.

George thought, What the hell? Why did I mention money? Idiot! Did I hear right. Did she say the three of us will meet up in two days time? I'll believe than when I see it.

The bus arrived in Dalman, and George alighted and made straight for the phone box. Using the phone card he had acquired at the post office, he rang Mary; she picked up the phone immediately.

'George, I was expecting you to ring earlier. I've been sitting here on tender hooks waiting for you to call.'

'Sorry, love. I had nothing to report until now.' Having carefully thought out what he was about to say, he proceeded to update Mary on the Easy situation, omitting his visit to the police station and the conversation with Helen, basically playing for time at least by telling Mary about the injury to Easy; he was preparing her for what he thought was inevitable, the dog's demise.

'Did you give her the money?'

'Yes,' George lied.

'We need her connection in Holland, regarding the British quarantine laws,' she reminded him.

'Yes! I know. Don't worry, I'm on top of everything, Mary. Leave it to me, and I'll call you Saturday when I have seen the dog,' said George, playing for time. 'You take care and stop worrying as everything's in hand. Bye! Talk to you soon.' Putting the phone down, George took a deep breath, thinking, I've two days to come up with a plausible story.

Eleven o'clock prompt, the next day, George range Katie; it seemed like an eternity before she answered. She's probably attending to the dogs, who am I kidding? thought George . . . come on, Katie, pick up. Finally, a click and a voice said, 'Hello.'

'Hi! Katie, it's me, George. How is Easy doing?'

'George! Oh George . . . Easy! Yes, he's getting there.' This sounded evasive to George, and her next words really frightened him. 'When exactly are you going back to England?' she asked.

She's evading the issue, thought George; heckles up, he blurted out, 'I can't go back until I've seen the dog. Mary will go mad, and hop on the first available flight. She's beside herself with worry over the injury he has incurred. I've managed to convince her, it's just a minor setback.'

'Oh, I see!' came the reply. George hurried on, 'That's why I need to see Easy as soon as possible; otherwise, all hell will break loose.' In for a penny in for a pound, he thought. However, knowing Mary's love of wildlife, he was telling the truth. Where animals were concerned, George thought Mary was somewhat over the top.

'So you can appreciate the delicate position that I'm in Katie . . . '

No reply! George thought he had lost the connection. Then Katie answered, 'Um! Yes! Right!' Her tone softened. 'Must be very difficult for you,' another pause, 'tell you what. Can we meet tomorrow sometime?'

George grabbed his chance and replied eagerly, 'Whenever. I'm free all day.'

'How about the same time and place as before?'

'That's great!'

'Easy is still a little lame, but hopefully, by tomorrow, he should be well enough to travel . . . There are a couple of things I have to do first, so I may be a little late but rest assured I'll be there. Oh and by the way, you did mention Mary had sent some money over with you.'

'That's right, I'll have it with me tomorrow,' said George. 'See you tomorrow then Katie. Bye for now, bye . . . ' Putting down the receiver, George could hardly contain himself.

The fact she had mentioned money must weigh in his favour, she obviously knew he wouldn't part with cash unless he saw the pup. Feeling somewhat relieved, maybe just maybe the pup was alive, and he had totally misjudged her. All will be revealed tomorrow, he thought, but the doubts still lingered.

The evidence was stacked against her, bearing in mind what he had learned from the police and Helen. The whole situation was stressing him out, so he decided to spend the rest of the day by the pool with his book and try to relax.

Chapter 32

The revelation that Bill was once top dog surprised Easy to say the least. By his own admission, Bill claimed to be five or six years of age, he wasn't sure, as two years incarcerated in this concrete prison had taken its toll. When they had first met, the impression that registered with Easy was of a much older dog, nearing the end of his days, even when helping him bury his friend Boris, the amount of effort it took Bill to help drag the animal into the undergrowth left him exhausted, depleted of what little energy he had. As he lay resting, Easy could see how frail and thin his companion looked; areas of fur were missing, sores covered his poor emaciated body, unable to digest food. Even when standing, his body shook with the effort. It crossed Easy's mind that he may well be burying another friend in the near future.

Was he heading in the same direction, would the lack of nutrition and disease have the same effect on his body? His instincts told him yes; his mind said no way. That old cow wouldn't reduce him to a trembling wreck, waiting to die. He doubled his resolve to find a way out of the hellhole.

Three weeks had passed since Easy's bid for freedom; he was well on the mend. The beating handed out by her was still fresh in his memory. With Bill's help, he had managed to retain his status as top dog, even though every day new animals arrived. None had seen fit to challenge his authority, once they heard how he dealt the Len the Lurcher.

Easy was no fool; he knew time was not on his side. Eventually, some enterprising young whippersnapper would seize his opportunity leaving him relegated to the ranks. At the moment, those dogs that were able still paid their dues with scraps of food for his protection.

During his three weeks of recovery, Easy had time to observe the day-to-day events of his living hell. He was still not convinced that those dogs that unfortunately had gone to meet their maker, within range of the back door and deadly hook, were in fact chopped up, cooked, and fed back to the starving animals the next day.

What he did know, once, sometimes, twice a week, Katie would enter the compound with her two well-fed and well-trained guard dogs and route around the compound for any dead carcasses, load them into a wheelbarrow, which she left just inside the Iron gates built into the brick wall. The two gates opened inwardly to reveal a van with its doors already opened backed tightly up against the wall so as to form a seal, leaving not an inch of space around the gates.

The underside of the vehicle could not be seen as the gates were set in the wall about fifteen centimetres above ground level. She would load the dead dogs into the vehicle, close the gates, and lock them. Having done that, she and her dogs would enter the rear of the house, making sure to bolt and chain the door behind them. A few moments later, the van would start up and pull away a few feet and stop, leaving room to close the vehicle's doors, then take off for its destination. This action convinced Easy that in fact Katie was taking the bodies somewhere to dump them.

Bill would have none of it; he still maintained she was chopping them up and feeding them back to the rest of the starving dogs.

Days passed into weeks; during that time, his recovery was complete, though his body weight had dropped dramatically. But nature was on his side; during that healing time, there had been several downpours of rain, though not enough to completely quench the incarcerated animals' thirst. Their daily squabble's still continued at the rusty water tap, the stronger dogs fighting their way to the front, and the older and wiser dogs waiting till the moon shone before attempting to drink from it.

At full strength and as well as he would ever be, Easy was fully aware time was running out, as for his companion, Bill's time had run its course, he was hardly able to walk, his body almost hairless and covered in sores.

He was immobile and lying on his own; he presented a pitiful sight. Easy avoided eye contact with him for fear of conveying what his friend already knew, the ferryman was waiting. In his lucid moments, Bill confided he was ready to meet his maker, the agony and suffering now just a memory as father time waited to close the door.

There had to be a way of escaping. There just has to be, thought Easy. As he lay there pondering his fate, the beginnings of an idea filtered through what if he organised a rebellion? The next time the old hag came with her dogs to retrieve the dead carcasses, they attacked them en masse, killing them if necessary. Brilliant, absolutely brilliant, but hang on a minute; even if they succeeded in subduing them, there was still no way out of the compound. How stupid can I get, he thought. There again if all the inmates barked and howled in unison, someone was bound to hear them and investigate.

During this time of convalescing, a female had befriended him, licking his wounds, tending to his needs. She was called Gypsy, having been disowned and left on the streets to fend for herself, till finally she fell into Katie's hands, and in a matter of months, she was pregnant, but her body unable to sustain the pregnancy, she miscarried, and now because of malnourishment and her general condition, she was incapable of sustaining another pregnancy. She said, 'If mother nature had allowed her to give birth, Easy would have been her ideal son.'

It was nice having someone to fuss over you, but Easy, being Easy, found her somewhat overprotective. He had a faint recollection of his real mother, and already, time spent with his foster mum was a distant memory.

As conversation with Bill was virtually impossible, he decided to confide in Gypsy as to the possibilities of his newly thought-out plan. Her input was . . . well there wasn't any. All she said was, 'If you think it will work, dear, then you go ahead.'

'I need you to help me put the word about and see how much support I can expect.'

'Yes, of course, dear . . . What do you want me to do?' came the reply.

With a touch of annoyance in his bark, Easy said, 'I've just told you. Go around and tell all your friends about my idea, and I'll do the same thing.'

'What, now, dear?'

'Yes, now!' He almost said you stupid bitch, but caught himself in time. Instead he said,

'Off you go, and meet me back here in an hour.'

The first dog he encountered was Len the Lurcher. My God, he thought, how the mighty have fallen.

Poor Len had aged compared to their first meeting and looked quite apprehensive; as Easy approached him, he cowered down.

'What can I do for you?' Len asked.

Outlining his idea, Easy waited for a reaction. Knowing that he wasn't about to be attacked Len said, 'It might work.' Feeling even bolder, he added, 'But it will have to be carefully coordinated, and to install confidence in the pack, you will have to lead by example.'

'No problem,' said Easy with an air of confidence but thinking why me? Then realising, as Bill always reminded him, if you're top dog, the others expect you to lead.

Leaving Len, Easy continued his rounds; all in all, the reaction was positive. On returning to his waterhole, he found Gypsy waiting.

'Where have you been?' she barked. 'I've been worried stiff.'

'Never mind that,' he retorted. 'How did you get on?'

'Every dog I spoke to seemed to be in favour of the plan. Those who were fit enough said they would support your lead.'

'Good! Then tomorrow, we will execute phase two.'

'Yes, dear, whatever you say,' replied Gypsy.

That night for the first time in ages, Easy slept well, not before checking on how Bill was faring; there was nothing he could do for him, as he slipped in and out of consciousness, other than to let him know he was there for him. In his more lucid moments, Bill would softly bark, 'I don't want to die alone.'

To which Easy would reply, 'I'm here with you, Bill. You're not alone.'

Gypsy would look on not knowing what to do.

Easy woke to the sound of a thunderclap as the heavens opened. The force of the deluge made a pinging noise as it struck the concrete patio and rebounded; in a matter of minutes, his dug-hole was full. Some twenty minutes later, the cloud disappeared, leaving a clear blue sky and a burning sun.

Looking over at Bill, he noted his left ear twitching, also the laboured rise and fall of his ribcage, as he struggled to breath. Still hanging in there, he thought, though in reality he hoped that Bill would pass away. As he looked at the soggy brown mess that had once been a healthy vibrant dog, he thought, In a few months, that could be me.

'Snap out of it,' he barked. 'Don't allow yourself to think along those lines.' The resounding sound woke Gypsy.

'You're up early, dear.'

'Yes, it's time to put phase two into operation.'

'Yes, if you say so, dear,' she replied. Once again, Easy had to bite his tongue.

'What do you want me to do, dear?' she asked.

'Simply backtrack and visit the dogs you spoke to yesterday. Tell them to meet at the water tap tonight as soon as the sun goes down. I will address the assembly and explain their part in the operation. When you're done, meet me back here.'

'Right now, dear?'

'Yes! The sooner the better before they have second thoughts. I'm off to do the same.'

That evening, just before dusk, Easy positioned himself in the undergrowth a few metres distant from the tap, making sure he was well concealed and waited for developments.

The usual melee of thirsty dogs were already snapping and jostling for position, exactly what Easy had expected all part of phase two. The sky was very overcast; conditions couldn't be better.

Easy reasoned should Katie or anyone else for that matter be looking out of the window, their vision would be impaired by the lack of direct light, this achieving two objectives: one, it would be difficult to ascertain how many dogs were in attendance; two, should the dogs cause any additional noise, they would assume the fighting was louder than usual at the dripping tap.

As the minutes ticked by, the numbers of dogs increased, milling around with an air of expectancy. Time to make an appearance, thought Easy. He stood up and strode purposely toward the rear door steps; he stood on the highest one, silent and still, an old trick his mentor had taught him; gradually, the noise quietened to a low buzz.

Easy barked, 'Thank you for attending this rather impromptu meeting and a special thanks to those of you who though suffering made the effort to be here. I'll keep what I have to say short, as we don't want to draw undue attention to ourselves. As you are all aware no animal has ever escaped from this hellhole, though many have tried. What I have to offer is no guarantee of freedom, just a chance, and in my book, even the slightest of chances is worth taking. You all have experienced the agonies and sorrow, the feelings of helplessness, as you watched your nearest and dearest suffer the pangs of hunger and thirst as their bodies slowly cease to function, In short, they die of dehydration and malnutrition.

What I propose to do is, the next time the old hag comes around to collect the carcasses in her barrow, the ones she can't reach with the hook, we wait until she opens the iron gates, then en-masse, we create as much noise as possible in hope of attracting someone's attention to our plight.

As we can never be sure, as to what day that will be. If any of you lose a friend or family member, report to me immediately, and I will take up residence as near to the gate as possible. Once those gates are open, I will emit a signal to inform you all. Your job is to congregate on the patio, 'creating as much fuss as possible. Is that clear?' The pack began to bark amongst themselves, an old brown Doberman, standing on three legs with a droopy tail, barked, 'How will we know the signal?'

Easy replied, 'I will howl twice,' at the same time thinking, very unusual to see a Doberman with a tail.

'Any questions?' The pack barked their agreement to Easy's plan.

A small cairn terrier cross piped up, 'The upstairs light is on.' And with some urgency, he barked, 'The window is opening.'

'Everybody scat,' barked Easy furiously. Most of the dogs dashed to the undergrowth, a few lingered by the tap.

Easy was about to make an exit when a voice bellowed, 'What are you up to, you miserable excuse for a dog? You're that black-and-white mongrel who invaded my house. I thought you were dead.'

Easy let her have it full blast, barking his defiance, before dashing off. The strains of her voice ringing in his ears.

'You filthy lump of shit, I'll hunt you down. Mark my words. There's no way you can hide from me, and when I find you, you're dead meat.'

Back at his dug-hole, Easy was greeted by Gypsy.

'That was a fine speech you made, dear, but you really shouldn't antagonise that woman.'

'Antagonise her! Should I ever get the chance, I'll take her leg off.'

'Now, now, dear, temper! Temper.'

Easy checked on Bill, who was awake and coherent, 'How are you, old-timer?'

'Fair to middling,' came the reply, 'won't be long now.'

'Anything I can do,' said Easy.

'No! Just sit with me a while. I'm scared.'

'Sure I will. You just rest yourself,' Easy sat next to Bill until once again he faded into unconsciousness.

Chapter 33

Time passed, as hours dragged into days; two more street dogs were thrown into the concrete prison, both under the illusion they were entering a reputable charity until they had to fight to gain any sustenance. None of them saw fit to challenge Easy's authority. The stress of waiting began to tell the constant tension never abated; he felt like a coiled spring. Old Bill was still hanging on, while Gypsy's fussing was driving him mad.

Then it happened, the three-legged Doberman checked in to say his friend, an old German Shepherd, had died near the water tap—too far and much too heavy for the jailer's hook.

This is it, thought Easy, telling the Dobi and Gypsy to pass the word around to the others to prepare themselves and be ready for the signal.

Easy positioned himself as close as he could to the iron gates, out of sight of any prying eyes, and waited. But having to lie still in the searing heat was seriously dehydrating him. By mid-afternoon, he was about to give up when he heard the van being backed up; in a matter of minutes, the backdoor of the house opened and Katie appeared with her dogs, careful to close and lock the door. She made straight for the wheelbarrow, pushing it towards the dead German shepherd, and telling her dogs to sit and guard, she endeavoured to lift the Shepherd into the barrow. Emaciated as it was and certainly half its natural body weight, she was having considerable difficulty loading the carcass. Finally, she made it, huffing and puffing, and she pushed the barrow to the gate.

Easy waited, tense, poised for action; she turned the key in the lock, the gates swung inward to reveal the van, backed up to fill the opening; moving towards the barrow, she was stopped by a piercing howl quickly followed by another.

'What the hell was that!' she exclaimed, the words were barely out of her mouth when an enormous weight bundled her over; she hit the patio with a heavy thud expelling the air from her lungs. As she tried to get on her feet, she felt a searing pain in her left ankle.

As the doors swung open, Easy was already in full flight when he smacked into Katie, seizing the opportunity as she lay winded, he clamped his teeth on to her ankle. Then all hell broke loose, the patio was a seething mass of barking, howling dogs. Her two dogs,' having not received any new commands, sat there watching it all. Kicking out with her right foot, she landed a hefty blow on Easy's head, forcing him to release his grip on her.

She stood up as Easy tumbled backwards, dazed. The cacophony of sound had reached a crescendo.

It took Katie a full minute to take in the scene that was unfolding before her eyes, a mass of half-starved dogs, yapping, snapping, barking, and howling. Gathering her wits, she ordered her dogs to kill. They sprang into action as the weakened pack ran to safety in the undergrowth, leaving Easy to scramble to his feet and follow . . . not before Katie caught sight of him.

'You! You little bastard, you're the instigator of this madness. I warned you before, you'll pay for this charade if it's the last thing I do. I'll make you suffer, you piss taking wretch. There's nowhere you can hide. Just you wait, and when I catch you, killing you will be too simple, I'll flay you alive.' But Easy was gone, hidden in the safety of the tangled mass of bushes, trees, and undergrowth.

The following days were a nightmare for the ill-fated animals, as Katie, with her left ankle, heavily strapped combed the wooded area with her dogs looking for Easy. It was a hopeless task due to the density of the overgrown compound.

The animals waited for some outside intervention. One day, two days, three had passed . . . nothing. The starving dogs kept a low profile; by the seventh day, Easy's popularity was on the wane, as the hungry dogs had not received any scraps of food from Kate.

The German Shepherd's body had been removed; his place taken by two more unfortunate animals that had succumbed to malnutrition and disease.

Easy was deflated, hungry, and subdued. Bill was still hanging on, much to Gypsy's surprise. For once she had a calming influence over Easy, saying by next week things would be back to how they were; she had seen it before when the pack got out of hand, Katie withheld their food until everything settled down.

Gypsy was right; two days into the second week, the first floor window opened and the food scraps thrown out to the hungry hounds, and, much to Easy's surprise and delight, he received his dues.

Still Bill hung on. Gypsy said, 'He won't go till his maker is ready for him.'

Now that Easy was back in favour, his brain was still working, trying to come up with a new plan of escape. Time was not on his side, but the fickle hand of fate was about to intervene.

That night, Bill seemed to brighten up; he called to Easy saying, 'I have an idea!'

Thinking his friend was delirious, he listened with half an ear, too preoccupied with his own thoughts, until Bill said, 'The only way out of here is in the van dead . . . That is, if she thinks you're dead.' Bill gave a gasp and shuddered, his breathing laboured.

Once again, he made a tremendous effort to speak. Easy, now fully alert, put his ear closer to Bill's snout.

'I won't make it through the night . . . Easy.'

'Of course, you will. There's life in the old dog, yet eh! Bill,' said Easy, trying to lighten the mood.

'My time has come. I've seen the ferryman,' gasped Bill, his bark barely a whisper. 'Listen to me. I need a favour from you.'

'Anything, anything at all,' said Easy.

Bill's bark was now very faint as Easy strained to hear what he was saying.

'Tomorrow drag my body out on the patio before daybreak, away from the backdoor and hook. Then position yourself near the gate and lie comatose, keep your breathing shallow. That way, she will think you're dead and load us both in the barrow and into the van.'

'I can't do that, Bill. When it's your time, I'll bury you.'

'No, you won't. Please let me die knowing my life has not been wasted. Do this for me. Do it for me.' Bill's voice faded as he drifted into unconsciousness.

Easy thought that the whole idea of dragging his friend onto the patio macabre and an act of barbarism.

Leaving Bill's side, he sat by his dug-hole, deep in thought. Gypsy gave a soft bark to catch his attention; she had heard most of what Bill had said until his bark failed.

'If you want my opinion, son . . . '

'I don't, and I'm not your son,' he barked harshly.

'Sorry, dear,' said Gypsy. There was a strained silence . . .

'I'm the one, who should apologise. I'm sorry for being so rude. Tell me what I should do, Gypsy?'

'Well . . . ' she replied, 'when Bill first arrived, he was an older edition of you—tough, energetic, confident and above all had total belief in his ability to escape. Look at him now! He has offered you a way out and that's his dying wish. You owe it to him. He needs the satisfaction that his last two years on this earth were not wasted.'

Easy curled himself up into a tight ball, not wanting anybody, not even Gypsy, to see his sorrow and heartache he felt. His mind was in turmoil as he contemplated what he knew he must do, if he was ever to escape. Eventually, tiredness overtook him and he drifted into an uneasy sleep. Gypsy woke him at sunrise, gently barking,

'You know what you have to do, Easy.'

'Yes, I know and I will, when the time comes.'

'That time is now,' came the reply.

'What do you mean?'

'Bill passed away soon after you fell asleep.'

'Why didn't you wake me, Gypsy? I promised to stay by his side till the end, and I've failed him.'

'No, you haven't. His last words to me were, "Let the pup sleep, he needs to rest, to prepare himself for what must be done to keep the promise he made to me".' Gypsy was lying because Bill had said nothing to her. He never regained consciousness, just faded away. She was sure that if Easy knew the truth he would falter in fulfilling Bills last request.

'Up you get, and together, we'll move the body out on to the concrete, then position yourself a few metres away near the doors and play dead.'

'I don't think I can do this, Gypsy.'

'You must, a promise is exactly that, a promise! Now buck up before the sun is fully up.'

Together, they dragged Bill's body out onto the patio.

Easy couldn't help but notice that Bill's features were relaxed, and he looked at peace with himself.

'Now, you position yourself and get your breathing under control and good luck,' said 'Gypsy as she made her way back to the overgrown compound.'

Easy positioned himself close to the wall by the gate; this would afford him some shade, until the sun moved across the sky leaving him exposed to the scorching heat.

How long would he have to wait before Katie collected the bodies was anyone's guess; equally how long could he tolerate the fierce unrelenting sunrays, not being able to move or pant, Easy had no idea.

Time passed and the heat had become unbearable. Easy was thinking to himself, I can't go on. I'm slowly cooking. I'll have to move; otherwise, I will fry. Having made a decision to give up, it was then he heard the sound of an engine. That must be the van reversing up to the wall, then silence, followed by the noise of a door slamming shut.

This is it, thought Easy. Don't panic, control my breathing and wait. When she approaches, take a deep breathe and hold it. He felt the tension mounting, at the same time reasoning that in a few minutes he could be out of there. His sensitive ears picked up the click as the key turned in the backdoor lock followed by the rasping noise as the bolts were withdrawn. Unable to see, he waited . . .

Katie's voice gave the order, 'Guard!'

That must be her dogs, thought Easy. Then came the inevitable double click as she relocked the door.

Hearing her footsteps moving toward the barrow, then the sound of wheels on concrete, moving closer, Easy thought, Stay calm a few more minutes. I'll be out of here. The noise stopped and Katie's voice was heard to say, 'Not much meat on this one. Shouldn't be too heavy,' then a thump!

That would be Bills body being dumped into the barrow, thought Easy. The noise of the wheels grew closer; as she halted by Easy, she said, 'This one looks somewhat fatter, wonder what killed him then.' With his tongue hanging out of his jaws, his ribcage still, he waited.

Katie stooped down to grasp Easy, then she stopped, exclaiming,

'I do believe this is the little runt that's been giving me grief, the bastard's dead. Shame I had plans for him.' With that she directed a powerful kick into Easy's midriff, saying, 'Take that you mangy cur.'

Catching him unawares, with the force of the blow, he was unprepared and unable to control a yelp as he jumped to his feet.

'You! You! Sneaky little bastard,' she screamed, 'thought you could fool me did you?' aiming yet another hefty kick, but missed, at the same time ordering her dogs to kill.

Too late, Easy was on his feet heading for the undergrowth, with Katie's hounds in hot pursuit. He knew the grounds like the back of his paws. In a matter of minutes, he'd lost the pursuing dogs.

Sometime later, back at the dug-hole, bruised but not broken, he collapsed on the ground, having spent much energy in losing Katie's dogs. As he lay there panting, he heard Gypsy say, 'Never mind, dear, you'll have better luck next time.'

Gasping for breath; 'There won't be a next time. She recognised me, you stupid bitch.' The words hardly out of his snout, he immediately apologised, 'Sorry Gypsy, I feel so frustrated.'

'Never mind, dear, we'll think of something.'

Easy didn't reply; he was too deep in thought, thinking about his bad luck. If only I hadn't tried to escape before, if only I had not been seen on the steps, if only . . . The voice of his old mentor entered his head; 'Stop it! Once in that mode of thought, if only this, if only that, you will drive yourself mad, plus it's so none productive.' Yes, he's right, thought Easy. Something will come along. There has to be a way out of here. There just has to be . . .

Weeks passed into months, though still top dog Easy was progressively getting weaker.

Gypsy had shaken off her mortal coil some time ago, leaving him alone. He had decided to play a lone hand as he felt he was unable to master the mental energy to sustain any form of relationship, he could just about look after himself. He also knew the day was soon to arrive when he would be challenged for his leadership.

Plagued by the persistence of the woman he hated so much, true to her word, each time she entered the compound to remove the carcasses, the old hag made a point of searching for him.

He was constantly on the move, changing his dug-holes, trying to stay one step ahead. Sure, he had an edge; once the door of the compound opened, his ears pricked up, senses alert, ever vigilant, always on the move, another reason for him to go it alone..

The seasons passed slowly. Easy was aware that the days had shortened, as the sun went down and the night chill set in; he reasoned that a year had passed.

The once all-consuming passion to escape, the one thing that held him together, the confidence he had in his ability to find a way out, had began to dwindle.

In spite of the lack of food, he was almost fully grown, though about half the body weight one would expect for a dog of his size. More or less resigned to his fate, Easy reasoned that there's a strong possibility he would not last another year.

Then, it happened; one day, as he lay amongst the weeds and brambles, watching the usual squabbling at the dripping water tap, the latch clicked.

Easy's ears picked up to the rasping, as the bolts were drawn; the door swung open. He expected to see Katie standing there. No! Was this another chance to escape! His body was tense as he watched and waited.

Before he had time to contemplate a course of action, a large meat bone landed at the foot of the steps with a dull thud. Easy and the dogs milling around the tap were stunned into silence. Was she trying to lure him out of his hiding place! There's no way that's going to happen, he thought. He stood up ready to beat a hasty retreat, but froze in disbelief, as his worst nightmare was realised. Bounding down the steps came Big Bob, the Bull Mastiff, from Dalman, grasping the bone in his huge jaws whilst holding it down with his massive paws, at the same time raising his large, yellow, teeth to rip what little meat there was on the bone. In a matter of minutes, there was nothing left. With spittle drooling from his mouth forming a small frothy pool, Bill lay on his side and fell asleep.

Fascinated by what he had just witnessed and his attention riveted on Bob, Easy failed to see Katie, standing in the doorway; she glanced down at Bob, then locked and bolted the door. One again, the ailing dogs were penned in, cut off from the outside world. Easy made his way back to his latest dug-hole. As he lay there dozing, he remembered it was Saturday; how could he have forgotten the day! Not only was his body wasting away, he was becoming senile. He waited for his usual donations that came after Katie's visit to the butchers, which she threw to the waiting animals.

An hour had passed and nothing. What's going on? thought Easy. He had heard the other dogs fighting over the scraps. Why the delay? Something was amiss. A noise in the undergrowth caught his attention;

'At last, better late than never.' Sheree appeared, one of the bitches under his protection.

'Easy, I'm sorry to be the one to tell you!'

'Tell me what?' he interrupted.

'Well, it's that new dog Bob,' she said hesitantly.

'What about Bob?' asked Easy.

'He's . . . ! He's put the frighteners on me and the others, demanding their meagre amount of food they had salvaged. Either they hand it over or receive a severe beating or even death.' Sheree went on to say the other dogs were expecting him to sort Bill out.

Thanking her for the information, he replied, 'Spread the word. In a day or two, things will be back to normal,' thinking whatever that is.

It was quite obvious to Easy that something had to be done, as top dog it was expected of him. He knew that he was no match for the mastiff. Even fully fit, the dog was twice his size and healthy. The only thing in his favour was the element of surprise to pick the time and place for the confrontation or slink off and relinquish his position without a fight. There was no way he could dodge the issue; anyway his ego wouldn't allow that.

The next day, Easy rose at sun up and made his way to the tap. Standing in the foliage, he watched the dogs up to their usual antics. He hadn't long to wait before the mastiff was on the scene, barking and snapping and demanding priority at the slowly dripping water spout. Easy stepped onto the concrete, stood erect, his tail in the air, and barked, with the loudest voice he could muster, 'Stop! I said stop!'

The Mastiff turned slowly, with an air of confidence, drew himself up to his full height, barking, 'Are you talking to me,' as he padded forward to within three metres of Easy, his body tense.

'There's only one big ugly mutt standing on my patch. Yes, I am talking to you,' came the reply.

Bob couldn't believe his ears. Now somewhat wary, thinking, Who would have the audacity to challenge his authority. At heart, the Mastiff was a big coward, relying on his size, and belligerent approach to either frighten his opponents or make them slink off. Very rarely did he have to do battle, but here was this skinny animal, black in colour with a white torso and four white paws, fronting him out. Immediately, the mastiff's pinball brain reacted, this dog standing in front of him must have a gang to back him up.

'I know what you're thinking thicko, but you're wrong, I'm on my own, just you and me, you piece of shit.'

If this was true, which he doubted Bob had nothing to worry about. Maybe the dog facing him had lost his senses . . . It only took half a brain to see in a one-to-one situation, this black bag of bones wouldn't last two minutes.

'You're obviously sick. Do yourself a favour and hop it.' Being a coward, Bob knew he could easily overcome this scarecrow, but in the melee, he might get bitten and catch something.

'Sick, I may be but not sick enough to see off your ugly mug.'

Bob was bewildered; this was a blatant challenge.

Easy was relying on Bob's hesitancy, and as while they were barking at each other, he was slowly creeping forward. The other dogs stood quietely and waited for the outcome between the two antagonists.

'Well, I'll be.' said Bob. 'You're the little runt who used to run with Bernie in Dalman. You tried to join my gang, you little punk. True you've grown, grown into a bag of bones, but you're no match for me.' That said, it gave Easy a way out.

For him, there was no way out. This clash of leadership had to be settled now. He saw Bob visibly relaxing, no longer bothered by this would-be protagonist. This was his chance, Easy sped forward and jumped over the mastiff's back, under his legs, and fastened his jaws firmly on the underside of his neck.

Taken complete by surprise, it was a full five seconds before the mastiff realised what had happened, then he leapt into action. Shaking his head vigorously, he tried to dislodge Easy who was hanging on from grim death.

It was then that fate intervened, a voice from the upstairs window shouted, 'What's going on down there?' In that split second, Easy slackened his already tiring grip.

With a mighty shrug from his massive head, Bob was free. Free to set about mutilating this bag of bones, holding the weakened dog down, with his massive paws, he bit into Easy's flesh, tearing and ripping with pent-up fury. Easy had no defence; he was taking a hell of a beating and thinking, I won't come out of this alive.

Once again, fate intervened. The backdoor flew open and Katie gave the order to kill. Her hounds bounded down the steps to attack the mastiff. Realising that he was the target, Bob released his grip on Easy and turned to face the two would-be killers; already exhausted, he knew he had to move. A coward at heart, Bob legged into the undergrowth. The order came: 'Cease.' The hounds halted, followed by, 'Home,' and they trotted back in the house.

Before closing the door, Easy heard Kate say to herself, 'I don't want that runt killed. That pleasure is all mine.'

Easy lay in agony unable to move, the bites were open, bleeding wounds, half of his fur was missing. Totally exhausted, he awaited his fate; all through the day and chilly night, he expected Kate to drag him in and put him out of his misery.

Nothing happened, as the sun came up, Easy became aware of insects feeding off the blood that was seeping from his open wounds, ants crawling all over his body, picking and carrying off flakes of skin.

Utterly defeated and full of despair, he prayed for a quick death. His body already weakened through the lack of food and vitamins, had no more resistance and no means of repairing itself. This was the end, his body broken and his mind telling him his time was now.

Chapter 34

Katie looked at the photograph that George had given her; she recognised the woman she was sitting next to. Between them lay a pup with a black coat, his chest white, the same as his four paws. Over the last year, many dogs had passed through her hands or passed away. What she did remember was this couple from England had sent her plenty of money, and George was about to part with some more.

He had made it quite clear that he was prepared to stay for as long as it took to see the runt. She had already paved the way for the dog's demise by saying he'd been in a fight and was too ill to travel.

Mind you, she did say the last time he rang, that tomorrow he will have recovered enough, and she would meet George at the cafe as usual with the dog He sounded pleased saying he would bring the cash with him.

She had to either turn up with the dog or convince George he had taken a turn for the worse and passed away during the night. But then how would she get him to part with the money? Simple, she would convince him, she would use the cash to have a nice wooden coffin made and the dog buried in the animal cemetery. It was either that or turn up he animalt, which of course was impossible. Her mind was made up; she was sure that convincing George of the dogs overnight demise would not be a problem.

A quick glance through the window confirmed what she already knew, the troublesome runt was dying on the patio, and if not dead, it would be by the time she returned. Checking her watch, she noted it was ten thirty.

Knowing it would take half an hour or so to reach the café by cycle, she thought, I'd better make a move. I don't want to be late.

Closing and locking the front door, she mounted her tricycle and headed towards the rendezvous point. As she rode along, she thought through the story she was soon to tell George; convinced he would believe it, she smiled happily.

But something was bothering her; there was a nagging doubt. Fifteen minutes into her journey, she stopped, as images of the photo flicked through her mind concluding with the picture of the injured dog on her patio.

'How could I be so stupid!' she exclaimed. 'It's the same animal.'

She quickly realised George might well up the money to bury the dog, but the likelihood of him donating more in the future, she was unsure about. On the other hand, if she produced the dog injured, as a result of the fight with the Mastiff, she would say the money would help with the vet's bills, and once George returned to the UK, Katie could ask for more, implying it was needed to maintain the dog's upkeep; it was in her interest to keep the dog alive. Turning her cycle around, she peddled furiously back to the house. Letting herself in and calling her hounds to guard, she opened the backdoor, showing no compassion as she stood over the black-and-white, bleeding mess that lay at her feet. Instead, she looked toward the sky praying, 'Please, God, let this dog live.'

Easy heard the door open and, through his painful haze, was aware of Kate standing over him. That's it, he thought, she's here to finish me off. That would be a blessed relief. Tired and exhausted the wounds giving him unbearable pain, he wondered if his body would end up in the cooking pot; at least some of the other unfortunate animals would benefit. Regardless to what Bill had implied, Easy thought, Nobody could possibly be that callous to actually cook a dead dog, then feed its flesh to the animal friends.

Though in pain, Easy realised Kate was kneeling over him crying, crying real tears, saying, 'You poor little thing, please don't die. Katie will look after you.'

Easy thought, She's up to something. As his large brown eyes looked at her, he whimpered, 'You, evil bastard, there's not an ounce of compassion in you, so why the crocodile tears?'

Next thing he knew she had gathered him up, carried through the door and laid him gently on the kitchen table. Making sure the door was locked and bolted and her hounds inside, she put the kettle on and left the room. A few moments later, she re-entered the kitchen, carrying lint and cotton wool, plus a bottle of disinfectant. Pouring the hot water into a bowl, she added a few drops of the liquid and proceeded to clean his wounds.

Ten minutes later, she thought, Well, that's the best I can do, adding, if you last another two hours, I'll have you back here, and with any luck, the recipient of a healthy donation from George, to cover your upkeep for the following year.

'Look at the time, I'm already forty-five minutes late.' she said out loud.

Pulling a cushion off the sofa and gathering Easy in her arms, she passed through the front door, dropping the cushion into the basket of her tricycle and placing Easy on top. She then looped a heavy chain around his neck, held by a running noose. The remainder dumped unceremoniously in the basket on top of Easy, who once again whimpered; the weight of the chain lying heavily on his wounds.

Ordering her dogs to 'guard', she closed the front door, mounted her cycle, and peddled frantically towards the town, with Easy bumping up and down painfully in the basket.

George was seated in the cafe at ten forty-five. Having ordered coffee, he settled down for a long wait, as he knew from experience Kate would be late. The previous evening he had dined with his friends and confided in them, asking what he should do. The general opinion was Kate was stringing him along, and they all had doubts as to whether she would turn up with the dog and advised him not to part with anymore money until he saw the animal.

Tracey had offered to accompany him today as she thought, faced with another woman, asking awkward questions, they might be able to prise the truth out of her. George declined the offer saying that he preferred to play a lone hand.

Looking at his watch, he realised already she was twenty minutes late. It was quite possible she might not turn up at all. The police had told him outright that they were unable to build a case against her through the lack of witnesses and hard evidence of money changing hands.

George was stumped; his main concern was how to break the news to Mary that the dog had died, and he knew that she would be heartbroken.

Easy wondered why Kate had dressed his wounds; it didn't make sense. One thing he knew for sure; he was too weak to jump out of the basket and wherever she was heading could only mean she was taking him somewhere away from prying eyes, so as to take her revenge by torturing him and ultimately disposing of his body. If that was the case, why dress his wounds.

Every bump the cycle passed over was agony, sending shooting pains throughout his entire body, the heavy chain scraping his open wounds. Finally, they came to a stop; Kate dismounted and lifted Easy out of the basket.

Looking around, Easy became aware that this place was familiar; his sense of smell told him they were in the vicinity of the sea.

'Come along, darling. We haven't far to go,' she said sweetly, at the same time pulling savagely on the chain, muttering, 'Don't you dare peg out on me now, you mangy bastard, after all I've done for you.'

What's wrong with this woman? Easy thought. It was obvious she wasn't right in the head, and certainly had violent mood swings. She dragged him along the deserted streets, probably to avoid other people, thought Easy, in case they remarked on his condition. His mind was made up; should the chain slacken, he would summon his remaining strength and take a bite out of her body, anywhere would do, just to leave her with a painful reminder of his existence.

For the umpteenth time, George looked at his watch. She's already over an hour late; perhaps she's not coming after all. The waiter came over saying, 'Would sir like another coffee?' But really meaning you can't sit here all day without ordering some food.

George got the message and asked him for the bill. Having settled with the waiter George stood up, not sure what to do. Then out of the corner of his eye, he spotted Kate making her way towards him through the palm trees that were dotted around the dock. She waved at George; he returned the gesture. As she neared, he realised she was dragging something on the end of a chain.

Could it be? George thought, as his heart upped the pace. Yes, it was a dog. Stupid, what else would she be pulling along! She reached the table and sat down.

'How are you?' She said, 'Sorry to be so late. When you're looking after so many animals times not your own.'

'Yes! Quite!' George replied, his eyes transfixed on what appeared to be a seriously underfed, emaciated animal, with open wounds seeping blood, and, if he was not mistaken, insects living and crawling all over its body.

George stood up, his face a mask of fury, his heart hammering in his chest, his hands clenched into fists. Trying to control the rage he felt. The urge to throttle the life out of this evil women, threatened to overtake him. He said through gritted teeth, 'Order whatever you like, Kate, I'll have a coffee. You must excuse me as I have an urgent need for the toilet. Be back in a minute.' Turning, he strode purposely toward the Gents. Once through the door, George's frustration boiled over into an uncontrollable rage. Pounding the cubicle door with both fists, he let vent to his anger. 'How could she. The woman's inhuman.' Thump! Thump! I feel like smashing her face in, better still throw her in the dock and let her drown.

As his mind wrestled with endless possibilities of what he should do to Katie, George realised he had stopped thumping the toilet door.

'Are you all right in there?' came a voice.

'What?' replied George.

'I said, are you okay?'

'Er! Yes, I'm fine. I slipped over and bumped my head. No problem.'

The outer door slammed shut. George's heart rate was slowing towards its normal pace. Already swollen, the pain he felt in his grazed knuckles of his right hand made George focus. How am I going to explain that away, he thought.

Now much calmer, George realised he had to think things through before returning. His first priority was to take charge of the pup; why he kept referring to Easy as a pup: heaven knows. True, the poor thing is a bag of bones and well under weight, but a year had passed since George had last seen him; his height had doubled and now he is almost fully grown. Secondly, as Mary had said, don't upset Katie, as we need the connection she has in Holland regarding the British quarantine laws.

Don't upset her, if Mary could see the state of the poor animal, she would probably kill Kate herself.

George knew he had spent far too long in the toilet. Also, there really wasn't any point in trying to plan a strategy as he had no idea as to which way Katie would bounce

Forcing a smile on his face, George returned to the table to a lukewarm coffee and Kate sipping a soda.

'Sorry, I was so long, must be something I ate this morning,' said George, avoiding looking at the dog and lifting the cup with his left hand.

'Touch of Delhi belly,' said Katie with a smile. Inwardly fuming, George smiled back. Katie went on, 'As you can see, the dog is still recovering from the fight. It really took a lot out of him. A few weeks of TLC, and he'll be fine.'

George nodded, not trusting himself to open his mouth. Looking at the poor wasted animal, it was blatantly obvious that Easy was undernourished; if he weighed seven kilos, that would be an overestimation. Filled with anger and frustration, he blurted out, 'He's so thin and looks very ill.'

'Oh, that's because of the dysentery he contracted from the other dogs. That's why I need the money to pay the vet for treatment. Have you brought it with you?'

Still struggling with his anger, George reached into his inside pocket with his left hand, withdrew the three hundred pounds, and handed it over.

Once again, his anger threatened to explode, but remembering Mary's parting words;

'We need her connection in Holland.'

George suppressed the urge to strangle Kate and asked about her Dutch friends.

'No problem,' came the reply, 'but it will be expensive.'

'How expensive?' asked George.

'I need to get the dog fit and well first, and then I'll make a few calls and let you know.'

It all seemed quite plausible, but as his eyes took in the pitiable condition of his dog lying between them with the heavy chain around his neck. He felt like saying, What happened to the new collar and leash that me and Mary had brought? but he kept quiet.

George knew in his heart of hearts he had to get the dog away from this evil woman. Picking the chain off the floor and gently patting the dog, it occurred to him not once had she mentioned Easy by name or did she attempt to pet him.

George knew he had the right dog, the markings were the same as in the photographs; four white paws, the chest and nose the same colour. He stood up left, left enough money on the table for the waiter plus a healthy tip, and made to move off.

'Where are you taking him?' Kate asked, with a hint of alarm in her voice.

'I thought Easy and I would spend the rest of the day together and get re-acquainted. I'll probably stay the night and meet you here tomorrow the same time.'

'Oh! I see. Yes, of course, right, you and Easy,' she said, hesitatingly.

Once again, George thought that's the first time she had mentioned the dog's name. He walked off towards the water fountain, thinking, there's no way Easy was going back to that monster.

Chapter 35

Easy, though very weak, realised he was free from that terrible woman, and if he was not mistaken, it was the same man that rescued him last year.

Walking was very painful, and to make matters worse, the weight of the chain slowed his pace and chafed his neck.

The circular parapet that surrounded the fountain was insurmountable for him, in his weakened state. He didn't have the energy or the strength to lift himself over. The thought of all that fresh water waiting for him added to his frustration. He lay against the fountain, thinking, a year ago he would have jumped over the wall, splashed around, and drank till his thirst was sated. All he could manage now was to lie down and listen as the water swirled and splattered in its concrete fountain..

'What's the matter, boy, not thirsty?' said George as Easy slumped down, his tongue hanging from his jaws.

Easy whined and gave a low bark trying to wag his tail to communicate his desperate plight.

George looked down at the neglected dog, not sure what to do; he had no experience with animals. Surely, the thought, the dog must be thirsty. The temperature is well into the nineties, so why is he lying there, maybe he's happy just being here.

Taking out his camera George fired off a few shots, thinking the photos may well be useful if the police ever got Kate into a courtroom.

The unremitting whining had George worried, not knowing what to do with the animal. There's one thing, I can do, that is to get rid of this awful chain, reaching down, George lifted the chain from around Easy's neck, thinking I'll keep hold of that, might well be useful as evidence.

With the weight of the chain no longer dragging him down, Easy made an effort to mount the parapet but fell back in an untidy heap. Seeing this made George think, Maybe the dog's too weak to clamber over, that's it! How could I be so stupid? Bending down, he gently lifted Easy and placed him in the fountain, the whining stopped.

Easy lapped greedily at the cool liquid and drank his fill; the swirling motion of the water as it moved around the fountain cooled his aching body and washed his open wounds. Easy lay down and enjoyed the soothing effect of the whole experience.

'Stay!' said George, 'Stay there, boy, I'll be back in a minute with a new collar and leash for you.' Not understanding the command, Easy was content to sit in the fountain, as there was no way could he get out unaided.

George remembered the pet shop from his previous visits, situated next to the hardware store. He thought, I had better hurry in case the dog runs away. Idiot, the dogs not going anywhere. He's too ill.

Five minutes later, George was back with a new collar, leash, and a bag of dog biscuits.

Gently lifting the dog out of the fountain, George opened the biscuits and offered the animal some.

Shaking the surplus water from his soaking body, Easy could hardly believe his luck, first the water and now the food; even in his weakened state, he greedily gobbled down the biscuits and sat looking with his brown eyes pleading for more.

George was about to oblige, when it occurred to him that the dog was obviously severely undernourished, and if he fed him too much, on a shrunken stomach, there was a strong possibility he might do more harm than good.

'Steady, boy, more later. Let's get you to Dalman and let the vet take a look at you,' he said, placing the collar around his neck. Then George made his way slowly to the taxi rank that stood adjacent to the bus station.

Approaching the leading car, he inquired how much it would cost to take him to where he was staying in Dalman.

'Forty euros,' came the reply, 'but if you intend to take the dog, it will be a further one hundred and fifty.'

'That's outrageous,' exclaimed George. 'Why so much?'

'With those wounds seeping blood, I will have to clean my cab out, which will take time and cost me money in fares,' the driver answered.

George thought, That's far too expensive, I'll go by bus. Having made the journey before, he knew the price to be fifty Turkish Lira.

Leaving Easy tied to a lamppost, he approached the bus driver;

'Can my dog travel with me?'

'Yes,' came the reply, 'but he will have to ride in the luggage compartment. It's well ventilated. We leave in five minutes.'

Walking back to where he had left Easy, he unhitched the dog and made his way to the rear of the bus, trying to shield him from the eyes of the driver.

'He's in a bit of a state,' said the man.

'I know. He's been in an accident and I'm taking him to a vet in Dalman,' replied George, lying through his teeth.

'Lucky for you the bus is half full, and the luggage compartment is empty.'

George lifted Easy in to the compartment, the driver closed the door. Entering the small bus, George counted fifteen seats, and finding a seat at the rear of the bus, George sat down somewhat relieved.

Like the ferries, the buses were run by the corporation and most of the drivers were able to converse in passable English. Thirty minutes later, the bus pulled into the station at Dalman.

George paid the driver, waited till the vehicle was empty, and then disembarked himself. As he quickly lifted Easy out of the luggage compartment, he noticed an old rug. He asked the driver if he might have it to wrap Easy in. 'You're welcome,' came the reply. Carrying Easy, he headed towards the vet's; he felt the animal wriggling and realised it was uncomfortable, probably to hot for him, plus the blanket was rubbing against his sore skin. Dropping the rug in the nearest bin, he placed Easy on the pavement and made his way slowly to the vet's, located next door to the pet shop opposite the petrol station. George noticed that people were giving him funny looks, as if he was to blame for the dog's condition.

Giving Easy two more biscuits, he said, 'I'll soon have you there boy, then we'll get you treated and make you well again.'

They arrived some ten minutes later and, to George's consternation, found the door closed. Tying Easy to the hitching post, he entered the pet shop next door to inquire what time the vet opened.

'Not till Monday morning,' came the reply.

Monday morning, of course, today is Sunday, he realised. Leaving the pet shop, he checked on the business hours posted on the inside of the vet's door. Nine o'clock was opening time; he would have to revise his plans.

Unhitching Easy and feeding him two more biscuits, he slowly made his way to the Aparto Hotel, where he was staying. Tying Easy to the lamp post, George made his way to the reception desk to explain his predicament he was in and could Easy stay in his room till tomorrow morning.

The receptionist was very sympathetic, but unfortunately, he was not able to grant George's request, adding, the Manager was, but would be back shortly, adding that the owner's office was located across the road in the other hotel complex, next to the bakery. Thanking the man, George walked down the marble stairs, untied Easy, and made his way across the road to the English tea shop opposite the hotel. Sitting outside, he ordered tea and cream scones, plus a bowl of water for the dog.

Gilly, the English waitress, served him and listened to his story. Full of concern for the dog, she remarked if she wasn't mistaken that's the same dog that used to beg outside the shop last year.

Easy lay down in the shade, under the table, once again grateful for the water and a few biscuits the man had fed him, not understanding why he wasn't given more. Yes, he thought, this is definitely the same place. It was here the English people had their afternoon tea. His mind drifted back to when he ran free; it must have been about this time last year, when that little girl petted and fed him. He looked across the road and noticed the flower beds where he and his old mentor used to sleep. His damaged body hurt, but his mind was saying, I'm free, free at last.

During the last months of his incarceration, he had all but given up on his attempts to escape from that awful woman, who seemed hell bent on destroying him. One thing he was sure of, in a matter of days, this man would return to his country and probably leave him in the care of someone else. What if! Here I go again, he thought, What if, stop it, there's no point in speculating as to the future. His mind was made up; he would stay with this man as long as possible, and hopefully, he would have sufficient time to build his strength up, and then escape. Once back on the streets, he knew that fending for himself was his sole responsibility. In spite of his aches and pains, Easy found himself drifting into a contented sleep.

Noticing this, George asked Gilly to keep an eye on his hound, whilst he sought out the hotel owner.

Walking down the road and across the junction George found his office next to the bakery, adjacent to where the hotel buses stood, in a neat uniform line.

The office door was open; he tapped smartly on the glass.

'Come in,' said a voice.

George entered; to his right was a young lady sitting behind a desk, pouring over a computer. At the rear end of the office behind a large oak desk sat a somewhat oversized man, with a mobile up to his ear, in a deep conversation, speaking in his native language Turkish. Gesturing to George to sit, at the same time holding up one finger indicating he would be finished on the phone soon.

The owner was a jovial man, capable of speaking several languages, self-made and proud of it. George could not help but notice two huge piles of money on either side of his desk; one pile was euros and the other Turkish Lira, obviously waiting to be counted.

Finishing his conversation, the owner stood up and shook Georges hand firmly, saying, 'What can I do for you, George?' One of Mr Yuris attributes was he never forgot a name, this giving the impression that his guests were very important to him and he, personally was there to tend to their every need.

George briefly outlined his situation and asked if Easy could be allowed to stay in his room till the vet opened in the morning. Slapping George heartily on the back, the owner boomed, 'No problem, no problem at all, providing the animal doesn't upset my other guest.'

As Georges friends were staying on the same floor, he knew they wouldn't mind. Thanking the owner, George hurried back to the cafe to collect Easy. Crossing the road to the hotel with the dog and mounting the stairs to the reception, George noticed Easy was having problems climbing the marble stairs. In fact, he was unable to mount even the first step. Perhaps he's too weak, thought George, or the steps are too high. Then it dawned on him. His nails, the dog's nails, they were too long; he was unable to gain any purchase on the marble and was slipping and sliding. Gathering Easy in his arms, George spoke to the receptionist telling him that Mr Yuris had given the okay for the dog to stay. The man nodded and smiled. With Easy safely in his arms, George made his way up to his room, at the same time thinking this animal barely weighs seven kilos, at his age he should be nearer twenty five.

Once in the room, George took the spare blanket from the top of the wardrobe and placed Easy on it.

As Easy sank into the soft blanket, he thought, Luxury, what a difference from his old dug-hole, and immediately fell asleep. Sometime later, he was woken by George who had showered and changed.

'Come on, boy, we're going to eat,'

Easy's body ached all over as he stood up and yawned. He tried to stretch but couldn't; it hurt so much. I need a pee, he thought. Looking at George, he whined.

Gathering the dog in his arms George closed the door and made his way down to the reception, where the others of his group where waiting.

'Shan't be a minute. I think Easy needs to do something. See you outside,' he said to no one in particular.

The group followed him out.

Placing Easy on the ground, George gently led him along the flower beds, to the piece of open ground.

Having relieved himself, Easy thought, I needed that, as he was led back to where the group was waiting,

George realised the dog's movements were slow and laborious.

Addressing his friends, he said, 'I'll give it a miss if you don't mind. I know it's our last evening together, but the dog needs to rest. I'll order a pizza and eat in my room. Enjoy your meal.'

Tracey said, 'That's okay, George. We understand. Catch you later.'

They had decided to eat at Abrahams. He found them a table outside the restaurant in the corner under the canopy. They all decided to treat themselves to a steak platter. The food was served on a rectangular wooden board, the outer edge completely surrounded by twirls of creamed potatoes; on one side, the steak lay, cooked the way each individual liked it. On the other side were sauté potatoes, fresh asparagus, diced carrots, and runner beans, and the steak was topped with a sauce of the diners' own choosing.

The conversation soon turned to the dog . . . What were George's plans? And how would Mary react to Easy's condition?

Later that evening, after eating and taking Easy once again for a pooh and pee, George settled him down on the soft blanket. It was time he called Mary. She answered immediately, first inquiring as to the dog's welfare, then, as an afterthought how he was keeping. George thought, Charming. Already the dog was first in line for Mary's affections. Outlining the events of the day, George chose to tell her only of Easy's general condition relating to his injuries incurred whilst fighting the mastiff, adding he was seeing the vet at nine the next morning to have his wounds treated and, depending on the vet's examination, whatever else he suggested or he deemed necessary, reminding Mary that Easy had been badly mauled and it was touch and go as to whether he would make it, thus once again, paving the way if the dog had to be put down. Saying goodnight to Mary, George put down the phone; it rang immediately.

'George,' said a lady's voice, 'It's me, Tracey.'

'Hi, Trace, how are you?'

'Well, but quite tired,' came the reply.

Tracey was a recovering alcoholic and drug user, who had finally got her act together.

'George, it occurred to me that in the morning, you won't be able to take the dog into the dining room.'

Interrupting, George said, 'I'll forgo breakfast and go straight to the vet's.'

'No need for that. If you meet me outside at eight o'clock, I'll sit with Easy while you have breakfast. Then you can take over and head for the vet's.'

'Never thought of that. Thanks, Trace. See you at eight o'clock then. Night . . . '

Chapter 36

In the back recesses of his mind, Easy heard his name being called . . .
'Easy, wake up, boy,' then with more urgency, 'Good boy! Wake up.'

Slowly, he drifted into consciousness, aware that someone was calling
him; his eyes flickered and opened; he felt disorientated not able to adjust
to what he saw. Moments passed before he realised that his body lay on a
soft surface and not in his usual dug-hole. Now fully awake, his eyes told
him he was lying in the man's room. Seconds passed as he familiarised
himself with the previous day's events. Was he free, really free? His inner
eye conjured up images of the concrete hellhole, the slow and painful
degeneration of both mind and body, the futile attempts to escape, pictures
of his old friends and their last few hours as they faded away, and the battle
with Big Bob that could only have one outcome. He inwardly he winced as
each blow from the steel rod wielded by that evil crone, thudded into his
emaciated body. Stop it, Easy . . . It's over. You're free, but what about the
others? They are still suffering? The sound of the man's voice echoed in his
head, 'Get up, boy! Get up! I'm taking you to the vet.'

Shaking with the effort, he managed to stand, Now, fully awake and
aware of his lacerated body, he tried to lick the patches where his fur had
been torn out, but they were far too sore.

Bringing his mind into focus as the man connected the leash to his
collar, Easy thought, Vet! What's vet?

'Good boy, its breakfast time. You can have a few biscuits now. I know you are hungry, but you'll have to take it steady until your digestive system can adjust to regular food. Drink some water. You'll feel better.'

Easy greedily lapped at the bowl of fresh water lying beside him; his thirst sated, he looked at the kind man, who stooped down and gently cradled him in his arms and left the room. As they approached the marble stairs, Easy felt safe in the mans arms knowing he was unable to negotiate them due to his long nails. Once outside the hotel, George met with Tracey who was sitting on a bench located outside the main entrance.

'Morning, Trace, sleep well?'

'Yes, thanks, George. How is the poor thing?'

'Better for a night's sleep, but he's obviously in pain.'

Putting him gently down next to Tracey, who Easy remembered from the night before, the man said, 'Stay there, boy. Shan't be long. A quick breakfast, then off to the vet.'

Vet, the same word again, it must be for my own good, thought Easy. I'll find out when we get there.

George never much of a breakfast man, drank two cups of coffee, ate a few pieces of melon followed by a bowl of cereal. Having exchanged pleasantries with the rest of his travelling companions, he was back outside the hotel to relieve Tracey.

'Thanks, Trace,' said George.

'No problem,' she said, noting the strained tension on George's face. 'You take care and good luck at the vet's,' she said, thinking he needed more than luck.

Tracey had been around animals all her life, and in her opinion, the dog's chances of survival were not good, best not to voice her concern, which would only succeed in adding further stress to an already overburdened George.

'Remember, the hotel bus leaves at seven for the airport,' she added.

'Er! Yes, right,' said George, his mind pre-occupied with Easy's condition and the possible consequences and options open to him after the vet had examined the animal.

'Come on, boy! Up! We're off to the vet's.' Gently helping Easy to his feet, he said, 'The sooner he checks you out, the quicker he can make you better.'

There it was again, thought Easy, the word 'vet'. Struggling to his feet and wagging his tail, he made to follow George's lead. Every step was a painful reminder of the hardship and trauma he had suffered during the last year, yet somehow he knew this vet was going to help him.

Some ten minutes later, George announced, 'Here we are. You've made it.' At this point, Easy was unable to control his bowel movements and defecated outside the door.

George entered, apologising for Easy's unfortunate accident.

'Not to worry!' exclaimed the vet, calling on his assistant to fetch a pail of water and broom and wash down the pavement.

George briefly explained the situation leading up to present time, omitting to say the acute embarrassment he felt as people muttered, 'What a state the dog is in' and the accusing eyes as they passed. One out-spoken woman had accosted him saying, she would report him to the authorities. George felt obliged to stop and explain the situation; she immediately apologised and said how she admired George's dedication to the poor animal.

The vet ushered George into a small office and pointed to a chair inviting him to sit, with Easy lying by his side. In broken English, he asked what he could do. George started to relate once again the whole sordid business but quickly realised the vet was having considerable difficulty in understanding what was being said and what George wanted. Watching the man's reaction, George could see the concern in his eyes; it certainly looked quiet discouraging.

The vet indicated for George to stay where he was and left through the front door. George sat and waited gently murmuring words of encouragement to his dog at the same time thinking there's no way the dog could understand him; the few commands he might be familiar with would obviously be in Turkish. George hoped the tone of his voice would at least sound reassuring.

A few minutes past and the vet returned, followed by a tall, lean, weather-beaten man, who introduced himself as Ronald originally from Sweden, who owned a restaurant a few doors along from the vet's establishment. Having lived in Turkey for the past thirty years, he was fluent in his command of the language.

George quickly updated Ronald as to the situation and the need for a full examination to access Easy's condition.

Ronald related to the vet what was needed, who promptly led the dog into his surgery. George passed the time, talking to the restaurant owner, and offered to pay for his time. Ronald would have none of it, saying most of his customers were expats and he was only too pleased to help.

Once in the surgery, Easy was lifted onto a metal table and was subjected to all manner of tests. Lights shone in his eyes, a metal probe inserted inside his ears, then a round flat object placed on his chest that was attached to two lengths of tubing terminating in each of the vet's ears. His chest and legs were felt by the vet's hands and rather indignantly his rear end was probed. Finally, as he laid on the table, a square type of machine was passed over his body as the vet moved him in various positions.

Lifting him off the table, he was taken through to the office, where the two men were waiting. Through Ronald, the vet explained there were no broken bones, only superficial injuries, but he was unable to tell how his vital organs were functioning until he received the results of the blood test. At this stage, he wasn't prepared to comment on Easy's chances of survival. Should the dog survive, George intended to take him out of Turkey and a passport was needed. This required immunisation for Rabies and vaccinations for other various common diseases associated with dogs, plus a microchip to be inserted into the animal's neck. All this information was passed on through Ronald.

Pressing the vet once again, George asked, 'What were the dog's chances?'

Noting the urgency in George's voice, he replied, 'If all his vital organs are functioning, with vitamin injections and nursing, his chances are good,' once again stressing that the vital organs had to be okay, and it would involve George in a great deal of expense.

George thanked Ronald for his assistance.

'Glad to be of some help. If you need any further assistance, here's my phone number,' he said, handing George a business card.

'That's very kind of you.' I'm leaving for London this evening, so I will need someone to liaise with the vet if you don't mind.

'No problem,' came the reply, 'ring any time.' He offered his hand to George, who shook it warmly.

'Well, I must be off. I have a restaurant to run. Talk to you soon.'

'Just before you go, would you mind asking the vet to give me some idea as to the cost of treatment plus the boarding of Easy for three weeks, as I intend to return. Hopefully, the dog will be on the mend, should it survive.' Could you also tell him I will pay half the fees now and the rest on my return. If he is unable to save the dog, I will send the outstanding balance via Western Union.

Ronald spoke to the vet who nodded in agreement and immediately started to write on the desk pad.

'It will take a while,' said Ronald.

'Okay, I'll pop down to the bank while he's sorting it out. Could you tell him that?'

'Sure' said Ronald. 'He'll have the cost ready for you by the time you return.'

'Thanks,' said George as Ronald disappeared through the door.

George stood up, patted Easy gently who was lying on the floor, then he left.

Easy lay there confused, Was the kind man leaving him here with this other person who moments ago was pushing and prodding him. Maybe he's the vet I keep hearing about. He seems kind enough and that other room had a nice clean smell to it. Whatever happens to me, it has to be better than that hellhole. Perhaps, this vet man will feed me and treat my wounds. I hope so . . .

George was back from the bank in twenty minutes, much to Easy's surprise who wagged his tail and barked.

'Miss me already?' said George, patting Easy gently.

Addressing the vet, George asked about the cost. The vet handed him a sheet of paper on the left side written in Turkish appeared a column of words presumably a list of treatments, next to these the cost in Liras at the bottom of the page, the figure of seven hundred euros; a lot less than George had expected. Handing the vet four hundred as a deposit indicating by pointing at the calendar hanging on the wall, he would settle the rest on his return in three weeks.

Ronald having explained to the vet George's intentions, the vet smiled his approval and wrote out a receipt, handing it to George's his face beaming.

They shook hands.

Bending down, George patted Easy, saying 'You're safe now.' Knowing full well the dog did not understand, adding, 'I'll will be back to collect you.' He departed with tears in his eyes.

Not knowing what was happening, once again Easy was thrown into uncertainty as to his future, and he lay on the floor whining. Stop it, he said to himself, this is stupid. I'm far better off considering the trauma of the past year. The feeling of loneliness threatened to engulf him. The kind man is gone. I've been passed on to someone else. I'll bide my time, and when fit and well, I'll re-appraise my situation, he thought, with the possibility of escape never far from his mind.

George hastened back to the hotel to pack, now committed to returning; he knew Mary would agree with his decision. As free agents, they had discussed buying a motorhome and touring Europe, sometime in the near future, why not now? Why wait?

Over the preceding months, George having checked out various vehicles, one in particular had caught his eye; one owner, low mileage, immaculate condition, a full service record. There was a strong possibility it may still be available because the asking price was well over the market value.

Should his worst fears become apparent and Easy did not survive, George had made up his mind; this is one tourist who would have his day in court when that woman was prosecuted, whatever the cost; he would be there to give evidence.

Back at the hotel, he called Mary to update her, as to the outcome of his visit to the vet being careful not to alarm her, but using Katie's excuse saying the animal had contracted dysentery and the vet had taken some blood samples to ascertain its general health, thus preparing her should the dog not survive.

Mary now aware that George was committed, and had to return to Turkey, she greeted his suggestion to bring forward the purchase of a motorhome with great enthusiasm.

'Let's do it!' she exclaimed. 'As soon as you return, we'll buy that one that took your fancy if it is still available.'

Chapter 37

So the idea of escaping was put on the back-burner. His rescuer had left leaving him with the vet-man. He was somewhat nervous but happy to be out of Kats's hands. Easy thought, I'll wait and see how events unfold. The kind man had barely left when the vet untied the leash and led him through the back room into a much larger enclosed area. His eyes took in the surroundings; four large metal cages were sited along one wall, about a metre apart, two were empty, the third occupied by a dachshund with his rear left leg encased in what appeared to be a white substance, he was later to find out was plaster; around the small dog's neck appeared to be a large funnel; the dog was asleep.

Easy's leash was undone, then he was gently ushered into the cage. For a brief moment he felt the urge to panic and in his weakened state started to struggle.

'It's okay, boy. Nobody is going to hurt you,' said the soothing voice of the vet, in native language as the metal door closed behind him.

Immediately, Easy noticed the floor was covered in fresh-smelling straw and a large bowl of water stood in the corner. Plenty of light shone through the metal bars which penetrated through the large glass windows set in the surrounding walls. Well, at least I'm warm and comfortable, he thought.

The vet departed closing the door behind him. Lying down and making himself comfortable, he was aware that his tummy had started to rumble. My! I am hungry. A muted bark caught his attention; the other dog, two cages along had woken up and somewhat irritably was asking, 'Who are you?'

Not liking his attitude, Easy replied with a louder bark, 'Never mind me. Who are you?'

'I asked first,' came the reply. 'Now answer my question. What's your name?'

Easy's heckles rose this cheeky little excuse for a dog, looking more like a salami sausage, was trying to dominate him; a year in Kate's hellhole if nothing else had taught him how to handle these little whip-a-snappers. Barking even louder, he said, 'I'm not interested in who asked who first. I'm telling you, you miserable little runt, and why have you got your head stuck through a funnel?'

'Who are you calling a runt, you skinny, flea-bitten street dog? I'll have you know that I'm a thoroughbred.'

'More like a loaf of bread, I could put you between two slices and eat you for lunch.'

'What?' came the reply. 'I'll have you know I'm high born and have a long line of ancesters, so you don't want to mess with me, as for the so-called funnel around my neck, it's to stop me chewing on the plaster around my broken leg.'

'High born are you . . . Yes, of course, you are. All that inbreeding has obviously left you a little retarded, so shut it, I want to sleep.'

With an even louder bark, the dog said, 'Who are you calling retarded? I'll have you know that I have a high IQ'

'That may well be, but street wise you're a dumbo, so be quiet and let me sleep.'

Easy waited for a reply . . . nothing, silence. In truth, the barking exchange with the little sausage dog had drained him mentally; this plus his physical condition left him exhausted. With nothing coming back from the sausage, Easy drifted into a deep sleep.

Sometime later, he woke with a start with the noise of the cage opening disturbed his slumber. The vet-man attached a leash to his collar and led him into the surgery, then lifted him onto the metal table.

'There's a good boy,' said the vet. 'This won't hurt. I'm going to give you a vitamin shot to help build up your strength. Soon, you'll be on solid food and feeling a lot better.'

Not knowing what was going on, Easy lay still his senses told him that this vet-man was helping him. Much to his surprise, he was lifted off the table and taken through to the back room. He expected to be returned to his cage, but no he was led through the back door, which opened onto a large garden. As if talking to himself, the vet-man said, 'A twenty minute walk will help the vitamins to circulate into your system more quickly.'

Easy felt quite happy to walk, even though he was still in some pain; it even gave him time for a pooh and pee.

Once settled back in his cage, he found fresh water in his bowl and a small quantity of a mashed mixture in a second container that had been placed next to the water. Somebody must have put it there when I was out walking, thought Easy. The mixture looked disgusting, but smelt nice and tasted even better as he gobbled it all down.

A soft bark caught his attention.

'How are you?' inquired the dachshund.

Expecting another boisterous exchange, Easy barked curtly, 'None the better for your asking.'

'I'm sorry to hear that,' came the reply. 'I would like to apologise for my behaviour this morning. It was not befitting for a dog of my stature to act that way.'

Here we go again, thought Easy. His snooty attitude reminded him of Harry the Husky he used to run with. Harry had no conception as to how the other half lived their lives and had to learn the hard way on the streets of Dalman. As his mind drifted back to the days before he was unfortunate to fall into the hands of Kate and the cruelty he suffered, his inner eye conjured up pictures of Jack, Bernie, and Barney, his old mentor. Their images now fading, the sadness he felt threatened to overwhelm him. Stop it, Easy. Stop it now! he said to himself. There's nothing to be gained dwelling in the past.

A soft bark interrupted his reminiscing, once again saying, 'Are you sure you're okay. You had me worried with your silence?'

'Yes! Yes! I'm quite all right. Thanks for your concern.'

'My name's Molly by the way. I've been here for three days and unable to exercise because of my broken leg, which itches terribly, and with this blasted contraption around my neck, I'm unable to scratch it. That's what made me so irritable this morning, and you just happened to be in the line of fire.'

'Apology accepted,' replied Easy. 'I must admit I've been through a tough time myself.'

'I'm sorry to hear that,' replied Molly. 'You look so thin and undernourished. How did that come about?'

Easy was about to launch into the whole sordid story but thought better of it. Changing the subject, he inquired,

'When do you get to go home?'

'Tomorrow,' came the reply. 'My owners are coming to collect me, and you?' Molly asked.

'I don't know what will happen to me. I'll have to wait until I'm fit and well.'

The next day, once again, Easy was taken into the surgery for more injections, only this time the vet's assistant led him out for a walk. As he passed Molly's cage, she wished him luck, saying, 'I'll probably be gone by the time you get back. Hope everything works out for you.'

This time, his walk lasted longer, and having finished his ablutions, he was led back.

Although very tired, the pain he had been enduring seemed to diminish, and already, he was feeling better.

The fact that Molly was no longer present made him feel a little sad.

Much to his surprise, sometime later, he was once again led into the surgery, only this time he was placed in a tank and sprayed with some smelly liquid by the vet. Not liking this, he tried to jump out, but the vet's assistant held him firmly at the same time whispering words of encouragement. Not that he was afraid of water, more the fear of the unknown. At least, the liquid was warm, and after the initial shock, he found the experience quite pleasant.

Images flooded back to the time he hurt his leg and was told to sit in the marina and the children playing thought he was drowning, after lifting him out in all good faith handed him to the dog catchers. He was lucky to escape; if his memory served him right, it was one of Big Bob's band that latched on to the catchers ankle who promptly dropped him, and in that split second, he was able to run off and avoid capture. In Easy's mind, that event seemed to have happened ages ago.

His mind returned to the present; the assistant hoisted him out of the tank and placed him on the metal table. There was a gentle flow of warm air emanating from a metal object held by the assistant. Once again, he found this new experience very comforting as his body and fur slowly dried out.

Having now got used to a routine, on the fourth day, everything changed. Once again, he was placed on the metal table, the difference being a small nozzle was placed over his snout as he lay on his side. This he found quite disturbing; the urge to panic threatened to overwhelm him. Fighting his natural instinct to struggle, he felt the tension slip away from his body, as he drifted off to sleep. Pictures flickered through his mind, a kaleidoscope of images seemingly unconnected, until finally, nothing . . .

Sometime later, Easy awoke to find himself lying in his cage. As he slowly returned to consciousness, he realised strapped around his neck was a funnel, similar to the one that hung on Molly. To add to his confusion, there was some minor pain between his back legs plus an urge to scratch that particular area.

It would be a further two days before the funnel was taken off and Easy realised a vital part of his anatomy was missing . . .

Chapter 38

The flight back to England was uneventful. As promised, Mary was there to meet him. The group, having agreed to meet the following Friday, shook hands, said their goodbyes, and went their separate ways.

Mary was chomping at the bit for news about Easy.

'How's the dog?' she asked.

'Yes, I had a great trip back. Thank you,' came the rather sardonic reply.

'Sorry, George, it's just that I'm so concerned about him.'

George couldn't resist the need to say, 'I know, dear. As usual, I'm number two in the pecking order.'

'Oh, don't be so silly, you daft man.'

As they drove back to Barnes, South West London, George brought Mary up to date on Easy's situation, careful not to alarm her but at the same time reminding her of the serious nature regarding the dog's condition.

'I promised the vet I would return in three weeks to collect Easy, giving him time to thoroughly check out his condition. If the results of the blood test are positive, we can vaccinate him against any local diseases plus a rabies jab and insert a microchip. He was quite positive he would have the blood test results through, and if all was well, his passport would be ready when we collect him. Apparently we need it to take the dog out of Turkey into an EU country. I thought we might head for Spain to your brother's and spend Christmas with him and the family. The trip should be relatively simple if I follow the Mediterranean coast and at the same time visiting all those wonderful places we promised ourselves . . . '

'But, George, this is all so sudden,' interrupted Mary. 'We need time to prepare for such a long journey. We're nearly home. Now let's think it through and talk about it after a good night's sleep.'

The very next morning, Mary was full of questions; she had had a sleepless night and risen an hour before George to prepare a list of things that needed to be sorted before they left England. She found it difficult to contain her enthusiasm during breakfast; as soon as they had finished and cleared the table Mary began, 'Well, George, this is how I see the situation: first, there's a passport that has to be issued by an EU country, otherwise, Easy will have to be quarantined in England for six months, which I'm not happy with. The poor dog locked in a cage, let out twice a day for exercise, an animal like Easy would end up with psychological problems. There again, Kate said she had contacts in Holland who had ways around the DEFRA rules. Then we need to by a motor caravan immediately, direct debits will have to be set up, our finances sorted, someone to keep an eye on the house. Mind you, we could let it through an agency depending how long we intend to be in Europe.'

'Whoa! Mary, you are going to fast. Let me ring that lady in Essex. You know the motor caravan we looked at last month, it was overpriced but in beautiful condition. Then, I'll call Tim and Paulo in Spain. I'm sure they will be delighted for us to spend Christmas with them, plus we could use their vet for the passport, as I have a strong feeling that Kate's Holland connection is a red herring designed to extract even more money from us.'

'But! But!'

'No buts, Mary. First things first.'

Picking up the phone, George dialled. Three rings later, a voice said, 'Hello.'

'Oh, hi! My name is George. I came to view your vehicle last month. Have you sold it yet . . . ? You haven't, well I'm very interested in buying it and would like to drive down to discuss it with you . . . Tomorrow would be fine, say around twelve. That way, we will miss the rush hour this end.'

George had already made up his mind about the vehicle and thought he would be able to negotiate a lower price with the one lady owner, a retired church minister whose husband had passed on and had no further use for the vehicle.

His next call was to the bank to arrange a banker's draft to cover two-thirds of the asking price; the rest he would pay in cash.

Then he rang Tim in Spain, briefly outlining his plan and informing him about the dog.

'Terrific!' said Tim. 'The downstairs of the house has been completely renovated, so the upstairs flat is vacant and at your disposal, and I'll talk to my vet about the passport. I have to take Scrappy for a check up tomorrow . . . '

'Scrappy?' George interrupted.

'Yes, he's an abandoned dog we found.'

'So, now you have three cats and two dogs?'

'Yes, that's right,' said Tim.

Mary's brother, who worked for himself as an engineer, was fluent in Spanish which would be very handy should any unforeseen difficulties arise in Spain concerning Easy.

'Look forward to seeing you,' said Tim.

'Great,' replied George, 'we'll keep you updated as things progress. Must rush. Regards to the family, talk to you soon, bye-bye.'

The next call was made to Wayne, George's eldest son, a builder by trade; no reply, so he left a message on his mobile to call back.

Mary sat listening patiently; as she opened her mouth to speak, George said,

'Mary . . . once we have brought the vehicle and set a date to leave, then we can attend to the other things that need sorting.' The next thing to be done was to ring Ronald in Turkey to see how the dog was faring. Mary was unaware of the desperate plight of the dog.

Ronald answered immediately.

'Hi! Ronald, it's me George . . . Yes, I'm in England. Would you mind checking with the vet as to how my dog is making out . . . You call back in an hour . . . okay, thanks.'

The next hour seemed like a lifetime to George, not knowing if the dog had survived.

Mary sensed the tension surrounding George; he had warned her about Easy's condition due to the fight with mastiff. She was unaware of Easy's true situation as she waited patiently. The silence was deafening.

The phone rang; they both jumped startled by the ringing. Picking up the receiver, George feared the worst. 'Hello . . . Yes, it's me Ronald . . . he is, are you sure, thanks for all your help.'

Replacing the receiver, George turned to Mary and said, 'Mary, Easy is okay.'

Mary broke down in tears of relief.

The following day after collecting the draft from the bank, George and Mary set off to Wickford to purchase the motor caravan. He had checked it out on his previous visit and was very happy with the vehicle's condition and service record.

The journey would take them along the busy North Circular Road, then on to the A12 to their destination. By George's reckoning, the trip should take approximately two hours. They drove in silence for a while, each absorbed in their own thoughts.

It occurred to George the enormity of the task they were taking on, with the cost of the vehicle and the amount of money needed to support them whilst touring, would totally deplete their savings. The major factor being the length of time spent in Europe, waiting for the dog's passport, at least six months, probably nearer nine before they were able to return to England. What the hell, he thought, I'm not getting any younger and who knows I might not wake up tomorrow.

They arrived shortly after twelve. Having introduced themselves, George made a cursory check over the vehicle, mainly to assure himself he hadn't overlooked anything. He noted since his last visit some three weeks ago that an additional three hundred miles appeared on the milometer, quite acceptable for that amount of time.

The preliminaries over George made an offer a thousand pounds under the asking price. He completed the deal, saving six hundred pounds, still well over the market value, but George was secure in the knowledge that the vehicle was faultless. He drove it back home; Mary followed in the family car.

Having arrived back safely and both vehicles parked, George checked his phone; there was a message from Wayne to say he was working in the area and would be around about seven that evening.

Seven o'clock sharp, a ring at the door announced Wayne had arrived. Very much like George, he was a stickler for time. Having explained the entire situation to him, Wayne was quite happy to keep an eye on things and asked his dad if he could use the house from time to time when working in the area.

'Feel free,' said George giving him a set of keys.

Mary reminding him to water the plants, Wayne said goodbye to George and his step-mum, not before adding, 'You must be bonkers, all that way to Turkey to rescue a street dog.'

Mary and George sat down.

'Let's see the list of things to be done,' said George.

Mary opened her notebook.

Three days later, they were on their way to Dover, booked on the eleven o'clock ferry to Calais. Prior to leaving, George had phoned Ronald to ask him to let the vet know they would arrive later than promised.

Once on French soil, George set the 'satnav' for Istanbul, and by his reckoning, from there, they would head south to Dalman; the whole journey was some five thousand kilometres.

Travelling through seven countries, the entire trip was relatively simple, as the satnav kept them on the motorways until they reached Turkey.

They overnighted in petrol stations where they also ate, thus saving time, having not to prepare their meals themselves, and they were on the road at daybreak, stopping only for petrol and food, driving until early evening.

While passing through France, Belgium, and Germany, there were no problems, but a little difficulty in Austria; somehow, they found themselves driving up the mountains with sheer drops on either side. The scenery was wonderful according to Mary, who kept up a running commentary, while

George, eyes glued to the road in front, listened; having always suffered with vertigo, the he found the concentration quite exhausting.

Prior to leaving England, they had agreed to share the driving; unfortunately, Mary had a sprained ankle, leaving George no alternative; until her ankle repaired itself, he would have to do it all.

The trip was not without its problems. They reached Serbia, and the country was non-EU—that meant their green card (travel insurance) was not recognised. This in itself caused a three-hour delay, whilst they purchased one at the border. What they found extremely irritating was being sent to one place for the card, then on to another building some two hundred metres further to have the card stamped, then finally a third building to pay for it.

The second problem occurred when the satnav decided to direct them to the centre of Belgrade in the morning rush-hour. They safely negotiated their way back to the motorway, by resetting the satnav, and once again started travelling in the right direction and were confronted by little old ladies, dressed entirely in black, crossing the motorway, on foot and loaded down with huge bundles of twigs resting precariously on their backs. Apparently, when building the six-lane highways with a central reservation, in certain areas, they ran through the centres of various villages. If that wasn't dangerous enough often, it was not unusual to come upon a two-wheel cart loaded down with vegetables being pulled along by a donkey, driven by a farmer—a nightmare for any driver.

The last obstacle was exiting Serbia into Bulgaria; they were stopped seven times at as many barriers to have their passports and vehicle documentation checked.

They arrived in Dalman late afternoon, having safely negotiated the rest of the journey. Mary was eager to collect Easy immediately, but as George pointed out, having driven all the way, it had left him completely exhausted and suggested they should check into the Aparta hotel, as being on the road so long he was tired and wanted to relax. The other option was to check into a campsite and pick the dog up in the morning. Mary, eager to see Easy, was somewhat disappointed but agreed.

They had to pass the vet's on their way to the hotel, so George decided to look in and find out as to the condition of the dog. He halted the motor home some hundred metres further on the opposite of the road saying, 'I'm just going to pop into Ronald's and thank him for his help. Just be a few minutes.' Armed with a bottle of old malt whiskey, he made to his way to the restaurant. Ronald was pleased to see him and shook his hand warmly. Once again thanking the man for all his help, George handed him the bottle of whisky saying, 'A small token of appreciation.'

'Glad, I was able to help,' said Ronald, and added, 'When you're rested up, pay us a visit. My chef has a excellent reputation for English food.'

Once again shaking Ronald's hand, George departed.

Feeling quite anxious, George made his way to the surgery; the vet recognised him straight away, and with a smile on his face, he told George all what he needed to know.

'Easy's fine, a huge improvement in his condition,' said the receptionist in perfect English. As promised, he's been chipped, all vaccinations completed, blood test clear, and passport ready. George was so relieved he could have kissed her; instead, he shook the vet's hand warmly saying he would be back in the morning at ten o'clock to settle up and collect the dog.

Making his way back to the motorhome, they headed for the hotel. Having checked in, it occurred to Mary it would be nice to spend a few days there and relax after their somewhat arduous journey. George agreed.

Chapter 39

By the end of the second week, Easy was feeling a lot better; his wounds and abrasions were rapidly healing, the fur that was missing from his emaciated body was growing back, and he had put on a little weight. But! And it was a big but, the boredom of the same routine was getting to him. Already the experience of the last horrific year had started to fade, and he yearned for his freedom. His mind was made up; as soon as he was fully fit, escape was the first thing on his agenda.

Things were about to change . . .

It was late afternoon when the vet's assistant arrived to take him on his usual walk; instead he was led out to a waiting van, placed in a cage and driven away.

What's going on? he thought. I hope I'm not being placed in another so called charity. I wonder where she's taking me. I Might have to delay my escape until I can sus-out the situation.

A short while later, the van halted outside a tall, wide, wooden door that had a mind of its own; it slid open, allowing the van pass through, then silently slipped back to its original position. A few moments later, the van stopped outside a single storey brick building. The van door swung open and the assistant reached into the cage, attached a leash to his collar, and then gently coaxed him out.

His first impression of his new surroundings was of a large green field bounded by a wire fence. Beyond the fence lay a smaller area covered in shingles; at one end stood a single storey, wooden building from which emanated the sound of dogs barking.

He felt a gentle pull on the leash; looking up, he noticed a man clothed in a brown anorak wearing green Wellington boots, standing in the doorway of the building. He spoke, 'So this is our latest recruit, good boy!' he said as the assistant handed him the leash.

'Come with me, let's settle you in,' he said in a kindly voice.

Easy trailed along as he was led across the field to the wooden structure. Once through the door, the noise from the dogs' barking grew louder. On one side of the structure stood a line of large kennels; on the other side, smaller ones which had slatted doors with gaps at the top, from which protruded the heads of little yapping sausages, as Easy liked to call the smaller dogs. The man ushered him into one of the larger cages, lined with fresh straw on which stood a bowl of water. The cage was roomy with slatted windows to allow the light to filter through.

'You'll soon feel at home,' said the man, and added, 'I bet you're hungry—it's nearly supper time, be patient, there's a good boy,' patting Easy's head and closing the kennel behind him.

A little while later, a bowl was pushed into the kennel. Having scoffed that down, it became apparent that the barking had decreased quite noticeably; it was obvious the other dogs were being fed. Soon all was quiet, Easy lay down and prepared for sleep, wondering what the next day would bring.

The next morning after being fed, the larger animals were let out onto the green area presumably to exercise. This suited Easy as it gave him time to inspect his new home and weigh-up his chances to escape. What he didn't expect was to be approached by a gruff Irish wolfhound who barked, 'Who are you?'

To which Easy replied, 'Who wants to know?'

'I do,' came the reply.

Easy, not liking the dogs attitude, barked even louder saying, 'Are you deaf? I asked who wants to know.'

The wolfhound snarled baring its teeth and barked, 'A little less lip, and tell me your name?'

Easy did not want to lose his street cred and he knew offence was the best way to tackle aggressive animals, but Easy was aware he was too weak to be lured into a physical confrontation and also he knew the other dog was trying to intimidate him.

'I won't ask you again,' he said the Irish hound.

'You won't what . . . Shut it, cloth ears, and answer my question,' barked Easy, drawing himself up to his full height.

'Answer your question, you undernourished piece of shit.'

'Undernourished I might well be, you fat lump . . . '

'Who are you calling fat? I'd chew your balls off it you had any to latch on to.'

Easy took a pace forward saying, 'I can't be bothered to argue with you, fatty, so piss off before I lose my temper and sink my teeth into your fat gut and rip out your entrails.' Secretly, Easy knew he was pushing his luck.

'You'll do what?!' exclaimed the Irish hound.

'You heard me, so can it.'

Just then, a loud voice interrupted the dogs' exchange, 'Larry! Quit it!'

Even more explosive, the man in the anorak and wellies roared, 'I said, "Quit, you two".'

Both dogs shrank back; as once again, directing his orders at Larry, the man said,

'Be off with you, and if I catch you throwing your weight around again, you will be disciplined.'

Larry cowered and slunk away, not before barking at Easy, 'Stay out of my way. I'm top dog here, and don't you forget it.'

What a let off, thought Easy as he moved toward the man wagging his tail.

'And you should know better getting into trouble on your first day here,' said Mr Anorak.

Easy sat with his head bowed, as the man walked away; left to his own devices and conscious of his close encounter with Larry, he decided to check out the field and introduce himself to the other occupants. As he trotted around the perimeter, he passed the large wooden door and the brick administration building where outside sat two parked vehicles. He noted on his first inspection how secure the area was; there appeared to be no avenue of escape. This experience in no way effected his determination to be free.

Having introduced himself to the other occupants of the large kennels, some of them playing, others lying in the warm sun, Easy was careful to keep out of Larry's way. He sat down to watch and wait, to see if there was a weak link in his new surroundings that he might be able to exploit.

The following days passed by peacefully. With regular food and exercise, he knew his strength was returning; all he had to do was stay patient until an opportunity arose for him to escape.

It must have been the fourth day when once again Easy was ushered into a van and driven through the sliding doors, where he was being taken he had no idea, but what he did know, once the vehicle stopped and the van door opened, if the man released the catch on the cage he would be off as fast as he could. But this was not to be, as the man pushed his hands through the cage bars, he attached the leash to his collar before opening the door. He found himself standing on a pavement and he noted he was on the other side of the road opposite the vet's.

The driver led him into a small open courtyard and hitched him to a tree that gave him some welcome shelter from the sun; a large bowl of water was placed close by. Left to his own devices, Easy sat and watched the man cross the road and enter the vet's surgery.

Chapter 40

George and Mary were up, showered, and down for breakfast early. George had slept for a solid ten hours, but Mary was so excited about being reunited with Easy that she was unable to settle. Bearing in mind what George had said about the animals condition, she was eager to see her dog and check him out.

Knowing Mary's love for all living creatures, prior to going to bed, George showed Mary the picture he took of Easy by the fountain in Balgarese.

'Poor thing,' she cried, 'how could a person be so cruel?'

The night before, George had thought long and hard before deciding to show Mary the photos and come to the conclusion that was the best option; that way, she wouldn't expect too much and be less shocked by the animal's injuries.

Having finished breakfast, they drove to the vet's to collect the dog, and once the formalities were over, they intended to motor on and make for Turtle beach to give the animal a good run and try to reacquaint themselves with him, after all one year had passed since Mary had last seen Easy.

George halted the motorhome outside the pet shop, suggesting to Mary they should buy some dog meat and biscuits to feed the animal, after the planned run. Mary agreed, and once inside, they made the necessary purchases plus two dog bowls.

Leaving the shopping in the motor home, they entered the vet's office who bade them to sit down. Opening the top right-hand draw of his desk, he produced the passport and in broken English did his best to explain the dates and stamps of the various vaccinations. All the entrees were written in Turkish which George found a little disconcerting. The vet seemed to anticipate this and produced an envelope from which he withdrew a sheet of paper, headed with his name, a registered company address written in English, outlining all vaccinations and their dates, including microchip number, rabies vaccination, and the results of the blood test. This had the effect of dispensing any worries George had about leaving Turkey. George opened his wallet to signify he wanted to pay the outstanding balance. The vet produced the invoice; it was detailed in English the cost of everything they had agreed, less the deposit. Having settled up, George asked the vet where the dog was.

'Follow me,' said the vet in stunted English, 'he's across the road in the courtyard opposite.'

Mary could hardly contain her excitement. They all left through the front door, leaving the assistant, head down busily typing and minding the premises.

Easy stood, as three people approached; he couldn't believe his eyes. The vet he knew, the tall man with grey hair was the person who rescued him from the concrete jungle, the female he wasn't sure about. He started wagging his tail furiously, at the same time barking as loud as he could and straining at the leash.

As the woman caught sight of him, she rushed into the courtyard, fell on her knees, and with tears streaming from her eyes, she cried,

'My poor little boy, has that nasty lady been cruel to you? Never mind, you're safe now. Mummy will look after you,' at the same time cradling his body in her arms. 'There! There I promised I would return to take care of you.'

It was then Easy realised this was the lady who fed and looked after him last year. Unable to control his gratitude, Easy let the lady smother him with kisses. He endeavoured to show his appreciation by licking her face. Stopping for a moment and addressing the two men, Mary said, 'How could she? How could she be so cruel?' Her countenance changed, eyes like steel blue chips, and through gritted teeth, she said out loud, to no-one in particular, 'I'll make her pay for this abuse on a poor defenceless animal if it's the last thing I do.'

This was a side of Mary that George had rarely saw, which he found quite disturbing, reasoning that in her emotional state, she was probably overreacting.

George untied the leash, which Mary took hold of. Once again having thanked the vet, they crossed the road to the motorhome.

Once inside, Easy found this new experience a little unnerving. Turning around in circles, he made himself comfortable on a nice soft rug he assumed was provided for his use.

'So Turtle beach it is, then?'

'Yes,' said Mary. 'This time of year, most of the tourists will have left. I can't get over how big he's grown, George.'

'He certainly has, but you can still see his ribcage protruding. Nothing that a healthy diet will soon put right, Mary.'

'True. Hopefully, the hardship he's had to endure hasn't left him with any psychological problems.'

'Only time will tell, Mary. We'll have to earn his trust.'

'Yes! Regular food and exercise with plenty of TLC should do the job, hopefully.'

Easy was still unsure as to what was going to happen to him; one thing he did know—at the first opportunity, he was off.

On arrival at Turtle beach, the door opened and he was let out with the man holding his leash. In a matter of minutes, the lady produced two bowls—one contained meat and biscuits and the other fresh water. Having not been fed this morning, both bowls were soon empty. With his tummy full, he felt a lot better. They walked him along the beach still attached to his leash. I'll bide my time, he thought, and see what happens.

The lady and man fell silent for a time. Then the man spoke, 'You see, Mary, the beach is nigh on empty and the dog needs to go to toilet.'

'Perhaps he's shy.'

'Mary I really don't think dogs have the same feelings as us, though he must want to go. I'll take the leash off and see what happens.'

'Are you sure? That's the sensible thing to do, George?'

'No! but nothing ventured nothing gained.'

Once unhitched, Easy was off like a rocked barking, 'I'm free—free!'

Running flat out towards the sand dunes away from the sea, he was bursting for a pooh and a pee, and he did like his privacy. Having finished his ablutions, he had a sniff around and settled in the shade to plan his future.

'Go and get him,' said Mary, 'otherwise, we will lose him.'

'Give him time. He'll come back when he's hungry.' They waited and waited until Mary, now quite agitated, said,

'Come on, George, let's look for him.'

Meanwhile, Easy lay down thinking, This is my big chance to escape, but I need to think this through. His old mentor had always advised him, 'When faced with an important decision, weigh up your options before proceeding.'

Easy, he said to himself, at the moment these kind people had fed me, taken off the leash enabling me to run free. The man had taken me to a vet who seemed concerned about my health. True, during my stay, I had to endure the indignity of having needles stuck in me, but I was fed regularly and exercised. My body once a mass of open wounds is repairing itself. The bald patches have started to grow hair. Finally, if these people let me off the leash once, they would do it again, so should the need to escape become necessary, I should have ample opportunity.

On the minus side, at the moment I have no idea where I am. If I could find my way back to my old hunting ground, Dalman, I would be left with two choices—one, join up with another gang or form one of my own. Either way, I would have to scavenge to stay alive and live with the constant fear of being caught by the council catchers who would ultimately electrocute me. The logical choice was to stay put.

'Easy! Easy! Come boy!' he heard the lady calling.

Leaping from behind the dunes, he bounded towards her, tail wagging, and he stopped and sat. Reaching into her pocket, she fed him a titbit. Blimey, he thought, if all I have to do is sit and wag my tail to get a tasty snippet of food, I'll do that again next time she calls. Having retrieved the dog, George drove back to town.

'George, I've been thinking, we should stay a while in Dalman until Easy is completely fit to travel before heading to Spain.'

'You must have read my mind, Mary. I was thinking the same. To be honest, I'm tired and a trifle peed off with driving. It was a long journey across Europe.'

'That's settled then,' said Mary, not revealing her true motive for wanting to stay longer.

The next few days, Easy and his new owners spent their time relaxing, long walks, regular food and sightseeing; all these things added to his rapid recovery.

One afternoon, as they ambled around town, Easy, with his new collar and leash, felt so proud; nothing had changed, Abraham's cafe was still open, though the tourist season was almost over. Usually, about this time of year, the dog catchers were working flat out to round up any strays they could catch. Those with a clean bill of health were tagged—the remainder put down. Easy felt so sorry for his old chums he used to run with, at the same time realising how fate had intervened to save him. A few dogs that had evaded capture, some he remembered, barked their acknowledgement and wished him luck; he noticed an element of envy as they exchanged pleasantries.

Some days later, Mary expressed a wish to visit the market and the local museum in Balgarese. George thought the museum, yes—the market, fat chance she was off on a buying spree.

The next morning, Mary was up early as she wanted to speak to the chambermaid Maria to ask a favour. Over the years, when visited Turkey and staying at the Aparta hotel, they had developed a friendship. Maria's language skills were such that she was able to converse quite fluently in English. When approached by Mary with her request, she was more than a little hesitant to grant it, but because of their long association, Maria gave in and granted Mary's request.

After breakfast, having taken Easy for his morning walk, they drove to Balgarese.

On arrival, Mary expressed her wish to visit the market first. George, who hated shopping, had the perfect excuse to avoid being pushed and shoved as he trampled around the stalls; it would not be practical to take the dog with them, and also, if they left him in the motorhome, he might feel abandoned. Mary raised no objections, so it was agreed that George and Easy would wait for her in an adjacent street. Having dropped Mary off, George parked up and settled down to read his book.

Though now into the middle of October, it was still pleasantly warm; knowing it would be at least two hours before Mary returned, George found himself dozing only to be awoken sometime later by a tapping on the window. He opened his eyes, and then closed them as Easy barked; now fully awake he was surprised to see a policeman standing there. It occurred to him that he had parked in a restricted area, which meant a fine on the spot. As he wound down the window to express his lack of knowledge in relation to the parking laws, the constable spoke in English.

'No reason to panic, sir.' The word panic sent an icy chill down his spine. The officer continued; 'We have your wife back at the constabulary as she's been arrested.'

'Arrested!' exclaimed George, his mind racing. 'Arrested? What on earth for?'

'If you would lock up your vehicle and follow me, all will be revealed at the station.'

Once more George asked, 'Arrested, what for?'

'I'm not at liberty to explain, sir.'

George's mind was in turmoil; had she been in an accident? Maybe shoplifting—No! not Mary.

On arrival at the station, George was shown into the charge room where Mary was sitting crying, with a woman officer trying to console her, who stood up allowing George to take her seat.

'Mary, what happened, tell me?' Between sobs, she revealed the reason for her arrest.

'I went to her house and painted the wall.'

Completely bewildered, George asked, 'Whose house, what, wall, where?'

'Her house.'

'Mary, you're not making sense,' he said gently. 'Take your time and tell me the whole story.'

At this point, George became aware, that except for the policeman sitting behind a desk, rifling through some paperwork, they were alone. Lowering her voice, Mary said, 'That evil woman's house.'

The reality dawned upon George.

'You mean Kate's house?'

'Yes!'

'How did you know where she lived?'

'I came to the police station and asked. They must have followed me there. I had just finished painting when I was arrested.'

It became apparent to George that Mary was not that upset as she had ceased crying.

'You had better start from the beginning.'

With a heavy sigh Mary began, 'After you dropped me at the market, I went to the local garage and brought two cans of red aerosol paint, then on to the police station to inquire where she lived, using the excuse that I had money to donate to her charity. Once there, I knocked on the door and waited for an answer, after about five minutes having knocked again, I was sure she was out. The funny thing was you would have thought her dogs would have reacted to the noise, but no, the house was silent. This was my chance, I thought. So I sprayed on the wall—"KILLER—BITCH" plus this other word.'

'What word, tell me?' Mary unclenched her fist to reveal, written in ink on the palm of her hand, the letters (Fahise).

'What does it mean?'

'I don't know, George. This morning, Marie wrote it down for me. I printed it on my hand so as to remember it.'

'Marie, who on earth is she?'

'You know, the chambermaid at the hotel, I asked her to tell me the most degrading word you could call a woman in Turkey. She was reticent to tell me at first, so I promised there was no way that I would implicate her should there be any repercussions. What do you think will happen, George?'

'I suppose you will be charged with criminal damage or something.'

Just then, a tall, lean, middle-aged man, dressed in plain clothes, walked through the door, and in perfect English said, 'Sir, follow me.'

George stood, was about to say 'what about Mary' when the man, obviously a senior officer, continued, 'You are to remain here,' pointing at Mary.

Mary, who had resumed crying, said, 'Will I go to prison?'

'That's for the judge to decide. I need to talk to your husband. While you're waiting, would you care for a cup of tea?'

Between sobs Mary replied, 'Oh, yes, please.' Turning to the officer at the desk, he spoke in Turkish; George assumed he was telling the man to fetch the tea.

George was ushered through the door, down the hallway into another rather well-furnished office, and was asked to sit down.

'Sir, your passports, please.'

'I'm sorry, but they're back at the hotel in Dalman.'

'We need your passports to complete the charge sheet,' came the reply, 'so please go and collect them and return ASAP.'

'But what about my partner?' asked George.

'She will remain in custody for the time being.'

George was back in two hours, not before talking to the hotel owner, Mr Yuris, who by chance, knew the mayor of Balgeres and promised to have a word with him.

Back at the police station, he was shown into the office where the plainclothes officer was speaking into the telephone. As George didn't understand a word, he assumed the language used was Turkish. Putting down the receiver, he held out his hand for the passports; he quickly perused through them, and then handed them to another policeman, who promptly left the room, undoubtedly to record the details on the charge sheet. The senior officer spoke, 'Please sit down, Mr Lewis. There's been a—let me say, a minor disturbance. Your wife is under arrest . . . '

'On what charge,' interrupted George.

'Malicious damage,' replied the officer.

'Malicious damage,' said George, 'how come?'

She was seen by two officers spraying obscene language on the wall of a house. The woman who owns the house is known to us. There have been many complaints made against her, mainly for taking money under false pretences, and cruelty to animals. We are unable to charge her as the people complaining will not attend as witnesses for the prosecution, because it can take up to six months before the accused appears before the judge and the people who have reported her are not prepared to come back to give evidence. As tourists, they would have to pay all their own expenses, so they cut their losses and put it down to experience. We brought the woman to the station, and when confronted by your wife, for obvious reasons, 'she denied all knowledge of her.'

George interrupted, 'That can't be true. We've had several conversations with her over the past year, plus a few weeks ago, I collected our dog, and handed over more money on top of what cash we sent to her via Western Union money orders for vet bills and a new kennel plus medication for her animals she said were unattainable in this country.'

'That may well be the case, but unless you can produce written evidence of these payments, and you are prepared to act for the prosecution, there is nothing we can do.'

George thought quickly; he was pretty certain he had retained the money order receipts back in the UK. He relayed this information to the officer, adding, 'I'm retired, and as we have to spend time in Europe, while waiting for an EU passport for the dog, coming back does not present a problem.'

The officer continued, 'As I mentioned, before the disturbance.'

'Tell me,' said George.

'When the woman saw your partner, she claimed she had no memory of them meeting and asked why she was conducting this vendetta against her. Well! You're wife went berserk and threatened to slit her throat. It took two of my officers to restrain her.'

'Oh!' said George. 'That's so unlike Mary.'

'We realised that she was overwrought and are prepared to over look the matter. Bearing in mind what we have just discussed, here's my card, whilst on your travels, keep in touch. Now collect your wife. You are free to go.'

Back in the charge room, Mary, wiping her eyes, looked up at George expectantly.

'Come, love, let's go. Easy's been stuck in the camper for hours and needs a walk.'

'Aren't they going to charge me?'

'Apparently not, let's go.'

George had a strong suspicion that Mr Yuris the hotel owner's conversation with the mayor of the town had some bearing on the matter.

They headed back to Dalman via Turtle Beach to give Easy a well-earned run. As they ambled along the seafront, Mary told George what happened at the station, after he left to fetch the passports.

'What I found surprising was their hospitality, offering me more tea, asking if I was hungry. Of course, I declined, feeling far too stressed to eat. Mind you I was bursting to use the loo, but too embarrassed to ask. Eventually, I confided in a police woman and she took me to the ladies. They all seemed to find the word I wrote on my hand very amusing, as every officer that came by looked and burst out laughing. Why they didn't charge me?'

'Heaven knows.'

'Probably because we are tourists, plus the amount of complaints that have been recorded against Kate and her so-called charity, and I wouldn't be surprised if Mr Yuris had something to do with it.'

'What do you mean?' Mary asked. George told her about the hotel owner's friendship with the local mayor.

'I don't know how you feel, Mary, but for me, a few more days staying in Dalman and I'll be ready to set off for Spain. As we have already agreed, we'll journey along the Mediterranean coast, and to cut down on the driving, by catching the ferry from Greece to Venice, then onto Spain, spend Christmas with Tim and Paula, and use their vet to acquire an EU passport for Easy.'

'I'm all for that. Let's stay three more days and then we leave.'

Having now made a definite decision to set off—little did they know the problems they would encounter once they reached their destination.

Having been cooped up in the camper for hours, Easy was out, free to run and do his business in private. This new-found freedom he loved. His mind was made up unless something unforeseen happened, his future rested with these kind people.

The whole new experience was magical, chasing seagulls that seemed to take pleasure in teasing him, digging down into the sand, trying to catch crabs, running until his legs ached with the effort, and finally the immense pleasure to be able to swim and eat until his belly was full.

Back at the hotel, word had already got around; everybody knew about Mary's escapade. Even Mr Yuris's wife usually uncommunicative was smiling and playfully threatening her husband with a knife. She had an intense dislike of cats and dogs as they tended to destroy her plants. But to Mary and George's amazement, she gently patted Easy on the head; Easy found this action a little disconcerting, as he remembered a year ago she would have chased him off with a broom.

Informing Mr Yuris that they were leaving in three days, George asked if he might settle the bill in advance. Once inside his office and having paid the money, George thanked the man for his timely intervention concerning Mary's arrest. George was sure that the hotel owner's friendship with the mayor of Balgarese led to the charges being dropped.

The last night of their stay, Mary had her usual problem, sleeping. George was out like a light; she read until the early hours until she noticed Easy twitching as he lay on his blanket. Squatting down beside him, she gently stroked his body, thinking how lucky she was to acquire such a lovely animal. Others might say Easy was the lucky one being rescued from that hellhole; as far as Mary was concerned, she knew that fate had intervened to bring them together. A tear fell from her eye as she remembered the cruelty that had been metered out to Easy. Quietly she whispered, 'A promise is a promise and once made must be kept. I'm back and you're safe now. Nobody will ever harm you again, not in my lifetime. You can look forward to a great new life. You'll be able to run free in Richmond Park—that's close to where you will live—chase the squirrels, play with other friendly dogs, swim in Beverley Brook, but you must never ever harass the deer, swans, or Canadia geese—that's a no-no.'

Easy didn't understand a word but knew instinctively by the tone of the ladies voice he was safe at last; emitting a heavy sigh, he fell back to sleep.

Chapter 41

The journey to Spain was uneventful, except for the incident on the ferry to Venice. Easy had to travel on the top deck in kennel hardly big enough for him to fit into. Every two hours, George went up to top deck to replenish the dog's water and lead him around the deck for a pee, which for some reason, he never seemed to want to do. On arrival, George and Mary were last to disembark. As their vehicle was first on, it followed they would be last off. During the whole trip, George found the staff very unhelpful. When it was their turn to leave, having carried Easy down from the top deck to the main foyer and placing him on the floor, the poor dog could not contain himself any longer and started to pee right opposite the checking in desk. Well, his peeing took forever, so long that the thick carpet was saturated and formed a puddle, much to George's dismay and the annoyance of the desk clerk. That will teach them a lesson, thought George for being so unhelpful.

They arrived a few days before Christmas and settled in the apartment that Tim and Paula's had placed at their disposal.

Their immediate concern was to acquire an EU passport for Easy that would enable them to enter England with him, thus avoiding quarantine which both George and Mary thought was cruel keeping an animal in a concrete cage for six months.

They knew that, on acquiring the passport, they would have to wait out the six months from the date of issue, before crossing the channel. They had made plans to tour Spain and eventually arrive at Calais after the allotted waiting period, twenty-four to forty-eight hours before departure on the Dover ferry as the dog had to be ticked and wormed and the passport stamped by the vet.

The Vet, Mary's brother used, admitted this was the first passport she had been involved in. Having administered the rabies vaccination, a blood test was taken and sent to the appropriate authorities.

Some three weeks later, Tim called the vet to ask about the outcome of the blood test, only to be told somehow the blood had become contaminated and another sample was necessary.

Six months to the day of the results of the second blood test, the passport was made available. George was reliably informed that to obtain a dog passport in Spain, you still have to wait for six months, but the animal did not have to be quarantined.

During that waiting period, they spent the time touring around the country sightseeing, constantly checking with Tim as to the availability of the document.

Finally, the big day arrived. They heard the news whilst visiting Valencia. By now, they had been in Europe nigh on ten months, leaving a large hole in their already depleted budget. Fortunately, Valencia was only seventy kilometres from Alzira where Tim and Paula lived.

They made their way to Tims, arriving on a Sunday. The family were eager to hear about their travels.

Mary felt somewhat frustrated, having to wait until Monday when the vet's opened to collect the passport.

The following morning, having said their goodbyes and thanking Tim and Paula for their hospitality, George and Mary drove to Alzira and collected the passport, then headed home to the mother country.

The three of them took a leisurely trip through France to Calais. Having checked into a campsite for a few days, George presented himself to the ferry booking office, only to find out, much to his annoyance, that Easy's passport was invalid. He tried his utmost to control his temper, while the booking clerk explained the reason why. The dates on the document were written in the wrong sequence. Apparently the microchip had to be inserted, a reading taken and dated, next a blood sample taken dated and sent to be analyse. Once the results were cleared and the vet received confirmation, the chip was read again and dated. George's frustration threatened to boil over. After all they had been through, and their life's savings all but spent, now to be thwarted by what George thought was petty bureaucracy was beyond belief. He now doubted the wisdom for taking on such a venture. His son Wayne had said at the outset he must be bonkers, going all the way to Turkey to rescue a dog. His one consolation was Mary's happiness.

Mary rang Tim who in turn rang the vet who suggested they post the passport back to her, and she would correct the errors she had made.

Some three anxious weeks later, Easy was being driven out of Dover seaport heading for Barnes, London.

Mary turned to George and said, 'Do you know it's ten months since we set foot on English soil?'

'Really, Mary, as long as that,' came the reply, George knowing full well how long they had been away from the mother country.

Easy looked out of the camper window spellbound by the amount of traffic and later was completely stunned by the beauty of the Kent countryside.

Mary turned and gently stroked her dog, whispering, 'Easy, your home is with us,' proudly adding, 'you're an English dog now.'

They arrived home safely; waiting there to welcome them was Wayne, George's eldest son. Mary noted the house was spotless; all her plants were well and watered, and a huge pile of correspondence needed George's attention. Wayne, true to form, had collated the mail in date order.

There was no immediate hurry to unpack, so while Wayne updated George on a few letters that needed his immediate attention, Mary took Easy for a pee and a pooh on Barnes common. The light was fading, Mary, not wanting to lose Easy, kept him on the leash. They arrived back as Wayne was leaving; once again thanking him for taking care of the house, she wished him goodnight.

Easy found it difficult to settle, wandering from room to room; he was unsure where to sleep. Having been kept in a confined space for the last ten months, he was spoilt for choice. Finally, he settled for the foot of the bed where George and Mary slept, not before wolfing down a bowl of meat and biscuits.

The following morning, having been fed and watered, he was taken out to the motorhome and driven to Richmond Park. They stopped in the first available parking space and opened the door to let Easy out, who bounded down the steps, then sat down.

His heart rate quickened as his eyes surveyed the panorama unfolding before him. Everywhere he looked was open spaced; tall trees standing proud, a hug expanse of ferns dotted the landscape, and strange smells wafted into his nostrils. In the distance, he could see brown four-legged animals with odd looking things growing out of their heads—he was later to find out that they were horns—little grey furry animals playing around in the grass, large birds making funny noises, but best of all, other dogs barking and wagging their tails. His ears picked up the sound of running water as he sat transfixed, taking in the vast area of Richmond Park.

A loud bark caught his attention; a few feet away trotting towards him was a Labrador. For a brief moment, he thought of Barney, his old mentor.

'Fancy a swim?' said the dog playfully. 'Follow me.'

Easy didn't need to be asked twice; he was off, hot on the tail of the Labrador. In seconds, the Lab seemed to fly through the air and landed on his belly with a loud splash, in the middle of a stream, followed by Easy.

'Where are we?' he asked.

'Beverly Brook,' came the reply.

Heaven, thought Easy.

The end.